WORSE
THAN A
THIEF

*Murder and Romance
In Kittery, Maine*

J. TRACKSLER

Llumina Press

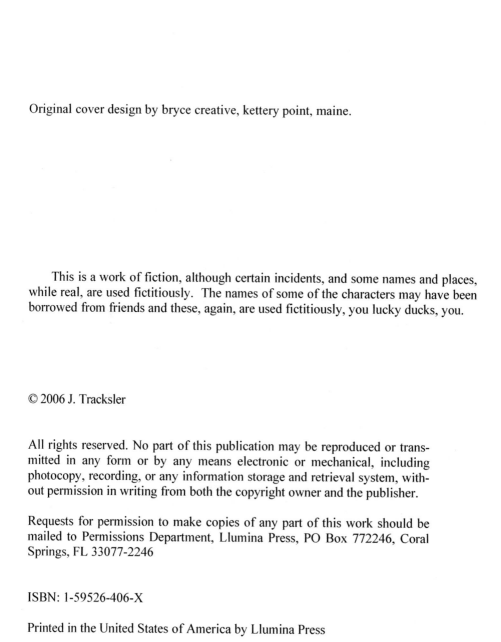

Original cover design by bryce creative, kettery point, maine.

This is a work of fiction, although certain incidents, and some names and places, while real, are used fictitiously. The names of some of the characters may have been borrowed from friends and these, again, are used fictitiously, you lucky ducks, you.

Requests for permission to make copies of any part of this work should be mailed to Permissions Department, Llumina Press, PO Box 772246, Coral Springs, FL 33077-2246

ISBN: 1-59526-406-X

Printed in the United States of America by Llumina Press

Library of Congress Control Number: 2006904599

WORSE

THAN A

THIEF

DEDICATION

This book is dedicated to the people of Kittery, Kittery Point and the Seacoast Area of Maine – the teachers, shopkeepers, entrepreneurs, customers, volunteers, postal workers, clergy, police and firefighters – and naturally, also to the folk who live in this hallowed place of unspoiled beauty.

And to my wonderful family and friends, this book is for you

CHAPTER ONE

Kittery Gazette

Our News Is Your News - Monday, August 7, 2000

STILL NO SUSPECTS IN MURDERS OF TWO WOMEN ONE YEAR AGO

By Nunzia Ciccola, News Editor

Kittery, Maine: One year to the date of the brutal murder that took place here, a reliable police source told this reporter "We have no suspects. This crime is still unsolved."

At about 9:30 PM, on the night of August 3, 1999, neighbors in the tiny residential neighborhood near Schooner Street in Kittery, Maine, were disturbed by the yowling of two cats. The cats made so much noise that several neighbors left their houses to see what was wrong. The cats were owned by two women who lived in the martini-olive-green shingle cottage at 236 Schooner Street. Led by the cats, neighbors found the front door ajar, entered the house and found Birta "Sunny" Sundergaard, heiress to the Sundergaard Munitions fortune and her house-mate, Catherine Black, brutally murdered in the living room of the house.

The Kittery Police were called immediately. Some person or persons unknown had hacked the bodies into dozens of pieces. "The room was covered with blood," said Carl Zumbo, of 240 Schooner Street, a neighbor who was one of the first on the scene. "You couldn't believe the blood...it was everywhere. On the walls, the furniture, soaked into the rug, even on the ceiling. It was as if a madman with incredible strength chopped those women up." Even now, a year later, the scene haunts Zumbo. "Those women were in twenty pieces each. You couldn't tell whose arm was whose; which head went where! It was a terrible sight!"

There were no weapons left at the scene of the crime and police have searched in vain for any clues to help solve this horrendous crime. Today, the file is still open, filled with hundreds of pieces of paper, but empty of any suggestion of who butchered these two young women.

This reporter asked Zumbo and other neighbors if they were afraid that the killer might return someday. Mrs. Hannah Clutterbuck, who was born in the house next door to the murder house and who has lived there for 85 years, told us: "There were never any further problems. We just don't know what happened. They were two nice young ladies, quiet...well, not too quiet, they liked to play their music and one of them had a banjo or a mandolin, but they never bothered anyone." Mrs. Clutterbuck shook her head. "And it was funny about the cats. I felt bad that the cats were left homeless, so I tried to find them and bring them home with me, but they were gone. They led us to the bodies and then they disappeared. It's a peculiar thing. Them cats were never seen again, although Carl Zumbo and my husband Elroy and a few others of us who live on Schooner Street swear that we hear them yowling now and then on a dark night." She shuddered and clutched her hand-knit sweater tighter around herself. "It's like ghosts, you know, them cats. Maybe to remind us about those killings."

Kittery Police Chief Alexander Bridge asks anyone with any information that can assist with these murders to call at 278-444-8484.

More pictures and Story on page 9A...

CHAPTER TWO

So trite to say that the wife is the last to know, but, in this case, I must have been dumber than I could have ever dreamed I might have been. After all, we'd been married for thirty-two years. Long enough, I guess, to get complacent. Certainly long enough to be the dumb, dumb wife, a cliché in most silly stories and TV Sitcoms.. The one that you feel sorry for, although you always have a bit of contempt for her. The wife...the one who should have lost a few pounds...had her face lifted...been a little more careful about her looks. That was me; the pathetic victim.

When Steve said he wanted to talk to me, I thought perhaps he was hoping to sweet-talk me into another vacation in Atlantic City. I hate going to Atlantic City. It's too...glitzy for someone like me. And Steve always loses more than we can afford and then drinks himself into a coma, and *then* gets surly for the next three days. Frantically, I tried to think of some excuse, some good reason why we shouldn't go, but my mind was a blank. So blank that when he told me he loved someone else and wanted a divorce, I was almost knocked off my feet. *Divorce? Someone else?* What was he *talking* about?

I swear that my mouth dropped open and my heart, actually, literally, stopped beating. All I could think of was that short story...you know, the one where the woman finds out her husband has been cheating on her and bops him over the head with the frozen leg of lamb. I started to giggle, caught in some hysteria known only to women whose husbands are leaving them. I didn't have a leg of lamb in the freezer. What was I supposed to do if I didn't have a leg of lamb?

Steve's voice went on, as if he'd memorized a speech. I looked at him. After those thirty-two years, I could tell; he *had* memorized a speech. "We've become incompatible, Regina." When he was really uncomfortable, he used my given name. Otherwise, he called me Reggie, like everyone else did. "Our lives together have no meaning any longer." Amazing. After thirty some-odd years all of a sudden we were incompatible. Amazing. As I'd babbled above several times, Steve and I had been married for a long time. Except for this sudden aberration, I usually knew what he was thinking and, Lordy knows, he was thinking furiously now. My stomach hurt and my throat felt closed up. I didn't know what to do with myself. Throw up? Die? Was my life over? He was *leaving* me, for God's sake! Divorcing me! What could I do? Start to scream? Kill him? *What?* I sat down, put my hands in my lap and looked up at him. He was sweating and his eyes were darting everywhere but at me. Good. I hoped the bastard choked. A tiny flame of something gleeful at his discomfort flickered in my heart. I was sort of proud of myself. Instead of a scene, instead of screaming, crying and never stopping, I sucked in my breath and managed to compose myself. How? I'll never know, but I did. My demeanor was very quiet and I kept a calm and interested expression on my face as he turned my entire life upside down. I thought I'd burst into tears, after all, here he was, ripping the familiar fabric of our marriage apart, ripping my life apart, but I didn't feel like crying. I felt like a stone had replaced my heart. A big, cruel, crushing stone. I tried to focus on what he was saying. Steve's words went on and on…something about us both being happier apart…blah, blah blah…fulfill our true potential…in the long run you'll be grateful…and I thought, *"Who is the other woman? What the hell is he really up to?"*

He was sweating and acutely uncomfortable. I could see the beads of perspiration on his face and his eyes darted every which way around the room. Everywhere but toward me. "Uh, I'll be moving in with Brianna." *Brianna? Brianna who? Brianna? What kind of a name was Brianna for an almost sixty year old man to be leaving his wife?* The stone that had replaced my heart shifted and my heart itself began to beat with erratic thumps. There was a real pain in my chest now. This must be what it was like to have a heart attack. When someone you love attacks you and your heart just dies. I bit my bottom lip and tried to breathe small, shallow breaths. I wouldn't give him the satisfaction of keeling over from any old heart attack and leaving him an easy way to get together with Brianna. Then he said something about dividing our assets. *Hmmmm? What machinations were going on in his computer-for-a brain?* Suddenly the pains stopped. I realized what was happening. The man was trying to screw me. *Screw me? Nah, he was trying to screw Brianna. He was trying to <u>divorce</u> me!* I sat up straight and turned my head in his direction, forcing him to have eye contact with me. I narrowed my own eyes and he began to sweat even more.

"And the children?" I asked him. He had the grace to look somewhat hunted. After all, he adored the girls and they adored him. "Who is going to tell them?"

His expression changed to the one he used when dealing with a recalcitrant subordinate. It usually worked with sales clerks and so forth, but I hardened my heart. After all, hadn't my heart already turned to stone? "I, uh, I thought that you...being their mother and all..." I shook my head. No. Nuh-oh, Steverino. Not me. He tried again and gave me one of his affronted expressions. Steve really did have great affronted expressions, but this time...this time it was different. He tried once more. "After all, don't you think it would be best...?" His face showed that he was trying to be reasonable. Another of his standard expressions to make me feel inadequate and cave in to whatever he wanted me to do. But not this time. I shook my head again, then stood up and reached for the phone. Steve looked hopeful. Perhaps he thought I'd fallen for the reasonable expression on his face. My own face was stony, just like my heart. And my soul? My soul was weeping, screaming, hysterical, dying. I dialed Jenna's number.

"Jenn? It's Mom." Steve blew his breath out, the way you do when you're really, really, *really* relieved. I still knew how his mind worked, even if he was leaving me for someone named Brianna. He thought that *I'd* tell Jenna the bad news. I cut off her usual cheerful greetings and said, "Hold on, dear, Dad wants to tell you something." I handed Steve the phone and waited until his mouth closed. "Don't forget to call Andrea next," I said to him as he stared at the receiver. Then, before I might begin to scream in some unstoppable, maniacal way, I went upstairs, packed a small suitcase and walked out the door.

◆ ◆ ◆

I drove my small, red Volkswagen bug to Route 1. At the Kittery Motor Lodge, *"We Never Close,"* overlooking the picturesque Kittery Truck Stop's gas pumps on one side and the Over the Moon Adult Book Store on the other, I took a room, using my United Airlines Visa Card. I presume my shell-shocked mind was still thinking about those Dividend Miles we usually used to fly to the Virgin Islands on our vacations. I was shown their best room, offering the slightly stale visage of an avocado green bedspreaded king sized bed, avocado green shag rug, large mirror, slick wood dresser, and a bathroom with a blue paper ribbon pasted across the toilet seat. Oh yes, and they had those plastic glasses. You know, the ones that they wrap in cellophane so you don't get someone else's germs on your lips.

I dialed Jenna's number. She was crying. "Mom, what's *happ*ening?

What is Daddy *talking* about? Who is this woman, Brianna?" I soothed her as best I could, reassuring her that I still loved her and that so did Steve. I hoped she didn't notice that I couldn't answer her questions.

"I don't exactly know what's going to happen now, honey, but Dad and I are going to work things out as best we can." I listened to her wails and calmed her down. "I'll call you tomorrow when I know a bit more about it all." My hands were shaking and I was certainly more shattered than I thought I'd be. Bri*anna*? Again, my dumbfounded mind wondered, what kind of a name was Brianna for a man Steve's age? Sounded like a teen-age pop star, for God's sake. What did she have that Steve needed more than he needed me? Smoother, younger skin? Poutier lips? Was she rich? Smarter than me? Better in bed? What was it that I didn't have any more? My own non-pouting lips began to tremble. Before I broke down, I chided myself for acting like a chump. I could get through this. I could, I could. Muttering, I dialed Andrea's number. She wasn't crying, but her normally sweet voice shook. I mentally cursed Steve for what he had done. Again, good Mommy that I was, I calmed my younger daughter and assured her that somehow, this would all pass.

It seems weird, but I was ravenously hungry after I hung up. Delayed shock? All I had to eat was a package of Spearmint Tic-Tacs that had been left in my make up kit. I chewed them down with a glass of water and stared at the wall, trying my hardest not to break down and bawl my head off. Suddenly shivering and cold, I took a shower, standing under the hot water for a long time, thinking about nothing at all. Then I got into my nightgown and sat in bed, making lists of what I was going to have to do to keep myself solvent and sane for the rest of my life.

◆ ◆ ◆

The next morning, I sustained a second shock, perhaps even worse than the one I'd gotten last night when Steve told me that our marriage was over.

Before I tell you about that, maybe I should fill you in a bit about what we were doing up here in Kittery, Maine.

Steve and I had married in our early twenties, a few years out of college. He was my first real love and, in those innocent days, the first man with whom I'd ever been intimate. Steve was considered a good catch. He was somewhat taller than me, had wavy brown hair and sincere brown eyes. He had charm, a decent sense of humor, and loved me. I loved him. We were both from moderately affluent families, me from a large, noisy Italian clan from Greenwich, Connecticut and Steve from a pleasant, but less-noisy WASP grouping from Lenox, Massachusetts. He went to Grad School at Boston University, and I played the young working wife, using my teaching degree to teach high school English to young hooligans in Greater Boston. We had an apartment, and then bought a house in Belmont, a pleasant Boston suburb of lovely old houses and tree-lined streets. Steve joined an investment firm and we had Jenna and Andrea. I stayed at home while the girls were growing up. Steve insisted and I agreed half-heartedly. "You don't earn enough to make any difference anyway, Reg," he'd said. "Your work isn't important. You don't need a career." I had loved teaching and had hoped that I could combine motherhood with working, but I caved in to Steve's desires. He told me, "My job is the vital one. You can stay home and watch the girls." I supposed he was right. His job was important and vital. I was less-vital, less-important, so I stayed home.

Steve worked hard, I'll have to cede that to him. He was an excellent salesman and his career blossomed with the investment firm. Soon, he was offered a partnership. We led a very nice, if unexciting life. The girls went to good schools; we socialized with young up-and-coming couples like ourselves, voted the Republican ticket with a few notable exceptions. We took vacations, went to Europe, the Virgin Islands, the inevitable trip to Disneyland…we were ordinary, rather happy people, or so I thought. Naturally, Jenn and Andrea went to college. Jenna married a boy she'd met at school and they moved to Rhode Island where Scott joined his father's dental practice. Jenn got a job at showing people around the mansions in Newport, and the newlyweds bought a condominium overlooking the water financing the downpayment with the generous gift we'd given them for their wedding. Andrea moved to Los Angeles, hoping to get into acting. She's still there, reading bit parts and going to auditions, hoping for that one big break. To keep herself in the style in which she feels she deserves, she waits on tables at an upscale Italian restaurant and mooches off Steve and me. They're good girls, crazy about their father, and always darling and lovely to me. Why shouldn't they be crazy about Steve? He'd given them everything he could, including his love and lots of money. Do I sound bitter or jealous? I don't mean to be. I love them dearly and they love me too. But they were always Daddy's Girls. Always wonderful and nice to me, but their hearts always belonged to Steve. I wonder how he'd explained to them what he'd told me. What had he said about his new plans? About Brianna, whoever she was, the bitch? And would he marry her as soon as he had gotten rid of me? And would Jenna and Andrea take to a new mother? Nah. They wouldn't be bowled over. Steve would have to really tap-dance to get them to forgive him for this one. Even if they were Daddy's girls. I wasn't too worried about Andrea and Jenna. They were both levelheaded and would keep on loving both of us, hopefully not taking sides one way or the other. They were adults now and, as normal adult women, had interesting lives of their own. Steve and I had often congratulated ourselves that Jenna and Andrea had successfully grown away from us in the years since school. We would all manage to get through this. After all, we were all civilized, weren't we?

Anyway, let me try to forget Brianna for a moment and get back to our history. After the girls left home, Steve began to urge me to move to Maine. He'd always wanted to live on the ocean and Maine was the one place where we might yet be able to snag a piece of land that we could afford. I didn't care where we lived. I'd wanted to go back to work, but Steve had again disparaged me out of anything resembling a job or career. "What's the point, Reggie? You can't do much that's worthwhile anyway." And so, I'd given in and never gone back to work, but spent my time working as a volunteer at The Red Cross. It was a useful charity, one that used its assets well, and Steve liked the cachet of having a wife who did community service work. I always felt that Steve ran the business end of our marriage, and he ran it well, without any input at all from me. Somehow, my achievements had been minimized to wife, mother and woman-who-volunteers. I guess I didn't have a very positive self-image. Maybe Brianna *was* what a successful man like Steve needed and wanted.

To get back once more to our history together…I'll get this over as quickly as I can… We bought a three and a half-acre property on Driftwood Island. Driftwood Island was an iffy-piffy private island off the coast of Kittery Point, Maine. Note that I said Kittery *Point*, not just plain old Kittery. There is a clear social divide between the old potato farmers, Navy Yard workers and lobstermen families who live in the very attractive, but older and a bit run down town of Kittery, and those with newer, greener, money, who reside on "the Point". It was very important to Steve that we reside, not live, and that the residing be done among the wealthy. Driftwood Island was the pinnacle of his goals. Steve sold his partnership in Massachusetts and opened a new office in Portsmouth, New Hampshire, just over the river from Kittery.

Until our new house, the house of Steve's dreams, could be built, we were living…ahem…residing…in a smallish condominium in Kittery Point, but barely one street over from Kittery. The condo was a stop-gap place to live, and we were both excited about starting to plan for the new house-to-be. We'd sold most of our furniture, and what was left, we'd crammed into the condo. We hadn't done much about blueprints or planning for the new house. Whenever the subject came up, Steve shrugged off any decision making and said that we had plenty of time. He told me that he'd spoken to a few designers, a few builders…but that nothing had been planned yet. I read a few new home magazines and dreamed of a smallish house with lots of nooks and crannies…something that looked as if it had nestled into its foundation forever. Steve dreamed of a huge place, with every modern gadget known to mankind. I didn't pay a lot of attention, and anyway, Steve was handling all of the details, whatever they might be. I didn't really know much about the plans or how things were proceeding. Being so ignorant about it all wasn't such a good idea, as I later found out. But that was then, when I was a fat, dumb and happy little wife who let her husband manage everything. Again, both of us agreed on what we were doing. I don't want you to think that Steve was the bad guy and I was the good wife. I was just as thrilled to dream about the new house, but maybe for some different reasons than Steve. Maybe. I want to be honest. Dumb, but honest.

And did I notice him drifting away? Not really, but perhaps, to punish myself, I could say that maybe I wasn't paying as much attention as I should. He did seem to work later at night. He did seem to be home less often. He traveled a bit more. But I truly had no idea. No idea at all. If I'd been more…what? Loving? Interesting? Thinner? Dressed a bit better? Drank more? Initiated some obscene sex games? What? What could I have done?

OK, that's the background part. Now we will get to my shock.

I drove back to the condo. I presumed Steve would be at work. I figured he'd call me and that we would discuss the parting of our ways, both conjugally and financially.

I opened the front door and stopped in my tracks. *Omygod*! We'd been robbed! The hallway and living room were nearly empty, denuded of the couch, the chairs, tables, the grandfather clock, the paintings on the wall, the expensive stereo system and the DVD player…almost everything had been stolen! I froze with my hand still on the doorknob with the door open behind me, listening hard to hear any sounds coming from inside the condo. The police always tell you to never go into a house that has been robbed. The robbers could still be there and they could be robbers who might hurt you. The condo seemed empty, but I didn't want to take any chances and I didn't want to spoil any finger-prints or whatever that the police might be able to use to catch the perpetrators. I could see a few sticks of furniture that the robbers had missed taking and my gut wrenched. I began to sob. On top of Steve's ultimatum, this pushed me over the edge.

I backed out of the house and called 911 on my car phone. A sym-pathetic dispatcher named Marsha made me stay on the phone…"Don't you dare go into the house, Mrs. Fornier," she ordered. "Just stay on the phone and talk with me until the police get there." We chatted for a few minutes, me – nervously, she – with great tact and patience. Marsha made me tell her what things I had noticed that were missing, and kept up a cheerful murmur to my distraught conversation. I guess they learn all about how to converse with moderately frantic housewives who have just been robbed and are waiting for the cops to arrive.

A police car drew up and two uniformed Kittery policemen got out of the car with their guns drawn. "Wow." I said to Marsha. "They have guns!" Unfazed, she asked to speak with one of the policemen and I handed the phone to the taller of them. He turned his head away from me and made some grunting sounds into the receiver. Then he pressed the disconnect button and handed me the phone.

"Stay here, Ma'am and we'll be right back." He motioned to his partner and the two of them went to the door of the condo. Their guns were held out, just as you'd see on some cops and robbers show on television. If I hadn't been so frightened, I might have been fascinated to watch them. The shorter one went around the side of the condo. The tall one opened the front door and went inside, leaving the door open behind him. I tiptoed up to the door and tried to look inside.

"What's happening?" Rose Nunn, my next door neighbor crept out of her doorway. "What's wrong?" Steve and I hadn't socialized with too many of the condo neighbors, but Rose and I had liked one another from the start. We'd exchanged greetings, drank a few cups of coffee together and traded chit-chat a few times, despite the fact that Steve thought she wasn't up to his social standards and discouraged any fa-miliarity. Fortunately, I liked Rose and we became friends.

"We were robbed!" I told her. "The police are in there now." She looked at me in a peculiar way, but I was so nervous, I guess I didn't pick up on it.

"Ummm, Reggie…" Rose's generally soft voice squeaked. "I, uh…last night….uh…" She caught hold of my sleeve and pulled at it. Her pink-cheeked, freckled face was concerned.

At that moment, the two policemen came out of my front doorway and I nearly leaped toward them. "Wait a minute, Rose." I said and ran to the door. The taller of the policemen had an envelope in his hand.

"Uh, Ma'am, Mrs., uh, Fornier. Uh, can you come inside the house?" His face was blotchy-red and he seemed uncomfortable. "Uh, now, please."

Rose followed us, walking right behind me, blinking nervously. "Uh. Just Mrs. Fornier, please." The shorter one waved Rose away. His face was pale and set and he obviously expected to be obeyed. After all, he had a gun. Rose nodded, biting her lip, and backed up a few steps. Her kind eyes, behind her glasses, gleamed in worry.

"I'll tell you all about it after. Thanks for your concern, Rose." I shrugged, waved to her and followed Tall and Short back into the condo. Rose stood on one foot and then shifted to the other, giving me back sort of a half-wave as I went into the door.

"Uh, Mrs. Fornier," Tall held the envelope in his hand. "Is, uh, Steve the first name of your husband?" I nodded my head like some demented hinged puppet. "Have you and, um, Mr. Fornier, um, had any, um…marital difficulties?" My mouth must have shown him my astonishment.

Marital difficulties? Was that what you call it when your husband leaves you for someone named Brianna? "What do you mean?" I asked Tall.

"Uh, this here's a letter to you. We, uh, read it. It was on the kitchen counter, um, and it was, uh, open." He handed me the piece of paper. "The furniture…all the stuff taken…. Steve, um. Your husband took it."

I guess I made some sort of mewing sound. Tall made a motion with his head and Short went into the kitchen and came back with a glass filled with water. I would have sat down abruptly, had there been anywhere left for me to sit. I drank a sip or two of the water. "Are you OK?" Short asked me. Both he and Tall looked extremely uncomfortable.

I nodded a few times, up and down, again like some helpless feminine marionette. "Son of a bitch," I said softly. "Son of a *bitch!* " Tall and Short nodded, seeming to agree with me. I felt foolish and stupid and vulnerable. The wife…the old wife. The stupid wife. Short patted me awkwardly on my arm. I guess my vulnerability showed like a buck-naked baby.

"Maybe you can go over to your neighbor's house," Short suggested. "Read the letter and then call your lawyer, or something." They shuffled their feet and mumbled a goodbye, glad to get away from me and the letter I held in my hands.

Reggie:
Brianna and I have taken the furniture we want. The rest is yours.
I gazed around bleakly. What "rest"? They'd taken damn near everything in the living room and kitchen.
I want the land on Tidewater Island. You can keep the condominium. I have left you $50,000 in our account at The Kennebunk Bank. You'll still have your share in the pension. I think I have been fair and considerate. You can contact me through my attorney……
A surge of blood red fury obscured my vision and I crumpled the letter in my hand. I forced myself to go up the stairs, needing to see the desolation, needing to hate him. Sonofabitchbastard! How *could* he? How *could* he do this to me? *Me!* His *wife!* After all, I had laughed with this man for most of my life, cried with him too, taken him, as I promised, for richer and for poorer, borne his children, for God's sake. We'd sat up together all night with the girls when they were sick, hugging one another and sharing our worries. We'd budgeted money to buy our first couch. We'd messed around on the kitchen table. We had been *married!*

The second floor was nearly empty; there wasn't much left. They had taken the computer and all of the furniture in the spare bedroom. They'd left a telephone and a bookcase and a spill of yellow files on the floor. In our bedroom, he'd taken all of his clothes, the bed, the armoire and the television set. My own clothes dangled obscenely from hangers, half on the rack and half on the floor of the closet. The bedclothes were heaped on the floor and he'd left me one dresser. Fair and considerate? I whimpered and ran to the bathroom and vomited into the toilet. Fortunately, he and his new *inamorata* hadn't been able to remove the toilet and had forgotten to take all of the towels and I was able to clean up after myself.

Rose was waiting for me. "Come in and have some coffee or maybe a drink," she offered with great sympathy. "I watched them last night, but I didn't want to interfere. He was with a younger woman…a blonde." She peered nervously at me. A younger woman and a blonde! The ultimate betrayal! I felt like such a jackass…the left-over old wife. Rose patted my hand. "What happened?"

I clutched at the hot mug of coffee and told her what little I knew. "Jeez," she said inadequately. "What are you going to do?" I shrugged, trying not to cry.

"I don't know. I…I just don't know…"

"Do you have a lawyer?" I shook my head. Steve had an attorney, but I presumed that one needed one's own in a case like this.

"I barely know anyone here in Kittery. I don't know what to do!" My voice rose in panic and the tears leaked out. Rose patted my shoulder. She'd been through a rough patch once in her life, I knew from past confidences. She understood my bewilderment and grief.

"I do know this lawyer. She represented my friend Maureen and she's supposed to be good. Do you want her phone number and address?" I mopped my eyes and nodded.

◆ ◆ ◆

I drove right over to the address Rose had given me. On the way, I stopped for gas. The gauge on my little VW was nearing empty. My shocks for the day were not yet over. My gas credit card was refused. "Sorry, Lady," the attendant informed me, giving me a scathing look and immediately pegging me as a career crook or a scam artist. "This here card is no good." I handed him the nine bucks while he watched me like a hawk, making sure that I didn't try to drive away before the transaction was completed. For the first time in many years, I had an acute consciousness of money, noting that I had about fifty dollars left in my purse together with a fistful of credit cards that were, I suspected, no longer of any use to me. Son of a bitch. I tried calling Jenna on my car phone, but, Steve had been a busy boy and now the car phone didn't work either. I presumed, and rightly, that he had cut off my ability to charge anything.

Steel replaced flesh and blood in the center of my chest. I might lose Steve, but I wasn't going to lose my mind, and I wasn't going to lose everything we had built in the 32 years we had been married. No siree, Bob. If I couldn't have Steve, and right this moment, I didn't ever want to *see* him again, much less be reconciled with him, I would have to be strong, resolute and sneaky. I *needed* this lawyer!

The Law Offices of Barbara Wyzinski and Associates were located in a small red brick building at the beginning of the Kittery Foreside Loop Road. The Loop Road was a one-way street running in almost a circle along the harbor in Kittery's original commercial district. It was an old, kind of funky part of town, with colorful buildings piled cozily against one another, occasionally showing glimpses of the water behind them. I passed the We Care Dry Cleaners, Saint Rocco's Roman Catholic Church with a connecting Parish Hall, a Tae Kwando studio, a bank, the imposing Rice Public Library, a masseuse, two hairdressers, a pizza restaurant, a flower shop and then the law office. It was an area that I'd never really explored. My half-numbed mind noted a used furniture and thrift store across the street from my destination. Maybe I could buy a few odds and ends there to replace the things that Steve and what's-her-name had stolen from the condo. But first things first.

Barbara Wyzinski was a giant of a woman, more than six feet tall and built like Mike Ditka. She had a gaunt, handsome face with dark, sympathetic eyes topped by a mop of frizzy black hair, monumental eyebrows and I liked her immediately. I knew she'd intimidate Steve completely in any courtroom battle. She sat me down across the desk and made some small talk. I knew she was sizing me up too. What did she see, this woman who made a career out of listening to people's problems? Obviously, she immediately saw my misery. Regina Sabatino Fornier. Fifty-five years old. Short hair, blow dried in a Dorothy Hammil sort of look, still light brown with the help of Preference Sandy Mist Number 24, medium height, medium weight, medium boring. Decent complexion, dark brown anxious eyes, a small upturned nose and a wide mouth that generally was smiling, but couldn't quite get the smile going today. A woman too old to be fascinating any more, someone whose breasts sagged a little, who wore a size 14, and whose face showed the lines of her years. Someone who had been kicked in the stomach and didn't know how to handle this situation.

She sat back and listened to my story, her strong face betraying shock and sympathy, and then she told me what to do. "Move the fifty thousand, if there really is fifty thousand, into a new account, one with your name only. Do that in the next five minutes after you leave here. Find out if he's closed any of your other accounts. If not, move any and all balances to a new account too. Is the car in your name?" I nodded. "Good. One less thing to bother about. We'll have to change the addresses on the registration and the insurance." She grabbed a pen and a yellow pad, ready to get to work. "Call each of the credit card companies. Find out if he's closed the accounts. Send each of them...no, I'll do that. You just give me a list of all your accounts and your account numbers." She sat back and rubbed her large hands together. "Do you want him back or are you glad to get rid of him?"

I sat back, startled. Did I want Steve back in my life? I thought of our life together...the girls...the ups and the downs...the love and the closeness that thirty-odd years had held. Then I thought of the humiliation I'd suffered today. The looks on the policemen's faces. The devastation of my life..."No. I don't want him back." I told her. She nodded, pleased with my answer.

"Good. We'll make him sorry he was born."

CHAPTER THREE

Jason Morant crept out of the house just before sunrise. He was keyed up, excited. This was going to be such a big adventure. None of the other guys would *believe* what he was going to do! Jason's freckled face grinned as he checked all of his equipment and stuffed everything into a rip-stop sack that he fastened onto the back of his bike with bungee cords. He rode off into the morning, munching on a large slab of his mother's banana bread, his ears filled with the raucous sounds of the Ramones spilling out of his CD player.

He biked onto the trail in the woods known to all his buddies as "mosquito alley". Slapping at the early morning bugs, he laughed aloud, relishing what lay ahead. It was dangerous…what worthwhile prank wasn't? It would be his *coup d'etat*, to quote Mademoiselle Corcoran, his French teacher at Traip Academy. His gift to the folklore of memorable senior class stunts. A legend, that's what he'd be…a legend. A little bit of worry niggled at him. It *was* a little dangerous. If he were caught, he'd be fined. Maybe even jailed. And his father would have a coronary! He might even be shitcanned out of college! But if he were successful…why the bragging rights would be worth a million bucks. He shouted into the morning air, "Watch out! Here I come!" and then giggled like a child for the sheer joy of it all.

He parked his bike in the shrubbery that edged the beach, dragging it into the bushes so that no one could see that anyone was here. This was the dangerous part. He put on his gear, checked again to be sure that no one had seen him, and slid into the water. His agile young body relished the tingle of the cold water.

After a vigorous ten minute swim, his whole body felt bubbly, as if he had ginger ale in his veins instead of blood. There! He sighted his quarry, jackknifed his slender, ropy body down and dove deeper. "Aha!" he mouthed silently. His excitement bubbled up through the cold water and he could barely keep himself from whooping out loud. "Gotcha!" Behind the mask, he grinned with exultation.

As he rose up from the dark green depths, the colors of the water changed like a turquoise rainbow. His head almost broke the surface.... "Agh! Wha..?" His voice gurgled in shock. What? What was *wrong?* "Agh!" He was trapped, unable to rise up any further. A heavy weight pressed down on his head.

He struggled, twisting frantically, jerking his nearly naked body back and forth...hampered by his treasures...and then...had the waters darkened or was his eyesight failing him? Helpless against the strong onslaught, his oxygen nearly gone, he opened his mouth to scream. Mistake. The salt water filled his throat and his head thrummed with a black roar. In a moment or two, his body went slack. The waves buffeted him, like a large strand of seaweed, to and fro. His fingers lost their ability to hold and his treasures were snatched away. Limp and unresisting, his body sank.

◆ ◆ ◆

Barbara...she'd asked me at once to call her that... made notes of everything I said. She listed every asset, stock, security and bank account and then made another list of the things Steve had whisked out of the condo. "Are there any credit cards in your name?" I shook my head sadly. I felt like such a failure. She smiled, a genuine grin. "Don't fret. We'll take care of getting you some gas cards and a few store credit cards...a girl should have credit cards of her own, right?" The puppet in my body nodded. Of *course* I should have had a credit card or two in my own name, but who would have ever thought.... Barbara soothed me, explaining that few married women ever bother to get their own credit cards. "They don't realize the dangers of having everything only in their husband's name. Not until something like this happens." Her frizzy head moved from side to side. "But we'll set you up anew, never fear, Reggie." She wrote a few more notations on the yellow pad that held my life on its blue lines. "I presume your health insurance is from Steve's company?"

Again, the puppet nodded. Everything belonged to Steve. I owed my very married-up-to-yesterday existence to Steve, didn't I? Wasn't that what you got with your part of the marriage?

Barbara made a few more notations. "We'll get him to continue your insurance for at least three more years." She made a few slashing lines with her pencil and I marveled at a woman who could make Steve do anything for at least three years. She didn't seem fazed at all at committing him to pay for insurance for me and I presumed she would be successful. That's how confident I felt about her. And I was right. She slapped the yellow pad down on the desk and stood up, looming over my huddled misery. "Let's get a bite to eat and then I'll get to work and formulate our strategy." I felt better; almost relieved that she was taking my problems and taming them into submission. Oh, how I loved this woman!

We walked along the sidewalk past the church and the thrift shop, then across the street to The Loop Café. The restaurant was bright and cheerful, with ten or so tables outside, overlooking the lobster pots and docks lining the harbor and had a similar number of tables inside. "The food here is terrific." I sniffed some appetizing smells and tried to remember when I'd last eaten.

The place was half-filled. A short harried man with slicked back dark hair, a coffee-colored complexion and an Omar Sharif moustache plopped two menus on the table and told us that he'd be right back. "He's the owner," Barbara told me. "Name of Gerjeet Simha. From India originally and then Pakistan. His family had to flee one of the terrorist regimes." I turned to watch Gerjeet as he frantically worked to wait on customers and cook at the same time. A young and lovely middle-eastern woman, with huge, nervous brown eyes, dressed in a sari-like outfit, hurriedly slapped dishes down on the counter and rang up sales on a cash register.

"They look busy."

"No help. No help today." The man returned, apologetic. Barbara told him that we were in no hurry and he grinned his relief. She introduced us: Reggie Sabatino Fornier meet Gerjeet Simha. Gerjeet saluted us with a half-bow and retreated to clear a table. We looked at the menu and I realized that I was starving. A bean and vegetable soup connected with my appestat and Barbara chose a meatloaf sandwich.

"Gerjeet makes everything from scratch. That's his wife, Anoop. She makes the soups." We watched them run from one side of the restaurant to the other like two frenzied ants. "I come here a lot. They do a great breakfast and a wonderful brunch. My husband and I stroll over on Sundays and sit for hours when the weather is good, watching the boats and reading the paper and eating." She grinned. "I eat a lot." Gerjeet skidded to a stop and took our orders, smiling and juggling three water glasses, the menus and the remainder of a plate of chili.

"Back to business," Barbara said. "Do you want to stay in your condominium?" I shook my head. Live in that place of dark emptiness redolent of humiliation? No. It was the last place I wanted to be. "OK. Do you want to sell it or rent it out?"

"I think I should sell it. What do you think?"

"I'd petition to have it put immediately into your name and then we'll get it right out on the market. Your husband...let's start right away calling him your ex..." She grinned wickedly at me, "or we could start to call him the shithead...." I grinned back. I really, really *liked* this woman. She sipped at her water and continued. "He seems to want that land on the island with a vengeance. It's a valuable parcel of land and he's hot for it." She questioned me. "Unless you yourself want it...?" I shook my head again. No. If I were going to have a new life, then I would have a new life. I wanted no part of the old one nor anything connected to Steve or what we'd had together, barring the girls, of course, and even that would be extremely different from now on. "Good. Then we'll have a great bargaining chip. The land is worth a fortune, Reggie. Are you sure...?" I shook my head even more emphatically. I would never feel comfortable on that land now. Not ever. Barbara nodded, as if I'd passed another one of her unwritten tests. "Naturally, we don't let on to him that you don't want it. We dangle it obscenely in front of him. It will be valuable, psychologically. And even more valuable in practical ways." My soup arrived in a blue tureen, accompanied by three hunks of thick-sliced bread and a yellow slab of butter. Barbara waved me on. "Start eating. Go ahead." She made some notes on a pad of paper and I spooned the soup up, letting the thick puree of warmth stream down my gullet. Funny thing. I felt a lot better. Barbara's sandwich came and we munched quietly for a few moments.

'What will you do for accommodations?" With my mouth filled with bread, I hunched my shoulders, mimicking uncertainty, and trying to push the wedge of panic down.

"Donno. I'll need to stay somewhere. I'm not going to spend the night at that empty condo." My face showed some delayed shock. "I...I guess I'll stay at the beautiful No-Tell Motel I stayed at last night and look for a place to rent tomorrow. Maybe something furnished. I don't even have a bed." I tried to chuckle, but the bean soup seemed to stick in my throat. "I saw that used furniture place down the street...I'll look there and then try..."

"You can stay with us tonight." My eyes flew open and I started to protest. "Don't even open your mouth, except to eat," she commanded, waving her pickle spear at me. "We have a big old house and plenty of spare beds. Horace and I would enjoy having you with us." I thought for a moment, then, with sincere humbleness, thanked her.

"Where do you live?"

"A few blocks from here, over on Admiral's Way. We bought an old house and are fixing it up little by little. We enjoy that sort of thing." Because she was a nice woman and because she sensed that I needed some time to get myself together, she rambled on for a bit. She told me some of the history of the Foreside Area. "When Kittery was still a fishing port three hundred years ago, this was the hot spot of the town. It went rapidly downhill when everyone moved away from town and Kittery Point became the place for all the new money. Then they built the outlet complex on Route 1, and the Foreside nearly died."

"I hate those outlets," I told her. "All the same stuff, only produced just for the outlets. Quasi-bargains and too much traffic."

She nodded. "Shoppers are starting to get smart; some of them anyway. There are so many unique shops that have opened around here. Shops that sell original items, not the mass-produced stuff that you see in every chain store." I nodded, tipping my bowl to get the last of my soup. "People are coming back here now, fixing up the old houses, roaming around all the neat little stores. It's become chic. Just look at the ambience here. The Foreside is enjoying a well-deserved renaissance and property values are going up. Look at Anoop and Gerjeet. This restaurant is a little goldmine for them. They live in that old house just behind the garage. Gerjeet's mother lives with them and she takes care of the house and their little girl. They are such sweet people and work so hard. The food is fabulous, but they don't have a clue about desserts. I think they stock some cellophane wrapped stuff and some stale pound cake." She took a last bite of the meatloaf. "Oh well," she mumbled, her mouth full, "maybe they'll find a good bakery one of these days. It's the only complaint I have about the place." She licked the last of the meatloaf from her fork. "Horace and I are thinking of buying another house here and using it as a rental. It would be a good investment." She pushed her plate away and seemed to come to some decision. Her homely face was speculative, "Are you squeamish?"

"Squeamish?"

"Mmmm. Would you live in a house where there have been a couple of violent deaths?"

I repeated my best shrugging act. "I don't know. What are you saying?"

She laughed, a booming sound that made several fellow lunchers turn and look at her with curious amusement. "There's a house nearby, a few streets from here. A beautiful old cottage that perches over the harbor. It's been empty, except for all the new furniture, for a year. My

19

law firm is the executor of the estate and we'd like to rent it out. It's a house that Horace and I are thinking of buying. Do you want to go and see it?"

"And the catch…?"

"The catch is that two women were killed last year in the house." She saw my eyes widen. "Oh, everything's been cleaned up, sanitized and repainted. It's sparkling clean and gleaming and a lovely little property." She spread her big hands out as if she were going to catch a football. "But…not everyone is anxious to live there."

"Uh." I didn't know what to say.

"Do you want to walk over?"

I was curious. Who wouldn't be? "Sure," I said. There was no harm in just looking, was there?

The tables were emptying and Gerjeet, with his shoulders slumped in weariness, came to the table. "Dessert, ladies?" Barbara shook her head.

"No thanks, Gerjeet. Just the check." He put down a tray and totaled up our lunch, then, with the delicacy born of repetition, placed the check in the exact center of the table. Barbara snatched it with a fierce glare, daring me to argue with her.

"I am so sorry, Mees Barbara, if the service was so slow. We were so busy today. Malik, that fool of a cousin on my uncle's side, decided that working here was beneath him. He has gone into Portsmouth to work on the telephones." His smooth face looked dejected. Even his moustache drooped. "It is too much work for Anoop and me. We need a new helper."

I thought of the fifty bucks in my purse. Fifty thousand dollars sounded like a lot of money in the bank, but not a lot for the rest of a lifetime. I didn't want to touch it. I stood up. "I worked as a waitress when I was in college. I always enjoyed it. If you'll have me, I can start tomorrow morning." I was delighted to see that Barbara's mouth could hang open too.

◆ ◆ ◆

We walked the three blocks to Schooner Street, passing the rather pleasant store front marked as Fair Tide. Barbara told me Fair Tide was a consignment shop that sold used clothing and furniture, with the profits earmarked for a local shelter home for temporarily displaced persons and battered women. Although I was sort of displaced, I certainly was happy that I wasn't a battered woman, at least not a physically battered one. I wondered if having one's husband leave you for a younger woman might just be considered psychological battering. Maybe, I thought to myself, blessing the facts that I wasn't destitute, had Barbara helping me, and now, even had a job. I vowed out loud to bring all my old stuff to Fair Tide and help a few ladies and gentlemen that were much worse off than I was. Barbara grinned at me. I know that I had passed another one of her informal tests. "I don't want anything associated with my old life." I emphasized. "I might find a few things there that I need. And I may as well do a bit of good at the same time."

Schooner Street was swimming in sunshine. The houses were all charming, small, old and higgle-piggle with porches that wound their way around and flowers growing everywhere. I sniffed honeysuckle in the air and the birds were almost noisy with chirping. I could smell the ocean and see small sailboats rocking at their moorings through gaps in the hedges. Across the harbor, in Portsmouth, I could see the old red brick buildings that had been shipping offices two hundred years ago. There was a glimpse of the channel that led to the ocean, fronted by the steel derricks and grey and green Government buildings of the Portsmouth Naval Shipyard. How could murder visit a place so charming? Barbara stopped at a rose arbor fronting a tiny path that led to Number 236. "Here it is," she gestured to me, and we turned, opened the gate and walked to the porch.

My first, second and third impressions were of a lovely garden, the sun shining and a sense of delight. Colorful flowers spilled out over the path and vines twined their way up drainpipes and hung over the eaves. The house itself was shingled, painted a mellow green with white trim. ters. The door was a shiny dark enameled black one with a unique stained glass window set in the middle. The other windows sparkled. It looked like a cottage out of a Disney movie. I expected to see chirpy, anthropomorphic bluebirds, dressed in little straw hats, on a branch singing some catchy zip-a-dee-doo-dah song. There was no sense of gloom or doom anywhere. Barbara fished in her handbag for the key, opened the door and went in. I followed with slow, hesitant steps.

We were in a tiny entrance hall and then I gasped as I saw the view. The entire first floor was one big room with wall to wall windows hanging out over the water. The walls were painted white, the floors gleamed with varnish. The furniture was old wicker, also painted white, with brilliantly colored cushions and pillows. The walls sported all kinds of funny shelves and cubbyholes. It was absolutely delightful, almost like being in a tiny ship of your own. Barbara stood quietly and grinned to herself as I was drawn to the windows and turned back to her with my own grin of sheer pleasure. As I turned, I noted a small kitchen tucked into the front corner of the room. The kitchen was a miniature marvel of stainless steel efficiency and I immediately saw myself at the oven, making all sorts of culinary concoctions. "Like it?" she asked.

"I love it!" I poked at the bookshelves that lined the walls under the windows. "Um, uh…where did it….I mean, what actually happened here?"

"There were two women who lived here. Nice people, although I myself didn't know them except to say hello. I think they were lesbians, not that it matters. Well-off, upstanding citizens. Generous women, good neighbors. Never any trouble or problems. Anyway, they were found in here," she gestured towards one of the couches, "bludgeoned to death. It was just about a year ago and the police still haven't any clue as to who killed them." She fingered the material on one of the cushions. "We had the whole place repainted and we replaced almost all of the furniture, even the beds and stuff upstairs."

"And no one else wants to live here?"

"No. Most people won't even come to look. Those that do, well…" She hunched her heavy shoulders, "don't want to stay."

I looked around carefully and actually sniffed the air. "There's no sense of bad karma." I touched one or two of the objects on top of a table, trying to feel a sense of the tragedy. The atmosphere was only calm and peaceful. "I can't believe you couldn't rent it." I watched a swarm of sun motes sparkle against the blue sky through the wavy window glass. A tall sailboat with starched white sails slipped by.

She shrugged. "I know. It's a really lovely view. However, people just don't seem to want to live here. Perhaps you're different, but I don't want to pressure you." Her big hands twisted together. "What do you think?"

"I like it. I think I'd like to see the upstairs." We trooped up the crooked staircase. At the top of the stairs, three doors opened off a small landing. One led to a gleaming old-fashioned bathroom with a massive claw foot tub in the middle of the floor, one led to a small bedroom that could be used as an office, and the last led to the main bedroom. It was a long, low room that went from the front of the house all the way to the back. Again, everything was painted white. White walls, white iron bedstead, white comforter. Only a few throw pillows in bright red and navy blue broke up the monochrome. At the back of the room, a set of French doors led to a small balcony which hung out over the water.

"Everything is brand new, except for a few kick-knacks and antique pieces that were so adorable we kept them." Barbara watched me to see how I felt about it all. I grinned and told her the furnishings were just right for me. "There's a lavatory downstairs and a washer and dryer in the basement." Barbara twitched the white curtains at the window. "What do you think?"

"I love it." I said. "Maybe I'm nuts, but I feel welcome here." She raised her heavy eyebrows and looked pleased. I prowled around, opening closet doors and peeking into the medicine cabinet. I found myself humming and I mentally placed a new computer on the little desk in the guest room. I could put a daybed in there and have room for Andrea to visit. *"...All covered with snow..."* I continued the tune as I went back into the main bedroom. Barbara followed me like a baby elephant, ducking her head as she went through the doorways.

"...For courting's a ple-aaa-sure..." She sang with me, her voice the alto to my wavering soprano. Then we both looked at one another as the music continued, a plinking guitar bringing up the melody. "Wha...! What's that? Where is the music *coming* from?"

We ran down the stairs, bumping against one another. The song tinkled on. *"And a false hearted loooo-ver, is worse than a thief...."* There, on the top of a square, obviously old table near the kitchen, a small, elderly Victrola, housed in a wooden case, poured forth a tune. *"For a thief will just roooo-oob you, and take what you have."* Barbara lifted the arm and the music stopped suddenly. The record, an old 78, whizzed round and round, faintly buzzing and clicking.

"That's odd," Barbara held the arm in the air, her face puzzled. "The Victrola was one of the things we left from...when...you know...before." She peered through her glasses at the scratched record label. "*On Top of Old Smokey*". That's all it says." Slowly, she set the arm back onto the record groove and the tune continued on its merry way, *"And you'll be for saaay-ken, and never know why-ee!"* Then, with a few more notes, the record came to its end and the arm bumped against the center post, kerchink, kerchink. I bit my lip and Barbara found the switch that turned the machine off.

"Did it just go on by itself?" I gave the Victrola a wary look. It was a really old-fashioned one with a metal plate showing Nipper, the RCA dog, listening to his Master's voice. I jiggled the controls, then turned the switch on again and put the stylus down at the beginning of the record. Plinky music began and then a scratchy, cowgirl sort of voice began to sing once more: *"On top of old Smooo-key, all covered with snow...."* I lifted the arm and shut the machine off again.

We looked at one another. "Weird," was all I could say.

"Do you think it's a ghost?" Barbara's sensible, scholarly face was perplexed. She giggled with jittery nervousness for such a big, tall lady.

"Bah!" I said. "We probably joggled it when we walked on the floorboards above." She nodded. Of course. What else could it be? I shrugged. What else *could* it be? People like Barbara and me didn't believe in ghosts, even in a house where murder had been committed, and why would a ghost be playing a Victrola anyway?

"Does it bother you? I can take the Victrola away." Barbara touched the table and the song began again.

I laughed. "I think a haunted Victrola is just what I need these days." I shut off the switch and patted the top of the cabinet. "Let's go outside," I changed the subject. For some reason, the scratchy music made me feel at home.

Barbara gave the record player a dubious look and then shrugged. We opened the back door and stepped out onto a long, low terrace that hugged the back of the house. "Did you plant all this stuff?" I gestured to the myriad of containers that lined the terrace, each overflowing with flowers. A large central planting sprouted tall yellow yarrow and stiff sheaths of goldenrod. Stalks of purple-headed Joe Pye weed waved and a few butterflies fluttered amidst the flowers. It was very attractive. "Or was it all here, um, before?"

"I have a black thumb. I confess that I called Jackie Norby...she operates a local landscaping business... and they came and did everything." She went down the shallow stone steps. "Do you like to garden?" I nodded, full of enthusiasm, itching to get my hands in the dirt, plant a few tomatoes, pick a few cukes. Barbara shrugged. "To each his own. Come and look over the cliff." We walked to the edge of the property and looked out over the rocks and mud of low tide in the harbor. 'Isn't this super?"

Enchanted, I gazed at the scene. "Can I afford to live here?"

"Sure, if you give good service at The Loop Café."

I giggled, feeling joyful for the first time in two days. Maybe Steve was right. Maybe I would be happier by myself. I snapped a yellow flower from a bush and stuck it into the hair next to my ear. I found myself humming the old cowgirl song again but this time there was no answering music coming from the house.

"Yoo Hoo!" An old lady in a flowered housedress was waving from next door. "Barbara!" She beckoned to us.

"That's Mrs. Clutterbuck. She's older than God and lives next door." Barbara waved back. "She's a sweetie and knows every single human being and every scrap of gossip about who lives in the Foreside. You'll love her." She waved again. "Coming, Mrs. Cee!" She turned and went back up the path. I lingered for a moment longer, hanging over the fence and hoping that I was making the right decision. The bush next to me trembled and a coal-black cat poked its head out. It blinked up at me and then wound itself around my ankles, purring loudly. I reached down to pat it on the head and another cat, this one white, appeared. The white cat sat down at my feet, leaning hard against my shin and watched the antics of its playmate.

"Hey, kitties." I cooed, making those silly sounds that people do. "Where do you two live, huh?" The black cat meowed, answering me.

"Reggie!" Barbara called and I looked up. I called out that I was coming and when I looked back down, the two cats had disappeared.

CHAPTER FOUR

P ropped up on two enormous pillows plumped at the head of a large, four-poster bed in one of Barbara and Horace's guestrooms, I reviewed the rest of the day. Barbara went back to her office, presumably to think up awful things to do to Steve and I went back to the condominium to pack a suitcase. Rose was waiting behind her curtains and came out as soon as she saw me, her eyes kind and concerned. I'd filled the suitcase and three cartons with things I thought I'd need, including two pair of khaki slacks and two dark blue tee-shirts which I figured I'd wear as waitress extrordinaire at my new job. Then I sat down with Rose for another cup of coffee and some female confidences. She was glad that I'd retained Barbara and promised to keep an eye on the empty condo. I told her about my new job, and she agreed that it might be just the thing to keep me busy and tide me over this time of woe. I gave her my extra key, told her to expect to see some real estate people in the next few days and said I'd be back later tomorrow afternoon. She kissed me lightly on the cheek, two women supporting one another. As I said, Steve had always sort of ignored her and the rest of the condo neighbors, scoring them as...well, not quite up to his standards. I hugged Rose again, thinking that once more, Steve's opinion counted for *bupkus*. I certainly thought that Rose was on a par or above me at this moment. I was grateful for her friendship.

I went to the bank and spent an embarrassing, but fruitful hour changing the joint accounts over to new ones in my name only. I was pleased to discover that Steve seemed to have forgotten about our checking account, and switched the seven thousand, four hundred twenty-six dollars and seventy-three cents into another new account sporting my name and only my name. I sat in the car afterwards and mused about how dependent a wife really is. Dumb and dependent. Whatever might happen in my future life, I vowed that I would take better care to be sure that, at least monetarily, I would always be my own master. I vowed that my daughters would learn from this and not end up like me. Ever! Wide awake, I rolled over and sipped at the glass of cold water on the bedside table. I lay back down. Useless. My eyeballs were stuck open.

I punched the pillows, wanting to sleep. I wiggled a bit until I was more comfortable and mentally shook myself. I tried to relax and made myself go over the events of the day. Barbara...the house...Horace...I chuckled as I recalled my surprise at meeting Horace Wyzinski. I guess we all make assumptions, and I had assumed that Barbara's husband would be a big, burly man to complement her. Was I ever wrong! Horace was small, about an inch or two shorter than I, which put the top of his head somewhere near Barbara's hefty collarbone. He had curly grey hair that circled his head like a wreath, pink apple cheeks and a grin like a ten year old boy. He'd brought home take-out Chinese food for supper...Barbara said that she was a terrible and indifferent cook...and we sat on the floor eating right out of the cardboard containers. Within three minutes, I was totally in love with Horace. His attention, however, although cheerful and polite to me, never wavered from Barbara's face. It was obvious that he adored her and she, in turn, watched him as if the sun and moon rested just above his sweet little head. He referred to her as his Queen and he touched her hand or shoulder at every opportunity.

Barbara put him *au courant* with my legal and domestic situation and he expressed a solemn regret for Steve. "She'll wipe the floor with him before you're finished," I believe was how he put it. "Barbara always does well for her clients."

He was delighted that I was taking the cottage on Schooner Street. "You'll chase away any thoughts of ghosts. It will be good to have someone in the place. It's been empty too long."

The word 'ghosts' reminded me of the Victrola and I mentioned the odd thing that had happened. The three of us agreed that old houses with uneven floorboards might set up vibrations that could do peculiar things. "I've heard of old houses that have windows and doors open and close when the tide comes in and out." Horace peered at me from under his bushy eyebrows. "Did it make you nervous?"

"Not at all. I kept waiting to feel peculiar, knowing what had happened, but there was no bad atmosphere of any kind in the house." Barbara nodded in agreement, "Or I'm just too insensitive or dumb to notice anything." We all laughed. "I am interested, however, in learning a little bit more about what happened."

Horace worked as a child psychiatrist in an office in Portsmouth. His building was right across the street from the newspaper offices. He promised to do some research on exactly what had happened a year ago. "I'll put a file together and bring it over." He ate a bit of lo mein. "Actually, the best person to talk to would be Mrs. Clutterbuck." Barbara and I had talked briefly with the old lady while standing in her backyard and she'd invited me to visit as soon as I had settled myself. "She's a pistol. Bright as a penny and she knew both the women. She's a nice old biddy anyway in addition to being a vast storehouse of any and all gossip." I promised to do my part. It would be good to get to know the neighbors. Already, I was feeling as if the little green house was mine and would be a good home.

A huge yawn interrupted my reminiscing and I rolled myself over into my favorite sleeping position. As I drifted off, I marveled that I hadn't missed Steve at all this afternoon and evening. Was that a good sign or a bad sign? Somehow, with my head cradled in the soft pillow, I didn't care.

◆ ◆ ◆

I left my suitcases at Barbara and Horace's and the boxes in my car. I walked to the restaurant and was greeted with great relief and enthusiasm by Gerjeet and Anoop. "We were afraid you might not come," they confided. They sat me down and fed me a cup of freshly brewed coffee and we talked a bit. They told me how they had saved every cent, how Anoop's family had given them money to help them immigrate to America, and how they opened the shop. Gerjeet did most of the talking. Anoop's huge eyes followed everything he said, and her hands, small and graceful, waved and moved in time to his words. Her wrists were adorned with thick, silver bracelets, hung with jangly charms and the metal chimed and clanged faintly. I felt very comfortable and happy listening to him and watching her. Anoop was dressed in a pink and purple sari and she had that dot-thing in the middle of her forehead. She looked like a Rajah's daughter and smelled heavenly with a clean, spice-like scent. Her hair was inky black, long and shiny and plaited in a big fat braid that flopped over one shoulder. I wondered if she put the dot-thing on every morning with, say, an eyebrow pencil, or if it was a sort of decal, but I didn't feel as if I should ask. Maybe in a week or so,

"Now, to the business." Gerjeet stood up and I mentally bounced on the balls of my sneakered feet. Anoop went into the kitchen and Gerjeet showed me what to do. In a half hour, I had learned the rudiments of where everything was kept and how the breakfast meal flowed. I set the ten inside tables with blue and white batik printed tablecloths, arranged the napkins and silverware, put out butter and condiments, wrapped the

28

blue and white apron that matched the tablecloths around my waist and was as ready as I could be when The Loop Café opened at seven.

I won't say I was perfect. I forgot to bring home fries to Gerjeet's steady customers, Lou and Cynthia Kochanek (they gently reminded me of my omission and I scooted, shamefaced, back to the kitchen to comply), spilled a cup of coffee over my sneaker, gave one elderly gentleman sausages instead of ham, and forgot to charge one professional-looking lady for the side of bacon she ate, but all in all, I managed. Everyone was kind, patient and friendly.

Most of the regular customers were the men and women who worked around the corner at the Portsmouth Navy Yard, four Post Office workers, and a few schoolteachers. Some of them even chatted for a few moments with me, introducing themselves and wanting to know a little bit about me, Regina Sabatini Fournier, new waitress and newly not-married-anymore woman.

I met Pauli Rines, the woman who ran the Continuing Education Department at Traip Academy, Kittery's high school, Mary Bogucki, a vice-president of some big company in Boston, Rachel Armstrong who headed up the Rice Library, the pastor of the local Methodist Church and Mike O'Brien, the local and very genial Postmaster.

The round table in the middle of the Café held a group of women who were starting three new businesses right down the street. Amid their bowls of fresh fruit with Anoop's home-made yogurt on top, they opened lap-tops and scribbled on business plans. A card and gift paper shop, to be called Papers, Ink. – clever name – would open in two weeks on the corner of Government Street, a just-started bistro with the unusual name of Anneke Jans, was planning an ad campaign, and an artist's co-op calling itself the original moniker of Just Us Chickens was refurbishing an old building and would be up and functioning next month. Another woman, a cute blonde with apple-cheeks rushed in and pulled another chair up. Everyone greeted her with a "Hi, Christa!"

Christa was another local woman-entrepreneur type. I watched, openmouthed, as she whipped out a laptop and showed the others her plans for a calling center to be built in nearby Eliot. I didn't even know what a calling center was! I was impressed.

Christa, and her last name was Heibel, was a transplant from International Falls, Minnesota and had chosen the Kittery/Eliot area as one that was ripe for business building. "I love the seashore!" she confessed to me. "We have lakes in Minnesota, but no seashore." She quickly fanned out a few presentation booklets on the table, asking the other women's opinions. "We have lakes and walleyed pike and lots of snow," she laughed. "I liked it there, but I needed a better market for the calling center and southern Maine seemed to have the best demographics."

Astounded and a bit overwhelmed by Christa's business jargon, I nodded and handed her a menu.

While Christa perused the menu, Debby somebody, a local artist who would be the driving force behind Just Us Chickens showed me a few of her haunting paintings of the lighthouses that dotted Kittery's shores. "Can you knit or paint, Reggie?" she asked me, inviting me to be a part of the creativity that was changing the face of the Foreside area. My reluctant headshake didn't daunt her. "Well, even if you can't to anything artistic, you can volunteer a few hours a week selling other people's stuff," she invited. I promised to think about it, if my time and weary feet allowed.

"If you can't be an artist or a volunteer, you can always come in and be a good customer." Debby nodded her head firmly and, impressed by these slick and professional women and properly cowed, I promised – *promised* - to show up and purchase things.

Christa chose the banana-stuffed French toast. I brought her order back to the kitchen and picked up Debby's dish of granola, some honey and a bowl of blueberries and wondered why I hadn't pushed myself before to befriend women like this. Mary, Debby, Christa, Rachel, Pauli…all lovely people and all seemingly with an interest in me – Regina, left-over wife. They didn't care that I'd once been married to Steve, a big hoo-hah businessman. They didn't care at all. They just seemed to like me. Me alone. Remarkable! I could use friends like these. I'd enjoy friends like these. I needed friends like these.

Perhaps I should have leaped out of my docile rut early in my marriage and become a more interesting woman. Maybe then Steve wouldn't have left me. Was Brianna a member of such a group of friends? Was this lack in me one of the reasons that Steve had left me?

These musings were interrupted by several tables of computer gurus who worked in downtown Portsmouth and wanted menus. I hustled, talked, chatted a little more with the business women and met more nice human beings than I had met in ten years of marriage with Steve. But was this his fault or mine? Mine, I thought. All I had to do was to climb out of the boring pot-hole I had made for myself. Ha! I had climbed out, hadn't I? Almost, I answered myself. I have one leg over the top and am pushing to reach the roadbed.

I got a lot of kind welcomes, a brochure of the Continuing Education classes from Pauli, a cheerful swat on my backside from old Judge Emery, a preliminary menu for the new restaurant, Anneke Jans, a business card from Christa, lots of potential new friendships and a comfortable pocketful of tips.

The Café emptied out about nine and I sat down for a moment with Gerjeet for a cup of coffee. Anoop shyly showed me a photo of Daria, their baby daughter. "Daria!" I exclaimed. "That's a family first-name in our big Italian family! I have a cousin named Daria, an aunt named Daria and a great-aunt named Daria!"

"Truly? It is a Hindu name. Is your family from India or Pakistan?" Anoop's eyes got even bigger and her jewelry flashed with her excitement.

"No, we are all Italian." I laughed. "The first time the name was used, that I know of, was 'way back more than a hundred and fifty years ago with my, um, let's see, Great-Uncle Dario who was a priest in Italy and wound up as a Monsignor in my home town. He came to the United States in…1902, I think."

"Such a coincidence!" Anoop clapped her hands. I took the photo and turned it this way and that. I saw a miniature of Anoop, with tumbled curls and a wide, toothless grin.

"She's just adorable." Anoop agreed with a slightly biased maternally fervent nod. "With those dark curls, she could be a member of my own family!" We laughed, instant friends with a common bond.

"I wanted to name her Daria. It was a name that I had dreamed of just before she was born." Anoop glanced quickly behind her to see Gerjeet working at the back of the restaurant. "Gerjeet and his mother wanted another name. I pretended to consider it, but when the time came, in the hospital, I insisted that my daughter take the name that I had chosen." She sat up a little straighter. "Gerjeet was not pleased and his mother was angry, but I didn't give in. In Pakistan, nice wives do not choose their daughter's names in opposition of their husband's desires. They always obey their husband. But we do not live in Pakistan now." Her dark eyes flashed and I sensed that women's lib was struggling to be heard above and beyond Anoop's traditional sari and the mark on her forehead. I patted her hand in understanding. Gerjeet came to the table, showing me the brunch menu. Anoop giggled nervously, then ran back to the house during the lull to give Daria her morning bath.

Gerjeet and I traded a few more snippets of our life stories and then the mid-morning crowd came in. I met several housewives, salesmen, and a few of the people who operated other businesses in the Loop area, most notably the two rival hairdressers, whose shops sat side by side. First came Rita of Rita's Beauty Parlor, a staid establishment that dated back almost twenty-five years. Rita handled the older crowd, matrons who wanted perms and rollers in their rinsed and blued hair. Two years ago, a second beauty parlor opened within a block of Rita's, an event that Rita would never forgive, even though the customers of Hair-Em, Scare-Em would never set foot in her establishment and vice-versa. The Hair-Em, Scare-Em crowd ran to punk hairdos, with pink and green highlights, unusually decorated scalps with symbols and signs of the Zodiac shaved out of the back and sides. The mistress of this particular boutique went by the name of Zee Pawlowski. Her real name was Deborah, she told me, but, "in the trade, I go by Zee." She tossed her head with its rather unusual hair-do of purple spikes crowned with sparkles on the ends. Even though she shook her head like a race-horse getting ready to run the Santa Anita Stakes, not one single hair moved on her head. "Deborah is just too ordinary." I nodded, fascinated. Nothing at all about Zee was ordinary. Needless to say, Zee and Rita sat at different tables and sniffed at one another's back. Nothing boring about these customers! I sensed a bit of drama and had listened to snippets of gossip all morning long. Barbara had hinted that this little Café was one of the hot-spots in town. Great! So many wonderful customers and potential confrontations already! I was comfortable and it seemed that I fit right in. I liked all of them and they seemed to like me. Me! Regina-by-herself. Not the old appendage of Steve's wife. I grinned and picked up a plate of pancakes and sausage and waltzed over to the four-top by the window. (Gerjeet had already clued me into restaurant speak…a four-top meant a table for four…a deuce, a table for two…see how well I was doing already?) I fluffed my hair back. I knew I was going to enjoy this job immensely.

As it was a beautiful day, Gerjeet opened up the outdoor seating area for lunch. A lot of customers liked to sit outside, especially as Gerjeet had declared that dogs were allowed to join their owners, as long as they (the dogs, that is) behaved themselves. He even offered large plastic bowls filled with water and a biscuit or two for his canine customers. Lunch went by in a blur of chili, pot roast, hot turkey sandwiches and salads. Again, I managed. I won't even pretend that I was efficient , but, as I said already, I managed. Barbara and Horace came in to offer me encouragement and leave me a five dollar tip for a ten dollar lunch and to tell me that the office had set up telephone service at 236 Schooner and that they'd see me later.

Just as lunch was ending, two enormous sunburned bearded men, carrying a bushel basket of lobsters, came into the restaurant. This was how I met my first two...how shall I say it?...suitors.

The last thing on my mind was men. I had been humiliated, bruised, embarrassed and stomped on - figuratively, but nonetheless stomped on - by my husband of thirty-odd years. All I wanted now was to find a cozy niche, lick my wounds, and learn how to live on my own again. Romance? Who needed all those problems?

And anyway, even if I dreamed about a new man in my life, who would look twice at me? Ordinary, a bit dumpy, 'way, 'way over the hill in figure and fashion. Who would even think of me as a desirable woman?

You'd be amazed. I was, too. Right off the bat, I was casually wooed by the lobstermen - Daniel and Jonah Bethany - better known locally as The Bethany Brothers. As soon as they set eyes on me, they literally twirled their matching red-gold moustaches like the villains in some old stage play. Their eyes lit up and they were loud and seemingly sincere about their admiration for me.

Looking almost like twins, even though they were three years apart, as I learned later from Barbara, the Bethany Brothers considered themselves, like their lobsters, quite a catch. They'd been born a few miles away, in an old Victorian house that backed up on the harbor, almost at the York town line. At the end of the land, a long pier and dock led to their lobster boat, lovingly called *The MaryAnn Seven*, in honor of their great-grandmother, who was born after the family had been given six sons. Even though their present boat wasn't the original one, I learned that fishermen never change the name of their boat, or bad luck would follow, so they told me. Daniel had been married three times, each marriage ending in a storm of fireworks, and Jonah had never been married, although he was rumored to have a long string of women who hoped that his hook would come their way. Since time immemorial, the Bethany men had always lobstered off the coast of Maine, and *The MaryAnn Seven* was rumored to be one of the most successful lobster boats in the state. Daniel's three disastrous marriages hadn't produced any children, and the brothers – unless there were some really big future surprises - were the last of their line. The two of them lived in a huge, ramshackle family house, and, if the tides were right, usually ate lunch at The Loop Café.

Anoop greeted them with cries of rapture. Evidentially, the brothers had a deal with the restaurant. When they caught more than they could sell at the market, they'd give the rest to Anoop and Gerjeet. Then the brothers would eat for free at the restaurant for a few weeks, and then the cycle would start all over again. "We have lobster stew now and lobster rolls on the menu tomorrow!" Anoop gleefully carted off the booty and I asked the brothers what they'd like for lunch.

Jonah, or at least I think it was Jonah, waggled his bushy eyebrows and told me what dish *he'd* really enjoy. It took me a second to realize that he was referring to me. My own eyebrows rose up nearly to the top of my skull. I wasn't used to this sort of thing. I backed up a bit, just out of their reach, and asked again. This time, I got an order for beef stew and a roast beef sandwich and another order for chili and a cheese steak with onion rings. As I backed away from the table, I almost heard the smacking of brotherly lips.

Anoop was giggling when I put the order in. "Those boys, they like you!" she snickered. "They like all women!"

"Pay no attention to them," Gerjeet's placid face tried to look fierce. "I will be sure that they do not bother you."

"I think I can manage." I swept up the chili and the stew, together with two coffees, and plonked them on the table, smiling nicely and adroitly managing to avoid a pat on the rear. I didn't mind Judge Emery's pat, which was friendly and absentminded, as if he were patting his dog. But this was different. These two guys seemed to be serious patters. I was clearly out of practice in the mating game. The Bethany Brothers were at their testosterone-laden apex.

I busied myself, cleaning tables and putting the restaurant in order in anticipation of closing. Meanwhile, I watched the two men out of the corner of my eye. They were handsome specimens of outdoor living, sunburned and well-muscled, about six feet and a few inches tall, with reddish-grey hair worn long and tied back into two ponytails. I mean one ponytail each. One of them had a gold earring and looked like a rakish pirate. Their features were strong and chiseled and their blue eyes twinkled with amusement as I tried to ignore them. They made little remarks about how good things were lookin' around here and I pretended not to hear them, but they did my poor, bruised ego a lot of good.

Daniel, I think it was Daniel, grabbed my hand when I served the sandwiches. "Aren't you gonna sit down and talk?" He asked. "You're the cutest waitress they've ever had here." Inasmuch as the last server had been Gerjeet's nephew, I didn't feel terribly flattered. I managed to sidle away, blushing like a fifteen year old Catholic school virgin. I was too old for this!

The brothers finished their lunches and motioned me to come over. I held their bill in my hand, and told them that Gerjeet had put it on their account. They grinned with brotherly cheer and Daniel told me that they meant no harm. "We'll be in to see you everyday that the tide is right, won't we, Jonah." Jonah smiled with great charm and nodded. He fished a ten dollar bill out of his yellow slicker and put it on the table.

"That's for the excellent service and the lovely, lovely view." He grinned at me, and it was hard not to grin back. They were so blatant, like two big overgrown dogs. Harmless, I guess. I grinned back and told them that I would look forward to serving them lunch again, but that was all that was being served. The two of them threw back their handsome heads at my pitiful joke and laughed.

They clomped over to the register and kissed Anoop soundly on her cheek, "Great lunch," Daniel burped and rubbed his belly. "Why don't you guys get some good desserts?" He lifted up a store-bought, cellophane wrapped pink-coconut-covered piece of cake and dropped it back down. "These things taste like cardboard." Anoop giggled, her bracelets jingling, and poked him in the region of his stomach.

"One day we get good stuff." She told him, with a dimpled smile. Did I sense a tiny bit of flirtatiousness? "You will see."

The brothers, in a testosterone-laden chorus, waved to me and told me that they'd see me tomorrow. I waved back faintly, nearly overwhelmed by so much…masculinity.

"They cute boys, no?" Anoop watched them clump away. She had a dreamy smile on her face. "I like them." Gerjeet scowled.

"Mmmm. Real cute," I said, turning to clear the deuce by the far wall.

◆ ◆ ◆

I returned to the condo to clean up and take the rest of my things. A huge box of left-over furnishings and several armloads of clothing were earmarked for Fair Tide. I emptied the refrigerator and boxed up all the food, including several boxes of cake mix. As I loaded the car, a plan began to bubble in my mind.

I dropped my leftovers at Fair Tide and was gratefully thanked by Julie and Lisa, the two selfless women who oversaw the running of the thrift store and served on its Board of Directors. We chatted for a few moments, and then I spied a nearly new bundt cake pan and two cookie sheets…each item priced at the munificent price of twenty-five cents. I quickly made my large purchase, thinking that my plan had just received an encouraging bolt from Heaven.

One more errand; leaving my dry cleaning at We Care Cleaners. Again, I made the acquaintance of my new neighbors in the Foreside, tall, smiling Ed and his handsome son, John. They promised to have my stuff ready in a day and assured me that they'd stroll down to the Café for lunch in a day or two. I felt at home. New friends and neighbors – a new life for me – and I began to sing as I got into my VW bug. *"And a false hearted looooo-ver, Is worse than a thief!"* Was I referring to Steve? Ha!

I stopped at Barbara's office to sign the lease and pick up the key. She wasn't there, but a handsome young man with the rather unusual name of Rodney Kuntz assisted me. Now if I had a name like Rodney Kuntz, I might have changed it, but this particular Rodney didn't seem to be fazed by the snicker implications of a name such as his. He stuck his hand out, shook my hand with a warm, firm grip and smiled. "Rod Kuntz," he confirmed. Rod was a lawyer-in-the-making, interning at Barbara's office and finishing his studies at the University of Maine Law School. He was the eldest son of English parents. His father was a surgeon at the local hospital. Rod had light brown hair, the kind that flops over his forehead, a bit like Cary Grant. He had bright blue eyes and an infectious smile. Always a mother, I mentally matched him up with Andrea. Of course she was on the West Coast and he was here, but…things could change. I asked him, as casually as I could, if he were married. "Gosh, no, Mrs. Fornier," he answered. "I haven't got a dime to my name now. I'll take the Boards in two months and if I pass, I'll start to work here and earn a pitiful salary." He grinned and I liked him more. "I'd need a rich woman." He jokingly leered at me and I planned to call Andrea and tell her about him. I wondered what she'd make of possibly being called Mrs. Kuntz.

Rodney told me that the utilities had been switched over to my name and that I could move right in. "What about the rent?" I asked. "Do you want a check now?"

"Don't worry just yet. Barbara is going to try to get your husband to pick up all your living expenses for a year."

"Really?" I was astonished.

"It's a common request. You know, man earns money, woman stays home. Then, when man sniffs around, woman gets compensated." He laughed. "Then the man gets to pay the price." He looked thoughtful. "I'll never mess around when I get married. It's too expensive and emasculating to go through all of this." I nodded in fervent agreement. "Especially for the man if he's in the wrong. Barbara will clean him like a chicken bone." On that pleasant thought, I left the office and went to my new little martini-olive green home.

CHAPTER FIVE

I parked in front of 236 and began to unload the car, putting the boxes and suitcases down in front of the door. On my last trip, I noticed the two cats I had previously seen in the backyard. They sat at the doorstep, the white one sitting up straight and the black one lying down. "Hey kitty-cats." I greeted them. I presumed they belonged to one of the neighbors.

I opened the door with my foot, trying to keep the cats from getting inside, but when I turned around, they were gone. I brought all my belongings inside and stood for a moment, almost in shock at how much my life had changed in a day or two. I spied a large blue and white vase on a shelf and emptied my apron pockets into it. I had a mountain of change, lots of dollar bills, and a few fives and tens. I made a decision to hoard all my tips and live on the four dollars an hour I was being paid. Perhaps I could manage, especially if poor Steve got stuck with my rent and utility bills.

I brought the suitcases upstairs, made the bed and put my clothes away. I went into the bathroom and made a list of all the things I needed to buy and then took a shower to get the smell of meatloaf off me. Feeling energetic, I dressed in shorts and a shirt and went down to the kitchen to begin working on my new idea.

What is it about cooking or baking as therapy for a broken heart? Whatever, I had the urge to create. Get my hands going on some batter, roll things out. I checked the fridge. Good. I had enough sour cream, eggs and other things to start my experiment. I rummaged in the closets and found cake tins and bowls and spatulas. I brought out my newish bundt pan and cookie sheets, preheated the oven and went to work.

My great grandmother had been a superb baker. She had learned her trade in Italy, under the supervision of a marvelous old lady who had opened her heart and her cooking skills to Great-Grandma Francesca. When the families came to America, Francesca had managed to start a flourishing baking business and now, several generations later, my cousin MJ still ran the bakery. Baking was in my blood. In the past, when I'd been upset or in a bad mood, I'd found great solace in kneading dough. Whipping up a few dozen chocolate chip cookies, an apple pie, my mother's sour cream cake, or a plate full of brownies had always made me feel better, and this afternoon, again, cooking didn't fail me.

I got out my own copy of Francesca's cookbook. Checking through the batter-stained pages, I made two sour cream cakes, using the bundt pan, layering each one with the rich, heavy sour cream batter alleviated with ribbons of chopped nuts, cinnamon and sugar. Then, I made a tray of *biscotti*, using dried apricots and macadamia nuts in place of the usual almonds, and to finish, mixed up some Cappuccino Squares. While they baked, I made two pie-plates of *torta di ricotta*[1], a great, never fail recipe that had been given to me by my cousin Julie, who was also superb cook and baker and now lived in Italy with her handsome husband and a brood of darling children.

As my confections lay cooling on the table, I made an inspection of the house, first tromping down the crooked steps into the basement. The basement was ancient, perhaps a few hundred years old. It was cut into the granite rock, with lichen-lined walls. In some spots, the rock had triumphed over the stonecutters and rose up in a medium sized boulder or two. There was a washer and dryer tucked into the alcove behind the complex-looking furnace, and wooden shelves holding gardening instruments lined one wall. I saw two bicycles leaning against a wall and pulled them into the middle of the room. One of them had two flat tires, but the other, an ancient red balloon-tired affair, seemed ready to go.

I headed back to the kitchen and the basement door slammed behind me. In the depths of the living room, I heard a click and then the tinny music started up again. The noise of the door slamming must have jarred the arm on the Victrola, I thought. That must have been what happened when Barbara and I were here before. The cowgirl voice began to sing. *"On top of Old Smooo-key..."* I laughed, thinking that this music was now stamped in my soul. The ghostly music on my Victrola would be good company. I began to wrap up my cooled cookies and cakes and sang along.

It was a funny thing, though. I'd sung *"On Top of Old Smokey"* a million and one times in my life, including my solo warbling this afternoon. I knew all the words. I mean, I'd even *heard* this record play the

---

[1] Please delight in the recipe at the end of the book.

day before, hadn't I? But this time, the words coming out of the Victrola were different…I cocked my head, puzzled, and listened…

"On top of that moun-tain
You pledged me your love,
You swore that you loved me
On the angels above."

And then it went into the familiar refrain. I shrugged. This must be a different recording than the one I was used to. I hummed along, wrapping the *biscotti* in clear Saran wrap. The record spun.

"You brought me such pleas-ure
Then you made me cry.
When you walked out of my life.
And bade me goodbye."

And the refrain plinked on. I warbled along with the cowgirl. If this inexplicable music was done by ghosts, they were friendly, old-country-standard singing ghosts. I kind of liked them. The record ended and the stylus went kerchink, kerchink. I went over to the table and played the song again. Inexpressibly cheered, I tried the telephone and found it working. I called my daughters and chatted with both of them, telling them about my new job, my new little house, my strange record player and my new life. Andrea's voice perked up when I told her about Rodney Kuntz.

"Eee-yow! What a horrible name!" I agreed that it was unusual, to say the least. "Is he really cute? You know how you are, Mom. Sometimes you think the dorkiest guys are cute."

"He's really cute, Andrea. I swear."

"Yeah, but Kuntz…yuk…You'd have to keep your own last name." She laughed. "But, seriously, Mom, how are you doing?" I smiled into the telephone and was sincerely able to assure her that seriously, I wasn't doing too badly.

◆ ◆ ◆

I brought the cakes, Cappuccino Squares, the *ricotta* pies and cookies with me the next morning. "Maybe you can see if anyone would buy them…" I was shy and hesitant as I offered them to Gerjeet and Anoop. They looked down at the table with their dark huge eyes wide and I thought that I had made a horrible cultural mistake. Perhaps they didn't want them. Perhaps I had stumbled over some huge Pakistani taboo and chocolate couldn't be served in their kitchen. Perhaps….

"Oh, how bee-yoo-ti-ful!" Anoop's voice was delighted. My breath whooshed out. "How won-der-ful!"

"You think they're OK?" I was biting at my bottom lip.

"Oh, my! Oh, my! Everyone will be so happy!" Gerjeet clapped his hands. "We will sell them all!"

We put the cakes and the pies on the counter and pyramided the squares on a plate. I had tied curly, bright ribbons around each of the wrapped *biscotti*, and we piled them in a basket. "Two dollars each!" cried Anoop. "And the cakes are three dollars."

"That's too much money," I protested. "How about we try a piece of cake or a square for two dollars and a buck for the *biscotti?*"

"Okey dokey, but you keep all the money," Gerjeet's face was stern.

"No, we split it. You get half and I get half. Let's see how they go. Maybe no one will even like them."

Gerjeet snorted. "Not *like* them? They will tear them apart and fight for the last crumb!"

"It is the one thing that we do not do well." Anoop's dangly ear-rings glittered as she shook her head in glee. "Soup, I can make, but cookies – no." She gazed hungrily at the pile of desserts. "These, they look so handsome and excellent."

"We will divide the money if you insist." Gerjeet decided. "Okey dokey, but, not so much for us." He shook his head. "You have to be paid more. You get two-thirds, we get a third." I shrugged and nodded. He smiled, a wide white grin. "They will be very, very popular, I am so certainly sure of that."

They sold…well, just like desserts and *biscotti* and hotcakes, if I may say so. We cut each cake and pie into 16 pieces, and at the end of the day, we'd sold all but two pieces. The Cappuccino Squares were completely gone, and only two *biscotti* were left in the basket. The customers fell upon the desserts like starved refugees. Barbara had come in with Rodney, and each of them had a square and took two more and a piece of cake back to the office with them. Pauli took six *biscotti* back to Traip Academy to share with her staff. Debby adored the ricotta pie, sighing that it brought her back to the lady that lived next door to her when she was a girl in Boston. Rita ate two pieces of sour cream cake, rapturously crying that it was just like her Russian grandmother's. The two men from Frisbee's store, the oldest continually operating family grocery store in the US of A, came in for lunch. Frankie and Ron each ate a Cappuccino Square, grinned at one another, sampled a *biscotti* and then a piece of sour cream cake. They took four *biscotti* each to go. As they paid me, they asked me if I would consider baking for their grocery store.

As flattered as I was, I had to decline. "If I ever consider baking full time, I'll let you know," I promised them. "But, right now, I am pretty busy."

The Bethany Brothers must have been caught in the tide, as they didn't come in. But if they had, I'm sure we would have had no desserts left at all. I went home on a cloud of delight, my apron full, clinking faintly with tips and *biscotti* bucks.

Well, actually, I went shopping first. I had the list of bathroom stuff that I needed and, in addition, I bought cream and butter and *ricotta* and chocolate and sour cream and eggs and apricots and almonds *and* macadamia nuts. I spent the early evening baking twice as much as I'd done the night before. I stored the extra two cakes, four pies and two batches of squares in the refrigerator, and put the *biscotti* into a large, metal tin for keeping. I also sat down to do some bookkeeping. I'd made one hundred twenty-one dollars in one day from my baking. Imagine that! I subtracted the cost of the ingredients and grinned to find that I had made a eighty-eight dollar profit. In one day. Plus my salary. Plus my tips. Not bad for a chick who had stayed home to watch the kids most of her life.

Barbara called to tell me she had written a letter to Steve's attorney and wanted me to read it and comment on it. Would I stop in after work tomorrow? She also had found a real estate agent that wanted to list the condominium. We could discuss that too.

As a thank-you for putting me up, I invited Barbara and Horace to join me for dinner on Saturday night and Barbara accepted. Now all I had to worry about what to serve, but I still had three days to decide.

I sat on the couch and called my family in Connecticut. I wanted to tell them about Steve before they heard it from anyone else. My darling Uncle Pat was first. He sniffed, commiserated with me, and confided that he'd never liked Steve anyway. Our large, affectionate Italian family does tend to stick together in matters like this. My cousin Angel said that she'd always known that Steve would screw me one way or the other. My cousin Joann said she'd pray for me, my cousin Lucy said that I'd get over it all with time, and to remember not to sign anything until my attorney checked it out, and my cousin Maddie told me that I was bound to meet someone better the next time around. I felt wrapped in cousinly love and smiled, then, reality hit me and I was glad that my mother and father were no longer alive to hear that their little Reggie had somehow messed up, marriage-wise. The night seemed oppressive all of a sudden.

A bit dejected now, I went upstairs, undressed and got ready for bed. I opened the door to the little porch and, after shutting out the light, went out to sit in the warm darkness. The perfume of the flowers rose to greet me and I leaned over the railing, watching the play of light on the water. I saw a movement below me, and saw the two cats sitting on the wall. They were both upright, like two sentinels, and I could swear that their eyes were locked into mine.

I lay in the soft, billowy bed and tried to close my eyes. I thought of Steve and the years that were gone. I rehashed the events of the last few days, then started to cry. I fell asleep, uneasy and restless, then awoke, frightened for no reason by the sound of a truck driving past the house. I closed my eyes firmly. As a rule, I don't dream much, but this night, perhaps because I was in unfamiliar territory and perhaps because I was upset, I had a nightmare.

It had to do with the cats, who assumed human shapes, the white one a tall woman with silvery blonde hair and the black cat as a darker-skinned beauty with long, straight black hair. The cat/women were dressed in beautiful gowns, but each sported a bushy cat-tail. Cowgirl music played crazily from an orchestra made up of smaller pussy cats, dressed in tuxedos. The two cat/women climbed my stairs and came into my bedroom with their bloodied heads held, like two horrible John-the-Baptist caricatures, on a tray in front of them. The trays were held by paws. But the faces were human. I heard another car or a truck backfire outside the house and I shuddered awake, sitting bolt upright. My body was hot and clammy and my heart pounded. I got up, peered out of the window into the night, but saw nothing at all except the shapes of bushes and leaves shimmering in the dark moonlight. I padded into the bathroom, drank a glass of water, sighed, and went back to sleep.

The next morning, I looked at the Victrola with disdain. I even spoke aloud to it. "Don't scare me anymore!" I scolded it, shaking my finger.

I gathered all of my previous night's baking and brought all of the cakes and confections to work. "I figure I have enough for two days and we can keep them fresh in your refrigerator." Anoop agreed, fervent with gratitude.

"So many customers say how happy they are!" Her pretty bracelets tinkled as she clasped her hands ecstatically under her chin. Today, she was wearing a bright orange sari and the dot on her forehead was outlined in orange and black. I almost asked her how she did it, but, at the last moment, was too shy. Maybe Barbara or someone with more knowledge than I would know.

Mid-morning brought my next admirer to the restaurant. His name was Bob Micklewright, and he was a CPA who had an office at the beginning of The Loop. "Oh, Bobby," caroled Anoop. "Come in, come in. Come to meet our new server lady!" She pulled him to a table and stood watching, while I came to take his order.

"He is nice, no?" Anoop asked me, when I told her that he wanted orange juice and two poached eggs with rye toast. "He is a very rich man." she assured me.

As I had said, for thirty years, no one looked at me with eyes that gleamed, but now, here in The Loop Café, I seemed to be magically changed into a femme fatale. Mature, to be sure, but nonetheless, a woman who got admiring glances. I was definitely a hit with the older male customers. It was amazing. And very, very good for my morale. And not bad for the tips, either.

Bob Micklewright's myopic eyes shone eagerly under his horn-rimmed glasses as he watched me. He smoothed the top of his sparse hair and adjusted his collar and looked like a trick dog about to come out into the circus ring. As he ate his toast, dipping it into the yolks of his eggs, he never stopped glancing at me with his admiring eyes. I didn't know whether to be flattered or annoyed. He was a pleasant looking man, perhaps in his mid-sixties, neatly dressed in a brown suit with a yellow and tan checked vest. He had thinning brown hair and soft brown, spaniel-like eyes. As I gave him his check, he coughed and sputtered, then asked me if he might take me to the movies one night. Dumbfounded, I could only stutter that I wasn't ready for those kind of thrills. Not just yet. . Undaunted, but with a sheen of sweat on his balding head, he plowed on. "There's a wonderful theater in downtown Portsmouth that shows lovely foreign films," he offered. "I'll find out what is playing and then, perhaps, you and I can attend one night." Again, I shook my head, hopefully communicating to him that it was too soon for such exotic pleasures. For a gabby girl, I was simply unable to speak a word. He got up and actually bowed to me as he left the restaurant. I watched him get into his dark blue pick-up truck to drive the two blocks to his office. Everyone around southern Maine drove a truck, it seemed, even rich accountants. I brooded, watching the truck execute a U-turn. I picked up his twenty-five cent tip...a mediocre, barely decent tip…nah, actually a cheap tip. No wonder he was successful at his business. My eyes narrowed. I truly despised anyone who was a cheapskate. And here I was, the newest sex-symbol aging waitress, who might be saddled with a cheapskate who wanted to take me out one of these days. I started to giggle a bit. And I marveled at the changes in my new life.

As the morning wore on, I saw many of my new-found friends and spent a few moments chatting with each of them. Then, the morning's peace was shattered by the loud rumble of a dilapidated truck pulling up to the Café. A large, scruffy lobster-man wearing a blue sweater climbed down, or at least it *looked* like a large lobster-man wearing a blue sweater. The blue-sweatered person clumped into the Café, swung a leg over a chair and grabbed at a menu.

"I'd better wait on him," I remarked, getting up. Anoop stared to giggle, grabbed at my arm and told me that this apparition wasn't a man as I had thought, but a woman.

"She looks like a big, old man, but she is a woman!" Anoop's eyes were wide. "An ugly, miserable, peculiar old woman!"

"A woman," I goggled. "Wow."

"Her name is Henrietta Ormond," Anoop whispered. "That is her real name, a girl's kind of name." She peeped at the lobster-person, put her graceful little hand to her mouth and spoke from behind it. "But do not – never at all – call her by the name Henrietta! Oh, no! That would not do at all. She would be very angry and yell at you!"

"Yell?"

"Oh, yes. She will be called 'Hank', a funny name, no? A name like a man would be called." Anoop's silvery laugh tinkled. "Like some cowboy who drives a tractor or rides into the town on a horse. She is Hank."

"No shit?" I wondered. "Hank."

"Oh, yes, shit," Anoop's command of English always delighted me. "She is Hank. Not even Miss Hank, but Hank. That's all."

"Hank, I see." I got up slowly and approached Henrietta, I mean Hank's table. Up close, one could see the ravages of the outdoor life that she obviously led. Coarse, grey hair in need of a good cut and condition, leathery skin with lines radiating from her eyes and the corners of her mouth, and large, square. masculine hands.

"Have you made up your mind?" I asked with my best smile.

"You're new here," she barked. "Never saw you before."

"I'm Reggie. Yes, I'm new. Pleased to meet you," I grinned my best grin and stuck out my hand.

She looked at it, ignored it and her face was grumpy. "Hmpf. Just bring me a cup of coffee – black – and a ham and cheese sandwich – toasted on wheat. And don't burn the toast." She handed me the menu and busied herself reading a magazine that had a picture of a bear being hunted on its cover.

I gave her order in to Gerjeet and he asked me if she'd been rude to me.

"Not really rude, just not too friendly."

He laughed., "She is one grumpy lady. Or more like a grumpy man!" He laughed again, pleased with his own joke.

After the Ormand woman left, with a roar of her truck's rickety engine, Gerjeet told me that she had lobstered as long as most of the men around Kittery. "She has a big boat that she runs with the help of one peculiar old man. They catch a lot of lobsters and I understand that she has much money hidden away in her house."

"She never spends one single dime if she can help herself," Anoop chimed in. "Did she leave you a good tip, Reggie?"

I shook my head. "Nope. A quarter. I figured she was related to Bob Micklewright!"

"She keeps all of the money under her bed. That is why she does not give money out in tips. She keeps it all."

"Amazing." What else could one say?

"Yes," Anoop nodded her head, "She would stab any person who comes near to her house or her boat. She has a big, wicked knife and one day she told me that she would kill anyone who tried to rob her." Anoop's dark eyes widened. "I believe her very words."

"I'll be polite to her and keep out of her way." I took a second cup of coffee to Mike O'Brien and thought thank goodness that most of our customers were sort of normal.

◆ ◆ ◆

I met another would-be-admirer that afternoon - a soft-spoken mechanic by the name of Phil Moore. Phil was Kittery born and bred and his family went back several generations to seafaring captains who had plied their trade in and around the Maine seacoast. He ordered three cups of coffee and four pieces of cake and sat at his table, mooning at me for an hour.

"My! He cannot stop looking at you!" Anoop approved. "He has his own gas station."

Impressed by that sort of grand munificence, I assured Anoop that I still wasn't ready to begin a life of romance, no matter how much wealth was waved at me. She told me to think these things over carefully. "All girls need a man," she advised. I promised to keep these things in the forefront of my mind.

By afternoon's end, I was exhausted and picked up some fried chicken at the local fast-food place at the outlets. I drove over to the condo and spent a few minutes chatting with Rose. I then cleaned the last of my clothing and personal goods from the condo and closed the door, hopefully, for the last time.

At Barbara's office, I read the letter she had prepared to send to Steve and his attorney. My eyes bulged out. According to Barbara's way of thinking, Steve's actions to me made him the equal of Atilla the Hun or Hitler. Her demands for me would nearly bankrupt him. She'd dangled the island property, however, and promised that if he'd accede to her/my wishes, that he'd get the property without any difficulty. This letter was hot! My hands felt scorched! "Will he go for this?" Barbara nodded, an evil grin on her face. "Woo," I said. "He's gonna shit."

"That's the general idea." Barbara buzzed her secretary and told her to mail the original to Steve and a copy to Steve's attorney, Certified Mail, Return Receipt Requested.

◆ ◆ ◆

I ate my chicken out on the back steps. The two cats appeared, probably drawn by my sticky hands and I fed them chunks of breast meat. As the daylight faded, I heard a "Yoo-Hoo" from the house next door. Mrs. Clutterbuck was calling me. I wiped my hands and covered the rest of the chicken. I didn't want the cats to eat the bones and get sick.

The cats walked part-way across the lawn with me, meowing and twining themselves between my legs. When I reached the gap in the hedge that separated my cottage from hers, the cats had disappeared. Again, I wondered to whom they belonged.

"Can you come in for some lemonade?" Hannah Clutterbuck was wearing a faded housedress and fishermen's boots on her feet. Her hair was a bird's nest of grey curls and her sparkling blue eyes looked as if they missed nothing. Of *course* I went inside. I was dying to see her house.

We clomped into the kitchen through the back door. I grinned and felt right at home. Her style of decorating and that of my mother were identical. Total mess and chaos from top to bottom. The ceiling was hung with hooks sporting old macramé plant holders with scraggly spider plants trailing dust and dried leaves, the windows were nearly blocked up with a profusion of more plants, the walls were plastered with photographs, calendars of years gone by, dusty portraits and children's drawings and every available horizontal surface was covered with bric-a-brac and crocheted doilies. When ordered to do so, I sat down on a painted kitchen chair only after removing a pile of saucepans from the seat.

Mrs. Clutterbuck took a pitcher of lemonade out of the refrigerator, which was an old GE with the motor on top. The pitcher had decals of cherries on it and matched the glass she gave to me. Her glass had a picture of a cow on it. "Home-made?" I asked. She nodded, of course. The lemonade was perfect. Exactly like my Aunt Fanny's.

After ten minutes, Ms. Clutterbuck knew everything there was to know about me. She knew the ages of my daughters and where they lived; she knew about every single operation and illness I'd ever had; and she knew all about Steve leaving me. "Men," she offered, shaking her head. "Sometimes they stink."

"Now's my turn," I told her. "Tell me about yourself, and then tell me about the women who lived in my house."

She nodded, acknowledging fair play, and then launched into her life story. Very interesting, too. She'd been born in this house, wed Elroy two days before he was shipped to France during World War I, birthed her first child upstairs in the big back bedroom while he was a prisoner of war, kept the household going while he was away by digging clams with her grandfather and ironing other peoples' clothes. When Elroy returned, minus his right leg, she'd encouraged him to become a schoolteacher. "We had seven more children. Mary, the youngest girl, died of diphtheria, but the rest are still around here." She drained her glass and wiped her lips daintily. "And we have thirteen grandchildren." She took me on a tour of the kitchen, showing me every single snapshot and portrait. I adored her already.

As we sat back down, an orangy-colored cat stalked into the room and plopped itself on my lap. "That's Ginger. She's just had another litter. Six kittens from a good neighborhood." Mrs. Clutterbuck laughed. "Want one?"

"No thanks. Not yet. I'm away too much right now." I kneaded Ginger's fat neck and she purred and batted my fingers. "I've seen two cats around my house. A white one and a black one. Are they yours?"

Mrs. Clutterbuck reared back in her chair. "You've seen the *cats*?" I nodded. "My land of Beulah!" She exclaimed, pressing her hand to her bosom. Her face brightened with fascination. "You've seen the *cats*!"

"What do you mean?"

"Well, the cats..." She trailed off, turning her empty glass around in her hands. "The cats..." She nodded her head a few times and then told me all she knew.

"About four years ago, old Mrs. Melillo died. She'd lived next door for more than twenty years. She didn't have any relatives. Left all her money to the Cat-lick Church down the street. They sold the house, just as it stood when they took her body out the front door. A real mess, it was. All her junk from twenty years." Mrs. Clutterbuck's indignation was sincere. She didn't seem to notice my slightly ironic smile as I gazed at the detritus piled everywhere in the kitchen. "This young lady bought the house. She was rich. Could have had any house she wanted anywhere, but the little green one was the house she chose. Her grandfather made a lot of money in both the big wars. Sold bullets and guns, I think. Anyway, Sunny…her real name was…some foreign name…let me see…" She scratched at her head. "Can't think…but it will come to me. Anyway, she said to call her Sunny, and we all did. And she was. A sunny, pretty, cheerful lady. Not a young girl, mind you, but maybe middle-aged. She had some men come in and cleaned the place out from stem to stern. Carted out piles of junk and furniture." She turned and pointed to a gate-legged table heaped with empty jelly jars, "She gave me that nice table there. Told me to come and get whatever I liked. I took that table, some jelly jars and Elroy took six boxes of tools." She shook her head. "And they're still down cellar. I don't think he ever even took them out of the boxes, fool man." She noticed that my glass was empty and sprang up to refill our glasses.

"She was alone? I thought there were two women?"

"Now wait a minnit. I got to tell you how it happened." She settled herself back down and Ginger leaped off my lap and onto hers. "Anyhow, she cleaned the house out and then brought in an army of men to paint and fix up. Painted everything white. She told me, 'Mrs. Cee,' …that's what she called me and you should too. 'Mrs. Cee, I want everything clean and white.' Well, goodness sake, it certainly was. White walls, white furniture. But it did look nice. A little bare and empty to my taste, but nice nonetheless."

"Long about two months later, this other lady, Catherine Black, came to live with her. We all called her Catherine, but Sunny called her 'Cat'. Once, I even heard her say 'Blackie the Cat'. I guess it was a little joke between them." She leaned over and her blue eyes gleamed at me. "They were girlfriends." Her eyebrows rose suggestively and I could clearly see the rambunctious girl she must have been, "Unnatural girlfriends."

"Oh," I said. "I understand, I think."

"Nowadays, they don't think nothin' about it all. They even have that television show. *Helen,* I think it's called." She sniffed. "In my day, they would be run out of town. But times they change and they *were* lovely neighbors. No matter what." She clasped her hands in front of her. "Elroy never got used to it. He'd always mutter about it all, but," she shrugged, "it didn't bother me much."

I decided not to pursue a discussion of alternate love life styles with Mrs. Cee. "And the cats?"

"Ah, yes, the cats. They went out and got two cats at the pound. One white one for Sunny and the black one for Catherine. Blackie the cat. Like her name. Nice kitties, too. Got along real well with Ginger here." Ginger arched her back and stood up, turned around in a circle and lay back down, draped across Mrs. Cee's lap like a boneless fur piece.

"So they were good neighbors. Always smiling, always saying hello and did we want them to get anything from the market, you know. They brought me flowers from their garden, they'd leave me a pot roast or some chicken soup with noodles if I was feeling poorly...nice ladies. They never...never, like..." her kind face looked embarrassed, "kissed or, um, anything else." She drew her head back. "Nothing like that. Elroy would have just died if he'd seen anything like that." She tittered. "But you could tell. Like they'd look at one another, or touch each other's arm. One of them played the banjo, and they both liked to sing old cowboy songs." My attention leaped. Did the "On Top Of Old Smokey" record belong to Sunny and Catherine? I made a mental note to ask Mrs. Clutterbuck about it after she finished telling me her story. She sighed and was quiet for a moment. "Tsk. Tsk." She made that sound that people make when they are regretful and continued, "Never any trouble at all there. They'd play their music and one would sing to the other. And they were sweet to one another. Little things." She shook her head. "Poor lambs, with what happened, I hope they did find love and affection with one another." She tsked again. "Such an awful thing."

"What happened?" I thought back to my dream – the cat/women and the heads. "How did they die?"

"Well," her voice dropped an octave and she leaned over the table. "It was just about a year ago. A nice day, bright and clear, and a pleasant night with a half moon. Elroy had gone fishing that morning with Old Jim Drawbridge. He usta be the police chief here before Alexander Bridge came along. They caught a bucket of fish and I was putting the fish in plastic bags to put in the freezer. Janie, that's my youngest girl, she was over. She'd brought me a bushel of rhubarb from her garden. She was washing the rhubarb and cutting it up and Elroy was sitting here with his leg unbuckled and his shoe off, resting and watching us work." She leaned back. "It was maybe nine-thirty or so. Late, but not too late, if you know what I mean. It was then we heard the cats." She sat back with a satisfied, expectant smile on her face.

I obliged. "The cats?"

"Mmmm. The cats. The black one and the white one. They was good-mannered kitties, always quiet and never any ruckus. Never before had they ever screeched or yowled. But this night, you would have thought somebody was stripping their fur off. They screeched. Loud, mind you. And they yowled. And they didn't stop! We were here and you could hear them from a mile away. After about five minutes of it, I said, 'Elroy, maybe you better go and see why them cats are making so much noise.'"

"The sounds were coming from the front of the house, so Elroy got fixed to go over there. Took him a while, with his leg and all, you know. I was getting nervous with all the commotion. Maybe its hindsight, but it seemed like there was electricity in the air, like before a storm, you know. So he went out the door and started to walk over. Janie and I stood at the front door and watched. Elroy only took three steps and there was that old fool Carl Zumbo from the other side of the street. He was running and grabbing at his heart and his face was as white as the moonlight. 'Help! Help!' Carl gasped. 'Call the police! They're dead! *Dead!*'"

"Well, we didn't know what he was talkin' about. 'Who? Who is dead?' Elroy asked him."

" 'Them! Next door! The ladies!' Old Carl was gasping and holding his heart. 'They're cut to pieces. There's blood everywhere!' "

"Janie called the police and then we ran over with Carl puffing behind." She stopped for a moment and clasped her hands together again, twisting them in remembered agitation. "When we got there, the door was wide open. There were the two cats, sitting on the doorstep, their heads up to the night sky and the moon, crying at the tops of their little cat voices." She shuddered. "We pushed the door open and...my land! They musta been sitting on the couch when it happened. Somebody...somebody strong and quick and with a sharp ax, or some big kind of knife...they were all cut up. There was a blonde head on the floor by the door and an arm...then a foot and then another part. Then another arm and then – oh, I'll never forget it - Catherine Black's poor head. That was on the sofa with a piece of leg and the banjo. All smashed together." She shuddered and tears came to her eyes. "It was

50

like...I never...." She slumped back, drained. "It was horrible." Her last words were whispers.

"What did the police do? Were they suspicious of anyone? What..." I touched her arm and it was chilly. "Is this a bad thing to talk about? Are you all right?"

She sat up and clutched her arms around herself. "No. It's all right, sweetheart. It was a year ago, after all. And I've seen a lot of things in my life." She sighed. "Like when my Uncle Angus chopped his own blamed hand off by mistake. Or when Hank Ormand's mother...have you met our lady lobster catcher yet?" I nodded, making that kind of face that says yes, you've met her and find her weird, and Mrs Cee made that kind of face back at me that said, yes, she certainly is a weird one. She scratched Ginger's soft fur and rolled on. "Well, Hank and her mother lived in the same old dilapidated house and never even spoke to one another for years. A feud, they called it. How in tarnation they ever lived together for all that time, I'll never know. Then, I guess the old lady died in bed one night and she – Hank, that is – never even called the doctor nor the police." My eyebrows expressed my surprise and she continued. "Waited until after she went fishing that day, waited until she'd come home, cleaned out the boat, toted the lobsters to the dock and then and only then, bothered to report that her mother had died. The Police Chief...have you met him yet?" I shook my head no and waited as the flow of reminiscing eddied around me. "He's a good man. Alexander Bridge. Good family, but...where was I? Oh, yes, Old Mrs. Ormand. Well, the Chief was new then. Just a young pup. He was kind of nervous about taking care of a dead female body." She chuckled, reminiscing. "He knew me from 'way back and asked me to come along to give a hand and I gladly went in the police car. I'd never ridden before in a police car and who knew what we were going to find, you know? Well, anyway, the old lady was certainly dead. Her poor body was soaked in pee and you-know-what!" I reared back, reacting as I should. "She'd been dead for at least a day or two and was just lying in her own filth! Stiff as an old shoe and smelling to high heaven! And her blamed daughter couldn't be bothered to call the police!" She shook her head at the memory. "Shoot! I've seen it all, darling." She kneaded Ginger between the ears and the cat rolled over on her lap, white belly showing.

"Oh, there have been bad things here. Indeed. Like when the Sainsbury boy lost his sweetheart to the Melton boy and went and blew his own fool head off, or when Crazy Joe Simmons went and hanged himself and I had to get my old stepladder out and lean it against the tree so

I could cut him down." Her face was resigned and sad. "I've seen a lot of bad things. But this…this thing with the two women. This was…Ah! I ought to try to forget it."

I leaned forward, dying to hear more.

The telephone rang and she got up, dumping Ginger out of her lap. "Hello? Oh, hello, Lucy…no, no…She's not supposed to bring the *cole* slaw. Sally Gerrish is bringing the cole slaw…" Mrs. Cee looked helplessly at me and gestured to the telephone.

I got up and made those kind of waving goodbye and walking away signs to her that I was going now. She turned away from the telephone and said, "I need to tell you about the cats. I'll talk with you tomorrow. Be careful, Reggie, dear. Make sure your door is locked." She spoke back into the receiver as I let myself out, "Not you, Lucy. I was saying goodbye to my new neighbor…Yes, she moved into the house next door…"

I let myself back into the back door, noting that I had left the door unlocked. I wasn't much for locked doors, especially when I was at home, but perhaps I should be on the alert. I stood with my back to the door and gazed anew at the big room. I tried to imagine the carnage that greeted Elroy and Mrs. Cee. I tried to feel the horror that they certainly felt. But the room simply looked spacious and tranquil. There was no sense of awfulness, no fear or clanking ghosts. No atmosphere of evil. It was a lovely room that looked over a lovely view.

I gazed out over the harbor and jumped. I had forgotten the chicken that I'd left out on the table. I snapped on the porch light, and completely forgetting my resolve to never leave the house without locking it first, went outside. The door slammed behind me. I groped around the table, but the plate and the chicken were gone. Maybe the black and the white cats had swiped it. I turned and let myself back into the house. The tinkly music was playing. Had the slam of the door jarred the turntable arm again? I went over to the Victrola. "…*But a false hearted looo-ver…Is worse than a thief…*"

That night, in half-slumber, I reached across the bed, anxious somehow to touch Steve's warm body. I sat up immediately, wide-awake. *There is no Steve*, I told myself. *Not for you. Not anymore.* I bunched the quilt up over my shoulders. *Steve is warming what's her name…Brianna Baby.* My eyes probed the darkness. Steve and Brianna. I guess I was feeling pretty sorry for myself. I got up, suddenly needing to use the bathroom. I couldn't get them out of my head. *Steve and Brianna. Up in a tree. K-I-S-S-I-N-G.* I poured myself a glass of water. "Go to bed, you idiot," I said aloud. "You are being stupid."

I got back into bed, but my feet were freezing now. I threw back the quilt and grabbed a pair of socks, slid them on, and heaped myself back. Too bad I didn't have a big, fat hairy cat to sleep on my feet and keep them warm. I blinked back tears of self-pity. Then I punched the pillow and rolled over, but it was a long time until I got back to sleep. The only good thing about that night was that I didn't dream at all.

♦ ♦ ♦

The next day was sunny and clear. The gloom of the night before had gone and I was able to laugh at my own pathetic behavior. I drank my orange juice standing in front of the refrigerator and as I didn't have to lug any cakes or cookies with me, I thought I might try to ride to work on the bike that I'd found in the basement. It had been years since I'd ridden a bike, but, after a wobble or two, I found the familiar rhythm and sailed along the streets, feeling like a child again. I rode down a few streets that I hadn't been on before and noted the beauty of the tiny, old cottages hugging the harbor. I saw a bank and a chocolate candy shop, which looked as if it had been closed since Columbus sailed the ocean blue. I noticed two more dry cleaners and a gaily painted blue and white building that announced that it was an Animal Hospital. I rode past another interesting looking shop that sold vintage clothing, whizzed past The Kittery Baptist Church and the minister's house next door, and then saw another adult video store on the other side of it.

I parked the bike at the entrance to the restaurant. There didn't seem to be any need to lock it or chain it up, and anyway, I didn't have a lock or any kind of chain.

After all, this was a small and kind community, wasn't it? I thought again about what had happened last year in the little green house and about my front door and wondered if I had remembered to lock it. I really must begin to be careful.

One of my new admirers, Bob Micklewright, was there for an early breakfast. He ordered his usual orange juice, two poached eggs and toast, but then, added a piece of my coffeecake to eat with his coffee. He gazed soulfully at me the entire time he was there. True to his CPA heart and soul, he again left me another twenty-five-cent tip. The way to a girl's heart was certainly not through his spendthrift generosity. Anoop tried to get me to tell her if I was interested, but I just said that it was much, much too early for a mature woman like myself to even *think* about such things.

Three men from the Portsmouth Naval Shipyard drove up in an inevitable pick-up truck, and took the table in the front, by the window.

They each ordered coffee and "some of the great coffeecake we hear you have". I was delighted to find that my baking prowess was bringing in customers. As I handed the men their plates, they asked me if I'd heard about the local boy who'd gone missing. Hearing their question, Gerjeet paused and told them that Police Chief Bridge had spoken to him earlier. Seems that a young boy by the name of Jason Morant hadn't been seen for three or four days.

"Could he have run away?" I asked.

"Maybe, but he was a good-natured boy who had just won a scholarship to Bowdoin College. Doesn't seem that he had much to run away from." One of the Shipyard workers told us that he knew the family. "Nice kid, nice family. I can't see Jason giving any kind of grief to his parents."

"Chief Bridge is doing an appeal on television tonight and there will be a big article in the Kittery Gazette newspaper asking anyone who has seen anything to come forward." Gerjeet told us. "The family is frantic, I hear. Oh, my. Such a terrible thing."

We all tsk-tsked. The shipyard men munched my cake and the talk turned to the ever-disappointing Red Sox.

Daniel and Jonah clumped in about eleven o'clock, bringing a pleasant smell of fresh seafood with them. Their collective eyes brightened and I could feel the admiration surrounding me. We bandied nonsense back and forth and they asked me if I'd join them at the Annual Ham and Bean Supper at the firehouse the following week. I could see Anoop smiling encouragingly out of the corner of my eye. With some regret, I told them that my state of single-ness was still too new for this sort of thing. "We'll wear you down, never fear," Daniel said. "Maybe one day, you can come out lobstering with us on the boat."

"That sounds like fun. One day I will." I smiled with what I hoped was a mysterious look.

"They are so handsome, no?" Anoop was anxious.

"Very handsome. A little too handsome." I tipped my head. "And there are *two* of them. I'd always feel as if I was doing something a bit racy, if you know what I mean." Anoop tried to look knowledgeable, but I could see that she didn't have any idea of what my decadent imagination could cook up.

The day stayed beautiful into the early afternoon and the outdoor table area was packed all day. Gerjeet told me that they had almost sold out of lobster rolls and lobster stew. About two o'clock, however, the sky began to grow grey and the wind sprang up. I began to take the tablecloths off the empty tables and hoped the customers who were still eating outside would finish before the rain came. As if in answer to my thoughts, the two parties paid their checks and left.

A thunderous noise came from the street as a noisy, raucous group of motorcyclists screeched to a stop. They parked their bikes a little too close to the restaurant as if to intimidate me. I noticed that two of the bikes had sidecars and that there was a large and vicious-looking dog in each of them.

As a generality, men on motorcycles are nice. I even had one once myself, when I was younger and lived in New York City. A motorcycle, I mean, not a man. A small one, but a true motorcycle nonetheless and my old roomie Jill and I had put-putted all over New York City. Motorcycles could be fun. But these particular guys were not so nice. From the moment they swaggered in, I knew they would be trouble.

I offered to seat them inside, but they wanted to sit on the terrace. "But it's going to rain," I explained.

"So what, honey." The fat one who had come in on one of the big Harleys that had a sidecar pushed three chairs together and then shoved two tables in front of them.

"So I thought you'd like to be dry." I was polite.

"So you let me do the thinkin'. You just do the servin'." Seven other riders sniggered at his witty riposte and elbowed one another. I shrugged and handed them menus. Gerjeet's worried face peered out of the door.

Mr. Fat looked over at him. "You got a problem, Chink Man?" Gerjeet shook his head. "Then go inside. This *lady*," his snarly voice dripped sarcasm, "will wait on us gentlemen." Again, his entourage snickered. Obviously Mr. Fat was their leader and resident comedian.

I smiled as calmly as I could at Gerjeet. "It will be fine. I'll take care of them." At this, the men started to laugh. Nasty laughs. I pretended not to notice and brought them glasses of water and took their orders. They wanted hamburgers and bowls of chili. I put the order in and stayed inside while Anoop filled the chili bowls.

"Are they bothering you, Reggie?" she hissed. "Do you want me to call the police?"

"They're OK, I think." I was a little worried, but thought I could avoid any real trouble. Gerjeet stood where he could watch them and told me he'd call the police if needed. I picked up the tray and brought the chili outside.

One of the dogs in the Harley sidecar began to howl and moan as I passed close by. The dog was tied to the sidecar with a thick rope around its neck. The rope was twisted around a stanchion and the dog was nearly choking. I went closer. The dog was gasping and had saliva coming out of its mouth. He was a huge dog, filthy with matted hair, and his eyes were wild with panic. I was afraid he might bite if I tried to loosen up his collar. 'Excuse me," I spoke to Mr. Fat, as I put the chili down. "I think your dog is in trouble."

He glared at me and yelled at the dog. "Shut up, you fuckin' beast!" The dog writhed and growled. "Mind your own beeswax, bimbo." His face leered dangerously at mine and his henchmen dutifully laughed at his remarks. The big, black dog in the second sidecar began to bark in sympathy. The men began to laugh. Mr. Fat glared at them and they subsided, snickering and poking at one another. Their conversation was littered with swear words and insinuations that I couldn't quite hear. I kept my face averted from their glances, vowing that I would only scream when this whole frightening episode was over. The black dog continued to bark, sharp, staccato barks that made me very nervous. The first dog, the hairy one, gave a strangled cry and tried to scrabble out of the sidecar.

"He don't wanna shut up." One of the other men sporting a NASCAR tee shirt said with a snicker that gave rise to answering snickers from the men. Annoyed, Mr. Fat stood up and pushed him back. The man in the NASCAR tee shirt's chair fell over and he crashed to the ground. Mr. Fat stood over him, his fist upraised. The hairy dog gave a loud yelp and tried again to get free, this time getting his front paws over the door of the sidecar.

"He's scratchin' yer paint." Another rider pointed towards Mr. Fat's bike. The dog was hanging over the door of the sidecar, frantically pawing as he tried to keep the rope from snuffing out his life. His claws dug into the shiny black expensive paint. Mr. Fat swore loudly and ran to his bike. He punched the dog's head, jerked the rope and tried to lift the dog away from the door. The dog squealed in fright, plunging and pawing in a frantic effort. Mr. Fat tried to shove the dog back and, terrified, the dog savagely bit his hand.

"Fuckin' dog!" Mr. Fat screamed. His hand began to bleed. He grabbed the door of the sidecar, wrenched it open, and hauled the dog out. He kicked the animal hard with a booted foot into the dog's ribs. The dog screamed with pain. The rope was twisted around the dog's legs and the animal was helpless against Mr. Fat's onslaught. The dog fell over on its side. The cyclists began to laugh. I started to go to help the dog, but a huge hand clamped down on my arm.

"Don't even think of moving." The man in the NASCAR shirt warned me. "He's really a mean one. He'll hurt you." I watched in horror, my hands twisted into my apron.

The dog lay still and limp on the ground. I thought it must be dead. Mr. Fat was berserk. He kicked at the dog and stomped on it, cursing and spitting. One of the blows loosened the rope slightly and the dog sucked in a breath of air. He rolled over and got to his feet, taking great gulps of air, wheezing and drooling. Mr. Fat kicked at the dog again, but this time, the dog lunged back at him, leaping at him and grabbing Mr. Fat's booted foot in his white-fanged mouth. In a twinkling, the dog had pulled Mr. Fat to the ground. The dog's jaws were huge and saliva dripped from them. He looked like an avenging Hound of the Baskervilles. Sensing freedom, the dog snarled and bit Mr. Fat savagely on the thigh, drawing blood. Mr. Fat screamed. Several of the other cyclists ran to help him. The dog lunged backwards, and the fraying rope around its neck broke. He bared his fangs at the men and advanced, stiff-legged and menacing. He growled, low and deep in his throat. The men backed away. The dog gave another low, snarling growl, turned and ran down the street. The black dog began to bark again.

"Son of a bitch! I'm poisoned!" Mr. Fat staggered to his feet. "Goddam dog probably had rabies! Son of a *bitch!*" He clutched at the table and saw me. "And *you,*" he roared, half in embarrassment and half in pain. "This is your goddam fault!" Furious, he grabbed at the table, overturned it, splaying chili everywhere. "Fuckin' bitch! Fuckin' place! Let's get the hell out of here!" He pushed three chairs over, glared at me again, and got onto his Harley. His henchmen followed, one of them overturning another table. I stood and watched, stunned, as they roared away.

"I presume," Gerjeet sniffed, "That they will not be wanting their hamburgers."

◆ ◆ ◆

We cleaned up the mess, grateful that the men hadn't caused any further damage or harm. As it was nearly closing time, we shut the door and collapsed into chairs. "Go home now," Anoop urged me. "Before the rain comes down too hard. Go and lie down. You had a bad shock." She shook her tiny fist in the air. "Such bad men. I will pray that they fall down or are bitten by spiders and die."

Hoping that Anoop's curse would come true, I got on my bicycle, eager to ride home before the storm hit. I admit that I was a little shaky. I simply wasn't used to people who acted like that. I rode a block or so and then heard a noise behind me. Nervous, I stopped and looked back. The big dog, filthy and wet, with the ragged rope trailing from his neck, was following behind me, his huge, hairy feet plodding on the wet sidewalk, his snout pointed my way. For a moment, my heart froze. Would he attack me? The dog stopped too. He sat down, looking weary, and raised his paw toward me. He whined, peering at me from under his scraggled eyebrows. His scrufty tail beat a hopeful tattoo on the sidewalk. He barked once, then sat up on his haunches and almost fell over. Awww! My heart puddled immediately and turned over, sagging in my breast. The big sweetheart! I dropped the bike and went to the animal. He whined with pleasure and buried his filthy snout against my chest, pushing against me, nearly knocking me over with joy. His tail whirled in an excess of happiness. I was in love immediately.

"OK, pal." I said to him, "I sort of feel responsible for you." The dog woofed, agreeing, I guess, in doggie language. "I can't just leave you here. You can come home with me until I can find out what to do with you." I pulled my bike up and pushed it along, my newfound friend plodding with exhaustion next to me. The animal was much too large for me to even consider trying to pick up. He probably weighed more than I did. As next best, I patted his matted head and my hand came away stained with blood.

"You're hurt, you poor thing. Come on. First things first," I conversed with the dog. He almost smiled at me with his whiskery dewlaps pulled back to show a long, red tongue and sharp white teeth. "Let's take you in for a look-see." Fortuitously, at the corner of the street, I remembered seeing a sign and a blue and white building. "Kittery Animal Hospital."

"Lead on, Macduff," I told him. "We'll get you fixed up here." We turned around, my new friend and I, and went up the steps and into the front door.

◆ ◆ ◆

Later on that night, as I lay in bed with the dog splayed across the end of the bed with his chin on my feet, I thought about how my life had changed in the space of one single week. The week had been like a balancing scale. On the minus side, I had lost a lot. My husband, my marriage, all my plans for a secure future, my status as a woman known as someone's wife, my charge cards, the prestigious new house we might have lived in until we got too old to dodder around together…and a familiar partner to keep me warm at night.

The scale didn't tip too crazily downward, however. Plonked onto the other side, like bright, heavy coins, were my new additions. Barbara. Barbara and Horace. My new job, Gerjeet and Anoop, and the pile of real live coins in the blue and white jar downstairs, this darling house with its two mysterious cats, my new-found independence, all the nice people that I'd met at the Café...and now, Macduff. "Hey, Bunky Boy." I said to him, patting the covers next to me. He responded with a lurch, thereby negating the negative of me not having a partner to keep me warm at night.

His bright black eyes, so like licorice drops, melted into mine. He squirmed closer to me, beat the bedspread with his now clean and plumy tail, groaned with pure happiness, and licked my arm. I wondered if he'd had doggy-type thoughts of a scale too. Maybe he had been happy before. Maybe Mr. Fat had been a good master...nah...never. The dog's scale was definitely weighted on my side. The other side of his own puppy scale was empty. I patted his head and thought that Macduff...for the name seemed to stick... and I were doing just fine.

He smelled rather nice now, after his stint in my bathtub with an entire bottle of Hawaiian White Ginger Shampoo and Cream Rinse. His filthy hair had been soaped and rinsed and now featured coarse black and brown hair with an amazing broad white stripe down the center of his face. He had two tan eyebrows crowned by tufts of unruly hair. His paws and the very tip of his bushy tail were also snowy white. I wondered if he'd ever been this clean before. His bruises and cuts had been attended to by two other new friends, two new people in my life that I had stumbled upon when Macduff and I, both wet and bedraggled, had gone into the Kittery Animal Hospital that afternoon.

◆ ◆ ◆

When the door jangled as we entered, Macduff and I saw a sparkling clean waiting area, with a worn, but polished tile floor. The entire place smelled like wet fur laced with disinfectant and Macduff sniffed rapturously. I didn't see anyone behind the high countertop that separated the office area from the waiting room. Holding Macduff by the frayed rope, we went in. His big, hairy, wet feet left splotches on the clean tile, but there was nothing I could do about the mess. There were two people in the waiting room, one middle-aged lady with an elderly white poodle on a pink leather leash, and a young man holding a cat carrier. The cat man was immersed in a magazine and didn't look up. The poodle and its owner eyed us with undisguised fear. Macduff and I looked scruffy, wet and unkempt, I guess. I sat down and Macduff sat down too, leaning hard into my leg. He eyed the poodle with some eagerness, but as the poodle withdrew up onto his mistress' lap, curling his, or her, poodle lip with disdain. Macduff seemed to lose interest. I patted the top of his head, and again, my hand came away smeared with blood.

"Is your dog hurt?" I looked up to see a young girl's head peeking over the counter. She appeared to be about ten years old, with frizzy red curls atop an animated, freckled face. "If he's bleeding, Grumpy can see him right away."

Grumpy? Cold and wet and tired, I couldn't really think. Grumpy? Was I in the middle of The Seven Dwarfs? I got up and Macduff got up too. He made a woofing sound and performed his sit up act for the little girl. She seemed as charmed by him as I had been. "He's really not my dog," I started. "He was strangled by a rope and then kicked. I think he's cut on his head and maybe hurt his ribs." The child's blue eyes widened in sympathy. She seemed to understand my incoherent explanation. "He followed me. I was on my bike and he came with me and then I noticed that he was bleeding." I hunched my shoulders, splaying my hands out. Macduff whacked his tail on the floor, almost grinning, and uttered another huge "Woof."

The girl disappeared for a moment and then re-appeared around the side of the counter. She was dressed in a tee shirt and jeans and had a long white lab coat wrapped around her. The lab coat was originally made for someone taller than she was, perhaps someone about six feet tall, and it dragged on the floor. She should have looked silly, but, even with her youth and drooping lab coat, she had an air of authority. "Come on." She motioned to me. "Bring him in here." The lady with the poodle seemed about to object, but the girl forestalled her. "We have to take an injured animal first, Mrs. Rigano," she informed the lady. "You realize that, don't you?" Mrs. Rigano subsided with bad grace. The little girl apologized. "Grumpy will be with you and GiGi in a few minutes."

The dog and I followed her into a small examination room. She bent and patted him, murmuring that everything would be fine once Grumpy came in. She turned and smiled at me with a grin that showed me that her two front teeth had recently been lost. She reminded me of my daughters when they had been young. "Wait a minute," she ordered, and then she went out. Macduff sighed a deep, patient doggy sigh and leaned wearily against my leg, nearly knocking me over.

In a moment, the door opened again and a large, bespectacled man came in. He had the same frizzy red hair as the child, but in his case, it encircled a large bald spot. He had a beaked nose and light blue eyes and the biggest hands that I had ever seen. "What have we here?" he boomed. "Tell me what happened?"

Macduff was lifted in his arms, like a puff of dandelion, up onto the table. The fact that he was wet and bedraggled and messed up the white hospital coat with mud and blood didn't seem to faze the doctor at all. The big, square fingers probed gently at the top of the dog's head as I told our tale. "Bruised ribs," He muttered. "Superficial cuts...Aha!" He showed me a gash on Macduff's leg. "We'll fix this up right away. Nice pup." Macduff groveled for him, licking at his hands and squirming with ecstasy as he was professionally fondled and examined. After a few moments, the man smiled and rubbed Macduff between the ears. The dog fawned at him slavishly. "Nice animal. Did you say he bit the fat man?" I told that part again with some relish, and the doctor's laugh rattled the instruments on the table. "Smart dog." He praised as he deftly cleaned the head wounds and applied a salve to the cut, then threaded a needle and executed a few stitches into Macduff's skin. Macduff suffered his ministrations stoically, even when the doctor said, "Steady, good pup. This will sting a bit." I watched, grinning idiotically, as if I'd taught the dog tricks myself.

The door opened and the little girl came in. "I put Mrs. Rigano and GiGi in the next room, Grumpy," she informed the doctor. "OK?" He nodded his approval. "How's your dog?" She came over and patted Macduff's messy, but now happy, whiskery face.

"I think he's fine. Thank you for helping us so quickly."

"I'm Sasha Stein," she offered me her hand. "What's the dog's name?"

"He's...Is it a he?" The doctor laughed again, a great roaring laugh, and nodded, showing me just how he knew. I blushed and then recovered. "His name is Macduff. I just named him. I mean, I don't know what he was called before this, but when he popped out of the bushes and lead me down the street, it seemed the right thing to call him."

"That's from Shakespeare, Sasha." The doctor said. "Macbeth." The little girl nodded dubiously. "Now you go and get me an ampoule for a rabies shot and one for leprosporosis." He turned to me as she scooted out the door. "I'm going to presume that Macduff has not had any shots. I have no way of knowing, but it is better to be wise than sorry on these things." He washed his hands at the small sink. "Just keep him up on the table while I go and take care of Mrs. Rigano and her detestable poodle. I'll be right back."

I patted Macduff and murmured soft nothings at him until Sasha returned carrying a tray with three hypodermic needles, a clump of cotton, several empty vials and a cardboard box. She looked up at me. "Grumpy told me about how the man mistreated him. My poor sweet Macduff." She crooned sympathetically to the dog. He licked her face. His tail twirled around like an airplane propeller, whacking the leg of the examining table and making the chair shudder. "If he's new, do you have any food for him for tonight?"

"No. I didn't expect to have a dog. But I'm glad he's joined me. I was a little lonely, you know. I can feed him some bread and milk until tomorrow. Will that be all right?"

"I'll give you some kibble to take with you when you go." She put the tray down carefully. "What's your name?" she asked me with the innocent curiosity of a ten year old.

"Reggie." I offered. "Reggie Sabatino Fornier."

"Hi, Reggie." Sasha waved at me, flashing her gap-toothed grin. "Pleased to meet you. Why were you a little lonely? Do you have a family, Reggie? Are you a married lady?" She rubbed noses with Macduff. "You need some fattening up."

I presumed she was talking about Macduff and not me. "You're very knowledgeable for a young girl, Sasha." I complimented her with sincerity, then tried to answer her friendly, but acutely personal questions. "I used to be a married lady, but now I'm all alone, as I said." Sasha's face took on a thoughtful look. I tried a question of my own. "Is the doctor your father?"

She began to giggle, as if I'd made the best joke ever. "No, Grumpy is my *grand*father. He takes care of the animals, and nowadays, I help him after school."

Grumpy…what *was* his name? His real name. One couldn't call him Doctor Grumpy, could one? Anyway, the doctor, still known only to me as Grumpy, came into the room again. "I got rid of her," he whispered conspiratorially. "And I got rid of Danny Hogan and his cat too. Easy one. Fur ball medicine."

"I'll take care of the billing in the morning." Sasha glared at him. "You forgot about it, didn't you?" He looked faintly abashed. She put her hands on her hips. "I brought you the syringes and I brought you the stuff to take blood. I thought you'd want to take care of that too. And the heartworm stuff, too." Sasha looked pleased with herself. "Grumpy, this lady's name is Reggie Sabatino Fornier. She's all alone except now she has Macduff. So it's good that she has him, right?" My face blushed scarlet. "And she can be friends with you and me, too.

OK?" He nodded, amused and gave me a kind smile. "And Reggie doesn't have any dog food 'cause she didn't know she was going to have a dog!" She laughed again at her own joke. "So I'm going to get her some to take home. OK?"

"Great idea, Sasha. What would I do without you?" He shook his bushy head in mock-wonderment. "Go get a box. Put some food in it, a little box of vitamins, and ten Keflex pills." She nodded importantly, winked at me and left.

"What a darling child she is!" I said impulsively. "You must adore her."

"Hold the dog's paw like this." He instructed me and his large, square hands held mine for an instant. I almost jerked away at the sudden jolt of heat I felt. Grumpy's eyes flashed at me for an instant and I wondered if he, too, had noticed the electricity. He made a harrumphing sound and got back to business. He expertly trimmed the hair from a spot and then withdrew a few droplets of blood into the three empty vials. "Thanks," he said absently, getting back to my remark. "She's my heart's treasure." His gruff voice softened as he injected Macduff with two hypodermics, one by one. "My daughter, Sasha's mother, died last year and Sasha had nowhere else to go but here. I thought...I didn't...." He sighed. "I don't know why I'm telling you all this...a perfect stranger..." I nodded idiotically as one does in these types of situations. I held my breath, hoping that he'd continue. For some reason, I wanted to know all about Sasha and her Grumpy Grandfather.

"My wife...my ex-wife...we're divorced... didn't want the child. This kind of a life, with me here working at all hours, I didn't think it was the best place for a little girl." My mouth flapped open and I tried to convey sympathy and understanding at the same time. Most likely, I conveyed lunacy, but he continued. "My mother lives with me, but she's getting on in years. When Sasha came...it seemed..." He sighed once more and waved his big hands. "I enrolled her in school and she was quiet and listless for a few months. Then, she started coming here and all of a sudden, she began to take charge of the office. She's a marvel." His handsome face beamed. "She tells me she wants to be a vet when she grows up. She's a different kid now. Happy and with friends. Her grades are up. Maybe it will all work out." I wanted to know what had happened to his daughter, but I couldn't figure out how to ask without seeming even more of an idiot than I appeared already.

Deftly, he finished working over Macduff. "OK, fella, down now." He heaved Macduff off the table. "And tell me about yourself, Reggie Sabatino Fornier. How did you come to be alone, as Sasha said?"

I told him. Briefly. And then I asked him what *his* name was. "After all my confidences, I ought to call you something other than 'Grumpy', no?"

Again, his laugh shook the syringes and nearly rolled them onto the floor. "It's Lincoln," he told me as he rescued the instruments. "Doctor Lincoln Fairweather. Known to Sasha as Grumpy, not Grampy, or whatever else one might call a grandfather. It was her own doing, ever since she was a baby." He grinned. "And you'll have to bring this monster back here again tomorrow afternoon so that I can be sure that he's going to be all right." I patted Macduff to try to hide the blush that consumed me. For some reason, I was delighted that I had been ordered to return to Doctor Grumpy's shop. My heart beat erratically and I chided myself for being a middle-aged idiot. The doctor was probably engaged to some gorgeous creature, or maybe he had six or seven women friends on a string. Anyway, I still was happy. I was going to have to come back.

Before I could disgrace myself with all this simpering and blushing, I asked, "What kind of dog do you think he is?" We both looked down at the large, hairy spectacle. Macduff's huge head was level with my ribcage. His ears, long and floppy, were set at rakish angles and looked as if they belonged on an oversized bunny rabbit. His coat was dark brindle, brown and black, coarse and ragged and his tail was long and curled over his back in a dripping tangle. He had longish hair that tangled over his eyes, a long snout and sharp, white, wicked looking teeth. I think that there was a white patch on his face, but he was really too dirty to see.

Doctor Grumpy rubbed his chin. "Hmmmm. Part camel, part donkey, with a bit of orangutan thrown in." He scratched his sandy head. "Maybe some sort of Irish Wolfhound with some Bernese Mountain Dog. He's got a blocky sort of body. Maybe some Airedale. Perhaps a bit of Sheepdog." Macduff looked up at him and woofed. "God knows. A melange of breeds, all large and all hairy." He put his hand under Macduff's chin and held his face steady. "But a nice pup, nonetheless."

"A *pup*? You mean he's going to get bigger?" My voice rose in protest.

Macduff licked at his hand. He laughed. "Yup. He's not quite two years old. If I'm correct, he'll grow a lot more. Be a bit bigger. Look at his paws." I looked down at the furry shovels. "You can always tell by the paws. He's going to be a monster when he grows up." There was great satisfaction and admiration in the doctor's voice. "Yes, he'll be a great big fella."

◆ ◆ ◆

I slid out of bed and Macduff whacked the bedspread with his tail. His eyes seemed to ask me where I was going. I patted the top of his head. I wondered where I was going, too, but maybe not quite the way Macduff meant. I went over to the dresser and pulled my wedding rings off. I looked at them...a diamond solitaire and a round, platinum circle. I thought back to that day, so long ago, when, in a blaze of happiness, Steve had put the rings on my finger. From then until now, I had never taken the rings off. Not even when I was in the hospital delivering Jenna and Andrea. Not even when I sprained my hand. Not ever. I wore very little jewelry, but the rings were sacrosanct. They represented my link with Steve. Two circles, unbroken. They were like a pledge. Steve, on the other hand, had stopped wearing the plain gold band that I had slid on to his finger so many years ago. "It bothers me," he'd complained a year or so into the marriage and the ring had disappeared. I jingled the two circlets in my hand for a moment, then put them in the top drawer, together with some other pieces of jewelry from a life that I didn't have any longer. I leaped back under the covers and Macduff rolled closer.

As Macduff and I fell asleep, we both thought about Sasha and Doctor Lincoln Fairweather. Probably not in quite the same way, though.

CHAPTER SIX

I woke up to Macduff's tongue licking my face. It was six o'clock and my first day off. Tonight, I was to entertain Barbara and Horace. I got up to let the dog out. He marched to the hydrangea bushes at the end of the yard as if he'd always belonged there. I turned the coffeepot on, singing, for some unknown reason, an old song. "Lincoln, Lincoln Bo-Bincon, Banana Fanna Fo Fin-con, Fee, Fi, Fo, Fin-con, Lin-i-i-coln."

Macduff woofed to be let in and I regained my senses.

◆ ◆ ◆

I shopped at the local food stores along Kittery's Food Alley - Carl's Meat Market, The Golden Harvest, the Beach-Pea Bakery and the Italian *salumaria* called *Enoteca*. I bought crackers and cheese, olives and some almonds, veal cutlets, wine, a box of risotto, heavy cream and butter, salad greens and two ferny green stalks of *finocchio*. I found the tiny shop that sold handmade chocolates – the one that I thought was closed – was now open, stopped in and made another new friend. The place was called *Cacao*, and a pink-cheeked woman with snapping eyes who told me to call her Susan presided over a huge copper vat of melted chocolate. My mouth made helpless noises and I bought two pounds of assorted chocolates-soft, bittersweet dollops, some with hot pepper, some with tea, some with spices. Oh my, they would do splendidly for after-dinner-coffee and liquors. I dithered over what to serve for a proper dessert, but then chose fresh raspberries and the makings for vanilla bean *panna cotta*. I would stun my two guests, I smirked.

At Ace Hardware, several cans of dog food, a large bag of kibble, a red leash and collar and three squeaky toys completed my shopping and I headed for home.

As I parked my car and was gathering my shopping bags, a large, dilapidated station wagon pulled up to my curb. Doctor Grumpy Fairweather got out of the driver's seat and Sasha tumbled out of the passenger's seat. "We came to see if Macduff is better!" she caroled to me. "And we want to take you and him shopping for doggie things!" I quickly hid the bag with the dog food and leash back in the car and wondered why I felt so delighted.

"What a great idea!" I gushed as I ushered them, trying to hide my newfound happiness, into the little green house.

Macduff went crazy, greeting them with barks of pleasure, frisking around Sasha and banging his exuberant tail into furniture. Doctor Fairweather ran his hands over the pup and announced that Macduff was a healthy animal and already healing nicely. "He's cleaned up beautifully. Look at his gorgeous markings."

"I love his eyebrows, Grumpy," Sasha rolled onto the floor, the better to inspect the dog.

"I hope you don't mind," he mouthed to me over Macduff and Sasha's heads. "She pestered me all morning to come here to see if you and the dog were managing OK." I smiled my pleasure and let him help me put the bags of groceries away.

"Are you having a party?" Sasha's eyes watched as I unpacked. "Are you having company?"

"Yes. My attorney and her husband are coming here for dinner tonight."

"What are you cooking?" I told her.

"Oh, veal," she breathed in ecstasy. "Grumpy loves veal." Her face was innocent. "Don't you, Grumpy?"

"Veal is one of my favorites, yes." His own face was pink with embarrassment and he coughed and changed the subject. "Um, uh, would you like to take the dog to the pet store?"

"What a good idea," I said, wondering if maybe I should ask Doctor Fairweather to join us tonight. I opened my mouth, but Sasha grabbed my hand.

"Goody! We can take him to The Pet Palace. They don't mind if you take your dog along." Sasha informed me. Then, after she had rolled on the floor for ten minutes with Macduff, she dusted herself off and began a leisurely inspection of the house. "What's this?" She opened the Victrola.

I showed her how to put the needle down on the record. The twangy voice sang out. Sasha sat down with Macduff at her feet, watching the record go 'round. She sang along with the record, only she sang the silly lyrics that talk about spaghetti and meatballs. Lincoln laughed at her, then prowled around the room himself. He poked in the kitchen, looked out of the windows and peered at the meager contents of my bookshelf. Steve had taken most of the books from the condominium, leaving me only my collection of English mysteries. "Nice house. Did you just move in?"

I nodded. "Do you know anything about the house?" I fished.

He nodded. "I took care of their cats."

"The cats are still around. I see them all the time." His bushy eyebrows rose. "I fed them some chicken the other night. But I can't seem to pin them down. One minute they appear, and the next minute, they're gone."

He started to speak, but Sasha bounded up. The song was over. "Come on, Grumpy. Let's go!" Lincoln and I looked at each other and we began to laugh. "What's so funny?" Sasha asked, but I couldn't seem to explain it.

◆ ◆ ◆

Sasha paraded Macduff proudly up and down the aisles of The Pet Palace. Several people asked her what kind of dog he was, and each time she answered differently. "He's a Certified Maine Wolfhound." Or, "He's a Shakespearean Cross Breed." And again, "He's a Macbeth Lurcher." She was having the time of her life and Macduff acted like a proper gentleman, sniffing politely at each hand that petted him and wagging his plumy tail. We bought another red leash and collar, a huge bag of kibble, a case of canned dog food, two large stainless steel dog dishes, a detangle comb and brush, four squeaky toys, as we couldn't agree on which ones we liked best, a cedar-chip filled floor cushion and a braided rope throw. Sasha put the collar and leash on Macduff and walked him out to the car while I paid the man behind the counter a huge sum equal to the all the tips I'd made on Friday. Secretly, I figured I could take the first red collar that I had just purchased back and trade it in for more food. I'd do that later, much later, after Dr. Grumpy and grandchild had departed.

Lincoln and I walked out to the parking lot with me pushing a carriage filled with doggie stuff and him staggering with fifty pounds of kibble in his arms. "Do you really like veal?" I asked him bravely.

"Sasha has a big mouth for such a little girl." His face blushed. It was an endearing thing to see on such a masculine visage. "Please…uh, don't pay any attention to her blatherings."

"Yes or no to veal?" I couldn't believe the words that were spilling out of my mouth. Only a week since I'd been dumped, and here I was, asking another man to join me at a dinner party.

He shifted the bag of kibble and slowed his steps, turning toward me. "Yes to the veal." His blue eyes gleamed. "If you didn't ask, I was going to beg you." My face flamed. What did he mean? He rested his chin on top of the bag of dog food. "There's definitely something in the air between us, Reggie, don't you think?" His head tipped sideways and my heart lurched. Known the world 'round for my brilliant ripostes, I could only stare at him, speechless. He laughed, a loud, triumphant shout, and almost dropped the bag of kibble. "Let's get you home so you can cook, woman." We piled my purchases in the back of the station wagon, shoved Macduff into the back and drove to 236 Schooner Street.

◆ ◆ ◆

As it turned out, Lincoln also knew Barbara and Horace. "We've seen one another at town meetings and Ham and Bean Suppers," Barbara said. Her Santa-Claus eyebrows nearly rose off the top of her head when Lincoln came into the house a few minutes after she did, carrying two bottles of wine. I intercepted one of those wife-to-husband looks between Horace and Barbara and knew that they were wondering what little game was afoot. I stifled a giggle and wondered myself, but I thanked some unknown God watching over me who had insisted that I get the hand-made chocolates.

Over nibbles and drinks, we shared the newspaper clippings that Horace had brought with him – the ones about last year's murders here at my new hacienda. Lincoln told me what he knew about Sunny Sundergaard and Catherine Black and the four of us speculated on just what might have happened in this self-same room a year ago. Macduff lay on the floor in front of the couch, his head on Lincoln's knee, his tail waving in front of Barbara's face. Horace sat on the floor, sharing the rug with the dog. On entering the house, the Wyzinskis had been physically introduced to Macduff when he nearly knocked them down in delight. There seemed to be great mutual admiration. After hearing the story of how Macduff and I became joined at the hip, Horace couldn't stop rumpling his fur and telling him what a brave dog he was. And if a dog's face could be said to smirk, albeit modestly, Macduff's did.

As I got up to get another round of drinks, the Victrola suddenly came to life. We all listened to the plaintive song. "Do you think it's the ghosts of Sunny and Catherine?" I asked. "Are they trying to tell me something?" I made the sound of a macabre laugh.

"I think it's more like the ghosts of a sagging old house." Horace chuckled.

Barbara wrinkled her nose. "It is a bit weird, though."

"I kind of like the idea of ghosts." I sipped at my wine. "The Victrola and the cats seem to be linked in some mysterious way."

"And where are the cats?" Lincoln unfolded his bulk from the couch and peered out the back windows. "We need the cats to complete the ghostly scenario."

"Let's see if we can scare them up, so to speak," I joked feebly. My audience groaned appreciatively. "Come on, Macduff, go get 'em, boy." I opened the back door and the dog bounded out. We stood on the terrace while he modestly trotted behind the hydrangea bushes. In a moment, he returned, obligingly accompanied by a black cat and a white cat. We goggled, all of us with our mouths open.

"What the...!" Horace's eyes were round with astonishment. "I don't *believe* it!"

"If this were a movie, an organ would begin to play 'Da da da DA'!" Lincoln boomed out a bit of Beethoven. "Here kitty." He bent down and held his hand out. Macduff and the two cats nosed at it. He stroked the black cat and the animal began to wind around his legs. The white cat sat at his feet and stared up at him. He scratched its head and then began to run his hands over both cats in a professional manner. "Good cats. Nice cats. Let me see...." Macduff watched, with a silly expression on his face, as if to say, "See what I brought to you."

Lincoln probed and prodded. "They seem in good health. Nice kitty, kitty." Lincoln patted them again and stood up. "I wonder where they've been keeping themselves this past year?"

"And who has fed them?" Barbara bent to pet the cats. "They look sleek and cared for. Do you think Mrs. Clutterbuck has been taking care of them?"

I shook my head no. "She was surprised to hear that they had appeared. She told me that she wanted to look for them after...after, um, what happened. She said she was worried about them. But she couldn't find them." The cats cocked their heads, as if listening to some ghostly sounds. They meowed to me and I got up to let them out into the back garden. They touched their noses to my hand, then, in tandem, they ran into the bushes. My company strolled outside into the cool evening air. Macduff barked once, watching the cats go, then, with indifference, lay down in the grass.

Horace walked over to the bush where the cats disappeared. He poked and peered, but the cats were gone. "Mrs. Cee also told me that she hears them yowling once in a while. I think it brings back bad memories to her."

My dinner was a complete success. They ate every morsel and praised everything, especially the braised *finocchio*,[2] a dish that none of them had ever encountered. I blushed and grinned at the accolades, for some reason feeling like a sixteen-year old girl at her first triumphant dance.

The conversation at the table never flagged. We talked about the murders which had taken place last year, wondered at the whereabouts of young Jason Morant, lamented the rising taxes in Maine, and debated whether or not upcoming legislation banning a casino would pass or not.

Barbara and Horace left first, hugging me and complimenting me once again on a marvelous evening and my superlative cooking (their heavenly words, not mine). As I shut the door after them, I turned and saw Lincoln watching me with speculative eyes. All of a sudden, I felt awkward. I wanted to say something, but my tongue was stuck to the roof of my mouth. He stood up. "This was a wonderful time for me. I don't usually go...I don't..." He put his hands on my forearms and my heart stopped still. The skin where his hands were resting was tingling, as if little electric shocks were jolting up and down the tops of my arms. I dropped my eyes to his shiny loafers and tried to swallow. "Reggie," he said.

"Uh," I said, raising my eyes to his knees and then to his belt buckle. "Uh."

"Reggie." I heard his voice smiling. I looked at his blue button-down shirt, and then to his face. "You know that courting *is* a pleasure." Before I could reply, he bent and quickly kissed my cheek. "And if I were your lover, I'd never be false-hearted. Good night, my dear." And he was gone before I could close my astounded mouth.

---

[2] Please delight in the recipe at the end of the book.

CHAPTER SEVEN

O ne would think that I might have laid awake, thinking whatever treacherous thoughts a woman might have after …lusting, I think the word might be….lusting… after a new man exactly one week after having a thirty-two year relationship end. One might think that, but, contrary to popular opinion, I slept well, a long dreamless sleep, awakening to Macduff's grunts.

The two cats were waiting outside my back door. Mentally, I was referring to them as Sunny and Blackie the Cat. I guess the ghosts of the two murdered ladies were in the air, or I was becoming soft in the head. Maybe both. The cats ran off behind the hydrangeas with the dog. I set out Macduff's new food bowls on the kitchen floor, added two soup bowls, and mushed up canned food and kibble for all three animals. I wasn't sure if the cats would come in again, but they trotted silently through the back door beside the dog. The three of them crowded contentedly around the food. The cats ate standing up, but Macduff flopped down and ate from a supine position on the floor.

I made myself a cup of coffee and luxuriated in having a late morning to myself. I wasn't due at work until 9:30. Sundays was brunch only; my first working brunch.

Andrea called me and joyfully informed me that she had gotten a walk-on part in a TV soap opera called "The California Life." She was to play a girl in a bar. "I get picked up by this character named Blaine. He's one of the regular heartthrobs." I made motherly congratulatory noises and asked her how many days she would be working. "Two or three. I'm just a pick-up chick." I snorted with indignation. Mothers don't want their daughters to be pick-up chicks, not even in a soap opera situation. "But I'm trying valiantly to make a great impression on Blaine. I think she…my character's name is Alexandra…. Anyway, I think Alexandra isn't just a cheap babe." I grinned into my phone. "She really likes Blaine, you see, and she's been dying to meet him for ages." I nodded, trying to picture the scene. "So even though he picks her up in a bar, she's happy."

"Do you think the people...the producers? The directors? Which-ever. Do you think they can be persuaded to give Alexandra a long life?"

"I'm going to give it all I can, Mom. How's that guy with the weird name?"

I assured her that Rodney Kuntz was just as cute as ever.

She laughed, "I gotta go now." She made kissing sounds into the phone. "You take care of yourself. I love you, Mom. I'll let you know how it goes. Byee."

"Byee. I love you, honey." Smiling and saying the kinds of prayers that mothers say when they hope God will be good to their children, I let all the animals out just before I left. Only Macduff came back. Once again, I wondered where the kitties went when they weren't here.

I drove over the little bridge to Portsmouth, made a quick stop at the local bookstore, River Run, and bought a few paperback mysteries to keep me company at night. Tom, the genial proprietor, welcomed me as a new reader and customer by adding my name and address to his mailing list. When asked, he recommended that I try the Joe Gunther series by Archer Mayor, a writer from Brattleboro, Vermont. I pur-chased the first two Gunther books, a Peter Robinson English mystery, a new Donna Leon Venetian mystery and a used copy of an Agatha Christie familiar oldie, *And Then There Were None*. I invited Tom to stop in at The Loop Café one morning and have a cup of coffee on me. Happy now that I was armed with some reading material, I went back over the little bridge and back to Maine.

Gerjeet went over the brunch menu again with me. It was a glori-fied breakfast menu, featuring quiches, eggs benedict and a couple of other fancy things. "I think we will sell all of your cakes today." Ger-jeet rubbed his hands together happily. "They are hotsy-totsy sellers."

The morning was sunny and bright and the outdoor tables filled up rapidly. Judge Emery was there, with his hound-dog, Marvin, at his feet, making avuncular noises and trying to pat me anywhere he could. Marvin lifted his head and thumped his tail in pleasure to see his master so frisky. I brought him – Marvin - not the Judge, a big bowl of water and three dog biscuits and he rolled over and waved his paws in doggie glee. The judge smiled, his long yellow teeth glistening, looking much like a hound-dog himself.

Two of the Naval Shipyard men that I had met last week drove up in a yellow pick up truck, parked just outside the Café and introduced themselves. One was named Dave Holt and the other was named

Jimmy Van Wart. The Van Wart one tried to flirt with me. I think the Holt one was married. He was wearing a ring anyway and was simply pleasant and smiling. I was professional and polite. No matter how many men fell at my feet, I wasn't going to let it go to my head. Chuckling at my own poor internal joke, I re-set the table in the window.

My new chocolate genius friend Susan came in, bringing her husband, Ron, and two of her neighbors from Wells, a small coastal town about twenty miles up the road. They took four menus, and then went outside to sit as George and Laurie McGilvery, the aforesaid neighbors, had brought two cats on leashes to brunch. A lot of dogs came to sit outside at the Loop Café, but these two felines were our first. Enchanted at the two good-mannered kitties, I went outside to take their orders, say hi to Susan and Ron and to get acquainted with the McGilverys and the cats. The cats, Frankie and Johnny, politely allowed me to pat their soft heads, perhaps sniffing the scent of my own two ghost cats. I fished two dog biscuits out of my apron pocket, and the cats mouthed them and lay down to munch.

Susan told me that the McGilverys had just returned from a trip to Antarctica to see the penguin colonies. "We love to travel," Laurie told me. She was a petite brunette with saucy hazel eyes, somewhat younger than her husband who sported a crewcut and a handsome moustache. "We went to Tahiti and Bora-Bora last fall."

As I verbally envied them their ability to travel the world, the four of them ordered Gerjeet's Calcutta Spinach and Feta Omelets, which he served with puffy Nan bread and a special chutney. From what the other customers had told me, no one knew what was in the chutney, but it was damned good and everyone begged, so far in vain, for his recipe. George speculated that there were mangoes and some kind of plums in it, and Laurie suspected some cinnamon and perhaps a teeny touch of cumin. I shrugged and spread my hands out helplessly. I had no idea, and thus, could not be bribed. Despite my inability to give them the secret, they left me a great tip and promised to return.

As I watched them and the cats leave, a great wave of satisfaction washed over me. I really *liked* working here. Here, in The Loop Café and in my new life, I had friends, new friends who seemed to enjoy my company, my ability to bake and give them good service, people who wanted to talk with me and genuinely seemed interested in what I had to say. It was so different from my married life with Steve. Then, in my old life, I was Steve's wife...Andrea's mother...Jenna's mom...a woman who depended on others for my identity. Here, I was Reggie.

Liked for myself. Sought out to converse with as an equal human being. It was a delicious thing for me and I *liked* it all.

Into this happy frame of mind, Barbara and Horace drifted in. I grinned and threw my arms around Barbara, my first and best friend in this new and newly satisfactory phase of my life. Horace kissed me soundly, "Mmmmm, Reg, you smell delicious." He nuzzled my neck. "Just like some harem girl...wearing some foreign spice."

Getting down to her detective mode as an attorney and prosecutor, Barbara tried to get me to talk about Doctor Grumpy and how and why he'd been a dinner guest last night. I shushed her and told her that we might, just might, talk later. She shook out a pile of newspapers, showing me that they would be sitting around for a long time. "There's a big story about that boy who is missing," she shook her head. "I hope they find him soon."

"Me too. I'll sit down with you later. Do you want anything else?" They ordered second cups of coffee and dove into The Kittery Gazette and The New York Times. I grinned and went to take Judge Emery's order for a piece of sour cream cake to go with his coffee.

Dressed in a navy blue pullover, tight jeans and yellow rubber boots, and carrying a tote of squirming lobsters, Daniel Bethany sauntered in all by himself. "I didn't recognize you without your shadow." I greeted him.

"Jonah has a big date today," Daniel snickered. "Even you, my little Tootsie, couldn't drag him away from this one." I made my face look regretful. Gerjeet bustled over to him, jabbering his thanks for the lobsters. Out of the corner of my eye, I spied Barbara and Horace watching.

"How about you and I doing something exciting this afternoon?" Daniel's smile was broad and suggestive.

I shrugged modestly. "Not just yet, Daniel. I told you that my life needs some solitude before I can leap back into the fray." I handed him a menu. "Want some orange juice?"

"Don't you think we should stop playing around?" His grin slipped and his eyes were stormy. I was amazed at the instantaneous change.

"What do you mean?" I set down the coffeepot and my hands went to my hips. "What are you suggesting?"

"I mean you and me." I gaped at him. He seemed to realize his mistake and tried to get the smiling look back into his eyes.

"Daniel." My voice was low and steady. "There *is* no you and me. Up until a little bit more than a week ago, I was a married woman. You and *me,* whatever that means, met only a week ago. We have had sev-

eral minutes of conversation over meat loaf and hamburgers. I scarcely
think I have led you on, or tried to get you into any situation. You are a
customer here, in the place where I work. Not a boyfriend. Not
an…*anything!*" My calm slipped slightly and my temper rose to the
top. Daniel pushed his hands out and made an apologetic-looking face.
Out of the corner of my eye, I could see Barbara watching me, her eyebrows up to the top of her hairline.

"Hey, babe, I'm sorry if I came on strong. I thought you and I…you
and me…" My head shook slowly from side to side. "No? Well, I
thought…. No, huh?"

"No."

"Too early for you, huh?" The man couldn't seem to comprehend
that I might not be interested in a romance with him. He brightened.
"OK. We'll just have to get to know one another better. I got a lotta
charm and patience, babe. I'll just be here and you'll get used to me."

I tried to lighten the air. "Let's just forget the whole conversation."
He looked glum and annoyed at the same time. "Now. Do you want
orange juice?"

He grinned sheepishly and ordered his breakfast. When I served
him, he still seemed a little angry. Just a bit put-off. I wondered if it
was because I hadn't fallen for his line…his fishing line, ha ha. At any
rate, he ate his breakfast without any further fuss, left me a five-dollar
tip, winked, and said he'd be seeing me soon.

The rush of customers precluded any further chit-chat, and I ran my
buns off filling coffee cups and serving food. The strange lobster-
woman, Hank Ormand, came clumping in just after most of the customers had cleared out. Again, she ordered her ham and cheese
sandwich and her black coffee, and again, she totally snubbed and ignored any attempts of friendliness on my part. The only change in her
behavior was that she left me two dimes for a tip instead of last week's
twenty-five cents. Had I displeased her even further? Who could know.

She certainly seemed annoyed, leaving in a rumble of engine noise,
driving her battered truck away and never looking back.

At three o'clock, the tables were nearly empty. Only Barbara and
Horace remained, still sipping coffee and reading the last of The New
York Times. I poured myself a glass of iced tea and joined them.
"Whassup?"

"You tell us. We've been waiting for three hours! Come on! What's
the story on Dishy Doctor Lincoln and what was up with the Bethany
Brute?"

"There's nothing to tell." I spread my hands out innocently. "I met Doctor Fairweather when Macduff got hurt the other night. We were right outside his office and went in for some help. He just took care of Macduff. He knew I was making veal for dinner, he likes veal, so I thought it would be nice to ask him to eat with us." My brown eyes were wide and guiless.

Barbara snorted. "Right."

I put my elbows on the table and leaned forward. "What about his daughter? What happened?"

"Sad story. She was their only child. I'm sure the divorce hit her hard. Was one of those kids who could never find herself. Drank in high school, got into lots of trouble, went away to college, met the wrong kind of guy, began to use really bad drugs, got pregnant...I will say that they did get married after the little girl was born...and then her life spiraled even further down the drain. The husband...boyfriend...whatever, was an even bigger druggie. Got her hooked on cocaine and then she became very sick."

"AIDS?" I asked with sympathy.

"Noooo, but some kind of hepatitis. Her health was precarious and she simply couldn't stave off the infections. I hear that Lincoln moved heaven and earth to try to get her well. All the big clinics, the best doctors...but she died. I think she was in her late twenties. It broke his heart."

"What about the ex?"

Barbara looked at me with pity. "Not interested at all, huh? Ha!"

Horace chuckled and shook his head - his expression said "Women." I poked him in his shoulder and bent back over the table.

"Lincoln's family goes back centuries around here. He went to school in Canada...McGill, I think...always wanted to be a local vet. *She* was into finance...money...status. I heard that she wanted him to set up practice in New York City or Boston and be a society dog vet. You know, treat pampered pooches who had neuroses." She rolled her eyes and made mincing gestures with her football-player-sized hands. Horace chuckled again, giving her a look of adoration.

"So?" I wasn't able to hide my fascination.

"So, I guess they quarreled. This was while Gwen was still a child. The mother took her when they separated and they stayed in Boston. Maybe that's why Gwen was so screwed up. The wife, I can't remember her name..." She turned inquiringly to Horace who wrinkled up his face and shrugged. He didn't know either. "Oh, well, it isn't important. The wife came from big money and demanded a big settlement and alimony.

Lincoln came back here and bought the animal hospital. I don't think money ever interested him. The house on Ghost Pony Road was his family's place and when his father died, his mother moved in with him. When Gwen got sick, she came to live here for a little while, bringing Sasha with her. The mother had given up on her years ago. I don't even think she showed up for Gwen's funeral. Anyway, she wanted nothing to do with Sasha, so Lincoln took her."

"What happened to Gwen's husband? Didn't he want Sasha?"

Barbara snorted again. "I don't think his brain functions at all nowadays. I think he's either in some jail or some mental hospital." Her face became soft. "No, the little girl is in the best hands with Lincoln." She sneaked a look at me. "However, I have to warn you, Lincoln is considered *the* catch of Southern Maine." I gazed with feigned interest at the brownies displayed on the white shelf under the window. "Don't think I didn't notice those moony looks between you two last night." She giggled in her booming way. "You are too much, Reg. The King is dead…long live The King!"

"Oh, come on." I knew my face was beet red. "He's a nice man, and Sasha is a dear little soul. That's all." Even Horace didn't believe that one. I dried a corner of the table with my apron. "Ghost Pony Road? What an interesting name?"

Barbara just grinned. Horace told me that it was one of the oldest roads in town. "I think it has something to do with pirates and haunted ships or something."

"And what was happening with Daniel the Lobster King?" Barbara wasn't about to be put off by mere geographical discussions of avoidance. "He seemed to be angry."

"He thinks he's God's gift to a poor working girl." I laughed. "I told him that I wasn't interested."

"He's got quite a reputation. A bad temper. Watch out for him."

"I can handle him." I wiggled my shoulders, trying to ease the kinks in my upper back. "Oooh. I'm tired. And my feet hurt!"

"Too many men! I swear, Reggie, you are a sex-magnet!" Horace brushed imaginary sweat from his brow. "You're hot stuff."

Barbara chuckled and then spoke softly. "I can't say too much…a professional thing…but I mean it when I say Daniel can be overly persistent and could be dangerous."

"What do you mean? He seems harmless?"

"Not so harmless. I can't talk about it because of client confidentiality, but he could be a problem." Her homely face was serious. "His brother is even worse. The two of them…rotten tempers. And even Bob Micklewright can be nasty when he's thwarted." Her booming voice laughed. "We've handled a few complaints about him making threats to some of his customers. You've gotta watch all those men that you are attracting, Reg." I snorted and stuck my tongue out at her.

"I'll be careful. I promise." I patted her hand.

"Well, keep an eye on them. And be sure not to be fooled by Bob Micklewright," Barbara made a hideous moue, "He looks so prim and proper, but I could tell you a thing or two about Mister Prim."

"Yeah?" I said. "What else did he do? Swindle some old lady out of her life's savings?"

"A little worse than that." Barbara tried to look mysterious, but only succeeded in looking like she had a tummy ache. "One of these days, I'll tell you more."

"I don't give a boop about Bob Micklewright," I assured her and opened The Kittery Gazette. They hadn't found the Morant boy and the Sox had lost again to the Yankees.

◆ ◆ ◆

I spent the rest of the afternoon baking. In my silly state of mind, I overdid it. I made four sour cream cakes, a chocolate jelly roll with whipped cream filling, a lemon cheesecake, four dozen brownies, two dozen Moon Pies, an apricot brioche, which recipe had been in my family for generations, three sets of *biscotti,* and a batch of Scottish shortbread. As everything cooled, I called Jenna. She was upset.

"Mom, Dad wants to bring *her* here next weekend!" What should I do?"

Was that a flare of jealousy I felt? Probably. Who could figure us chicks out? I tried to be calm. "Just go ahead. You've got to meet her sooner or later. She's probably very nice."

"Huh! She's probably younger than I am!"

I changed the subject, asking about Scott. As usual, anything about Scott sent Jenna into newlywed rhapsodies and I listened with one ear while wrapping cookies. We hung up after telling each other "I love you." I wondered how the meeting with Brianna would go…and would Jenna tell me about her. I tried to call Andrea, but there was no answer. I left her a message telling her that I loved her and that things were going well. I wondered how the TV scene at the bar had gone and whether Andrea could bring her character to a long TV-type life.

I was tired and went to bed early. Macduff flopped beside me and promptly fell asleep. I tossed and turned, restless. Vivid half-dreams filled my head. Steve and me on one of our beach vacations with the girls. While Jenna and Andrea played in the waves, Steve drew a big heart encircling "Reggie and Steve" in the wet sand. Steve and me dancing together – so proud – at Jenna and Scott's wedding. Steve telling me that he loved someone else. I tried to ignore the last scene and recapture the scenes of happiness. Steve and me on the beach. I tried hard, but realized that I really couldn't remember anything about what had happened that day, only the fact of the scene itself. A picture. That's what it was. I was remembering a *picture*! We had a photo of the four of us posing, and then another one of Steve's sand heart with Jenna and Andrea in the background. The next photo was of Steve and me dancing at the wedding. Again, I couldn't remember a thing about the wedding. Only what was portrayed in the photo.

I could, however, remember everything about Steve telling me he was leaving. Every word from his cheating mouth, every despicable expression on his lying face. I shuddered. Was this what time and one's emotions did to one's memory?

I got up and took a cool drink of water. The phone rang. It was Lincoln. There was no question that my heart leaped. I could feel it jump from the place in my chest that it usually resides, up into my throat. I tried hard to get my words past its living lump. "How are you?" I blurted, always the brilliant conversationalist.

He told me again how much he'd enjoyed the veal. "And the whole evening." His chuckle warmed me even more than Macduff's furry body. "I plan to reciprocate very soon. Do you like opera, Reggie?"

"I love opera, Lincoln." It felt so nice to say his name. I noticed that the lump slid back to where it belonged.

"The Pickwick Theater in Portsmouth is having a performance of *La Boheme* in two weeks. On a Saturday night. Can you join me?"

Should I leap out of my self-imposed huddle and have a date? Was it too soon for me to be seen in public with a man? Before I could formulate my answer, Lincoln sort of changed the scene. "My mother's club has bought a bunch of tickets. She's going, Sasha and her best friend Eva are going to try to see if they can sit through a night of singing, and I have asked Horace and Barbara too. I hope you can join us."

Ah, *us*…not just me. Under those slightly unromantic dampening circumstances, I said I'd love to. A little voice inside me wondered if Lincoln would sit next to me. We spoke for a few more minutes, taking about Sasha and her antics and then discussed Macduff's continuing good health. When we said goodbye, I was smiling and soft, dreamless sleep came right away

Unearthly screeching awoke me. I leaped out of bed. Macduff began to bark frantically, growling and baring his teeth. The cats! I heard them screaming! There was the frightening sound of a truck or a car with a noisy engine in front of the house. I grabbed my robe and Macduff ran down the stairs ahead of me, barking and whining. Without even thinking, I opened the front door. It was dark, pitch dark. The red eyes of taillights were disappearing down at the end of the street. Macduff ran out, growling and gave chase as far as the street. There, on the front doormat, were the two cats agitatedly pacing and clawing at the door.

Macduff came back. He was upset and his hair was on end and he made sounds at the back of his throat. The cats twined themselves around his legs, nervous and meowing with frantic cries. I stood in the doorway and wondered what the hell had just gone on. A kerchunk sound behind me made me turn. The record dropped down and the Victrola began to play. *"For a thief will just rooooob you...."*

I shivered. Macduff whined and crowded close to my knees. The cats had disappeared again. I could never quite understand how they were underfoot one second, and the next they were nowhere to be seen. Could they really be the ghostly reminders of the two murdered women? Muttering to myself, uneasy, I locked the door and went back inside. For some reason, the thought of Hank Ormand with her big, red work-hardened clumsy hands came into my head. I snorted, telling myself not to be such a silly, but the night seemed even chillier and I had goosebumps for at least ten minutes.

I stood in front of the Victrola for a long time, fingering the switches and running my hand on the smooth circle of the record. Once again, I thought about Sunny Sundergaard and Catherine Black and the terrible way they had died. I wondered if Hank was a lesbian as well as a very masculine woman and if that had anything to do with Sunny and Catherine. I shook my head and told myself to stop being so nutsy.

I took the folder that Horace had given me and climbed the stirs to the bedroom. Macduff plodded after me, his capacious snoot a millimeter from my knees. He was panting, a nervous huff-huff and was still agitated. I slung off my clothing, leaving it for once in a heap on the side of the bed, yanked on my Yankees sleep shirt and climbed under the covers. Macduff leaped up and pushed his hairy body as close as he could. I was happy for his heavy nearness, but shoved his paw off my lap and opened the folder. I had already read the contents, the voluminous newspaper clippings trumpeting last year's murder mystery, but now, I read them again, with even more care to detail.

The clippings were dreadful, telling the reader of a vicious crime, a horrendous murder scene, and the utter failure of the police to find the killer or killers, despite hours and hours and hours of tedious work by the detectives who worked the crime. I scrutinized the photos, many of my now immaculate living room, but mostly, I pondered the information about the two women. Their backgrounds, the story of their lives before they were butchered. Had I not known that they were partners in life, I might not have realized their relationship from the newspapers. Was that important at all? Was there a maniac or a group of crazed citizens who hated lesbians? Someone who blamed Sunny Sundergaard for the bullets and weapons that her family manufactured?

A small manila envelope held copies of financial information. Sunny had been a very wealthy woman. Her Will had left everything to Catherine Black, and Black's Will, while not leaving such a huge estate, left everything to Sunny. As they had died simultaneously, the disposition of their estates reverted to the next beneficiary. In Sunny's case, all of her money had been divided between two first cousins, a Mary (Mrs. Dennis) Molchan and a Christa (Mrs. Richard) Vermierin, both of Berlin, Germany. I presumed that the police had checked to see if either Mary, Dennis, Christa or Richard had made any quick trips over the ocean to Kittery last year. Catherine's money went to the ASPCA. I nodded. It seemed fitting.

Suddenly exhausted, I closed the file and tossed it to the floor. As it thudded down, the Victrola sprang to life. The cat/women nightmare spectacle loomed in my imagination, fed by the horrors that I had just read. Macduff seemed to sense my inner distress and snuggled even closer, licking my hand and wiggling. The record reached the end, kerchunked a few times and then started up again. How could it happen? I lay in bed, listening to the familiar words, wondering what all of it meant.

And then Macduff and I went into uneasy slumbers.

◆ ◆ ◆

Zee, the wild-haired proprietress of the Hair-Em Scare-Em Boutique, "*We do Unisex Stuff*", sipped her late morning coffee. It was the lull between breakfast and lunch and the Café was empty except for her. I liked Zee a lot. I admit I was a bit prejudiced because of the way she looked. I always tried to see her without the protective covering of her punk hairdo and nose rings, to ignore her oddness. In truth, she was a cute little thing. However, the nose things got in my way. I guess I was just too old to appreciate facial punctures.

Zee tipped her exotic head and looked at me. "You need a do," she declared. "There's no one here for you to slave over. Come to the shop now and I'll make a new woman of you."

I shuddered as I thought of what she had in mind and tried to mumble that I was due to have my hair done in a few weeks. She grinned. "I won't shave your head or anything. I promise. Come on…You'll love it! I can do very respectable stuff. Come on!" Gerjeet and Anoop joined her in trying to convince me. Was my hair that bad?

And so I found myself being shampooed among posters that showed people with bright pink lightning zig-zags cut into their scalps, people…I didn't know whether they were men or women…with their hair painted in leopard stripes, or with green hair standing straight a foot up in the air. I admit it…I was a bit nervous.

"Re-lax!" Zee scolded me. Then she massaged some gorgeous smelling goop into my scalp and I did. Relax, that is. Her glittery blue tipped talons did a very creditable job. I felt my tensions melting…melting. Then she wrapped a towel around my head and spun me up. Her eyes and mine met in the mirror as she prowled around me, grabbing hanks of my dripping hair this way and that. 'Don't worry. I'm going to make you gooor-geous, just gooor-geous!" I made some sort of whimpering noise, but she paid no attention.

She mixed up some foaming stuff in a plastic bowl and then painted my hair with it, tipping her head and spinning me around to get it just the way she wanted. "Sit there for ten minutes and then I'll cut it a bit." She disappeared into the back of the shop and came back out with two cold cans of beer. We popped the tops and sipped. For some reason, it felt just right. I wondered what my daughters might think if they saw me here, at 10 o'clock in the morning, my hair painted with foam, guzzling a Budweiser.

"I've *got* to look weird, Reg." Zee told me, poking her own hair higher in the air. "If I want customers, they have to feel that I'm, so to speak, on the cutting edge." We both chuckled. "Really. They need to think that no one else will think of the things I can think of to do with their hair." I eyeballed the posters and assured her that I certainly wouldn't have thought of any of those particular things to do with my hair. She looked pleased.

She shampooed the stuff off my hair, toweled it dry and then sprayed another kind of goop on me. Tipping her head, she tousled my hair into ringlets. "You have naturally curly hair!" she squeaked delightedly. "Why don't you wear it natural?" She messed up my hair a bit more. "People *die* to have hair this curly!"

"I always hated my curly hair. When I was a kid, all my cousins called me 'Poodle Head'. Yuk! I always brushed it smooth. I always slept with those big rollers poking grooves into my scalp." I looked into the mirror. I looked like a demented and older Shirley Temple with blonde streaks. "I always thought I looked, you know, just fine." She gave me a look of disdain.

"Give me a shot. Let me play a little." She combed and snipped and then turned the chair so that I couldn't see my reflection. Sternly, she forbade me from looking in the mirror. "Don't wiggle!" she admonished. "And don't worry. I'm in charge here." What the hell was she *doing* to me? I was a rejected wife of fifty-five, not some bimbo on MTV.

She fussed, snipping and poking, her face mirroring her concentration. Then she stepped back. "Fan-fuckin' tastic!" she gloated. "You look super!" She spun me around. "Ta DA!"

I looked fearfully at my face and hair. Son of a gun...I looked...well, fan-fuckin' tastic. She'd shaded my hair blonder, and picked out golden highlights. She'd cut it so that my curls tumbled around my face like a Botticelli cherub. In the warmth of the studio, my cheeks bloomed pink and my eyes sparkled. I looked ten years younger and pretty damn good. "You are a genius!" I cried. I couldn't believe how wonderful I felt.

"Wheee-ooo!" Zee screamed. "Wheee-ooo!"

◆ ◆ ◆

I was a sensation, if I do say so, at lunch. Gerjeet whistled when I came back in and Anoop clapped her little hands and danced around me. Bob Micklewright was so stunned that he left me a thirty five cent tip, the guys from the Shipyard were verbally appreciative, Jack Burke, one of the local cops, gave me a whistle and Judge Emery forgot to pat my rear end. I made more money in tips than I ever did. Wheee-ooo!

But the best part...the very best part... came when I went to do a bit of grocery shopping on my way home from work. There, in the fresh vegetable aisle of The Golden Harvest, I ran into Steve and Brianna. Who was more embarrassed? It was a tossup. I gulped and backed into a shopping cart. Steve reacted like a cat on a bed of coals, almost jumped into the air and literally staggered into the fresh fruit, toppling three grapefruits. "Reggie!" He gibbered. "Reggie! You...You look...What have you done?...Reggie!" He goggled and stammered and I blessed Zee and God and whoever was responsible for the random chance that I looked so good.

"Hey, Steve." I waved and then turned to poke the Swiss chard. I pretended to be absorbed in each and every stalk, but my ears were straining to hear the furious whispering going on between Steve and The Bitch. I sneaked a peek at her from between the leaves. She was blonde...very blonde...and slender...really slender. I could see the bones at her neck sticking out. She had that...Karen Carpenter kind of look...a toothpick with huge boobs...and she was very, very pretty and very, very, very young. She was dressed in an obviously couturier designed, expensive business suit and looked extremely chic and elegant. I was dressed in my working outfit of jeans and a tee shirt. She was wearing soft black leather, expensive-looking pumps, with heels higher than I'd ever dare wear. She looked very professional, a walking illustration of what the up-and-coming woman executive should look like. I looked like the dog's dinner...but thanks to Zee and Providence, my hair looked great. She was tall, almost as tall as Steve and her make-up was perfect. I was short and dumpy and wearing sneakers splashed with ketchup. A smear of lip gloss was my only concession to make-up. A sharp pain stabbed me somewhere in the vicinity of my heart and I forced myself not to start crying.

Steve seemed to be drawn toward me. "Uh, Reggie, uh. Uh, how are you?" The pain abated a bit as I saw Brianna poke Steve sharply. "Uh, Brianna, this is my wife. I mean, uh, this is Reggie." My mood brightened a bit. Steve was definitely not at his best here.

Graciously, I nodded. "Brianna". Stupid name for a grown up. I left the conversational ball lying in a pool of water on his side.

She eyed me from top to toe. Somehow, despite the jeans, I wasn't quite the way she expected me to be. "Hello, Regina." Frosty. Definitely frosty.

"I, uh, hear that you've taken a job as a waitress," Steve tried mightily to get back in the game. "I didn't think you'd...I mean, *a waitress*, for God's sake, Reggie."

I laughed and the pain dissolved. "You are such a dork, Steve."

And then God truly and really and royally smiled on me. I felt a hot stab of glory, a touch on my arm and a deep voice said, "Ready, Reg, my dear? I've picked out the wine." He hefted a bottle of Merlot with his big hands, leaned into my shoulder and I looked up at his strong, smiling face. Somehow, Steve looked shorter than he'd ever looked. Not only shorter, but less masculine, less assured and more stunned than I'd ever seen him. Brianna looked at Lincoln with undisguised interest. Steve noticed and it made him even more pathetic.

"Then let's go, Lincoln." I nodded regally to Brianna's open mouth. Lincoln smiled distantly at the two of them and we walked away. As I said before, Weeee-ooo!

◆ ◆ ◆

"I presume that was the former husband?" Lincoln put my groceries in my VW.

"That was him." I dangled my keys. "Barbara refers to him as the shithead." I chuckled.

"You seem to be OK with it all." His face was somber.

"I was…it was a bit…yeah, I think I am just fine." I grinned, relieved. A huge weight flew from my subconscious into the heavens.

"And the new girlfriend?" Lincoln's mood was brighter.

"That was her." I sighed. "Dishy, wasn't she?"

"Not as dishy as you. Too skinny. I hate skinny women." He dismissed the reason my marriage had gone south with a shake of his head. "But *you*! You *femme fatale*, you! Not that you don't always look toothsome. But today, you look different…what? Ah, your hair…" He prowled back, turning me this way and that. "Nice. I like it. It suits you better…." His reddish-grey eyebrows leered up and down like Groucho Marx, "You look…cute. Adorable." He laughed and then pushed me into the car. "Here they come. You can't leave me yet. I'm the new suitor. Let's see how jealous we can make him. Let's go." He walked around to the other side and climbed into my passenger seat. He put his arm around my shoulders and I felt that peculiar jolt of heat again. I kept my head facing forward, but sneaked a peek out of the corner of my eye into the rear view mirror. Steve was staring at us and Brianna's face was visibly annoyed. I put the car into gear and drove off with Lincoln's gentle fingers caressing my fan-fuckin' tastic hair.

'Where are we going?" I checked the rear view mirror again. Steve and Brianna had driven off the other way. Lincoln's fingers stopped touching me and I felt a bit bereft.

"We need a drink, don't you think?' I nodded emphatically. "Let's go to Captain Simeon's." He directed me to a local pub behind Frisbee's store overlooking the water.

We sat at a small table, shared a dish of popcorn and the stories of our lives. He heard everything about me, from my early days as a happy child in a warm and loving Italian-American family to the abrupt end of my marriage. I heard about his early days, his college years, his marriage and its dissolution. He told me of the bleakness of Gwen's short, confused life, and the rage and sorrow that he carried in his heart, together with bittersweet memories of her. "I couldn't seem to help her and it tore me apart." I put my hand on top of his. "I'm determined to give Sasha a different kind of life. I don't exactly know how to do it, but I am damned if she'll wind up...sick and sad." He curled his fist around mine. "Thanks, Reggie." He sighed. "I needed to talk about this. Thanks for listening."

A waiter waved menus at us. "Hungry?" I nodded. "Me too. All this soul-baring makes one ravenous." We ordered steamers and boiled lobsters then ate with our fingers. Butter ran down our chins and the food was delicious. I watched him picking at the elusive meat stuck in a claw. His face was absorbed and I felt my heart turning over inside me. He looked up and caught me staring at him. He smiled.

"You feel it too." It was a statement. I couldn't pretend not to know what he was talking about. I nodded. He popped a piece of lobster into his mouth and chewed. "From the instant I saw you, wet and bedraggled, with that hairy monster at your feet," He shook his head slowly from side to side. "I was pole-axed." I giggled, a little muzzy with my third drink and a little muzzy with happiness. I'd have a huge black coffee now and sober up before I brought him back to his car. "I saw your wedding rings and my stomach dropped." I glanced down at my hand, glad that I had taken the damn things off.

"And then Sasha asked me all those questions." I sat back, almost gloating.

"I love Sasha. And I love her curious little mind." We both laughed. "And her big little mouth." He picked up my hand. "When she confirmed that you were all alone, I had to suppress my shout of triumph."

"Really?"

"Really. Really and truly." He dropped the banter and looked at me intently. "Reggie..."

"Coffee and dessert?" Our waiter chirped. We both sat back and began to laugh. "What's so funny?" the waiter asked. "Did I miss a joke?"

CHAPTER EIGHT

C andace Chabot loved to ride her new motorscooter. Richie, her husband of fifty-one years, had given it to her for her seventy-second birthday last March. Ever since Richie had gone to the doctor with male-type problems and the doctor had prescribed Viagra, Richie had been giving her presents left and right. Silky, frilly nightgowns, suitable for a much younger and skinnier lady, a diamond necklace, a trip to Las Vegas, and the scooter. The nightgowns made her chuckle. Hey, if Richie enjoyed them on her, well, wasn't that fun. The trips were exciting and the diamond necklace was the envy of her sister-in-law Cheryl. But the scooter was the best of all. A 50cc Yamaha Vino, shiny and blue, was the joy of Candace's latter stage of middle-aged life.

Every morning, she'd plop her helmet over her permed curls, hop on, rev up the engine, and zoom around for an hour or so of two-wheeled bliss. She knew the neighbors referred to her as that nutty old lady with the motor scooter. Who cared what those fossils thought! If they gossiped about her and her little scooter, the heck with them. The whole situation only made her laugh with gusto and delight.

She loved riding the roads in the early hours. There were animals and birds to see, leaves changing, a neighbor or two walking, envying her scooter and willing to chat for a moment. It was the best of times, even on a morning like today, with a rainstorm imminent. The leaves were shimmering as the wind picked up. Candace gripped the handle-bars and made herself be careful about driving around the pot holes.

She grinned and slowed down when she saw the Mamma-doe and her two teen-aged fawns in the middle of the road. The beasts looked at her as she stopped the scooter and the Mamma nervously checked the woods, making certain that a quick escape was near. Candace sat back and let her sneakered feet rest in the dirt. "Hey, doe," she whispered, somehow feeling honored that Mother Nature had allowed her to see these three treasures. The doe watched her intently, velvet ears cocking back and forth. The fawns were splay-legged and dainty, with freckled spots across their backs. Their stumpy tails wig-wagged and their little faces watched her with astounded curiosity.

A roar split the moment, and a truck barreled around the corner, weaving in a drunken manner, completely out of control. Swift and protective, the mamma doe nudged her babies and ran across the road. One of the babies followed, but the other stood, awkward and stupefied, and the high, hard bumper of the truck smacked it into the air. The fawn crumpled and lay still and Candace screamed out. The truck skidded, recovered, fish-tailed and nearly drove off the road as it sped away.

Candace leaped off her scooter, jammed the stand down and quickly wrote the license number of the truck in the dirt with her finger. "Son-of-a-bitch!" she yelled. "I got you, you cowardly bum, you!" She ran to the fawn. Clearly, it was dead, the soft brown eye already turning opaque and cloudy. Candace began to cry. Madder than she could bear, she turned to remount her scooter. The rain had started and her tears melded with the raindrops. Angry beyond belief, Candace squared her shoulders resolutely. She'd ride right to the police station and have the monster arrested. Son-of-a-bitch.

As she throttled around the corner, she gave a gasp of fright. The truck was coming back, aiming straight for her. It hit her obliquely, knocking her off the scooter. As her head thudded against the road, she thanked God for her helmet. "Ufff!" she cried. Her head bounced hard as it hit the road. Pain split through her, but she kept alert. She groaned and tried to roll to her feet. She pushed her arms out and grabbed the fender of her motor scooter. She heard the truck stop and the pound of heavy feet. And then, even though the helmet had kept her from injuring her head, it couldn't help her when heavy hands grabbed her. She was pushed down into the dirt, rolled over and a small, heavy rock smashed into her face, over and over and over again.

The rain beat down harder. Her assailant pulled on the gloves and an old yellow jacket that were always kept in the back of the truck and rolled Candace's body into the vegetation at the edge of the road, and then pushed her further into the brush. The scooter followed. Screened by the bushes and trees, her assailant dragged Candace's body through a thicket and then pushed her over the bank of a small ravine, not noticing that a shred of the sleeve of the yellow jacket ripped on a tree branch and hung, drooping in the rain and misery.

Panting with exertion, the attacker dragged the scooter down the same path, and then sent it rolling and careening madly down the bank where it came to rest, obliterating most of Candace's body from view. Breathing heavily, dusting off gloved hands, the assailant reversed tracks, making sure not to leave anything behind that might leave an identifying clue, then climbed back into the truck and turned on the radio. Somehow, in all the frenzied haste, Candace's killer missed seeing the small scrap of yellow fabric. The truck roared off and the now teeming downpour obliterated any traces of tire marks or signs of the incident. It also obliterated the license plate numbers that Candace had scratched into the dirt at the side of the road.

Two nights later, a curious opossum's attention was caught by the shiny yellow scrap of cloth. The opossum scratched at the cloth, enchanted by the way it reflected the moonlight. The cloth broke free from the twig that imprisoned it and floated to the ground. A night noise interrupted the opossum's game and it froze in place for a few moments. Deciding that any danger had passed, the opossum ran away into the night.

In the morning, a large crow spied the yellow cloth, flew down to the forest floor, watched warily, and then pecked at the scrap. The crow cawed, an eerie cry, picked up the cloth in its beak and flew away to decorate her nest with the trophy. Three other crows were drawn to the area, but they flew straight to the ravine to investigate the strange, but delicious object thrown there.

◆ ◆ ◆

I made the orange *torta* three nights before the Ham and Bean Supper. Mrs. Cee had given me orders to make some kind of a dessert. "A nice gooey one," she had said. "It always goes." And so I whipped up what was a treasured family recipe. Family stories said that the cake recipe had been handed down from the one my Great Grandma Francesca made when she was an abandoned bride in Italy. Such a tale, the story of Francesca and her trip across the ocean with her five little children, only to find that her husband, the nasty Carlo, had taken up with another woman.[3] Were these stories true? I guess so, after all, here was the *torta d'arancha* to prove it. It was the most complex, gooiest, most imposing thing that I knew how to make. And so, to please Mrs. Cee, and to impress the good people of Kittery, I did. I froze the *torta* to keep the rum ricotta cream fresh and stiff and defrosted it an hour or so before we were to leave for the Supper. Whistling along to the Victrola, I sliced the candied oranges that decorated the top, made the swirls of cream, and twisted each orange slice into a curlicue of citrusy delight.

---

[3] Read Francesca's amazing story in *The Tears of San'Antonio*

The Annual Ham and Bean Supper at the Kittery Fire House, so I was informed, was one of the big social events on the Kittery scene. Oh, for sure, Kittery Point had a gala ball at the Yacht Club every summer, but those who attended the ball were merely newcomers. Maybe rich newcomers, but newcomers, nonetheless. And the Kittery folk looked down at their noses at newcomers, no matter how wealthy they were. Only my standing as a waitress at The Loop Café admitted me to the hallowed circle of the Ham and Bean Supper. Yessir, pound for pound, you couldn't beat the Ham and Bean fest for authenticity and true social standing. Everyone who was anyone would be there. And this year, me too.

I was astonished, but honored to have been asked by 1) The Bethany Brothers, 2) Bob Micklewright, 3) Jimmy Van Wart, 4) David Wessell, the nice newly-divorced man with a delicious British accent who worked at the hardware store , 5) Phil Moore, the garage-owning fellow, and 6) good old Grumpy. I turned everyone down, even Lincoln. Why? Because it really was too new. Having Lincoln at my house with a few other people, going to an opera with a crowd versus showing up in public as his date were two horses of two different colors – one pink, one green. And I would never have gone out with any of the others anyway. So here I was, all dressed up, going to the dance with my elderly neighbors, and riding in the back seat of the Clutterbuck Oldsmobile, excited as a young orphan girl going to the Ball.

It was a balmy summer evening, one that had fireflies dancing. Elroy drove. He had a special kind of transmission in the car, one that let a one-legged man with a metal leg and foot drive safely. And he did drive very safely. At fourteen miles per hour, all the way, we drove in sedate splendor to the firehouse. The parking lot was filled with cars and chattering people. Elroy, with the privilege of the disabled, was able to snag a good handicapped parking space right up at the front.

Mrs. Cee was spiffy in an electric blue two piece pantsuit. She bragged, and I had no reason not to believe her, that she'd had it for more than twenty years. Elroy wore dark blue pants and a plaid shirt, and I was gussied up in a coral colored linen dress with spaghetti straps and a flouncy hem. Elroy told me that I looked like one of them petunias.

Mrs. Cee carried her tried and true seven-bean casserole wrapped up in newspapers to keep it hot. "If I don't bring it, everyone groans and asks me where it is. It goes fast. Not like some of them casseroles that some others bring." I nodded, understanding perfectly and prayed to some Ham and Bean God that my *torta* wouldn't wither on one of the tables uneaten.

The firehouse had been transformed. The engines were parked out in the back, the place had been cleaned up and there were tables lined up and down in the bays. Lights had been strung up and twinkled overhead, and huge industrial fans blew cool air over the foodstuffs. There were twelve tables laden with casseroles, beanpots of varying sizes, slabs of beef, hams, turkeys, vegetables and one table alone held at least twenty baskets of home-baked rolls. I turned to Elroy. "Mmmmm-*mmmm!*" I opined.

"Hot diggity," he agreed.

Mrs. Cee took my precious *torta* from me and ceremoniously carried it to the center of the five tables that held desserts. "This here is to go on a nice raised dish," she ordered. The lady who took it from her was in complete accord, and I smiled as they cleared away a Jell-O mold or two to make way for my masterpiece. Before I could observe any more, Horace and Barbara swept me into dual hugs.

The Clutterbucks commanded the best table with the sure knowledge that comes from many years successful negotiations at Ham and Bean Suppers. We were close enough to the food to be able to get first pickings, far enough away so as to not be bothered by those who were still foraging, in the path of the cool air of the fans, yet not so close as to have the fans bother us, close enough to have a great view of the dance floor, and far enough away so that the band wouldn't be drumming in our ears. I was impressed. Barbara and Horace quickly put their stamp on the two chairs next to mine. No fools them.

I saw Bob Micklewright and an older woman go by. He saw me and nodded in a cool manner as he held the elbow of his date's arm. Jimmy Van Wart was with a bunch of men from the shipyard. David Wessell was with an attractive, blond-haired woman. I noticed a lot of my customers…I waved at them and they waved at me… and then Gerjeet and Anoop were at my side. "So many people, no?" Anoop goggled. "We have a big table over there. All of our cousins are here." I saw a table awash with the color of bright saris and waved to Gerjeet's mother who was wearing a deep purple sari with one of those things on her forehead to match. As a matter of fact, almost all of the ladies at the Simha table were similarly outfitted.

"Barbara," I asked. "What do they call that dot thing on their foreheads?" I gestured toward Anoop. "And what is it for?"

Horace grinned and answered. "It's called a *bindi*, and it's a Hindu symbol. I don't know what it represents, though. Maybe something to do with good luck."

"More than that." Barbara told me. "When a girl gets married, then she can put one on. I think you can either paint it on with a sort of eyebrow pencil, or they also have these little stick-on ones. I guess it's a symbol of growing up." I nodded, not completely understanding, but a lot more informed than before. Horace promised me that he would research the matter so that we'd all be a bit smarter.

"I suppose I could just ask Anoop, but I was afraid of offending her." Horace started to answer me, but we were momentarily stunned into silence by the entrance of the Bethany Brothers. They nearly pranced into the Fire House, both of them with their arms around the waists of their respective dates for the evening. The men strutted in, each wearing brand-new fancy-dress western jeans, tight fitting, and sporting copper rivets up and down each leg. On top, they each wore a freshly starched rodeo shirt, Daniel in lavender and Jonah in buttercup yellow. The shirts were embroidered with flower motifs and strained over their muscled forearms. On their heads, the obligatory white Stetson hats. My eyebrows climbed at their splendor. The brothers were accompanied by two very pretty women, fancily dressed in square dancing duds, with scoop necked, peasant blouses and yards and yards of starched skirts. The women looked a bit older then the brothers, but nonetheless were very attractive in a hard way. Jonah winked at me as they passed our table and I waved my fingers back. "My!" Barbara said, fanning herself.

"You said it!" I agreed, stunned at their glory.

The band, consisting of a semi-professional group of locals dressed in tattered dungarees and plaid shirts, as if they were going to a hoedown, climbed onto the platform. A large, cocoa-colored dog accompanied them. I figured that the fellow playing the bass fiddle was more than a hundred years old. I couldn't wait for the music to start and the crowd seemed full of anticipation. The leader, the only one who wasn't in overalls, tapped the mike and asked everyone to be seated. Actually, he was wearing rather preppy Bermuda shorts and a button down shirt. He introduced himself as Bill Bowman and told us the professional name of the band was Nerdy Ned and His Nine Nasty Nosepickers. The crowd cheered. Obviously, the Nosepickers had played for this group before. The dog barked and lay down in front of the microphone and the Nosepickers began to strum and tune their instruments.

As we took our chairs, I was amused to find that Lincoln, Sasha, and a little girl with long blonde hair called Eva, one of Sasha's friends, were sitting at the other side of our table. Sasha was adorable in a pink sundress, and Eva wore a similar outfit in pale blue. An older woman sat next to Sasha. Lincoln stood and bowed, and introduced his mother to me. Regina Sabatino Fornier meet Mrs. H. Jacques Fairweather. Sasha giggled and wiggled her fingers to me, and Mrs. Fairweather, an older, more feminine version of Lincoln nodded regally, also waggling her fingers. "Please call me Maisie," she smiled. Lincoln came over, moving his eyebrows up and down like some ferocious movie villain and mentioned that I looked great. I grinned. The music burst into a rousing version of "Ain't She Sweet."

We ate until we couldn't possibly stuff one more bean into our mouths, all the while entertained by the Nine who played old favorites from the 30's and 40's. Then came coffee and desserts. I was pleased to see that someone had prepped Lincoln and he had the sense to have a largish piece of my *torta* in the middle of his plate. Sasha had heaped ice cream and strawberry Jell-O on her plate. Eva had fifteen – I counted them – fifteen - huge chocolate-covered strawberries. Mrs. Fairweather – Maisie, I mean - had angel food cake with strawberries and a small piece of my *torta*. Horace and Barbara, the Clutterbucks and Lucy, the Clutterbuck's daughter, had snagged what was left of my masterpiece. I sat back, fat and happy, knowing that the *torta* had passed the supreme Kittery Ham and Bean Supper test.

The wives of the firemen cleared the debris off the tables and the band took a short break. Fire Chief Eugene Kievit sold raffle tickets and nearly everyone bought an "arms length" for five dollars. Half of the money to go to a winner, half for the firehouse. We all applauded loudly when Judge Emery won the raffle, and even louder when he donated his entire share back to the boys in the firehouse. The cash bar was opened and bottles of beer appeared everywhere.

I was greeted with a big hello by Rodney Kuntz. His date was a stunning young woman with very short black hair, almost a crew-cut. She was nearly a foot taller than he was and wore stiletto high heels and a tight purple dress. Was everyone at the law office into shorter men and taller women? Rod introduced her: "Reggie, this is Diane." Diane smiled, very nicely, I must say, and bent over to greet me. She was gorgeous. Her tight skirt slid up over three admirable yards of polished thigh and every man on our side of the firehouse breathed a happy sigh. I made mental notes so that I could describe it all to Andrea and Jenna.

And then the dancing started. I sat out the first dance, entranced at Elroy and Hannah's prowess in doing a little number that was called the Peabody. They moved around the floor in stately precision, turning and quick-stepping, more intricate and graceful than the Rockettes. Elroy was amazing on his artificial leg and Hannah was a picture of dignity combined with rhythm. They got a standing ovation from the crowd as Elroy twirled Hannah back into her seat. "I need a cold brew and I need to sit down for the rest of the night!" Elroy gasped as the music stilled. I offered to get him a beer, but Lincoln was faster than I and slapped a cold one into Elroy's waiting hand..

A tap on my shoulder. It was Jonah Bethany. "How about it?" he asked and I was swept into the intricacies of "My Blue Heaven." As I had suspected, Jonah was a good dancer. He held me firmly, but not too tightly, and I duly admired his outfit. He grinned his thanks, but saved his breath for the dancing. He led masterfully and managed to sashay me right back into my chair at the last note. I thanked him with delight.

"You look good enough to eat, girl. We gotta get together." He kissed my hand and vanished back to his table. I refrained from looking at Lincoln, but Barbara told me later that he glowered.

That was the last moment that I sat down. The Nosepickers played their gol-darned nose-picking hearts out. The dog slumped on the floor, beating time with its dusty tail and the crowd danced and danced some more. I, myself, danced with my Doctor Grumpy, Horace, Judge Emery, Susan-from-the-candy shop's husband Ron, Jonah again, Daniel, Jimmy Van Wart, Dave Holt, Lincoln again, three other men from the Naval Yard, two of the firemen whose names I didn't remember, the Kittery Point Postmaster, Mike O'Brien and the Police Chief, Alexander Bridge. I did a jig with Sasha and her friend, Eva to the tune of "The Too Fat Polka", jitterbugged with Fire Chief Kievit, was pointedly ignored by Bob Micklewright, and then wiggled through the Chicken Dance with Lincoln, laughing the entire time as neither of us had any idea of how to perform it. I watched Barbara and Horace dance almost every dance. Barbara was outfitted with a red checked dirndl skirt with a white blouse on top and medium high heels with a strap across her instep. Horace wore blue jeans and a checked shirt. When they danced, Horace barely came up to her shoulder. They might have looked ludicrous, but they didn't. They just looked sweet.

Eva and Sasha cavorted with a group of youngsters, pushing each other around and giggling and having what seemed like a great time.

Even though I was dancing with lots of others, I was always aware of Lincoln. I caught him watching me, too. Whenever his smiling blue eyes touched mine, my heart lurched. What was this supposed to mean?

I just…it hadn't been enough time…How could I feel like this? I shook my head and my partner, Dave Holt, asked me if I was OK. I laughed and assured him that I was fine…simply fine.

At intermission, Maisie Fairweather sat next to me and in five seconds, knew all there was to know. She was a handsome woman, tall and tanned, with freckles on her face and hands. Her hair was grey, streaked with strands of red, and her nose was slightly beaked and aristocratic. She sipped at a Diet Coke and told me that Sasha thought I was wonderful. I blushed, then composed myself and told her that I thought Sasha was wonderful too. "It hasn't been an easy time," she confided. "My granddaughter's death was tragic. Absolutely tragic." Her blue eyes sought mine. "I understand that Lincoln has told you a little about it all?" I nodded and her hand touched mine. "Sasha is his salvation. She's enabled him to enjoy life again." She made a tsk-ing sound. "I thought I'd never hear him laugh again." I squeezed her hand. She was about to say something more to me, but Lincoln came back to the table. Maisie patted my hand as if to say "later". He brought over four foaming beers, plonked one in front of me, gave one each to Hannah and Elroy and tipped one to his own mouth.

"You don't have to work on Saturday, do you?" I shook my head no. "Good," he said. "We're going to spend that day on and in the water. I'm sorry to ask you so late, but I wasn't sure if I had to work on Saturday. I don't, as it happens, so I'm free too. Sasha and Eva and I are going to take you clamming."

"Clamming?"

"Yup. The tide will be just about right at eleven. Sasha and I will introduce you to Kittery's great sport. You'll have to stop in at the Town Hall one morning before Saturday and get a clamming license." I nodded OK. "And can you drive over to my house?" Again I nodded. "And dress in messy clothes. You'll get filthy."

"Sounds like fun." I grinned back my pleasure. "How do I get to your place?" He drew me a detailed map of how to get to Ghost Pony Road on a piece of napkin. "What's the story behind the name of your road?"

"I'll explain it all when we go clamming." I nodded. "I think the clamming license costs fifteen bucks"

"I can take it out of my tips," I said with a lofty air.

"You probably should wear a bathing suit under some old shorts," Maisie suggested. "That's what I used to do when I was spry enough to clam. Wear some thick socks and we'll find you a pair of rubber boots to fit over them."

"Can I bring anything? Coffee? Lunch?"

"Nah. We'll supply everything. And supper will be a mess of steamers." He sighed with happy anticipation. "Nothing will taste as good. You'll see."

The Nosepickers began to strum and plink out bits of song. Bill Bowman got up from the table, kissed his wife, Jo, burped, rubbed his stomach and climbed back up on the stage. The hound dog sat up and scratched its belly. People set down their beers and sodas and Lincoln swooped me onto the floor as they began to sing "Has Anybody Seen My Gal?" Could I have been happier? I think not.

Then Daniel danced with me again to the tune of "There's a Tavern in the Town", then Gerjeet – we did a slow, rather awkward waltz - then Mike O'Brien, huffing and puffing, twirled me around to a breathless polka tune. Jonah grabbed me right out of Mike's arms as the Nosepickers segued into "How Much is that Doggie in the Window" and everyone barked along, laughing. And then, and then…I danced with so many people… and then Lincoln slid in just before Daniel to take me to the floor for the last dance. It was – what else? - "Goodnight, Sweetheart". He held me lightly, but I could still feel the hot impressions of the tips of his fingers where they touched my bare skin. Lincoln whispered all kinds of funny, racy things in my ear, including the fact that I looked good enough to nibble on. I think I was glowing. Oh, let's face it. I was lit up like the Brooklyn Bridge on a summer evening!

As we drove home, again at fourteen miles an hour, I decided that I'd had a wonderful time. An absolutely wonderful time.

CHAPTER NINE

Kittery Gazette

Our News Is Your News Monday, August 28, 2000

TWO KITTERY RESIDENTS MISSING! HAS ANYONE SEEN JASON MORANT OR CANDACE CHABOT? POLICE SEEK INFO!

By Nunzia Ciccola, News Editor

Kittery, Maine: Jason Moran, age 18, missing since Wednesday, Candace Chabot, age 72, missing since Friday.

Where are they?

Police Chief Alexander Bridge is seeking any information as to the whereabouts of two town residents who are missing. The two cases do not seem to be related.

Bridge's office was notified late Wednesday afternoon by Thomas Morant, father of the young man, that Jason had not returned from a bicycle ride taken in the early morning on August 16th. "Jason left the house about 7:30 AM. He took his bicycle," his father stated. "It was a normal thing for him to do, take a ride." When he didn't come home by noon, his family began to worry. "Jason is a good boy. He wouldn't worry me or his mother," the elder Morant said. "He'd call us if there was any problem at all."

The boy was riding a blue Schwinn bicycle. It is likely that he was wearing blue jeans and a red tee shirt. Jason is 6'1" with dark blonde hair and blue eyes. Most likely, he was also wearing a baseball cap, dark blue with a Bowdoin College logo. A June graduate of Traip Academy in Kittery, Jason was very familiar with the roads and landmarks of the area.

"We're afraid that he rode into the woods somewhere and is injured and unable to get help." His father appealed to anyone who might have seen Jason that morning or afternoon to call 911. "His mother and I are frantic. We are assembling a search party tomorrow morning and welcome any assistance to help our son."

Chief Bridge is in charge of the search party, which will consist of police officers, firemen, first aid volunteers, citizen volunteers and volunteers from the Portsmouth Naval Yard. Anyone who can assist is welcome. Please call 278-444-8484.

On Friday morning, August 25, Candace Chabot, age 72 and wife of Richard R. Chabot, of 704 State Highway 1, took an early morning motorscooter ride, as she often did. When she didn't return home after several hours, her husband called the authorities, worried that his wife had been in an accident.

Police searched every Kittery and Kittery Point street, but there was no sign of Mrs. Chabot nor any sign of her motorscooter. A heavy downpour made visibility difficult, but "we looked everywhere," Chief Bridge stated. "No one saw her or her scooter."

Candace Chabot is 5'4", has short, wavy grey hair and was wearing a dark green tracksuit, white sneakers and a dark blue motorcycle helmet. The motorscooter is a dark blue Yamaha Vino, with a brown leather seat. The license is ME 1375 MC.

"No way that Candace would disappear like that," her husband stated. "She was always home by 9 o'clock. She must have had some kind of accident."

The search party that will comb the woods and sea-shore looking for Jason Morant will also search for any sign of Candace Chabot.

"Again," Chief Bridge implored the public, "If anyone has seen anything – anything at all that can help us with either of these two missing persons, call the Kittery Police immediately at 278-444-8484. "And again, we welcome all the help we can get. There's a lot of wood-land and seashore in our town and we need every person who can assist us in finding Jason and Candace.

CHAPTER TEN

The phone rang as I was brushing my teeth. It was Jenna. "Mom, it was awful! She was awful! I hate her and I hate Dad for doing this to you and to all of us!"

Was I a horrible person to say that I felt a rush of satisfaction? Maybe, but I must admit that I grinned, toothpaste and all. "Oh, honeybunch, I'm so sorry that you are upset. What happened?"

"She...she came." Jenna's voice was shaky. I tried to make soothing noises. "I tied to be nice, but, oh, Mommy, I hate her!" Jen's voice wailed. "He paraded her in like she was The Queen of Sheba or something!" I stifled a snort of laughter and told Jen to take a deep breath. I heard her breathe in and out. "I'm OK now. It was just...she was..."

"Come on, Jenna. Just tell me. Take it one thing at a time."

Jenna sighed and started all over. "They were supposed to be here at seven. We were going to have a cook-out. I figured if we cooked burgers and hot dogs, that it would give us something to do." I nodded into the telephone. As if she could see me, Jenna said. "I knew you'd understand, Mom. I was so nervous and I didn't know how to handle it all." I made a soothing noise. Poor Jenna. It truly must have been a difficult evening for her. Her beloved father and his...date.

"So what happened next?"

"They arrived twenty minutes late. That sort of made me upset. Daddy is never late for anything and I expected them to be here on time. Poor Scott was pacing the floor and I gulped a vodka and tonic in five minutes." Her voice rose. "And then they got here. He almost carried her in, Mom. Like he expected us to applaud!"

"Mmmm-hmmm." I kept my tone noncommittal.

"She was overdressed. I mean it was a *cook-out*. Scott was wearing shorts and a tee shirt – a nice tee shirt with a collar and all and I was wearing my new blue striped capris with a white crop top." Jenna was always the detailed one. "Dad was nicely dressed," she said with a touch of asperity, "but *she* was gussied up like she was going to dinner at the Ritz!"

"What was she wearing?" I couldn't resist.

"A pair of very tight slacks, turquoise silk. Silk, Mom!" I snickered. I couldn't help it. Luckily, Jenna sailed on without having heard me. "And a jeweled silvery top. With a big Fendi logo made out of *sequins*!"

"No!"

"Uh huh. And she had high, high heels. Strappy sandal ones…and they were gold leather!" My gasp made her happy. "And her hair was all up in a fancy do, and she had those dangly chandelier earrings. Like J Lo!" I began to laugh. I couldn't help it. Jenna forgot to be upset and started to laugh too. "She looked like a hooker, Mom!"

"Oh, sweetheart. What else happened?"

"I think Dad was aware that I was stunned and less than admiring. He looked really uncomfortable." Jenna sighed. "The conversation was heavy going. No one knew what to say." I made some noise and she continued. "She took a hamburger and a tiny spoon of potato salad. She took three bites of the hamburger. That's all she ate. She didn't even try the dessert. And I'd made my best brownies! The ones from your recipe!" Jenna was indignant. "And then, Mom, she asked to use the bathroom." There was an expectant pause.

"And?"

"And she was in there for a long time. I was sort of concerned. I mean, she might have been ill or something."

"So?"

"So she was vomiting!" Jenna was jubilant. "She was making herself puke!"

"No!" I cradled the phone and my mind boggled.

"She's bulimic, Mom! A puker!" Jenna started to laugh. I thought of all the mother and daughter discussions I'd had with Jen and Andrea. Trying to discourage them from feeling that their body image was important enough to starve themselves. I was lucky, though. Neither girl was heavy. Anorexia and bulimia hadn't been problems, thank God. But Brianna! Is that why she was so thin? I was stunned.

"Are you sure? I mean, she might have genuinely been ill."

"Nah. She was sticking her finger down her throat!" Jenna was ruthless. The rest of the evening hadn't gone well. "Dad was squirming. He knew it was a mistake to bring her over. They left early and they weren't even speaking to one another. She's a creep and Daddy will come back to you. You'll see. He won't be able to stay with someone like her." Jenna was triumphant.

"But, Jen," I spoke softly. "I don't think I want Daddy to come back to me."

"B...but...You *don't?*" Her newly matured voice squeaked. "Why not?"

"I'm sorry, darling. You mustn't think that it will all go back the way it was. I had a bad shock when Daddy left, but after a few weeks, I realized that he was probably right. We *have* grown away from one another." Jenna sucked in her breath. "I have a new life now. One that doesn't include your father anymore."

We talked for a few more minutes and then hung up, telling each other I love you. Jenna was subdued. I knew she would call Andrea and the two of them would hash all of this over. They would help each other and that was good.

I hung up the phone with gentle wonder. I hadn't planned to feel this way, but it was true. I didn't want Steve at all any more. I wanted Lincoln.

How could that be? We barely knew one another! Macduff's muzzle licked my hand as we went upstairs to go to bed. We jostled each other for the coziest spot under the covers. I petted his wooly head in an absentminded way. Lincoln, Lincoln, Bo-Bincon.

I tried to remember what it was like...I mean when Steve and I just met. There *had* been sparks and fireworks and weren't we in love? What had happened to the feelings? Had they gradually disappeared? Did he stop loving me years ago, or did it take Brianna's pointy chest to change him? Certainly I had been smitten when Steve and I met. There were bells and whistles and...well, you know. I mean it wasn't always fireworks. Especially after the years had gone by. But I had thought that we were normal and still wanted to be married to one another. How had it gone so wrong? I sighed and bit at my lower lip.

And me? Had I also really stopped caring years ago? Did we just go through the motions of a marriage? My hand stilled and I touched myself on the spot on my throat where my pulse beat. Macduff pawed at my hand and I sighed and began to scratch his ears. Blissful, he fell asleep. In an hour or two, my eyes closed, but I was restless and hot all night.

◆ ◆ ◆

I fed Macduff, let him out to do his business, shut him up in the house and, as it was a lovely day, decided to ride my bike to work. I saw Mrs. Cee out in the front yard and she waved to me. As I passed her, I noted that Elroy had backed the car out. I presumed that they were going on an early morning errand. I hadn't listened to the news that morning. However, as soon as I arrived at The Loop Café, it became evident that something unusual was happening.

There were two patrol cars parked outside. Four policemen were inside. One of them was the tall policeman who had been at the condo. He gave me a friendly, but quizzical glance, one of those looks to say that he knew me, but couldn't quite place where we'd met. Gerjeet was making up several large containers of coffee. He put a dozen pieces of cake and several brownies into a box. "Here, these are for the searchers." The policemen thanked him and left.

"What's happening?"

Gerjeet pointed to the front page of The Kittery Gazette and I sat down with a cup of coffee in my hand to read about Jason Morant and Candace Chabot.

"Oh my! Those poor families! I wonder what's happened to them?"

"Perhaps they have been kidnapped," Gerjeet offered. "Or maybe they insulted someone in a high political office." I made a dubious face. "Or they had malaria."

"Two people? In the same week?" Anoop nodded, sure that this suggestion held the solution.

It was the talk of the day. People came in and ate. Everyone had a theory, some even more peculiar than Gerjeet's.

Barbara and Horace stopped by for lunch. Naturally, the first thing talked about were the two missing people. Horace was taking the afternoon off and joining the volunteer searchers. "I did some legal work for Candace and Richard," Barbara told me. "She was a lovely woman, cute as can be on her little scooter." Barbara sipped her soup thoughtfully. "She must have had some kind of terrible accident."

"But why hasn't anyone found her?"

Barbara shrugged her strong shoulders and looked doleful. Horace patted her hand. "We'll find her…whatever." It wasn't very reassuring.

"Oh, I almost forgot with all this," Barbara hesitated a moment as she got up to leave. "Good news. The condo is sold."

"Yippee!" I did a little jig. I never wanted to see that condo again.

"We got full price." She grinned triumphantly. "Any regrets?"

"No sir! I'm glad to get rid of the blamed thing." I stacked a few dishes onto a tray. "It represents everything that I want to forget."

"You'll be a rich woman now, you won't have to work."

"Nah." I gestured dramatically to the tables and chairs. "This has been the best thing that happened to me. I really enjoy this job. I have good friends, a lot of fun, and for the first time in my life, I'm sort of supporting myself." I had the grace to look slightly abashed. "With the help of Steve, of course."

"He owes you the courtesy of a few bucks," Barbara made a sour face. "Don't sell your life as a wife and mother short."

"I know. I deserve a little bit of help from him. But soon, I plan to let him off the hook and manage by myself." Barbara looked dubious. "I mean it. I can live on what I make here, especially with the bakery stuff selling so well. And as for the condo money, I'll sock away it away for my creaky old age or for my grandchildren, should I ever get any."

Barbara shrugged her shoulders. "I'd keep him squirming for a while."

I laughed, hugged Barbara and Horace and wished him luck in his search. "I pray that you find them," I patted his arm, suddenly somber. He nodded with a heavy sigh and then I realized just what we all were thinking. "Anyway," I muttered, "I'm praying."

◆ ◆ ◆

As I approached 236 Schooner Street, I was delighted to see Lincoln's station wagon at my curb. Lincoln, Sasha and her friend Eva were sitting on the hood, obviously waiting for me to appear. Sasha jumped down and went running towards me. I swooped her up and her warm, little girl sticky arms hugged me around my neck. "I thought you were *never* coming home!" I put her down and she dragged me toward the car. "We want to take you and Macduff to York Beach for a frozen banana! Can you come?"

"A frozen banana! What delight!" I smiled at Lincoln. His steady gaze made me feel hot.

"We were in the need for some refreshment. Eva suggested York Beach and frozen bananas."

"Sounds great to me. Let me get the hound and wash my hands." The girls skipped at my side and then went into raptures over Macduff. Macduff returned their enthusiasm, ran out to do his hydrangea duty, and then presented himself for the ride. I sat up front with Lincoln, and Macduff shared the back seat, hogging the driver's side window.

Sasha wanted to make sure that I liked Eva as well as she did. In her half-little-girl, half-boss-of-the-office prattle, she informed me that Eva's mother made salsa. "And the salsa is named for Eva. It says so on the lid."

"I never knew anyone who had salsa named for them." I was impressed. "Is good salsa?"

"Delicious," Sasha assured me, "Even though it is too spicy for me."

Eva, a delightfully shy long-legged blonde sprite, giggled. Her gap-toothed grin matched Sasha's. I guess ten years old was an optimum time for a few lost teeth. "How can you say if it's good if you don't eat it?" She challenged Sasha.

"Because your mother says it is." Sasha's logic was firm. I sat with my elbow out the window and wondered if Sasha missed her own mother.

York Beach was a funky, seaside type of place, kiddie rides, a petting zoo, skee-ball emporiums and a taffy-making machine placed strategically in front of a plate glass window. The smell of the taffy and the mesmerizing sight of the dual armed taffy machine winding and winding and stretching the goo made our taste buds sing. We bought a bag of assorted taffy, a cup of vanilla ice cream for Macduff, and a frozen banana, chocolate dipped, and on a stick, for each of the humans. Lincoln and I sat on the rocks bounding one side of the beach, while the girls and Macduff cavorted in the sand and waves.

"Is the salsa good?" I stuffed the last bite of my banana into my mouth. Lincoln looked at me and then wiped a spot of chocolate off my chin with his fingertip. He then put his fingertip into his mouth and licked it clean. I watched his finger like a sleepwalker and felt a hot puddle of mush inside of me. I wanted to…something. Instead, I asked again about the salsa.

"It's very good." Lincoln seemed consumed by some inner mirth. "I'll bring some over to you."

I didn't know what to say. I wanted to touch him. Touch his fingers, his hands. His hands were large and capable looking; his forearms were covered with wiry gold-blonde hairs. The mush inside me was spreading. In a downward way. I didn't think I would be capable of such feelings. Not yet. But I was. He watched me. "What is it Reggie?"

What could a girl say? I want you to kiss me? I want you to hold me? I opened my mouth. "Isn't Eva a pretty name?" Actually, that wasn't what I really wanted to say, but it popped out. Probably better than what I was thinking.

"It's a beautiful name." Lincoln gave the question his sincere thought. "Almost as pretty as Regina."

I was still rather flustered. I began to babble. "You know, there is a test. A test to see if a name is a good one. You are supposed to do it when you have a baby. The test. To see if the name is going to be OK throughout the baby's life." He raised his thick eyebrows at me. I think he was suppressing a grin. I plowed on. "So if you were going to name a baby Eva, you'd do this test. You'd use the name in a few different situations. First, you'd say, 'Baby Eva! Come to Mommy, Eva!' And if that sounded good, then you'd say, "Mrs. Jones, or whatever, can Eva come out and play?' And then you'd say, 'Eva, congratulations on your diploma.'" I couldn't seem to meet his eyes. "And then, you'd say, 'Eva, I love you', and then 'Eva, will you marry me', and the last test is 'Eva, we'd like you to accept the Vice-Presidency.' If the name sounds good in all those situations, then it is a good name for the baby."

"Hmmmm. Let's see if I have it right," Lincoln picked up my hand. The jolt of warmth felt electric. "I start like this, 'Baby Reggie. Come to Daddy', right?" I nodded like a puppet. "Then, 'Can Reggie come out and play?'." His voice was deep and his thumb rubbed the top of my thumb. "Then 'Reggie, will you marry me?' and then 'Reggie, will you accept the Vice-Presidency'. Did I forget anything?"

"You forgot one." I whispered.

"And what was that one?"

"The one about love."

"Ah, the one about love." I knew he was teasing me. Sweetly teasing me. Even so, my insides were churning. He brought my hand up to his lips, turned it over and kissed the palm. My mouth opened and I thought I might die. "The one that says, 'Reggie, I love you." He kissed my palm again, then gently held my chin and kissed my open mouth.

"Grumpy!" Sasha squealed. "You're kissing Reggie!" Eva's mouth was open even further than mine. Macduff seemed to take the whole thing in his stride and sniffed at some desirable spot on the rocks, then anointed it. All this romance was of no interest to him.

As we drove home, Lincoln's pager went off. A cat had been hit by a car and he was needed in surgery. He dropped Macduff and me at the curb, kissed me on the cheek to the giggles from the back seat and told me that he would call me as soon as he could. With that, Macduff and I had to be satisfied. Macduff was fine with it all. I was not.

◆ ◆ ◆

There was a message on my answering machine from Andrea. She loved me and she'd heard from Jenna. Dad was a stupid shithead and she never wanted to meet Brianna. No matter what. "Oh, and Mom, guess what? The producer liked the way I played Alexandra. Blaine is going to see her...I mean me...again! I'm going to be in at least three more episodes! I am so thrilled, Mom." I grinned into the answering machine. Me too, Andrea. "I'll try to call you tomorrow. I love you, Mom. Byeee!"

I made the telephone rounds of calling my Greenwich relatives.

Uncle Pat was extremely encouraging, telling me that he was proud that I was standing on my own two feet. MJ promised to send me a few of her prize recipes from her bakery and Cousin Joann wanted to know all the juicy details about the new man in my life. I hung up with a decidedly warm glow. Family was always family and our family was one of the best. Even from several hundred miles away, their love cocooned and sustained me. I grinned and waltzed into the kitchen.

I was too wound up to sleep. I made three batches of cookies, molasses and clove this time. Then, I climbed into bed at midnight, the phone rang. "Did I wake you?" It was Lincoln. He'd been on emergency duty and had just finished stitching up a rooster that had fallen a-foul (his joke, ha ha) of two jealous hens. I asked him just how one stitched up a rooster and he answered, "Very carefully". On this hysterical note, we talked for a few moments. About nothing, really. He ended the conversation by telling me that he was going to be busy all day tomorrow and he had a meeting tomorrow evening. "But I am certainly looking forward to our date." My face glowed at the word date. He continued, "Did you get your clamming license?" I assured him that the paper was in hand.

"Would they really put me in jail if I didn't have a license?"

"It would be a serious misdemeanor. They don't mess around with serious crime here." We both chuckled, wished each other a good night, sleep tight, and hung up.

I tried to settle down and sleep, but the evening played over and over again in my head. The thing about when his hand touched me. The hot flash that accompanied every touch. The warmth I felt when we talked on the telephone. I sighed. I guess this was what all of my relatives had meant.

You know that I came from a big Italian family. A big Italian family with big Italian superstitions. There was this thing...the Sabatino Electric Tingle. It was supposed to run throughout the family, going back to the year whenever, when my Great-Great Aunt Carina met my Great-Great Uncle Rafael. She felt this tingle. This hot, electric shock feeling when his hand touched her. And Rafe felt it too. So much that they stared into each other's eyes and vowed to be wed, right then and there, or so I have been told. And supposedly, the Sabatino Tingle had been passed down through all of us. I'd never had any such feeling, mind you. I'd asked around. Who had the tingle and who didn't? My cousin Carrie confided that she hadn't felt it when she married her first husband. She thought the whole thing was hooey until she met Alister, the man who would eventually be her second husband. Then, she'd said, the tingle was definitely there. And her daughter also tingled. My daughter Jenna said that she felt a definite warmth, with Scott but not an electric shock. Who knew if this thing – this tingle – really meant anything or not.

My cousin Julie swore to me that the tingle really existed. My cousin Maddie agreed, and so did my cousin Joann. My Zia Carina said she tingled still with Uncle Mike, even though they were both in their eighties. My cousin Angel had told me that every man she met gave her the tingle. My second cousins Jessica, Jody, Mia and Laura were too young. No tingle had come their way yet, but they were hopeful that the future would be good to them. MJ was still looking for the man who might make her tingle. On the other hand, my cousin Kathy said she tingled whenever she even looked at her husband, Adam.

So, at last, after all those non-tingle years, I finally seemed to be following along the Sabatino pathway. Lincoln's touch burned. Singed. Tingled. I smiled with utter satisfaction, threw my leg over Macduff's hairy back and went to sleep.

◆ ◆ ◆

I drove to work on Friday, bringing my three batches of molasses-clove cookies, a large tin of Scottish shortbread, six dozen Raspberry Jelly Linzer Cookies - the kind with the hole on the top with the jelly that peeks out - and two sour cream coffee cakes.

Before I went to the Loop, I turned the car toward Tidewater Island. I drove down the narrow dirt roads to the lot that Steve and I had purchased. The place that should have been our dream home. The lot that Steve nearly gave his soul to keep. Why? I couldn't explain. I just wanted to see...I stopped the car.

And there it was. A huge house already in the first stages of construction. Piles of lumber, the basement cemented in. A big sign declaring that a contractor named Swanik Custom Builders was going to put up this new house and that it had been designed by some architect named Thane Pearson. My mouth fell open and evil thoughts began to churn. How the heck had Steve gotten the house started so soon? We had discussed plans, but never made any firm decisions. He must have moved fast. *Fast!* Shoot...he moved like greased lightning! This house was obviously planned, designed and arranged-for long before Steve had given me my walking papers. I bit at my lip, wondering how I could have been so stupid...so oblivious to what must have been going on around me. Steve contacting an architect, designing this house, planning for everything, including a builder and a hot little number to share the new bedroom with!   And me, little Reggie…not knowing one thing about any of it. I really *was* a dumb broad, wasn't I?

I tested the idea in my mind. Did I care? Was I upset that he had made such an ass of me and our marriage? My mind shed a tear or two and then shook itself and squared its shoulders. My mind and I didn't really seem to care at all. Good for me.

As I sat in my car, going over all of these earth-shaking matters, I noticed a large grey Volvo was parked in the dirt driveway area. Gee, I hope it wasn't Steve. I'd be mightily embarrassed if it were. Imagine Steve showing off his new castle to Brianna and me being discovered snooping around. I froze as I saw a young girl with short blonde hair come out from behind a huge stack of boards. She was followed by two huge black dogs…Newfoundlands, I think they were called. To me, they were as big as two grizzly bears. The girl saw me and waved and smiled.

I fluttered my hand in a feeble hello, put the car in gear and got the heck out of there. I certainly was slightly embarrassed and my poor heart beat with a vulnerable thud. Who was she? A neighbor, snooping too?

I drove away. As I crossed over the little bridge, leaving Driftwood Island and Steve's house behind me, I stopped the car and looked back. Other than my acute mortification of having whoever the girl with her two big dogs was see me, I felt nothing at all. No jealousy, no sadness. No wistfulness that the big house going up might have been mine. It was as if I had driven past the new house of total strangers. As indeed I had. I turned the car around and went back along the private road. Back to my new life.

CHAPTER ELEVEN

When I got to work, everyone was talking about the search. I felt bad. In my selfishness over my own life, I'd forgotten that two nice people seemed to be missing. "What happened?"

"They found the boy's bicycle," Anoop told me as she dusted the tops of my cookies with confectioner's sugar, then put them on a decorative plate. "It was in the bushes near the beach." Her huge eyes looked mournful. "But no boy. They could not find any trace of him. The air has swallowed him away."

"And the lady? Candace?"

Anoop shook her head again and her bangles and chains flew. "No one. No lady to see. There was no one else there."

◆ ◆ ◆

I was happy to see my former condo-neighbor, Rose Nunn at one of the tables. She was sitting with another woman who looked familiar, and had a tiny scrap of fluffy dog sitting on the floor beneath her chair. I tied my apron behind my back and went to greet them. The other woman was tall and slender, with blonde hair combed into a casual do. Her name was Joan Grasser. The reason she looked so familiar was that she worked at the Rice Library and had checked out books for me. The scrap of fluff was introduced to me as Shotzy and I learned that she was a Miniature Schnauzer for whom Doctor Grumpy Fairweather cared. Rose was delighted to hear that the condo had been sold. "And at such a good price. It made all of us feel good. Nice to know that one's investment is doing OK. Everyone at the condos asked for you. Everyone is happy for you, Reg," her happy face smiled. "You know. Get that memory out of your life," was how she put it. I nodded and brought them their eggs.

The morning rush slowed for a moment and I was able to sit with Joan and Rose for two seconds of gossip. Shotzy's eyes melted into orbs of happiness as I passed a tiny piece of buttered toast into her polite little mouth. We all...well, maybe not Shotzy... worried and speculated about the young boy and the lady that were missing. Joan was fascinated by my transition from married woman to scorned woman to rather happy waitress. I told her that it, on balance, was probably the best thing that had ever happened to me, "Although it has taken me a few weeks or so to realize how good it can be." I tried to be honest.

"Rose told me about the scene at your condo…when all your furniture disappeared." Joan gave me a look of sympathy.

I laughed. "It seemed like a tragedy then, but now, I think it was sort of funny."

"Funny?" They gasped.

"Yeah. Like some movie scene." I tried to make them understand. "It was horrendous and embarrassing then, but now…I can look back and laugh."

Joan's face took on a wistful look. "My marriage crumbled," she confided. "I can't get over it all yet." I patted her hand. "My ex – I guess we are getting a divorce – hasn't supported me at all since he left. I work, but the Library job isn't exactly the best paying job in the world." She bit down on her lip. "I have health benefits, thank goodness, but I worry about money all the time." She told us that she had trained as a bookkeeper, but the Library job was the best she could find. "Shotzy keeps me sane." She patted her lap and the little dog leaped up and curled herself into a bright-eyed ball. "If I didn't have her, I'd go crazy." Her face was rueful and I could see the prickling of tears behind her lop-sided smile.

"I understand completely. I've acquired a pooch too. A large mutt named Macduff." I laughed out loud. "He's the man in my bed these days." I pressed my nose down to Shotzy's black buttoned one and promised to see if anyone I knew was looking for part-time help. Rose suggested that Joan seek Barbara Wyzinski's legal advice and I chimed in with fervent agreement. "If it hadn't been for Barbara, I'd be in big trouble. She's a great lawyer and will help you, I promise." I scribbled Barbara's telephone number on a napkin. "Call her, Joan. She can help." I chuckled inwardly as I thought of what Barbara would soon do to upset the life and pocketbook of Joan's ex.

Three tables of customers came in and I got up to sling hash. Joan and Rose gathered their packages and Shotzy's leash and left, promising to let me know how Joan fared. I made a mental note to call Barbara, and then was swept up in eggs, sunny side up, with a side of bacon, bagels and cream cheese and all the other delights that pleased the morning patrons of The Loop Café.

My social standing drooped a bit at ten o'clock as Bob Micklewright brought his stiff-haired lady friend in for breakfast. The one that he'd escorted to the Ham and Bean Supper. I wondered if they'd spent the night together...then snickered inwardly at the clinically comical mental image that was conjured up by my over-active and irreverent imagination. Although I greeted him in a cordial and professional manner, he pretended that I was only an employee, someone beneath his dignity to chit-chat with. He didn't introduce us. He hung over his companion, patting her hand and all but cutting up her bacon for her. She, in turn, gazed devotedly at him. Anoop commiserated with me. "She has stabbed you in the back, Reggie. Taken your man from you." Her huge black eyes were sad. I told Anoop that love knew no boundaries, love knew no rules.

"If he loves her, I won't stand in her way." I all but smote my brow. Anoop looked at me with great respect. I certainly was a woman of the world, wasn't I?

True to his nature, Micklewright left me twenty-five cents for the two breakfasts. As he and his new babe drove away in his truck, Anoop scowled, upset by the perfidies of men.

◆ ◆ ◆

Mrs. Cee dropped in with some chocolate cookies. "I've been dying to see what you've done with the house," she confessed. I showed her everything and she nodded with approval. "Looks good. You'd never know there was blood all over only a year or so ago." I nodded thoughtfully at her observation, thought I would have shivered, but didn't, and went to put the kettle on for tea.

Mrs. Cee poked her head into every cupboard and then helped me to set the table. As she plunked down the teapot, the Victrola leaped into motion.

"*On top of old Smoooo-key...*" She gasped, clutched at her throat and got to her feet.

"My lands! It's the ladies!" She stared at the spinning record.

"*...Is worse than a thief.*" Mrs. Cee's head cocked and she listened carefully, her hand held up to ward off my comment. The record ground to a halt. Mrs. Cee watched the stylus bump and scratch and then turned to me.

"It's them." Her head shook back and forth and she seemed a little pale.

"Who?"

"The ladies. Sunny and Catherine. It's them singing." Eyeing it with a great deal of suspicion, she shut the Victrola off and sat back down at the table. "They made that record. Great land of Beulah! It's like hearing ghosts!"

"It really is their voices?" My own voice squeaked upwards. "Really?"

"I can't get over it." She palpitated the vast area of her comfortable bosom, sipped at her cup and picked up a cookie. "Like they were coming back from the dead. Many a time they would sing for me. I told you, they had this mandolin." She strummed an imaginary instrument. "And they loved to sing them old cowgirl songs." She tsk'd and slapped her thigh. "What a peculiar thing!"

I told her about the cats and how they kept popping into my life and then out of it. She shivered again, "Brrr. Maybe them cats are the ghosts of Sunny and Blackie the Cat." I laughed, a bit hollowly, hoping that Mrs. Cee would never find out that I had similar thoughts of the cats and ghosts and who-knows-what too. "Well, now, there are stranger things, you know…" She looked back at the Victrola and rolled her eyes.

"Too bad the cats can't tell us what happened last year." I humored her a bit, although maybe I was fooling myself. "It would be a miracle if they would speak. Tell us just what happened; tell us who the murderers were."

She looked at me for a long moment, her eyes sad. "Maybe they are trying to tell us, but we can't understand what they mean."

◆ ◆ ◆

Macduff and I woke to bright sunshine on Saturday morning. I know I wasn't supposed to bring along any food, but my mother had brought me up as a good girl. Even attending a clamming party, I was a polite guest. And besides, I wanted to show off my baking skills a little bit too. I'd prepared another family stunner, one that we called Cheryl's Buns. Easy recipe, using frozen bread dough, butterscotch pudding and pecans. When plopped together correctly, they produced a mile-high gooey coffee cake confection that looked a great deal more complicated than it was.

Macduff had been invited along and I packed him a little picnic basket of his own. Kibble and fresh water and some biscuits. I put on some new underwear, trying to make sure that I looked good under any circumstances…and who knew what might come up?… I covered myself with old cut-off shorts and a sleeveless top, put a pair of heavy socks and my black tank bathing suit on top of Macduff's basket, pulled on an old pair of sneakers and off we went.

Ghost Pony Road was located on the Pepperell Cove Peninsula part of town. Kittery's coast protected the Portsmouth Harbor and had done so for several hundred years. There were old fortifications and gun towers and mind-boggling views of lifeboat stations and old lighthouses. I drove slowly, enjoying the scenery and Macduff stuck his hairy head out of the front window and enjoyed the breeze blowing his ears back. I turned the car over a small bridge and dodged the potholes down onto a dirt road. Another turn brought me onto Ghost Pony Road. The houses here were largish and old, with mature trees and flowering bushes and backyards that sloped down to the rocky shoreline. The car bumped over another small wooden bridge and a weathered red mailbox told me that this was where the Fairweathers lived.

Number Five was a shingle house that had been built a long time ago. It was vaguely colonial, with a big porch and humpy eyebrow windows that stuck out here and there. A widow's walk crowned the house and, as we drove up the driveway, Sasha and Eva came screaming out of the house to greet us. I noticed that the driveway was crowded with cars. I parked the VW in the only space left, next to Lincoln's disreputable station wagon. Shoed in next to it was an elderly, but gleaming, butter-yellow Mercedes-Benz, a glamorous silvery Cadillac, and a monstrous newish truck, one of those enormous ones that has a front and a back seat, a flatbed back and is a hazard to everything else on the road.

Macduff, in a frenzy to meet the girls, climbed himself out of the front window of my car. He turned at my astonished gasp, gave me an apologetic look, and then collapsed in Sasha's arms.

Laughing at Macduff's more-than-human expression, I disentangled myself from the car, backing out, rump first. I heard a piercing wolf-whistle from the area of the front door and, slightly embarrassed, turned, tugging at the frayed hem of my shorts. The front door was dark with the grey-green leaves of the rose arbor that clustered around it and I couldn't clearly separate the shadows of the people who stood there. Lincoln's hearty laugh made me grin and I grabbed all my stuff from the front seat, sticking my tongue out at him. Sasha grabbed me around the waist, nearly knocking Macduff's basket out of my arms. Eva danced alongside, grabbing at my hand, and Macduff barked and frisked and added to the pandemonium.

The shadows separated. "My, my. Who is this little ragamuffin? The babysitter? Your cleaning lady?" The voice was cool and dripped vitriol. I held Sasha in a hug and watched as an elegant vision in a pink suit and white sandals came into the sunlight. She was older - tall and attractive, with blonde hair done up in an immaculate chignon. She was dressed in the height of fashion and looked expensive and soigné. Lincoln followed her. She held his arm in a proprietary grip and I loathed her on sight.

Sasha's head pillowed into my waist. I swung her up and heard her fierce whisper, "I hate her. I *hate* her." I gripped Sasha harder and felt the heat of Eva's damp fingers on my forearm.

"Who *is* this?" the vision drawled, "Your cleaning lady?"

Lincoln laughed, albeit a bit hollowly, I thought. "Reggie. Hello, my dear."

My eyes narrowed. The vision looked slightly taken aback.

"Hi, Lincoln." I dragged my baggage with me and closed in.

"Reggie, this is Athena. My, um, ah…ex-sister-in-law." He was nervous. Definitely nervous. I nodded to the vision. "Athena Hamilton…Reggie Fornier." His jaw was at a peculiar angle and I couldn't tell if he was jittery or laughing inside. Sasha burrowed her head further against me and Eva moved closer. Macduff sensed some tension and stood still, watching me with doggie concern. "We're all going clamming."

The vision smiled then, a perfectly charming smile. "How nice. Clamming." She made it sound as if we were going to roll in garbage. Her voice tinkled. I had read that once in a story, about a voice that tinkled. I never knew exactly what it sounded like. But I knew now. "Pleased to meet you."

I nodded pleasantly, shifting Sasha's weight slightly.

"I mustn't keep you. It's such a lovely day to grub around in the mud." She smiled again and held onto Lincoln's arm, guiding him away from us. "Good-bye. Good-bye Sasha. Please try to remember to act more like a lady." Sasha's grip tightened, threatening to strangle me and I felt a surge of love for the child. I wanted to protect her from…what?

"Good-bye." My burden and I walked toward the front door.

"Sasha, say good-bye to Aunt Athena." Lincoln patted Sasha's shoulder.

She squirmed around and muttered "Bye." Eva, a staunch buddy, just hung on. Macduff turned his head to watch Athena and Lincoln, waited a moment, and then galloped after me.

We reached the front steps. "Ooof," I groaned theatrically. "You weigh a ton." I dropped Sasha down and pretended to gather my parcels around me as I peeked to spy on Lincoln. He and the delectable Ms.

Hamilton were at the door of the Cadillac, murmuring together. Lincoln's head was bent down and he held her elbow as she got into her car. Sasha and Eva watched and I pretended to scratch Macduff's furry ears as I, too, watched to see what was happening.

The car door slammed and then Athena started the engine and backed the Cadillac out of the driveway.

"I *hate* her." Sasha said again. Lincoln waved as the Cadillac drove away. He loped casually toward us.

"What a beautiful day!" he exclaimed, a little too cheerful. "Perfect to catch lots of clammies."

Sasha's breath whooshed out. "Perfect now that *she's* gone." She began to laugh. Eva and I joined in. I probably shouldn't have, but I did. With relish.

◆ ◆ ◆

Sasha and Eva dragged me all over the house, showing me everything and chattering like two little birds. Sasha's bedroom was at the top of the house. A typical young girl's rat's nest of clothes, dolls, a computer and a few posters of juvenile rock stars on the walls. A silver picture frame stood on her nightstand. "This is a picture of my mother," Sasha picked it up to show me. "She was really pretty, wasn't she?"

"She was, darling. She was. She was beautiful." I gazed at an older version of what Sasha would look like in ten years or so. Lovely.

Lincoln's bedroom was on the floor below, neat in dark blue and green plaid. There were no personal pictures on his dresser or bedside table, other than one large one of Sasha, maybe age three. I know because I looked. His office was also immaculate and impersonal.

The house was charming, a hodge-podge of styles. The furniture was old and comfortable and almost every window showed a view of the water. The kitchen was obviously the heart of this home, with a huge commercial range, scarred wooden floors, and plants decorating every sill. I could have moved right in.

We had coffee (the grownups, that is…the girls had milk) and my contribution of Cheryl's Buns was loudly appreciated. Eva and Sasha thought the "buns" part was a hoot. No one mentioned Aunt Athena. It seemed to me, however, that her immaculately groomed essence hovered in the air with a tiny bit of tension affecting everyone.

The girls wore old, faded shorts topped with ratty tee shirts. Their feet, like mine, were encased in heavy socks topped by rubber boots. Lincoln also wore a pair of faded shorts and I kept sneaking glances at his long, pretty-good-looking legs. I think he was scouting out my underpinnings too.

With Maisie watching us, we gathered assorted gloves, battered metal baskets, and several bottles of cold water. From a bin in the garage, Lincoln issued each of us a wickedly sharp short garden harrow-like instrument. "It's a clam rake," Eva informed me. I held it out, wondering what kind of giant clam needed such a thing to be caught. Lincoln watched my expression of horror and laughed.

"You'll see. You need it to pry up the mud." He gestured with his rake and I nodded, not quite understanding what I might have gotten myself into.

Maisie and Macduff waved us off. Macduff had initially been annoyed that he wasn't to join the party, but Maisie plunked a huge stew bone down on the floor and he forgot that the rest of us existed. "I'll see you in an hour or so," she blew a kiss at the expedition. "I'll have your picnic waiting for you."

We trooped out the back door, then walked, boots slapping, along a path that led over the rocks and down to the mudflats of Pepperell Inlet. It was one of those perfect summer mornings, bright and sunny with a sweet breeze that discouraged bugs and saved us from perspiration. As we squooshed down towards the water, I was glad that I was wearing somebody's old boots. Eva slipped in the mud and fell, screaming with laughter and Lincoln nearly fell on top of her as he picked her up.

Our mood was giggly. "Here, walk this way." Lincoln hunched into a burlesque of a walk and we all obliged, imitating him. We skirted the reeds at the edge of the mud and the sliding little waves began to play with our feet.

"Who owns the truck in your driveway?" I asked Lincoln. I had been wondering about it, but the vision of Auntie Athena had gotten in my way.

Lincoln looked embarrassed. "It's mine."

"*Yours*? You own a big truck like that?" My expression made him stop sloshing through the water. I giggled. "It just doesn't seem to fit you."

"It doesn't fit me at all." Lincoln began to laugh. "One of the farmers up in Emeryville owned me a ton of money. His sheep were in bad shape. I managed to save most of them, but the whole thing set him back a bit. Didn't have the cash, so he turned over the truck to me instead. He told me that the truck was worth a fortune, but that it guzzled so much gas that he wanted to get rid of it anyway." He shrugged. "It was the truck or a prolonged collection action. So I took the truck." He bent down and scooped up a handful of water, then splashed it over his head. "I have to get it listed for sale. I hate to drive it." His face was sheepish. "It scares me to death!"

"It sure looks like a gas-guzzler."

Lincoln laughed. "I've got to sell the dratted thing. I'm simply too busy to get around to it. I think I need someone in the office to help with taxes and finding time to do little extras. Sasha runs the office rather well, but she's in school most of the time. She's able to handle appointments, the billing and easy stuff, but she certainly couldn't cope with selling a truck. Everything else is sort of falling behind." His smile drooped for a moment, and my heart wanted to gather him to me and make him safe and warm and protected from anything bad. "I'm just too busy to bother with stuff like that."

Joan's face loomed in my mind. "Do you really need somebody?"

"I could use someone part time." Lincoln stepped over a large log that was at the water's edge. He held out his hand and helped me clamber over it. He kept hold of my hand as we walked after the girls and my heart skipped like a stone across the waves. As a matter of fact, my heart always seemed to be very active when I was with Lincoln. "If I had somebody else in the office, even two days a week, I wouldn't get into such messes. Somebody to take care of those overdue bills and other secretarial things."

"Really?"

"Really. Why? Do you want a part time job?" he teased.

"No, I'm fully occupied." I smiled up into his eyes. "But just yesterday, I met a woman who might be able to help you out. I'll call my friend and find out if she might be interested. Her name is Joan and I'll have her call you so you can interview her."

"Terrific." His hand squeezed mine and that heart of mine kept doing things that it didn't usually do when I wasn't with this man.

"Who belongs to the beautiful yellow car?" I figured I might as well ask all the questions that were stuck in my throat.

"My mother. She's had it for twenty-five years and I think it is still under the original warranty." Lincoln laughed like a schoolboy. "She drives it to church and back on alternate Sundays. I think the odometer is under fifteen thousand miles."

"Wow."

"Yeah. It's her pet. She calls it her banana cream pie." I wondered if he noticed the relief that blew through me. Old Aunt Athena was more than I could deal with. Thank goodness there wasn't another woman lurking about leaving her car at Lincoln's house.

"This looks like a good spot!" Sasha's voice rang out. We gathered around her.

"OK, Sash, tell Reggie what to do." he ordered.

Sasha obliged, explaining that the clams were hiding under the mud. "You look for their air holes…see!" She spied a group of holes in the slick, wet mud and showed me their patterns. "This is where they are." She picked up her rake, squatted with her rear end in the air and maneuvered the rake into the mud. She leaned hard on the handle and pushed, grunting with effort. I could already see that clamming wasn't an easy thing. "Oooof. You've gotta' be careful. You don't want to smush up the clam. Otherwise they're no good." The tines of her rake broke through the mud, bringing up a large shovelfull of grey-black mud and the faint smell of decay. There, at the tip of her rake, stuck in between two of the wicked tines, was a muddy clam, grey-whitish and yukky and sporting a yellow neck, which reminded me of…well, suffice it to say that I had been away from Steve and marital intimate stuff for awhile. I suppressed a grin. Lincoln had the same suppressed grin on his face too. Sasha grabbed the clam and the clam fought back, squirting a stream of water right at her face! Sasha screamed with glee. "That's the most fun, Reggie! When they pee on you!"

She deposited the clam in the bucket. "Now you have your first hole," she showed me. Her cute little face was screwed up with earnest effort and the hot sun had already brought her freckles out across her nose and on the tops of her cheeks. She wiped a strand of hair out of her eyes and left a streak of mud on her forehead. Eva's face was pink with the sun and her fascinated expression was earnest too. Sasha's lecture went on. "You stand in the hole and dig around yourself. Then bend down and start to scoop the mud away, sort of in a circle." She bent industriously and scooped, exposing two more clams. She handed them to me and I dutifully put them in the bucket with the first prisoner.

Sasha moved over and gestured to me that I should move into her spot and try to find some more. "Come on, Reggie. You can use this hole first." I stepped gingerly into the mud and squelched my feet into a comfortable position. "They hide in groups. We call them clam hotels. OK, Reg, let's see how you do."

I stuck my rake into the mud. It was surprisingly difficult to penetrate. I pushed down, lost my balance in the slippery scree, pinwheeled my arms in the air to keep my balance, lost the battle and fell on my hip in the mud. Everyone cheered and told me that I was a seasoned pro now. I sprawled over to push myself up and found myself sliding on my face. Ten minutes into the event and I was covered with gook. Good thing prissy old Aunt Athena wasn't here to see what a mess I was. Lincoln's strong arm pulled me up. I shook him off and I attacked the mud with maniacal strength. There! There he was, the little devil! I saw him! I scrabbled in the mud, careful not to break his shell. Aha! I grasped him gently, but firmly with my gloved fingers and brought him out! A magnificent creature, nearly three inches long, plump and dirty and peeing a stream of water into the air. I felt wonderful.

Sasha, Eva and Lincoln spread themselves out, each finding their own circle of holes. Sasha had her own style of digging, crouching down with her little bottom resting on the mud, scratching the surface like a dog, digging until the clams came to the surface. Lincoln bent from the waist, using his energy efficiently, bringing up clam after clam with machine-like regularity. Eva sat right down in the mud and raked the surface, bit by bit, until she unearthed her own clams. And me, well, suffice it to say that I slipped, slid, gouged myself, cut my fingernails to shreds and had the best time I'd ever had finding edibles on a beach.

The morning air rang with our triumphant cries as the buckets were heaped with bivalves. I slipped again, lathering myself with mud from head to toe, and Eva joined me, sliding completely down on her rear end and skidding into the water. It was terrific!

My original holes petered out and I searched now, on my own, for my own personal clam hotel. I found a pattern of holes a bit higher up on the beach. Lincoln watched me, then offered his advice that the clams were generally found closer to the water. Obviously, Lincoln didn't know how cussedly stubborn I could be. "I want to dig here." I told him.

"On your head, be it." He teased. "If you don't find any, don't blame me."

With that type of challenge, I nearly dug up the entire beach. Clams here, clams there, clams, clams everywhere. Not only did I find the biggest clam hotel, I found a whole town! "Oh, look!" I screeched. "Lookie, lookie!" I was dancing with joy, trying not to fall again. The clams were nearly jumping into my hands, two or three at a time. "Here's the Momma. Here's the Daddy. Here's Uncle Joe!"

Eva was near me, calling, "Here, clammie, clammie." She grinned at me, her blonde hair nearly white in the dazzle of the sun, her cute little face pink, sweaty and gap-toothed, and dug up three more.

Sasha moved closer to me and began to dig. She looked around to be sure that Lincoln wasn't within earshot. "Athena is a sneak and I hate her." She whispered. "She was married to my other Grandmother's brother." I tried to keep my expression neutral, but I was dying to hear about it all.

"Oh," I said, a bit lamely.

"Yeah." She grunted with effort, digging out two clams. "She comes around, issuing me orders, making dumb suggestions about how I look and I dress and how I shouldn't be working at the animal hospital."

"Really? I think your job there is vital." And I really did. "I know your Grumpy couldn't work efficiently without you." And that was true, too.

Sasha abandoned her digging and squatted next to me. "She's sneaky and nasty. Grammie Fair doesn't like her either."

I was hopeless. I know it isn't a good thing to gossip with a ten-year old, but, hey, I was curious. "What does she do?"

"She peeks at the stuff in Grumpy's office." My face must have shown surprise. "Honest! She opens his drawers and looks in his check-book." Her wiry hair bobbed in the sun as she nodded twice, up and down. "I saw her and she knows I saw her. Then she makes up something to make me look like I'm the one in the wrong!"

"Like what?"

"Oh, she told Grumpy that I was always spying on her. Then she laughed like this..." Sasha neighed in a donkey-like manner... "Then she said she dropped her bracelet behind his desk and was just trying to find it."

"How often does she...I mean, um," I wanted to know all about this Athena person, but really didn't want to ask too many questions. "Um, does she live near here?"

Sasha didn't seem to mind. "Nope, thank goodness. She lives in Boston." She pointed to a heap of mud that I had just dug up. "You missed one...over there." I looked and by golly, there was a huge one, just sitting on top of the mud. I grinned my thanks.

"And what happened to...? I mean, is she still married to your uncle?"

"Nope. Uncle Paul divorced her years ago. He's married to a Japanese lady now and they live in Paris. He's a doctor...a people doctor...over there."

"And," ...here was the crux of my curiosity... "Is Aunt Athena married now?"

"Nope again. I think she'd like to, you know, have Grumpy date her." I stopped digging and that heart of mine stopped dead. "I hate her and Grumpy knows it." She stuck her gloved finger into the wet mud. "I'd really rather that he dated you, Reggie. I really like you." Her head was down and I couldn't see her eyes. I put my muddy hand on top of hers and squeezed.

"I like you, too, Sasha. I like your Grannie Fair and I like your Grumpy too." Well, after all, it was true. I liked him just fine.

Sasha's hug knocked us both off our feet and we sprawled together in the mud, our faces just inches apart, and giggled. We helped each other up and shook hands, sealing a bargain that only women would understand, even if they were only ten years old. As Sasha scooted over to a new site, I sat back on my heels and pondered the soft feelings I had for the child. Maternal, soft feelings. Gooey, taking-care-of feelings. "Watch out, Reggie, my girl," I admonished myself. And then I looked down the beach to where Lincoln stooped, his rump clad in those disreputable, baggy striped shorts, and sticking up in the air Even like that, the man was sexy. Definitely soft feelings nearly overcame me, and not just maternal ones.

"We've dug up every clam in the town!" Lincoln dragged three buckets over to where Eva was digging. "Enough! Enough! Leave some for next time." We all were ready to stop, straightening our aching backs, gloating with satisfaction at our haul. "Lordy! We'll never get these buckets back up!"

"I never saw so many, Grumps." Sasha was trying to count the clams.

"Well, come on, intrepid clammers. Let's get these babies washed." Lincoln took two of the baskets and groaned as he lifted them. "Geez! There must be five hundred!"

I lifted the third bucket, amazed at the weight. Sasha and Eva carried the last bucket between them, the muddy edges bumping against their knees. Laughing and cheering ourselves, we trudged back to Lincoln's backyard.

"Oh, my!" Maisie was properly reverential. Macduff barked and wanted to eat the clams right then, but a biscuit convinced him to wait a while.

We rinsed the clams in running water, counting them and throwing away the few 'mudders' that managed to sneak into our haul. "I stopped counting at six hundred!" Lincoln marveled. "This is the most we've ever gotten."

"Its 'cause of Reggie." My staunch admirer Sasha boasted. "She brought us beginner's luck."

We left the clams soaking in plastic pails down in the cool depths of Lincoln's cellar. "We put them in clean salt water and add a little bit of cornmeal," he showed me. "The cornmeal makes them spit out any sand that might be left." He smiled and rubbed his belly. "Mmmm. *Mmm*! These are gonna be *good* tonight!"

"How do you cook them?" I loved clams and was eager to try them any old way.

"Just steam them in a bit of water. Then slurp them up with some butter and their natural juices." His eyes gleamed. "We should eat about 200 of them ourselves." My eyebrows asked really. He nodded with great pride. "Yup. And then my mother will steam up the rest. Some she'll batter up and then freeze for fried clams later on. Some she'll freeze in broth for clam chowder." He patted me on my shoulder. "You did real good, girl. Real good." He bent down and kissed me on the tip of my nose. Astonished, my mouth opened, but he just laughed and turned my shoulders toward the door.

The tide had been coming in steadily and the little beach where we'd been clamming was fast disappearing. We cleaned ourselves up, drank some iced tea and then changed out of our muddy clamming clothes and into our bathing suits. I used Lincoln's bedroom to change and felt kind of funny taking off my clothes there. It made me think of …well, you know…things. I pulled a long tee shirt over my bathing suit and told myself to stop being so silly.

As I came down the stairs, Lincoln's eyes gleamed. "Not bad," he said and waggled his eyebrows suggestively. Fortunately, my cheeks were already pink with sunburn, so I didn't look too blushingly school-girlish at his leer.

We collected our gear. Macduff was so slavishly enamored of Maisie and her foodstuffs that he didn't even notice that we were leaving him behind again.

The girls dragged two heavy picnic baskets over to the bleached wood dock that stuck out into the water. A small motor boat bobbed at the end of the dock. "Where are we going now?" I asked.

Sasha answered me. "We're going over to Bold Charlie's Island." At my blank stare, she continued. "It's a place where the pirates used to come hundreds of years ago. There's supposed to be buried treasure there."

Lincoln stowed the baskets of food into the boat. "Let's get going." Sasha and Eva leaped into the bow of the boat and I climbed, a bit more slowly, into the middle. Several hours of unaccustomed stooping and bending were taking their toll of my more-than-middle-aged body and its tender joints. Lincoln pulled at the starter and we roared away from the dock. Maisie waved goodbye at us and Macduff's expression was forlorn for an instant, but then, Maisie said something to him and he leaped in the air, nearly turning a circle and ran back to the house, without a further backward glance. So much for doggie fidelity.

As the little boat bumped over the water, I heard the story of Ghost Pony Road and the Dread Pirate Bold Charlie. Seems that Bold Charlie had been some kind of very handsome, dashing, but bad guy in the old days, robbing passing ships of their gold and bringing it here to Kittery Point to hide. It was rumored that he was ruthless and beheaded everyone on the ships he robbed, even killing the horses that were on board the vessels. People seemed to think it was worse that he killed the horses than the other passengers. Even to this day, the residents of Ghost Pony Road say that they hear the ghostly pounding of hoofs as the souls of the horses thunder past. "When you hear the hoof beats at night, it means something terrible is going to happen." Lincoln's narration was solemn and scary and Eva's blue eyes were round with fright.

"Really?" Her voice quavered.

"Maybe," he answered, and then grinned, breaking the spell. Eva and Sasha crept close to me, clambering over the seat and sitting right up against me. I could feel their warm, sticky bodies and smell the sweaty, pink, sweet little-girl smells of them – clean and innocent. I wanted to hug them and keep them safe from ghosts and wild horses and Aunt Athenas and anything that might cause them harm and terror.

Sasha's face peered out. "I've heard the horses," she whispered in a soft voice. "One time."

"Did not!" Eva challenged. Sasha simply shrugged. Lincoln looked at her speculatively and then Eva shouted. "There's the island!" We all looked up and saw a narrow spit of land. Lincoln steered the boat over and it glided over the sandy bottom to the edge of a small beach. He shut off the motor and tied the boat to a stake that had been pounded into the sand. We clambered out, forgetting Bold Charlie and his bloodthirsty crew.

The island was small, covered partially with scrub pine and rocks. We found a smooth stretch of sand and plunked the picnic baskets down. "I'm starved!" Sasha moaned. "What's to eat?"

Root beer and two cans of Micheloeb for Lincoln and me. Thick, messy sandwiches of mayo, lettuce and roast beef, a bag of nacho chips and a container of Eva's mother's masterpiece – Eva's Salsa. Pieces of fried chicken, crispy and smelling like heaven, marshmallows, graham crackers and Hershey bars to make S'mores, big ginger cookies, delicious – close to my own recipe, but a bit softer - and a plastic box filled with cubes of cheese. A feast! Just the right kind to replenish the stomachs of four intrepid clam hunters.

With my mouth stuffed with Eva's Salsa – I mentioned to her again that I had never eaten salsa named for anyone I knew – and a can of beer, I leaned back on the sand. I was a very happy person. I watched Lincoln pack an enormous amount of food into himself. He ate three sandwiches and two pieces of chicken, burped in a gentlemanly sort of way, and then ate four ginger cookies. The girls ate and ate and then got up to find driftwood to make a fire for the marshmallows.

"Was Bold Charlie the Pirate real?"

"Yup. I understand that he murdered hundreds of men and horses."

"Really?"

"It's an old rumor that there's gold and jewels buried all around this island." My eyebrows raised themselves. "Honest," Lincoln raised a sunburned hand. "Lots of people come out here and dig, or go SCUBA diving and excavating, trying to find his spoils."

"Has anything ever been found?"

"Not yet. But you never know, do you? Maybe, right underneath our blanket, there's a treasure!"

"Ha!"

"Well, it's *some*where." Lincoln winked.

"What happened to him?"

"Supposedly, he loved a woman. Her name was Lady Pamela and she was the wife of the richest man in Portsmouth, an Englishman, Admiral Lord Negus. He owned a fleet of ships that traveled back and forth from England to here." I rolled over on my stomach and propped my head on my arm. "He was tall and handsome and brave. There's a portrait of him in the Historical Museum."

I made some sort of hmmm-hmmm-ing noise and he continued. "Bold Charlie executed some treacherous maneuver and plundered old Admiral Lord Negus' ship and killed him, and, of course, all his men and their horses. Our government had enough of Bold Charlie and his nefarious doings. The Navy came after Charlie. They had him trapped. He was being chased by hundreds of sailors and boats and there was little chance that he could escape. Only by sneaking his boat past this island might he get away."

"What happened then?" I could visualize it all. The boats and their huge sails, the musket fire, the blood and the frightened neighing of horses, the shouts and the screams.

"He wouldn't leave without Lady Pamela. I guess he really loved her. I hear that she was a stunner with long black hair and glittering green eyes." Lincoln's face wore a lascivious moue. "He came back to get her, meeting her at the little cove on the other side of this island." He paused, deliberately, and ate a cube of cheese.

126

"What *happened*?" I threw a cookie at him. He caught it deftly and popped it in his mouth.

"She was waiting for him. Standing on the edge of the water with her cloak blowing in the night wind; her dark hair flowing over her collar. Old Charlie rowed his boat in to pick her up and they captured him. They killed him like the rogue that he was, then captured his ship and killed all his men."

"And Lady Pamela?"

"Ah, Lady Pamela." He laughed. "She was a survivor. She married the Governor of the State of Maine, had twelve children and died rich, fat, happy and old."

"Is this all true?" I demanded. "Didn't she mourn for Bold Charlie?"

"The whole story is all written up in the Kittery Naval Museum. I swear." He held his hand up. "Lady Pamela knew which side her bread was buttered. She was a beautiful woman, but a practical one. If she couldn't have Charlie, well, then the Governor would do fine."

"Honest?"

"Cross my heart." He made the obligatory mark on his chest. "Her portrait is in the museum too. In between Admiral Lord Negus and the Governor. Bold Charlie's portrait is in the back room." We shouted with laughter. "My grandmother was given a ring and a necklace that supposedly was given to the Lady Pamela by Bold Charlie."

"Really?" I breathed.

"Uh-huh. I'll show you the ring and bracelet. You can even ask my mother."

"What a great story." I sipped at my beer. "What did Sasha mean when she said she'd heard the horses?"

Lincoln turned my way, suddenly serious. "I think it was the night her mother died." He looked out over the ocean.

"Have you ever heard them?"

His voice came from far away. "A couple of times." There was silence for a few minutes. I wondered if Lincoln had also heard the hoofs on the night Gwen died. I didn't want to upset him or bring back bad memories, so I reached for another cookie and munched it. I thought I might broach the subject in a slightly different way. I'd, well, I'd approach the whole thing in a roundabout manner...maybe ask Lincoln about the history of the area. I turned to question him, but he, filled with food, had fallen asleep. His reddish hair was in disarray and his mouth slacked open slightly. There went my heart again, feeling those soft and tender sensations. I touched his face gently and then heaved myself up. If I didn't walk off some of the meal, I, too, would be snoozing.

I heard the girls yelping from across the rocks. I watched them, leaping and jumping, their arms filled with sticks. I waved and they waved back. I wondered where this whole relationship would go. I certainly had my hopes.

With a sigh, I turned and looked out over the water, musing about the things that had happened here so many years ago. The ghosts of the ponies and the ghosts of Bold Charlie and his cut-throat crew. I shivered a little despite the hot sun overhead. These beaches and shores had seen all kinds of things over the centuries. Funny things. Inexplicable things. Like my Victrola playing in the middle of the night and my ghostly cats that kept appearing and disappearing. Like the sounds of horses. I looked down and saw a dark grey, smooth, round stone. I bent and picked it up. It was warm and silky in my hand and I hoped it would be a lucky stone for me. The waves lapped at my bare toes and I walked, aimless, along the edge of the beach, ducking around logs and seaweed. I bent down again and picked up a particularly nice piece of driftwood. Macduff would enjoy playing with it, I thought.

A clump of sea pine barred my way. Too lazy to climb around it, I stepped into the water and waded out a few feet to go around. The water was cold and pleasant, slapping at my thighs. I found a few beach roses embedded in the pine and picked two of the blossoms, sticking them behind my ear, thinking that maybe Lincoln would think that I looked like a sexy island woman.

I rounded the clump and waded back to the beach. A huge log hung with flotsam barred my way. I leaned on the log, trying to pull myself around it...and then...and then...I screamed. And screamed and screamed and screamed! Ohmygod! Ohmy*god*!

CHAPTER TWELVE

I had never seen a dead body before. Oh, I really had, you know, seen people who were dead. Laid out. Dead in a funeral home. My mother and my father. My Auntie Jean. Countless relatives, mostly all old. One neighbor's child who died in an automobile accident. But not a dead body like this.

It was the Morant boy. I don't think I realized it at first. I just knew that there, in the seaweed, was a white...no not white, sort of bluish white, shape. It had arms and legs, but no fingers or toes. It was lying, face down, bobbing in the current, entwined with sticks and seaweed and there were tiny, translucent fishes that were underneath its head. Strands of hair bobbed with the slightest current. It was swollen and bloated and was simply horrible.

Lincoln came running, searching for me after hearing me scream. I saw him and saw the two girls, trailing after him. Somehow, I took possession of my hysteria. "Get the girls away!" I cried to Lincoln. "Keep them away!"

I couldn't get past the body, so I turned and lurched my way back, around the sea pine and the pink flowers of the beach roses. The water clawed at my thighs and I had to swallow my bile so that I wouldn't be sick. I dropped the piece of driftwood, but kept my fingers clutched tight around the smooth stone. I had to keep myself sane. Lincoln stood at the water's edge. 'What's wrong?"

I realized that he couldn't see what was on the other side of the log. I threw myself in his arms and held him hard to me. My heart thudded, hard and heavy. "It's a body! The boy! The boy who is missing! I think...I think...Oh, Lincoln! Oh, God!"

He held me tightly. I think his face nuzzled mine and then he put me aside and went into the water to see for himself. I watched him, with my hands clasped over my mouth. He came back, his face grim and sad.

The girls were huddled at the top of the beach. We gathered them to us and stood, in a circle, and we told them what we had found. They were shocked and cried and we went back to where the detritus of our picnic lay.

"Gather everything up, girls," Lincoln began to pack up. "Help me." He turned to me. "Can you operate a motorboat?" I shook my head, no. "OK, then you stay here and make sure nothing...um, happens." I nodded, my eyes wide and dry. "I'll take the girls back and get help. I'll be back in a half-hour or so. Will you be alright?" I nodded, tight with misery and grief.

When Lincoln's boat was out of sight, I walked back to where the body floated, caught in the fingers of the sea pine. I watched, unable to keep my eyes away. As I guarded over the pitiful remains of his strong young body, I heard someone keening and then realized that it was me.

◆ ◆ ◆

They came back in a police boat, Lincoln and Chief Bridge and three other men, one dressed in SCUBA gear. I was introduced to Joe Amaral, the SCUBA diver. A short, muscular man, he shook my hand and nodded somberly. "Sorry that you had to be the one to find this, Ma'am."

"The poor, sad child." I didn't know what else to say. Lincoln searched my face to see if I was alright, then helped Joe to unload the boat. They had plastic tarps and cameras and lots of other equipment. I pointed the way and they left me, walking with heavy, measured steps down to the water. Joe waded in and I turned away, unable to watch anymore.

After fifteen minutes, Chief Bridge came back and sat his bulky body down on the sand. He patted at a spot next to him and I sat down with him. He smiled at me in a kind way, his bloodhound face sad. "OK, Reggie, tell me slowly just what happened. What did you see? What did you touch? What did you do?"

I told him how I walked on the shore and how I found the body.

I told him that I hadn't touched anything, but that I had come back to watch over the body again. "Maybe to protect it from any further harm." I gulped, "And I guess I was morbidly curious."

He scratched at the bushy hair on his head, adjusted the granny glasses that were his trademark, then patted my arm. "Understandable. I appreciate you telling me. You never know what is important and what isn't." He wrote everything down in a little notebook and then sighed. "Poor kid. Poor young bastard. At the prime of his life...everything ahead of him." His voice broke, an experienced policeman, but a sad human being. "How am I going to tell his mother?" I didn't know how to answer him so I touched his hand and we watched the waves come and go.

◆ ◆ ◆

We had our clam supper, but the sunshine had gone from the day. We all ate, kind of mechanically, although the clams were buttery and delicious and we ate dozens and dozens of them. Lincoln called Eva's family and they came to get her. In the inane way that one speaks when one doesn't know what to say, I told Beth, Eva's mother, how much I had enjoyed her salsa. She nodded and clutched Eva close to her.

After Eva left, we all went into the living room and Lincoln lit the logs in his big fireplace. As the fire blazed up, Sasha crept onto the sofa next to me and cuddled against me. I put my arms around her and rocked her. Macduff curled up on the other side of her, his hairy head on her lap. She caressed his fur and was silent. In a short time, she fell asleep. Lincoln picked her up and carried her up to her bedroom. In that funny way that dogs have of doing just the right thing, Macduff padded up after them.

"Macduff is lying on top of her bed." Lincoln told me when he came down. "I hope she doesn't hear the horses tonight."

"I've heard them many a night." said Maisie. "I'll sleep in her room tonight," she mused. "That way, if she wakes up, I'll be there." Her son nodded. Maisie heaved herself up from the chair she was in. "As a matter of fact, I think I'll go up now." Lincoln stood up and I did too. Maisie came over to me and kissed my on my forehead. "Maybe you should stay here this evening. You can have my bed. I'll put a clean nightgown out for you." I nodded, not knowing what to say. I really didn't feel like going home. I didn't want to be alone. "What a thing to happen!" She shook her head in bewilderment. "Such a terrible thing." Kissing Lincoln, she climbed the stairs, her tread measured and slow.

Lincoln and I sat together on the sofa, his hand in mine. We stared at the flames. "Do you want to stay here tonight? I'd like you to." His arm went around me. "You shouldn't go home. It's a bad time to be by yourself."

"Maybe that's a good idea," I said. "I'll admit. I was really upset."

"And why shouldn't you be? Stay here, Reggie. We'll keep each other company until...well, until. And after all, my mother said it was OK."

I giggled and hit him with a pillow. He drew me close. Even closer. "Ah, Reggie..." he said. His face came closer and his lips found mine. And I felt bliss and heat and forgot, for a moment, what had happened. But only for a moment. We broke apart. "This just isn't the night, my dear," he said to me, holding me even closer. He stood up and pulled me to me feet. "Go on up to bed. I'll just sit here for a few more minutes and…well, I'll just sit here." His blue eyes were so sad. I was sure that he was remembering another death that happened to someone too young to die.

I hugged him hard and then ran my hand down the side of his face. His cheek was a tiny bit bristly with whiskers. My hand tingled. We kissed again, a dry, soft, passionless kiss of two friends who had shared something important. "Goodnight, Reggie, my darling." His voice was ragged.

I turned and climbed the stairs. I think he whispered, "Another time," as I went upstairs.

◆ ◆ ◆

In the morning, two policemen came to the door and wanted us to sign our statements. If they were surprised that I was still at the Fairweather's house, no one said anything.

The policemen had a cup of coffee while we read over our typed statements. The Chief had taken good notes and the statements were signed. Sasha came down as the policemen were leaving and Macduff plodded down the stairs after her. She seemed pale, but otherwise normal. "Oh, Reggie. I'm so glad you are still here." She hugged me hard. Lincoln smiled and put his hand over mine and my heart almost jumped out of my chest.

The daily newspaper thumped on the front porch and we all read about what we had seen. It *was* the body of Jason Morant, aged eighteen. Dead before he could fulfill all of the potential that a young boy should fulfill. It appeared that he had drowned. There were many bruises and small abrasions on his body, about what would be normal for a body that had been buffeted in the water for several days and nights. There was no obvious sign of any foul play. In the absence of any further information forthcoming from the autopsy, it was ruled an accident. A tragic accident.

◆ ◆ ◆

I drove home, showered and changed, fixed Macduff up for the morning, and then went to work. After all, brunch had to be served. The only peculiar thing that happened was that the Victrola kept coming on, playing its plaintive song over and over. I had to take the record off the turntable so that I could get dressed. For the first time, the music made me nervous and jumpy.

◆ ◆ ◆

Business was brisk at The Loop Café. Customers brought in piles of newspapers and everyone was talking and endlessly discussing what had happened. When the customers became aware that I was the one who had actually found the body, everyone wanted to talk with me. My face ached from saying over and over that I didn't know anything at all. Nothing.

Barbara and Horace came in and hugged me before settling down with their coffee. "We'll talk later." I nodded. Gerjeet and Anoop were hushed and almost reverent with me, treating me as if I had been ill. Even Bob Micklewright forgot to snub me and asked me if I was OK. I nodded somberly when he asked me how I was, hoping that he wouldn't ask me anything else. As the Café was busy, he couldn't really pin me down. As he left, he winked at me and left me his usual tip. I was glad that we seemed to back on our old footing. Him being cheap and me being polite.

My garage-owner admirer, Phil Moore, came in, drank two cups of coffee and ate a piece of my plum coffeecake. He hemmed and hawed and asked me if I would like to go out with him some night soon. I declined, explaining that I really didn't date. "Its just too soon for me, Phil," I explained with gentle firmness. His poor face was red and he stammered that he understood. I felt badly that I had hurt him. He was the right age, a nice man, pleasant and amusing, sort of handsome in a craggy way, certainly a good catch, but not for me. There just wasn't any tingle there at all. My heart was already occupied. There was no point at all in encouraging him or anyone else. Except, well, Lincoln.

There were dozens of Base employees in, and several of the Kittery Police stopped for coffee around noontime. Tom, from the River Run book store came in with his wife. They ate some of Gerjeet's Indian Rupee Pancakes with Golden Syrup, a new menu item. Gerjeet told me beforehand that they were just his old pancakes, but that he'd had a dream to re-name them as something exotic. His dream had been a good one, as the newly named pancakes were a huge success. I told Gerjeet that he should make note of all of his culinary dreams and that he could soon retire as a wealthy man.

More folk strolled in. Frankie and Ron were there from Frisbee's Store and my new friends and customers, George and Laurie McGilvery had driven down from Wells, eager to try more of Gerjeet's cooking. Their cats, however, had stayed home.

As we chatted, I admired the gorgeous antique diamond ring that Laurie flashed at me. "I love it!"

Laurie dimpled and confessed that she was a jewelry junkie. "I can't resist," she giggled. George smiled, a bit proudly, after all, he was the man who bought such baubles. They ordered the lobster salad and flipped out newspapers to keep themselves busy until their food was served.

As I placed the order for two lobster salads, I wondered if I wanted a husband who would buy me exquisite antique diamonds. Maybe. And then I wondered if I wanted a husband, whether I got diamonds or not. Was I still willing to take a chance? Maybe.

The tables were filled and I barely had time to chat. Anoop looked a little tired and my feet ached. It was good to be busy, but I couldn't wait until everyone had finished and gone home.

The door opened once again. The man who owned the adult book store came in, sat at the counter and read the newspapers that everyone else had discarded. I noticed that we were completely sold out of my baked goods, except for three slices of cake. I was glad. It would do me good to get my mind busy doing some baking this afternoon.

Laurie and George left with the three last pieces of cake wrapped to go. "We're having tea this afternoon with Michael Martins. Have you ever heard of him?" I expressed my ignorance. "He's a local actor." I still looked dumb. "He's with the Sanford Stage Company."

"Where's that?"

"Sanford, Maine."

"Oh," I sort of knew that Sanford was in the northerly direction. "Is he famous?"

"In a local way. He does a lot of plays there." Laurie hefted the bag with the cake slices in it. "When I was working up at the Portland Symphony, he helped with some fund raising. George and I always try to see all the shows that he's in."

"Is there a show that he's doing now?" I was always open to new cultural events and had always enjoyed theater.

"They're rehearsing for "The Fantastiks.""

"Ah," at last, I could contribute something brilliant. I began to sing, a little off-key, "Try to remember the kind of September..."

Laurie smiled and patted my arm. "It's a great play. I'll let you know when the tickets go on sale. And thanks for the cake. Michael has a voracious sweet tooth."

"Who was that?" Barbara wanted to know.

"Oh, just some new friends," I answered airily. "I get around you know!" She laughed and poked me. "So hurry up and finish with all of these blamed new friends and customers and sit down with your old buddies and tell me all about what happened on the island." Her voice changed and I was brought back, away from the thoughts of diamond rings and men who sang songs on a stage to the bleak reality of finding Jason's body.

◆ ◆ ◆

The morning seemed endless and I was only able to relax after the crowd left. Anoop brought a playpen into the restaurant and plopped little Daria into it while they cleaned up.

I sat for a few minutes with Barbara and Horace and, in the warmth of their friendship, was finally able to tell them everything that had happened. "Gee," was Horace's inadequate comment. "Things like this never happen in Kittery."

"How about the murders of Sunny and Catherine last year?" Barbara poked him. "You can't say nothing ever happens."

"You're right. I almost forgot." Horace sipped at his cooling coffee. "And there was that other guy...can't remember his name...Ed something, I think..." He squinted with effort. "He worked at the Shipyard....um, a year or so ago..."

"But he was only missing," Barbara corrected him. "No one knows what happened to him. He could have just disappeared." She looked up at the ceiling, seeking some inspiration. "What *was* his name?"

"Ed...Ed, um...Don't remember." Horace scratched his head. "He just disappeared. Like the lady a few weeks ago? What was *her* name?"

"Candace?" My voice was troubled. *I* was troubled. Too many people disappearing. Too many deaths. I kept seeing Jason's body... I got up, nervously agitated and went to the playpen. Daria stood up, hauling herself by the rails, and grabbed at my thumb. She made some happy burble and smiled at me. I patted her hand. It was so soft and smooth and I felt tears coming.

I spoke with Barbara about Joan, then used the Café's phone to call Joan and told her about Lincoln's need for some assistance. She was delighted, promised to call Barbara at once to set up a meeting, and also told me she would call Lincoln at the office to see if they could meet and talk.

There was a rumble of a truck's engine in the street. I jumped, nervous suddenly at the noise. I saw a dark shape pull up to the curb and felt goose bumps on my bare arms. The truck stopped and I watched Hank Ormand climbed down, dust off the seat of her pants and come into the Café. What was it about this peculiar woman that made my fur bristle?

She made her way to the counter and asked Gerjeet for a coffee to go. Without a smile, he handed her a waxed cup filled with hot black coffee. She took it, gave him one dollar and one quarter and stomped out, looking at no one and speaking to no one.

"So cheery to see a pleasant face," I commented, sticking my tongue out at Hank's departing back.

"She brightens up the world with her smile." Gerjeet opined. "Makes me want to puke, her type." We looked at each other and sighed. Hank's misery had infected the two of us.

My aura of solemn somberness changed as the Bethany Boys tromped in, bringing salt air, a high degree of masculinity, and a bushel of lobsters caught by the traps of the *Mary Ann Seven* through the door with them. They were in high spirits and ate huge lunches, praising Anoop's cooking and my clever way of serving. Barbara and Horace watched the drama unfold with ill-suppressed grins.

Outside on the terrace, the sun spread its warmth and business was booming. Rodney Kuntz and his spectacular girlfriend, Diane took a table, and then, Hannah Clutterbuck and her friend, Gladys Gomm trooped in for coffee.

Father Norton, from Saint Raphael's stopped in, wanting eggs and bacon, his clerical collar drooping a bit from the heat. He greeted me, mentioned that the heat was a blessing to the tomato crop and then sat with four firemen at the table overlooking the water. The firemen all ordered pancakes and waffles and informed Father Norton that the heat was a royal pain. As I rushed about in the unaccustomed afternoon business, I barely had time to talk with any of them.

A grey Volvo rolled into the curb and a young couple and two huge black dogs emerged. I recognized the girl and the dogs. They were the same ones who had been at Steve's property on Driftwood Island. Suddenly embarrassed, I hoped she hadn't recognized me as the snooping about-to-be-ex-wife. I greeted them with my face hidden in my chin. They were friendly and pleasant and she didn't seem to remember me nor my snooping ways, thank goodness. I brought out two soup bowls of water for the dogs and was introduced to their enormous, friendly faces. "This one is Murphy and this one is Acadia." The girl patted each huge head. 'We call them Murph and Cady and generally refer to them as 'the girls'."

I took their order and we chatted about how nice it was that Gerjeet and Anoop encouraged their patrons to bring pooches to the Café. I told them about the McGilvery's cats sitting out in the sunshine with their little cat-leashes. Murph seemed very intent when I mentioned the word cat. Laughing, Murph's owners ordered soup and chili and homemade bread. "And a couple of crackers for the girls, please."

Barbara and Horace were leaving as I brought the order out to the young couple. "Hey! Thane!" Horace greeted the man. *Thane, I thought? An unusual name. Wasn't that the name of the architect on the sign outside Steve's house?* I plunked the soup down and listened shamelessly. Barbara and the young girl, whose name was Holly, I discovered, were old friends, having served on the Kittery Chamber of Commerce Committee together. I was duly introduced. Holly, if she had any recollection of me gawking at the new house, was kind enough not to mention a word.

Gloom should have descended as Hank Ormand's truck roared up once again and she climbed down, looking, if possible, even more grungy than before. This time, however, the noise of her truck and the bleak look on her face gave me no sense of fright nor emotion. She was simply an old lady...a peculiar old lady, but an old lady nonetheless.

And this time she was a bit more friendly. She gave me a nod, a brief one, but at least it was civil. "See you've got those over-the-hill lobsters from those Bethany scamps," she ventured, almost spitting on the floor in her disdain.

"Over-the-hill? I thought they were fresh caught," I decided that being too nice to her didn't make any sense, so I just said what was on my mind.

"Fool you," she countered. "They take all the good ones and sell them for top price." She glanced at the menu. "They trade you the old, limp, almost dead ones." She sniffed. "I wouldn't be surprised if one of your customers got sick one of these days from their garbage. Give me my usual."

As I served her, she twisted around in her seat, poked at her hip pocket and brought out a huge knife. My heart stopped at the sight of it. She fingered the sharp edge and laughed at my expression. "What's the matter?" she almost sneered at me. "Never seen an equalizer?"

"An equalizer?" Naturally, I bit.

"Sure, girl. Some man tries to steal my lobsters, this here knife makes me as strong as he is." She swished it through the air. "Off with his head. Hee Hee." Her dry laugh made the hair on my arms stand up. "Now, we are equal!"

I put her coffee cup down as gently as I could and backed away. What *was* it about her that made me so nervous? Fortunately, she left without making any more conversation.

Gerjeet laughed at my telling of her comments. "She is a harmless old biddy. Very peculiar, yes, but harmless."

"I don't know. That knife frightened me."

"Oh, my. All those lobster catching people have those big knives. She is no different." He spread his hands out in supplication. "She's a jealous old bitch. She'd love to sell her lobsters here, but we already have enough."

She left me a fifty cent piece. I wondered if that was all she had with her or if I was warming her crusty heart. I laughed and then gave myself a mock shudder. Hank wasn't anyone that I wanted anywhere *near* my heart! And I didn't really want to be near hers, crusty, dusty, jealous, knife-wielding or not!

Kittery Point's faithful postmaster, Mike O'Brien was the last customer out the door. Wearily, we cleaned and re-set and swept and refilled salts and peppers. I was never so glad to be done with work. As much as I loved every moment and every customer, the day had been endless. I collected my generous tips and finally went home that afternoon, happy that my secret spying on Steve's new house was still my secret.

And speaking of tips, my blue jar overfloweth. It was filled to the brim. I gloated, wondering how much was stuffed in there. I vowed to stop in at the bank and get a bunch of those paper things that one rolled coins in. Until then, I needed a new vessel. I rooted around in the cupboards and found myself another new container, a large heavy pewter pitcher. The sound of change plunking into it was music to me. I set it back on the shelf and thought that I was doing fine…just fine.

I set out my ingredients and began to bake, making two batches of brownies, three sour cream cakes, several versions of *biscotti*, some with nuts and some not, as I had discovered some of the customers like Dave Holt had tender teeth. I made up an experimental batch of lemon squares and a bundt cake with a coffee filling and a mocha glaze. Then, still restless, I perused Francesca's recipe book and came up with one that I hadn't tasted in ages – a confection called *la testa della zingara vecchia,* or the head of an old gypsy. The *testas* were succulent domes of dense espresso-infused fudgy cake covered with a shiny coffee-liquor glaze. Francesca wrote that Zia Filomena, the old cook at the castle in San'Antonio where my ancestors used to reside, said that the dark chocolate lumps of goodness looked like the dusky heads of the gypsies that came every year to the *festa* in the village. As the *testas* baked, I re-read Francesca's spidery writing and smiled with delight. Not only did her recipe book outline how to cook the foods mentioned in it, but it often told long, rambling stories about how the foods got their names and even personal tales of what was going on while Francesca was learning to bake.

It seemed that way back in the old country, the dark, exotic gypsy women were lusted after by the village men-folk. Maybe even more than lusted after. Maybe the men-folk had visited a gaily painted gypsy caravan late at night to see for themselves what delights the women with coffee-colored faces and silky, inky black hair might offer. As I dripped the shiny Ganache glaze over the chocolate domes, I could understand how delicious the forbidden might be. Yum.[4]

I called Andrea and caught her just before she went to work. Her character, the silly little bar chick, had caught the attention of the director. "Mom, they're going to write Alexandra into at least six more episodes!" Andie was ecstatic. She calmed down enough to ask me about my own life and I told her that I had met someone nice. She squealed and wanted to know everything. "Tell me everything!" she ordered.

In a pig's eye, I murmured to myself, and then launched into a highly censored version of Lincoln and me. I debated, then told her about finding poor Jason's body and she cautioned me to be careful. "Let me know what happens, Mom." She was very curious to hear more about my new man, as she referred to Lincoln, and seemed genuinely happy that I was interested in someone. Unfortunately, for her rabid curiosity, she had to rush to work. I promised to tell her more when there was more to tell and we hung up with kisses and protestations of our love for each other.

Smiling in my own maternal way, I called Jenna and Scott. No one was at home, so I left a generic love-you message. I knew that Andrea would call her sister the first chance she got and the two of them would speculate on their old mother's love life. I chatted with Uncle Pat and my cousin Joann. The calls seemed to cheer me up and I immediately launched into more baking, turning out a tray of gingerbread and a batch of chocolate chip cookies. Macduff watched all of my exhortations hungrily and was awarded two cookies without any chips in them. I had heard that chocolate was bad for dogs. Macduff, however, hadn't heard any such thing, and when my back was turned, I found that he had sneaked three more cookies, all studded with chocolate chips. "You're gonna die!" I chided him. He only looked up at me with slavish devotion and beat the floor with his bushy tail.

I heard the noise of a truck coming down the street and the rumble of the engine again made me afraid for some unknown reason. Wide-eyed, I peeked out of the window and was astonished to find that Lin-

---

[4] Again, you will find the recipe at the end of the book.

coln was at my door and that he had driven there in his temporarily-owned monster vehicle.

I felt stupid at my nervousness and didn't mention to him that the sound of the truck motor had awakened some dormant fear in me. "Oh, you came in the truck." Was my only comment.

"The wagon smelled of wet cat," he explained. "I'm letting it air out for a day or two." He patted Macduff, kissed me in an offhand manner, and asked me if I was up to going out for a lobster roll.

"If you help me clean up," I agreed. He, too, hadn't heard that chocolate chips might be bad for one, and managed to eat six cookies while he washed up. He assured me that a few chocolate chips wouldn't hurt a dog of Macduff's poundage, but that yes, dogs in general should not be fed chocolate. Macduff ignored him.

I rushed upstairs, washed, and changed into clean, rather sexy underwear (again, who knew what might be in store for me), then slid a madras plaid sundress over my head. I shook out my curls and was ready to go.

Macduff's lip drooped when it became evident to him that he wasn't to be included on our excursion. Laughing at Macduff's woebegone expression, Lincoln helped me to heave myself into the cab of his monster truck and off we went. The seat of the truck was high in the air and I felt as if I were driving around in a skyscraper. I felt very foolish that the sound of a truck's motor had made me fearful. Silly me.

"Were you OK today? I mean, after all that happened yesterday?" Lincoln was tenderly solicitous. I assured him that I was fine, but admitted to a few tears, especially when I watched Daria's innocent sweetness.

"I feel so awful about Jason's death. His mother...I just can't imagine how she is going to bear it." He picked up my hand in his large paw and held it tenderly as we drove to Fox's Lobster and Ice Cream Spot, one of the apocryphal local clam huts that dotted the coast. Fox's was located at the top of a hill, overlooking the famous Nubble Light House. Lincoln helped me down from the front seat of the truck. His hand touching mine set off those sparks. My heart again began its jumping around.

Fox's was renowned for their lobster and ice cream, and rightly so. Being good Maniacs, we ordered properly, each downing a bowl of chowder, a butter-drenched lobster roll, then shared a gargantuan banana split, covered with gobs of freshly whipped cream and Fox's famous home churned ice cream. Sated with scrumptious food, I idly asked Lincoln why he and Sasha didn't have a dog.

He groaned. "Did Sasha put you up to this?" I shook my head, assuring him no, honest.

"I just wondered, from the very first day when you came over to see how Macduff was doing, why you didn't have a dog. I just never got around to asking you."

"I adore animals. Naturally. Otherwise I wouldn't be in this business that eats up so much of my time and makes me so little money." He reached over the table and picked up my hand. "There are so many dogs and cats that need homes. I vowed that if I couldn't take care of all of them, I wouldn't take just one. My mother has trouble keeping up the house, even with the help she has. And I'm too busy and Sasha, even though she begs me to keep every stray that comes our way, couldn't take good care of a puppy or kitten." He shook his head. "So we just love every one of them...just not at our house."

"Ah," I said, mesmerized by the heat from his fingers on the palm of my hand.

He gave me a peculiar look. "Maybe, one day, things will change and the situation...whatever it is...well, maybe one day we'll have a dog." My face must have shown some bewilderment and he coughed and stammered. "I...um...I'd *like* a dog, if things were, um, different." He stood up abruptly, dropping my hand. "Let's go. Let's get your pooch and take him for a run at the beach." He seemed all businesslike all of a sudden.

Macduff greeted us at the door, perfectly willing to forgive us for not including him on our dinner date. "Wanna got to the beach?" Beach was a word that Macduff understood completely. He nearly leaped in the air in a complete circle in his answer. I let him out for a run to the hydrangea bushes and got his leash and a few plastic bags to act as pooper-scoopers. The two cats, Blackie and Sunny, as they were now permanently named, came running inside with him.

"Hey, kitties," Lincoln bent down to them as they wound around his ankles. "Where have you two been?"

I patted the cats, scratching them behind their black and white ears, and then opened two cans of tuna fish. I put the cans outside the back door and watched as the cats crouched to gobble the food. I filled two bowls with water and we left them to eat and drink as I snapped the leash onto Macduff's collar and introduced him to Lincoln's new mode of transportation.

"By the way," Lincoln said as we drove to Seapoint Beach, "Your friend Joan called me. She's coming over in a day or two to talk about coming to work for me four evenings a week, after she finishes work at the Library. She sounds like she might work out just fine. Thank you, Regina, my queen."

I grinned back at him and bravely picked up his hand in mine. I'm not sure about this, but I think *his* heart was doing flip-flops at that point. I was amazed at myself. I didn't think I was a bold hussy, one of those women who went around grabbing at men. But, hey! I could learn, couldn't I?

We strolled on the beach with other people who were exercising their dogs, walking miles while Macduff loped beside us, occasionally going mad and chasing alongside another dog or cavorting in the waves. Most of the time, our hands were linked and most of the time, my heart was doing two things at once. We talked, telling each other more about our lives, our failed marriages, our children, our childhoods, our dreams, our failures and a tiny bit about our hopes. I felt like a young girl again, perhaps ready to…well, who knows? I know what I hoped, but…did he feel the same way? This was scary, uncharted territory and I was terrified of what might happen. Or of what might not happen.

The summer twilight dimmed and we climbed back into the truck, two of us a little nervous and one of us tired from running for two hours.

The one who was tired ate his kibble and collapsed on the floor in front of the Victrola. The nervous ones …well, I won't go into details, but nervousness didn't seem to be a problem any more.

CHAPTER THIRTEEN

I pushed Macduff's heavy paw off me and rolled over, propping myself up on my pillows. Lincoln's scent, a nice, spicy man-kind of smell, drifted up to me from the dent on the other side of the bed. I stroked the spot where he had lain and smiled to myself. A self-satisfied, smile, heavy with drowsy pleasure and remembrance. Sometime, in the middle of the night, Lincoln had heaved himself up, kissing me again and telling me that it would be better for us both, all around, if he went home before dawn. Macduff had shown a remarkable amount of doggie-tact, lying just outside the bedroom when a dog would have been in the way. After Lincoln got out of bed, Macduff leaped up, making himself a nest in the warm blankets. Lincoln used the bathroom and came back to dress, pushing Macduff over so that he could put his pants on. Lincoln's pants, I mean, not Macduff's...oh, you know what I mean.

His goodbye to me was filled with love and perhaps some kind of promise. I clung for a moment, wanting him to never leave me again.

The phone shrilled. It was Lincoln and he said all the wonderful and silly things that a new lover says and I answered in kind. We would see one another again that night.

◆ ◆ ◆

The day passed in a whirlwind. Joan Grasser stopped in and told me that she and Lincoln had met early in the morning. She had liked him and his set-up and he had liked her and her experience. She was hired and would be starting work on Monday afternoon. I hugged her with gladness, happy that two problems had cancelled themselves out.

The *testas* were a huge hit. They sold out in about seven minutes and each customer who shelled out five dollars to try one clamored for more. I told everyone the story of the gypsy ladies and promised those who missed out that I would make more and soon. "They sound like extremely interesting ladies," was Gerjeet's reverent comment as he licked the last drop of glaze from his moustache. "It is a shame that they do not live around this town."

"What would you want with gypsy ladies?" Anoop asked him. "They would be dirty and have not-washed faces."

He shrugged, grinning, "I would just want to meet them in their caravans, that's all."

In the afternoon, Rodney and his tall, stunning girlfriend came in for coffee and to bring me the papers that would eventually finalize my divorce. "About four to six weeks, Reggie." Rodney assured me. "It will be all over."

"So fast," I mused. "All over. So quickly, after so many years."

"Are you sorry?" Diane wanted to know. She gave Rodney a quick look.

I shook my head no. "It's amazing what a difference a few months can make." I put a huge slice of my sour cream cake in front of her and she smeared it with butter and jam. Diane was stick thin. She took an enormous bite, ingesting, oh, perhaps 700 calories at a gulp. If I ate like that, I'd gain fifty pounds in one day. But back to the divorce. "My life has done a one-eighty change." I dawdled at the table, rearranging a fork. "Things that were so important...well, they don't matter any more, except for my daughters. They're still first in my life and will always be." Rodney nodded. "And now... other things are important to me. People," I made a vague face and then gestured to Rodney. "You and Barbara. Horace. This place. Anoop and Gerjeet and the baby. All my new friends...My dog. Mrs. Cee... things that I didn't even know about...people that I didn't know..." I shook my head, thinking of so many things and then one special one. "I mean, my whole life has changed."

Diane took another gigantic bite of her cake. "How do you know?" she asked, her youth naked on her pretty face. "How can you be sure that a love is real and will be a forever love?" She touched Rodney's hand and bit at her lip.

He put his hand on top of hers. "We just have to have faith, right?" She nodded in a dubious manner.

"Even with faith and the best of intentions, life has some surprises." I found a touch of tears coming to my eyes. "I didn't mean to have my marriage end. I guess I would have gone on, not even realizing that...well, that...well..."

I polished and re-polished a spot on the table with my cleaning rag. "I mean...oh, goodness. Look at me! I'm nearly crying!" I sniffed.

"I think this is what is called an emotional moment," Rodney muttered with sweet insight beyond his years and experience. "When you realize that this is the beginning of the end of your marriage. It has to be tough, even if it's what you want." He drank the dregs of his coffee. "Maybe that's why Barbara asked me to bring you the papers. Maybe she wanted me to have this experience."

My eyebrows went up and I digested this idea. "I think you're right. She has to know that that actual papers, coupled with the word 'divorce' would make anyone jump back." A smile cracked the corners of my mouth. "That Barbara is one smooth woman."

"Whew!" Diane shook her head. I watched as her golden hoop earrings dangled and accentuated the slenderness of her neck. Rodney seemed mesmerized. "This is deep stuff. Tough."

"Tough, but..." I began to laugh. "Not that tough! Actually, it's *great!*" I made a whooping sound. "That's why Barbara sent you! So I could get used to it all. Look at me...I'm delighted! I just needed a moment to realize it!" The three of us began to giggle and customers turned to us, wondering what we were laughing about.

◆ ◆ ◆

The days sped by. My evenings began to change. Lincoln was there. Every night, every moment that we could, we were together. Oh, not alone all the time. No. Not even most of the time. Maisie and I became good friends and I treasured her quiet, but deadly wit. Sasha was fast becoming a part of my heart and Lincoln...Ah, Lincoln.

Oh, it was wonderful. You remember, don't you? When love is just starting? How every moment is crystal clear, every touch, every kiss is bliss. How you stare at each other and then laugh for no apparent reason, how you store up little memories. Like when MacDuff ate the turkey stuffing. Or when I went shopping with Eva and Sasha for Sasha's first bra. Or when Lincoln took me with him on a veterinarian type call to visit two alpacas at the alpaca farm (the object of the visit was to help the alpacas mate – an amazing thing to behold, especially when one was with one's new beau). Or when Maisie showed me the family albums. Or when Lincoln and I began to dance in the kitchen and we got to messing round and I burned an entire batch of *biscotti*. Or when Lincoln talked of us and the future. I was hooked. Falling in love...head over heels over head over heels.

I held the fledgling feelings to myself, only sharing the words with Lincoln. And even then, we never said the big "L" word. Oh, he called me darling, and sweetheart and even "my love". We talked about what we'd do next year, how we'd take a vacation together...what we'd do at Christmas, what we'd do on New year's Eve. But he didn't say that he loved me. And likewise, I never said it to him. Did he love me? I thought so. Did I love him? Oh, yes. Oh, yes. More and more every day.

Barbara watched me like a hawk, ready to pounce on a careless glance or messed up pillow case, or a man's razor in the wrong place. Her bushy eyebrows narrowed and she and Horace nudged one another all the time.

Andrea and Jenn seemed attuned to my happiness, asking me ceaseless questions. But I fobbed them all off, hugging my happiness like a child hugs a doll. I was afraid and hopeful and anxious and frightened and deliriously happy all at once.

◆ ◆ ◆

To celebrate the Pickwick Theater's performance of *La Boheme*, Barbara and I went shopping to buy ourselves new and spiffy outfits. We prowled the boutiques of Portsmouth, trying on dresses and jewelry, planning to outshine all of the competition. I bought a dress of yellow silk, severely cut on the bias, with a water-color iris that curled up my hip and ended just short of the low cut décolleté top. It made me look taller, bustier and more regal than I usually did. I bought new strappy sandals and a necklace with a deep purple pendant that echoed the purple in the iris.

"If that don't make him sit up and beg, I don't know what!" was Barbara's comment. I smiled mysteriously and held up the soft pink chiffon dress that she was dithering over. It was shirred at the top and softened her shoulders. She grinned. "I look almost dainty in this, don't I?"

"Almost." I agreed

◆ ◆ ◆

Opera had been fed to me along with my baby food. My great aunt, Antonina Sabatino, had been a rather famous diva [5] and my entire family was well-versed in all aspects of opera. I'd been to The Met often and once, on a vacation to Italy, saw Lucia Sargento and Giuseppi Luciano perform at La Scala. I knew every word and aria of *La Boheme*, and so, Saturday night loomed as a distinct pleasure.

We used Maisie's pampered antique Mercedes. Lincoln drove, with Maisie dressed in soft black velvet sitting up front with her son. I sat in the back with Sasha, who wore a darling pink two-piece dress, and Eva, who was clad in brown velvet with a matching band in her hair. The girls were a little nervous and anxious that they wouldn't understand the music.

---

[5] Antonina's career is chronicled in *Panis Angelicus*

"Will we be bored?" Sasha wanted to know.

"No, not if you know the story," I assured her. Eva looked skeptical, so I spent a few minutes telling them about the story, and regaling them with family tales about Antonina. "*La Boheme* was the very first opera she was in. She was thirteen or fourteen and had just begun taking singing lessons from Professor Fazzolini." Eva was convulsed over the funny name.

"Shut up, Eva," Sasha poked her friend and a cheerful giggling and shoving match ensued. "Come on," Sasha bounced on the seat. "Reggie, tell us more. I want to know *all* about Antonina." She rolled the syllables. "Antonina. Such a pretty name." I agreed, explaining that our family had a lot of Antons and Antoninas. "I love the names in your family," she bounced again on the seat. Tell me more about her." I obliged.

"Professor Fazzolini, funny name and all, was a very famous opera coach and all the aspiring singers wanted him to help them. All the opera houses wanted his protégées. He could pick and choose from singers all over the world, but he chose Antonina, a little girl. He had accidentally heard her sing and was so impressed that he insisted that she come and learn from him. He wouldn't let her sing a note in *La Boheme*, however. She could only be a part of the crowd. I'll show you tonight what part she played." My audience, including the giggling Eva, was enthralled.

"And she was famous? Really, really famous?" Eva wanted to know.

"Really, *really* famous." I assured her. "She was a person they call a *diva*. That means "divine"…one of the goddess. Only the best opera singers become *divas*. They were almost like saints to their adoring fans. Antonina sang all over the world. The finest operas, the best roles. She sang before kings and queens and presidents and emperors. She got presents from total strangers, priceless jewels, pedigreed dogs, exotic parrots, huge bouquets of flowers and men begged to drink champagne out of her shoes."

"Yuk." Sasha grimaced and the grown ups laughed.

"Crowds of people followed her everywhere. Sometimes, a group of admirers would pick her up and carry her into the theater, so that her feet wouldn't have to touch the ground." The girls were goggle-eyed.

"Did she have any children?" Eva wanted to know.

"Oh, yes. And that's a grand story which I'll tell you about another time." Maisie twisted around and raised her eyebrows at me. I winked back, making a face that said that it was a story for adults only. "She was a fascinating woman. As a matter of fact, the first time she played a starring role, it was because the opera star who *was* to have played the role was murdered on stage!"

"No kidding?" Lincoln asked.

"No kidding." The car pulled smoothly into a parking space near the front of the Theater. "I'll tell you more after the show."

The Pickwick Theater was an ancient stone edifice standing between two brick buildings on the shore of the Piscataqua River. The lobby was filled with well-dressed patrons and the air of expectancy was palpable. 'They do a grand job here," Maisie assured me as she waved to a group of friends across the room. I saw Barbara and Horace, Thane and Holly, Chief Alexander Bridge and his wife Claire and several other patrons of The Loop Café. Everyone was looking very spiffy, and Barbara and I gave each other the high-sign. Sasha and Eva were round-eyed with all the splendor, and each of them clutched one of my hands. We filed in and took our seats. Horace at the far end, then Barbara, then Maisie, then Lincoln, me, Sasha and Eva. A few ladies from Maisie's church filled up the rest of the row. We were all introduced and smiled our hellos. Puccini's music filled the theater. I glanced around…where was the orchestra? …and finally located it, up above the audience, perched in a balcony overhanging the topmost seats. Lincoln helped me to slide off the light topcoat I wore and his heavy eyebrows rose upward in a satisfyingly complimentary way as he admired my dress. I winked at Barbara and she winked back.

I showed the girls how to read the program. We looked at the photographs of the leading impresarios. The part of Mimi was played by a golden-haired beauty named Alexis Risdi and Rodolfo's alter ego was a bearded giant named Guido Parisi. I'd never heard of either of them, but their biographies seemed impressive. The little girl in the red velvet coat, Antonina's original role so many years ago, was played by a teenager named Isabella Lanterna-Lewis. I wondered if she would light up the stage as Antonina had done.

The lights dimmed and flashed to signal the start of the show. There was a sudden commotion as a few people filled the empty seats behind us. I whispered to Sasha that the opening scene would be an attic studio apartment in Paris, occupied by four young men, a poet, a musician, a philosopher and a painter.

My explanation was interrupted by a hand that reached over from the row behind us. The hand clasped Lincoln's shoulder in a most familiar way. The hand, attached to five red-tipped fingernails, belonged to Aunt Athena. My eyes narrowed and I felt my annoyance jump up.

"Lincoln," her voice was clear and acid. "My dear. What a surprise. You didn't mention that you'd be here." The orchestra crashed into the opening notes of the overture. Athena leaned forward, "Why don't you move back here next to me so we can talk and be cozy?"

Three people in the row behind her shushed her with annoyed murmurs. Lincoln's shoulders hunched as he turned slightly and whispered "Later."

I sat back to enjoy the show, determined to not let my own hot annoyance and chagrin interfere with Puccini's glorious music. The girls giggled at how the young Bohemians fooled their buffoonish landlord and sat, enchanted, watching Rodolfo fall in love over Mimi's frozen little hand.

Out of the corner of my eye, I saw another little hand, an unfrozen one, this one with vermillion-colored fingernails, touch Lincoln's collar again. I looked sideways up at him and saw that he, too, was looking sideways. Except that he was eyeing Athena's fingers. His face held a peculiar look. My imagination couldn't decide if the look was adoring or annoyed. Lincoln reached up and patted the hand, sort of brushing it back. I relaxed a little bit.

I tried my best to ignore her. After all, I was the one sitting with Lincoln. She was merely in the next row. But there was something about her that gnawed at my gut, something mean and frightening to me. I have heard people say that they felt someone's eyes boring into their back. And I could. Honestly. Her eyeballs were piercing me from behind, venomously digging into me. I felt her hatred and aggression clearly through the back of my neck. I hated her. I turned my face back to the stage and told myself not to be so silly.

In the café scene, I whispered to the girls, "See the girl in the red velvet? That's the part that Antonina played. She was a wonder. Even without singing a note, she glowed on stage, subduing everyone else, even the soprano that played Mimi." Sasha leaned forward and Eva's mouth dropped open. I knew how they were entranced, because it had happened to me the first time I saw *La Boheme*. Each of them was imagining that it was Eva or Sasha there on the stage, ready to be thrust into the spotlight of a wonderful operatic career.

The intermission light blinked on. "It's not bad." Judiciously, Sasha nodded. "I think I understood it all, even though the titles were awful to read."

Eva nodded in a dubious way.

"Who wants to get up and get a drink?" Lincoln asked the ladies in our row. I got up to help, ignoring Athena's peevish glare. As Lincoln, Eva, Sasha and I edged our way out, Athena pushed past three people and stood in the aisle, blocking our progress.

"Sasha," she looked down at the girls. "You should be in bed. It's much too late for a child like you to be attending." She put her hand on Sasha's shoulder and gave her a shake. Sasha blinked, opened her mouth to protest, saw Lincoln's face, and ducked her head.

"She's enjoying herself, Athena." Lincoln winked at the girls and the crowd pushed us out into the lobby.

"She can't be enjoying this sort of thing, Lincoln darling." Athena leaned against him, using the crowd as her excuse. "She's too young to understand anything. This is an *opera*, after all, not a children's matinee. She should be at home with that babysitter you employ." She turned herself so that her back was to me. "And, darling, I have so much to tell you since we talked the other night." My gut wrenched. "We must get our plans..." I couldn't quite hear what she said even though I practically leaned backwards..."can we talk? I want to make sure that we...." Although I strained mightily to hear, the lobby was so noisy that I missed the rest of her sentence.

Lincoln purchased several cups of soda, a bottle of water, and three glasses of wine. He handed the soda and water to Sasha and Eva and they turned back to deliver the refreshments to Maisie and her friends. I took a glass of wine from Lincoln and he handed Athena a glass. Her perfectly sculpted face made an expression if distaste. "This amateur production is terrible!" She sipped her wine, arching a look at Lincoln over the rim. "Why don't these country bumpkins do Little Red Riding Hood, if they can't do a professional job."

"I'm enjoying it a lot." I piped up.

She looked over at me, "Oh, this is your baby-sitter, isn't it? You should be taking better care of those two young children." She sniffed, ignoring me as if I were dust on the floor, and talked to Lincoln as if I were invisible. "What would she know of opera?" She spoke as if I wasn't there. I wanted to kick Athena right in her well-groomed, elegant posterior.

"Athena, you've met Reggie at my house." Lincoln's eyes were amused. Mine weren't but I tried not to let it show.

She paid no attention and linked arms with him, pulling him away from our circle. I hated her. Her body leaned into his and she clutched at his shirtfront. I hated her. I stood back and bumped into Barbara and Horace, who were watching the scenario play out. Barbara's eyes glittered and she cut in front of Athena, like a large buffalo shoving an overdressed, annoying rat. "Oh, Lincoln. I need a drink." She headed Lincoln back towards the little bar that had been set up in a corner of the lobby. "Can you get two beers?" She maneuvered her considerable body between Athena and Lincoln. Horace, not to be outdone, pulled me past Athena. The crowd was thick and everyone was eager to get to the bar. With three against one, it was easy to...well, perhaps the word is shove... Athena further and further away.

Lincoln laughed, although I thought his laugh was a bit hollow. "You'll have to forgive Athena. She's...well, she's herself."

Barbara said something under her breath and Horace laughed. Lincoln looked even more uncomfortable. I kept my eyes glued to the top of my glass. "Do you think the girls are enjoying the performance? Was it a mistake to expect them to understand?" Lincoln put his hand on my arm.

I decided to be a nice girl. To not make any kind of fuss. "I do. I think they understand the story...maybe not all of the nuances, but enough to follow, and I overheard Sasha whisper to Eva that the music was cool. I presume that's the ultimate compliment." We all chuckled, hoping that Puccini, from his spot in musical heaven, would understand.

Athena's high heels tapped back to Lincoln's side. She glared, seeing his hand on my arm. I felt smug inside, but tried to have a nonchalant expression on my face instead of one that trumpeted, "He's mine."

She went right into battle mode. "Lincoln, my darling man, please leave the baby sitter to do her work and come over here with me. We *must* talk, darling." She took his other arm and pulled him towards the bar. Her false tinkle of laughter floated back to me. My own poor arm felt denuded and chilly. As I said before, I hated her. Barbara made a hideous moue at Athena's narrow back.

"Bitch", she remarked.

"Now, now, girls," Horace hugged us both. "Let's get ourselves another drink and go back to our seats. The atmosphere won't get any better out here while she's determined to monopolize him." He was right, not that it made me feel any better. We got bottles of cold water and went back inside. I was a bit pissed at Lincoln. He should have made it clear to Athena that he was with me, and not have abandoned me to go and have an intimate conversation with her. *Although,* my silent voice reminded me, *he really isn't with just you, but with a group of people.* I shushed my silent voice and began to chat with the girls and Maisie.

As the curtain rose, Lincoln came back in, took his seat, and picked up my hand. He smiled at me and my toes curled. All my jealousy evaporated and, to my ultimate joy, Athena never came back to her seat.

◆ ◆ ◆

Afterwards, lying in bed by myself, my eyes gritty and my mind churning, I tried to analyze the evening. One thing I knew, I hated Athena and she hated me. Oh yes, we girls know right away who our sworn enemies are, and she would cheerfully have put a steak knife into my heart, twisted it, and then walked away without one of the sprayed and bleached hairs on her head getting messed up. And I would have done the same to her. Not that I felt deeply about it all! Not at all!

The opera had been marvelous. It hadn't been Antonina up there, but the cast was terrific, enthusiastic and believable. At the end, when Mimi lay dying, and tears were running down my face, I felt another tiny little hand creep into mine. Sasha sniffed audibly and I patted her hand in understanding. I heard a sniff or two from Eva and saw a tissue mop the tears from her eyes. Lincoln harrumphed and took out his own handkerchief. The players took three curtain calls and we cheered and clapped and yelled "Bravo! Bravo!" Sasha and Eva really liked that part and wanted to keep on yelling.

We went to have ice cream and coffee at Breaking New Grounds, a popular spot on Market Square. The evening was chilly, but we braved the oncoming autumn and sat outside, munching and sipping and rehashing the parts that the girls had liked best. "I'm very proud of you two," Maisie told them. "You behaved beautifully and were very grown-up." Sasha and Eva squirmed on their chairs, ecstatic at the praise.

"Maybe I'll be an opera singer when I grow up," Eva stated. "My teacher says that I have a good voice."

Sasha snorted. "Yeah, right. And I'll be the Queen of England!"

Eva punched Sasha's arm. The grown-up phase of the night seemed to be over. "I want to be like Musetta and have men kiss my little toe." She wiggled her foot and warbled Musetta's waltz music. "Men will carry me around and give me parrots and diamonds."

"OK," Sasha capitulated. "You can be Musetta and I'll be Mimi, although I'll make sure that I take some cough drops so that I won't get sick and die. We can sing together all the time and we'll be a big sensation all over the world."

"Oh, dear," Maisie's laughter shook the table. "Perhaps it's time for you two divas to be in bed. You can dream of being famous."

I told them the story of Antonina's first opera. "She was about your age and went to see *Aida* at the Metropolitan Opera in New York City.

"Ayeeda?" Sasha queried.

"It's about an Egyptian princess. A magnificent opera with live horses and camels on stage. There's a pyramid and a tomb and a huge procession of hundreds and hundreds of singers and live animals." The children were wide-eyed. "And Antonina loved it so much that she decided then and there to be an opera singer, just as you two have decided. When she went home and got into bed, she wrapped herself in a sheet, just like an Egyptian princess. Her mother, my great-grandmother Francesca, went to kiss her goodnight and found her singing an aria out loud, all wrapped up like a mummy."

Sasha gave me a wicked look. "Her mummy found her looking like a *mummy*!" At that, we all howled with laughter, picked up our sweaters and went home.

That is, I went home. By myself. Lincoln dropped me off, walked me to the door, kissed me hard and hot, and got back into the yellow Mercedes to bring the rest of his group home. I was there, in the little green house, by myself, with only Macduff and my jealousy and worries about Athena to keep me company until a fitful sleep finally overcame me.

CHAPTER FOURTEEN

Roberta Edna Taylor Winslow, age eighty-six and a little grumpy today, woke up on Sunday with a headache and the wisp of a wonderful dream. She thumped her pillow, trying to make herself comfortable enough to drift back...back to the lovely dream. A tail of an image misted back...It was a long time ago, she was seventeen and it was a summer evening. The night she met Eugene.

Ah, *Eugene!* The handsomest man she had ever known. Her eyes closed, her mind drifted and she was young again. She wore...what was it? A white organza dress, with pink and green flowers embroidered around the neckline and pink roses twined into her golden hair. A snatch of music was playing in the background...an orchestra, shimmering chandeliers. The Cotillion! The June Cotillion. *"Wild again...beguiled again...bewitched, dum-dum, da da dum da, am I...."* Roberta sighed, a happy sigh. She could envision it all, every detail ...and Eugene.., ah! He was leaning against the fireplace across the room, and just like in a romantic movie, his eyes and her eyes met. Ah, he was so debonair in his tuxedo, so handsome, just like Fred Astair. All the other girls watched in envy as he made his way across the dance floor and took her hand. How her heart had thudded in her breast, hot and heavy, changing her world from innocence to the beginnings of adult lust. Even now, knowing that it was only a dream, she felt herself flush with emotion. The music swelled... He drew her up and into his arms. *"Bonsoir, ma petite fleur,"* he had said to her, his voice velvet with his French accent. She'd heard the gossip earlier that night in the powder room. He was from France, a wealthy cousin of one of the Astors, slim and elegant, and every girl there had dreamed that he might ask her to dance. And here he was, waltzing with her...and her alone. Roberta smiled into her pillow and allowed the music to transport her across the polished floor in his strong arms. His lips brushed her hair and her girlish passion was aroused.

154

She heard a whine and the touch of a cold muzzle. The fantasy of her dream faded a bit. The dance floor receded, leaving her with the reality of being an elderly woman on a cold and dreary morning. She grasped at the tail of the dream. *Come back, Eugene,* she begged, refusing to open her eyes. The orchestra played...*Ah, good.* The music surged and once again, Eugene's arms steered her under the glittering chandeliers and out onto the patio and the warm, seductive summer air. She raised her arms to hold onto his shoulders and felt the real chill of the morning. With the goosebumps of reality, handsome Eugene, his touch, and the cotillion were gone.

"Drat!" she swore. A sharp bark answered her. Roberta groaned, ignoring the bark and humped herself back under the covers, punching her pillow into a more comfortable shape. "*Eugene, mon amor,*" she tried once more to get back. It was such a *good* dream! But it was too late, the dream, the music and the man were gone. Gone with the years and her youth and her suppleness and her life. "Rats", she said out loud. A whine again permeated her senses. Even so, she certainly didn't feel like getting up out of bed. And so, she didn't. *Eighty-six years old. Leave me alone!* Only Roberta's dog, a wide-awake Golden Retriever who sometimes answered to the name of Energizer...Gizer for short... felt differently about the morning's potential and activities. Gizer had no knowledge of Eugene's continental charms. He pawed at Roberta's recumbent body. When she didn't respond, Gizer jumped on the bed, barked once, whined and began scratching at the blanket. Gizer had his own agenda this morning and his agenda included getting outside and fast.

"All right, all right." Roberta gently cuffed Gizer's head with stoic resignation. "*Au revoir, Eugene.*" Gizer licked her face with his pink tongue, then waved his tail, exulting in winning the battle. He barked again, softly this time, a woof of celebration, and leaped back off the bed, ready to go. "Ooooh." Roberta groaned as she climbed out of bed, went to the bathroom, anxiously followed by Gizer's padding feet. She splashed water on her face. Jeans and a baby blue sweater, her favorite color...feet shoved into those comfortable walking shoes. An aspirin for her headache, a gulp of cold water, then a baby aspirin as a sop to that fool Doctor McCurdy who bugged her constantly about her heart and her aches and her cholesterol. Another gulp of water followed. One would think at eighty-six, doctors would leave a woman alone, she muttered, thinking of all the other little pills that she took every day. A glimpse in the mirror showed that age was creeping in, no matter how many pills she consumed or how much cream and gook she stroked on her face. Ah, well. She swished out her mouth, gave her hair a stroke or two of the brush and groaned, just a little, as she stepped onto the scale. Gizer gave Roberta a reminder of a bark. She patted the dog on the head, scratching the soft, amber fur between Gizer's ears. "Two seconds, pooch, Just give me two more seconds."

In the kitchen, the automatic coffee pot was sending out its aroma, and, on auto-pilot, Roberta grabbed a go-cup and poured it in, light and no sugar, jammed on the top of the cup, grabbed Gizer's leash and hooked her CD player around her neck. She locked a fanny pack around her waist and opened the door. In a frenzy now, Gizer was dancing with excitement and a full bladder.

Roberta pulled a dark blue woolen cap over her still-blonde-with-the-help-of-a-good-hairdresser hair and stretched her still generally slender eighty-six year old body in the cool morning air while the dog squatted in blissful relief at the side of the driveway. The stretching relaxed her muscles a bit. *"Not bad for an old broad,"* Roberta complimented herself, wondering how the years had treated Eugene. What had triggered that dream? Why today, of all days, should she think of that golden time, so long ago? Eugene. Was he still slim and elegant? Would his kiss still make her heart tremble? Was he still alive? Or had he succumbed to a stroke or a heart attack? Or even worse, had he gotten fat and balding? She laughed at herself. *Fool old woman!* Ah, but he had been so soigné, so ...so... perfect. She snorted. Hell, he was probably stuffed into a wheelchair somewhere. "And here I am, feisty and fine. Ready to take on the morning. Come on, Gizer. Let's go!"

She put a disc into the slot, the sound track to *The Music Man*, and adjusted her earpiece as Gizer, bladder comfortably empty now, sniffed at a few delectable smells, and then took off at a brisk lope, pausing only to leave his mark on a tree trunk or two. Roberta followed, pacing her walk to the music of *Seventy-Six Trombones*.

Despite the aspirin and the delicious remnants of her dream, Roberta's headache was taking it's time about leaving her, gradually being pushed out by the warming sunlight and the music. The road narrowed and the forest closed in. Although there was never a lot of traffic here on the lonely road, Roberta nonetheless, was watchful for a careless car. Gizer was well-trained and generally stopped dead in his tracks if a car approached, but Roberta was still careful of the dog's well-being. She walked rapidly in the middle of the road with Gizer snuffling the leaves that had begun to fall, lining the narrow lane. The solitude was soporific and in a few moments, her headache was nearly gone. She began to thoroughly enjoy the walk and even picked up the pace, starting to jog with a slow, rhythmic shuffle. Gizer trotted in perfect contentment at her heels and Roberta found her mind relaxing, rejecting the bliss of her dream of Eugene, turning more practically to the flea market that she would be participating in this afternoon. She was an expert at jewelry making. She had all her gleaming, glittering wares ready, pinned neatly into the glass show boxes, all priced and ready to go. It would only take fifteen or so minutes for her to get set up. Maybe this week, they'd give her a better table than last week. Maybe she'd make a few dollars more. Maybe she'd sell that amber piece with the silver filigree.

At the bend in the road, three runners appeared in the distance and Roberta waved her arms and picked up her jogging pace. Every morning, right about here, she'd meet her daughter Phyllis and her son-in-law Steve, running toward her from their house on the other side of the marsh. It wouldn't do to appear sluggardly to them. They might get some idiotic idea that she was getting old, for goodness sake. And who was the other runner, she wondered.

As they came closer, Phyllis, too, waved at her mother. Roberta slowed her pace. *Oh my word*, she gasped to herself, *it was Eugene!* Despite her age, her heart started to beat faster. She stopped, took off her woolen hat, and patted her hair, thanking some God of Romance who had insisted that she have her hair colored last week. *Eugene!*

You fool! She chided herself. *It's not Eugene. You are the silliest old lady in the world!* Far from Eugene's remembered elegance, this person, even in the distance, ran with a huffing and puffing gait, lumbering and clumsy. *Oh drat,* Roberta realized, it was that horrible man, Gilbert, who was visiting Phyllis's next door neighbor from some benighted city in the mid-west. She had made Gilbert's acquaintance a few nights earlier at a party and hoped that Gilbert and his obnoxious humor and opinions on anyone and anything would quickly return from whence he came. She considered herself a reasonable person, with a good attitude toward others, and she generally liked most people that she met. But this Gilbert however, had ruffled her fur with almost every remark that the bigoted idiot had said. Even easygoing Steve had looked annoyed with Gilbert's chatter most of the night. Ah, well, he'd be going home soon.

Gizer, much less discerning of other's character flaws than his mistress and scenting friends, dashed ahead frolicking around the group, knowing that a biscuit awaited him in Phyllis' pocket. He ran to her, frisking around her legs and she stopped to pet him, waiting for her mother to join them.

" 'sup, Roberta baby?" Gilbert slapped Roberta with annoying familiarity on the shoulder, sending a jolt of arthritic pain down her arm.

"Nothing much," she picked Gilbert's hand off her shoulder, much like she would pick a worm off the branch of an apple tree. She stepped away from him in case he decided to maul her further, unhooked her earpiece and shut off the CD. "I had the most unusual dream last night," Roberta turned to her daughter as she twisted the top of her go-mug and sipped a blast of hot and fragrant coffee.

Phyllis, who hated hearing anything about anyone's nocturnal meanderings, pretended not to hear her mother and began a series of stretching exercises. Gilbert, still puffing with exertion, took the opportunity to sit down on a portion of the stone wall on the side of the road. He was gasping and out of breath, Roberta was pleased to note, and his color was bright red. *Perhaps he'll have a heart attack*, she thought with wicked delight.

As the sun rose higher and warmed the back of their necks, Gizer realized that no one was paying a great deal of attention to him. Relishing a moment of freedom, he wandered into the woods, picking up the tantalizing scent of something interesting, just beyond the trees.

The joggers talked for a few moments more, hashing over last night's baseball game and the rising price of gasoline. Gilbert's glee at the Red Sox's loss irked Roberta and she turned around sharply to give him one of her best glares, triggering a nasty jolt to her neck and causing her recently departed headache to throb again. Fretful now and suddenly anxious to get home, she called, "Gizer! Here pup!" They could hear the dog, crashing through the woods. A sharp yelp echoed. She pursed her lips and tried a whistle. "Come on, Gizer. Where'd he go? Gizer! *Energizer!* Hey, *dog!*" A staccato series of barks answered. And then another. And another.

Roberta stood at the edge of the woods and peered through the branches and leaves. She called again. Gizer was an exuberant, but usually a well-behaved dog who had graduated at the top...well, near the top...of his obedience class. *"Come!"* Roberta's command was sharp. It was answered by a fusillade of barks and then a sharp whine that worried Roberta, sending a shiver of some nameless apprehension though her.

Phyllis asked, "What's the matter with him? Do you think he's hurt?"

"Well, I don't know, but I'd better go and...." Roberta pushed her way a few feet into the woods and peered through the thicket. Curious now, Phyllis and Steve followed. Gilbert watched them from his perch on the wall.

◆ ◆ ◆

Certainly he'd seen many dead bodies. It was his job, for chrissakes. A police chief, nearly forty-five years on the force. Of course, he'd seen them. Auto accidents, hangings, stabbings, heart attacks, the Morant kid drowning last week, peaceful death from old age, those ladies chopped to pieces last year, even a few really stomach wrenching suicides. But you never quite ever got used to them, did you? Alexander Bridge sighed and looked down into the gully.

Candace Chabot. The second dead body in Kittery in as many weeks, goddamn it. He figured she'd been lying there for more than ten days. Her body was sprawled in the gully, mostly underneath her beloved motor scooter. The little blue Yamaha lay under a mantle of leaves and branches and the back wheel rested on her arm and chest. Her jacket was ripped and shredded. Chief Bridge saw that her helmet was twisted and even from where he stood, he could ascertain the damage of the gaping, dried blood encrusted wounds that covered what was left of her face. Small forest animals and insects had found her first, then larger animals. Alexander thought that perhaps some foxes, a wolf or coyote, or maybe even that dreaded denizen of the night woods, a fisher cat, had feasted on her poor, dead flesh. One of her arms had been detached, perhaps by an animal, and it lay a few feet away, a mangled piece of bone and clothing and shredded gristle. Shit.

He'd gone to school with Richie Chabot's brother John and known Candace's family for his entire life. They were all nice family people. He'd talked to Richie only the night before last and knew that Richie still had some hope that Candace would be found, unharmed, but his own experience had been expecting something like this for the past week or so. Ah, well, at least now Richie would know what happened. Some freaking consolation.

Away from the gully, over in a clump of trees, Roberta Winslow stood, her golden dog wheeking and whining, cowering close to Roberta's leg. Phyllis and Steve Fox stood next to her, nervous and understandably upset. The fat one, the jerk from Kankakee, or wherever, had lost all control and vomited all over his three hundred dollar running shoes. The danged ole pudge was loudly complaining that he wanted to go home. *I'll keep him here for another hour, make him wish he'd never come to Maine!* Alexander had no patience with idiots. Bad enough that a body had been found...the rest of the group, including the old lady, were behaving well, considering what they'd stumbled over. But this fat jerk was bitching and complaining as if he'd been really inconvenienced. Tough shit.

Luckily, except for the dog that had nosed around Candace's body and then raised the alarm, the humans had only stood at the top of the gully and not tromped over the scene of death. Alexander wanted to say the scene of the crime, but, until his suspicions were confirmed, it was technically still only a scene of death. *Only* a scene of death? Ha. Alexander swallowed the bile in his mouth. Shit.

Three of his men were taping off the perimeter of the woods that might be pertinent to the scene – of death, of murder, of whatever. He turned at a sound behind him. The Medical Examiner's car and the Crime Lab crew had arrived.

"Alexander." Dr. Jack Murphy stepped over a rotted log and stood next to him, looking down. "What happened?" Murphy wore freshly pressed grey pants and a just-out-of-the-laundry blue button down shirt. *How the hell did he always manage to look so good?* Alexander wondered, brushing ineffectually at a coffee stain that marred his rumpled uniform shirt. No matter what the time of day or night, rain, snow and in between, Murphy looked like an advertisement for Jos. A. Bank. *I always look like the camels ran over me,* Bridge mused, *even if it's first thing in the morning, just when I leave my house, wearing a shirt that Clare just got out off the ironing board.*

Bridge rubbed his hand across his face, feeling the faint stubble on his cheeks. "It's Candace Chabot, I think. Or what's left of Candace Chabot. There's the Yamaha." He gestured with his chin.

"Hmmm. Not an accident, I don't think. No way she could have lost control and skidded all the way in here." Murphy stroked his own immaculately barbered chin. "Check the broken branches."

"Yeah. I figure she's been here since she went missing."

"Who found her?" Doctor Murphy looked back, as if he expected to see the perpetrator lurking in the bushes.

"A dog named Gizer and his lady owner, a Mrs Roberta, um, ah, Edna Taylor Winslow." The Chief read the names from his notebook. "They were taking their morning constitutional and the dog went off into the bushes, kept barking, and they all – she, Mrs. Winslow – was with three others – they all came over…no, wrong…" he peered at the scribbles he had made. "One of them stayed behind, and the other two – Mrs. Winslow's daughter and her husband – came over to the gully. I guess they could see that the news wasn't good, for thank goodness, they didn't go down and tromp around."

"No shit? A dog named Gizer. Cute name for a dog."

"No shit." Alexander sighed. He showed Murphy the trail of broken branches that led from the road to the top of the gully. "Somebody pushed her and the bike through here, I reckon." He fingered one of the branches. "Week or so? Whaddaya think?"

"You know me. I never have an original thought," Murphy's charming smile broke out. "How long has she been missing?"

" 'Bout two weeks."

"I'll check to see if she was killed here or her body moved at all, but don't expect anything definite until I get her on the table." Murphy went back to his car and took out a large suitcase and his medical bag.

The Chief motioned to Georgie Wood, one of his new patrolmen. "Tape off this area, Georgie." Gulping hard, trying not to disgrace himself, Georgie complied, making an effort not to look at the body or the flies and insects that still swarmed over it.

"Hey Chief," Georgie was trying to appear intelligent without throwing up, "The perpetrator would have to be someone strong, don'tcha think? I mean, to get the motor bike and her all the way into the woods?"

"Mmmpf." Bridge acknowledged. "Maybe."

With practiced action, Chief Bridge and Dr. Murphy took plastic booties out of the Crime Scene Kit. Bridge grunted as he bent over to tie them over his boots. "Uuuff. Gottta cut out those donuts," he groaned. Murphy gave him a sympathetic smile, bent effortlessly and slid his polished shoes into the booties. The two men slipped latex gloves on their hands and side-stepped down into the gully, trying to make as little disturbance as possible, so as to preserve whatever clues might still be around after ten or so days of rain, weather and the ravages of the hungry forest animals.

◆ ◆ ◆

Sunday morning found me tired and upset. I'd slept badly. I was angry that Lincoln hadn't come home with me. I was angry that he'd spent time, however brief, with Athena. I was angry that I hadn't called him to tell him that I was angry, and I was angry because I *was* jealous and angry. Green-meanies jealous. Jealous as I hadn't been since I was a sophomore in high school and Brad Hvolbeck had asked Janie Whidden to the Valentine Dance instead of me.

The weather wasn't helping my feelings. Instead of the beautiful Indian summer days we'd been luxuriating in, today was sullen and cold. A drizzle was in the air. I drank my coffee standing up, watching Macduff in the backyard. The cats were nowhere to be seen. Probably snug and cozy in whatever little cat den they disappeared into when I wasn't looking. Dispirited, I trudged to work.

My first customer for brunch was Bob Micklewright. Alone. I brought him a menu and he ordered juice, coffee and corned beef hash and eggs, poached hard on top. I nodded and tried to take the menu. He held on tight to it and then grabbed my hand. I was a little startled and tried to pull my hand away, but he hung on to it. "Reggie." His face was odd.

"Bob, let go of my hand." I pulled it away and glared at him.

"I dream of you," he told me. My eyes told him that I was stunned. He backpedaled a little. "You know that I have always been attracted to you, Reggie." Again, my eyes answered. I wasn't pleased at this declaration of his intent.

"Bob," I began, but he interrupted me.

"I want to take you out to dinner. Tonight. You'll have a good time with me, Reggie. I'm a gentleman and a generous man."

I couldn't help it. I snorted.

He grabbed my hand again. "I need you, Reggie. I told you. I dream of you. You and me."

I gathered my wits about me. What *was* it that made me attractive to him? My apron? The way I poured coffee? "Bob," I tried again. "You're a nice man and I like and respect you." My mind was reeling. *What are you saying, Reggie? You think that he's the world's biggest dork!*

"I don't want your friendship. I want to be, um, your, um, boyfriend." His eyes, behind his glasses, gazed intently at me and I got a chill. He looked almost menacing. "I want to be with you alone."

I shook off my silly fear. This was only Bob, the soft-bellied man who gave me a twenty-five or thirty cent tip every day, not some sex-maniac rapist. "Look," I shook his hand away. "I'm perfectly happy to serve you here. That's my job. I even think you are a pleasant person." Did I now? Did I still think he was nice? *Well, Reggie, my girl,* I told myself, *this isn't the time to tell him that you don't think he's nice.* "But, Bob, I am just not interested in dating you. I'm sorry." I whisked the menu away and almost ran into the kitchen to put his order in to Gerjeet.

I waited on a few more customers. I'll admit that Bob had shaken me more than I expected. Joan Grasser and Rose came in and I nearly babbled a hysterical good-morning to them. The Pearsons and their oversized canine "girls" sat outside, under the blue and white umbrellas, despite the faint drizzle. I buried my head into the soft black fur of Cady's head, trying to calm my still-fluttering heartbeats. Two of the firemen sat at the window table, each demolishing a plateful of pancakes and sausage. The Café's placid pace of a normal Sunday morning resumed. I hoped the drama was over. My breathing slowed and I brought Bob his platter of corned beef hash without a single word to him. He glared at me. "Bring me some hot coffee," he ordered in a nasty, peevish voice. I backed away, nodded, and with my face stiff and unsmiling, brought him a fresh, hot cup. He avoided my glance. As I turned around, I saw Lincoln come into the Café.

I know that my face lit up. I know that I was delighted beyond reason, and I know that it showed. Lincoln's wink and grin to me beamed through the morning, and if that wasn't enough, my heart turned over as Lincoln mouthed a kiss to me. I bit my lip in joy and confusion. I could feel the hot blush that rose from my collarbone up to my cheeks. When I took Rose and Joan their check, Rose's raised eyebrows, together with her observant and knowing expression told me that she had certainly noticed Lincoln's attention. I glanced around and saw that Bob Micklewright had noticed too.

The peace which I had fought to achieve crumbled. *Screw Bob Micklewright*, I thought to myself. Idiot man! I had never, *ever,* given him one iota of attention other than to bring him hashed brown potatoes. How *dare* he anticipate that I would pay him any amorous attention! How *dare* he! With a revitalized full head of steam, I brought Bob his breakfast, ready to do battle if he so much as touched me again. Again, he wouldn't meet my eyes. I gently placed his platter on the table and backed away. I had wanted to slam the entire breakfast over his head, but...well...it was better that I tried to be polite.

And now from annoyance to joy. I went to Lincoln's table, trying to keep from skipping and jumping. He took my hand in his paw. And gave me – you know – that kind of look. "We need to do a little bit of talking when you get finished here." I nodded, we did indeed. "Just bring me some coffee. I'm going to the office for an hour or so and I'll be back here at 2:30, OK?" His smile lit up my heart and several other regions of my body. I turned to get him a cup of coffee, and saw that Bob had left the Café without touching his breakfast. I heard the angry roar of his truck's muffler leaving and was relieved that he had gone. I cleared his table of the untouched food. There were three one-dollar bills and a five lying by the side of the table. The meal, together with coffee, juice and tax, came to $7.99.

After Lincoln left, the morning pace accelerated and I didn't have time to think of Reggie and her men and her anxiety. I only had so much room up in my brain, and bacon and eggs, mushroom quiche and Gerjeet's new popular addition of kedgeree kept me occupied. Horace and Barbara wandered in and sat outside with Holly and Thane and the girls. The drizzle had stopped and a watery sun was trying to peek through the clouds. Barbara looked exceptionally happy this morning. I wonder what nice thing had happened to her, but didn't get a moment to stop and chat, except to say that when all this breakfast stuff was over, we'd talk.

Daniel Bethany was the next to appear. He hefted a huge basket of lobsters and kissed Anoop soundly as he handed it over to her. She giggled and dimpled and looked as cute as a button. Gerjeet's smile was a bit strained, but Daniel only slapped him on the back and ordered two coffees and four buttered rolls to go.

"Jonah's waiting in the boat. We're going back out again. The lobsters are just jumpin' in the boat and we gotta make hay while the going is good." His wide, white grin included me, and Barbara and every other woman in the place. I shook my head. Dang, he *was* a good looking man. He winked at me. Danged if he didn't *know* that he was a good looking man.

As he clumped away and roared out of the street in his big truck, a patrol car rolled to a stop and parked right outside the door. The Tall policeman from my day of embarrassment at my condo got out and came into the Café. He went right to the counter without socializing with anyone and spent a few moments in intense discussion with Gerjeet. Every customer was aware of the tension that had entered with him, and the buzz of conversation ceased, with necks craned and ears stretched to find out what was happening. I stepped close to the counter and noted that Gerjeet's normally coffee-colored face was pale. He went into the back and came out with one of my sour cream cakes and a box of brownies. He gave them to Tall, who brought them to the patrol car. Gerjeet followed with two large carafes of coffee and fixings. Tall drove off.

"I will tell all you people what has happened," Gerjeet came back in and held his hands up, speaking to everyone in the Café. "It is most sad and you will all cry with me and the family. That nice lady, Candace Chabot, was found today. She is dead." A furor went up as we all began to talk and ask questions. Gerjeet waved his hands. "I do not know more. They found her in the woods and she has been dead for many days." He rubbed his chin. "Her poor husband will be crying and her family too."

◆ ◆ ◆

"What's up?" I asked Barbara, after we had commiserated on the tragedy of Candace's death. "You look like you swallowed a light bulb." I flopped in a chair between Barbara and Holly. Cady's tongue licked my kedgeree-smelling hand and I patted her and scratched between her ears.

"Oh, something nice. But it's a secret." Barbara managed to look coy.

"What?" I cajoled. "You can tell me."

"And me," Holly giggled. Barbara only shook her head as Horace looked amused.

"Not until tomorrow." Horace took her hand in his. "Our lips are sealed." And no amount of wheedling would make them change their minds, not even the promise of an extra piece of sour cream cake on the house.

"Well, if you're not going to share your innermost secrets, we're leaving," Holly snapped the leads on Cady and Murph. "Even if you did tell us, we're leaving anyway. Thane's mother is coming this afternoon." She rolled her eyes. "I can tell when I'm not wanted. Come on, Thane." Laughing, Thane got to his feet and stuffed the two huge dogs into the back of their Volvo. I watched as Thane backed out of the parking space and noticed that the poor Volvo was looking the worse for wear, with a few dents and rust spots. I supposed that carrying two monsters like the girls would sure wear an automobile out quickly. We waved goodbye and then I turned back to Barbara.

"OK, they're gone. You can tell me now." Barbara laughed, looking very attractive, but refused.

"I'll tell you what," she offered. "Come for supper tomorrow night and you'll hear all."

"What's for supper?"

"Steaks. Horace got a new Weber grill for his birthday."

"Your birthday?" I goggled. "I didn't know it was your birthday!" Horace laughed again and told me that it wasn't until September fifteenth.

"But I bought myself a nice, early present."

"A Weber grill!" I enthused. "I'll say it is nice! Hot dog! OK, I can come, but only if I can bake you a nice, gooey, birthday cake."

"Bring Lincoln and the cake and you're on." He checked his watch. "Good grief, it's after two! We've gotta go." He pulled some money out of his pocket, checked the bill, and left a small wad next to his plate. Barbara got up too.

"Come over about six. It will just be us four."

We hugged, then, the thought of Candace struck us simultaneously. We hugged again, this time harder.

◆ ◆ ◆

At two-thirty, the Café was empty. I cleared off the tables, refilled the salt and peppers and folded the tablecloths. The watery sun had overcome the clouds and a tiny, refreshing breeze made the air smell fresh and clean. I sat down, easing the ache in my shoulder blades and waiting for Lincoln to appear. Anoop carried Daria into the restaurant and set her on the floor near me. She sat down and her eyes were worried. "That Bob," she bit her lip, "he was bothersome to you, yes?"

"I think he has lost his mind." I agreed. "He simply went crazy!"

"Some men, they cannot believe that a woman would not want them, no matter how feeble they are." She fingered one of her silver bangles and slipped it off, holding it just above Daria's reach. Daria pulled herself up, clutching at Anoop's sari, and crowed with glee as she grabbed the bangle. Anoop scooped the little girl up and held her close. "Sometimes, men are so unjust." She buried her face in Daria's curls. "Women are only their slaves."

"You said it, Anoop." I held my arms out for the baby and swung her up in the air. She screeched with delight and that was how Lincoln found us.

◆ ◆ ◆

We went to my house. "Too many big and little ears –all female– at Chez Fairweather," Lincoln confided. I let Macduff out into the back yard, made us coffee and the two of us sat on the back steps, him on the top step and me one step below, watching the dog wander around. I kept my mouth shut and let Lincoln lead the way, whatever way we were about to travel. He picked up my hand.

"About Athena," he started. I made myself keep a neutral face. I wasn't going to scream that I hated her, *hated her*! His hand engulfed mine and he slowly rubbed his thumb across the ball of my hand. I wanted to grab him and throw him to the ground, to ravage his face with kisses, to….

"Yes," I murmured. And then shut up.

"She's a lonely, bitter woman."

166

Sure is, I thought, but kept silent. *Miserable bitch, too.*

"She's been on her own since Paul divorced her and she's unhappy. She's one of those women who really needs a man to make her life complete."

Mmmm, and she especially wants you, Lincoln, my man.

"She looks upon me as a ...uh...friend, um, that she can rely on." He bent closer and kissed the top of my head.

Bullshit, I thought to myself.

"Anyway, she's no one that I have any interest in at all." His lips nibbled at my ear. "It's only you, Reggie, my queen. Only you." I closed my eyes and bliss descended on me. *Athena? Athena who?*

CHAPTER FIFTEEN

I made Horace a *torta d'arachia* as a birthday cake and found a wonderful CD of Frank Sinatra's old Tommy Dorsey recordings (Horace was a Sinatra freak) to wrap as a gift. Lincoln got him a quart of single-malt, "A real gift," he commented, dismissing the CD as something not quite worth giving to a man that he respected and liked.

Barbara and Horace were outside in their backyard, stoking the flames of the new Weber grill. Its massive domed top sparkled in the afternoon sunlight. "Nice," Lincoln stroked the stainless steel hood of the grill, as only a man could stroke an inanimate object that cooked meat. Horace beamed and showed all of the features of his new purchase. Then, he dazzled us with four monstrous rib-eyes which would soon be sizzling on his birthday gift to himself. Barbara and I chuckled maternally at the antics of our men as she put my *torta* into the refrigerator to consume later.

We pulled our chairs up near the Weber and watched as Horace demonstrated more of the grill's finer points. It was a beauty, almost big enough to house a family of five, and I presume one could have barbecued an entire ox on its gleaming surface. Horace, twirling a new and obviously expensive cooking implement grilled us stuffed mushrooms and we sat eating them with slurps of appreciation while the baked potatoes cooked.

"So?" I finally chirped.

"So what?" Barbara pretended that she didn't remember that I was extremely curious about her secret, whatever it was. Nonchalant, she speared another bite of mushroom.

"Oh, come on," I urged. "What *is* it?" She and Horace gave each other one of those married looks and she actually giggled in a girlish way. "Whassup with you two? What's the big secret?"

"Well…" She drew out the syllable, making the most of her moment. I nearly got up to throttle her and Lincoln laughed at my impatience. Barbara took Horace's hand. "You tell them, sweetheart."

168

"OK. We do have a very wonderful secret," he started. Barbara's eyes were downcast and I couldn't figure out what the heck they were going to tell us. "You know, Barbara and I have been married for almost twelve years." His cherubic face got pinker and pinker. "In the beginning, we hoped that we'd have a family," I sucked in my breath, my eyes wide. "But, no matter how manfully I tried," he made a rueful face, half-joking, half-not, "Nothing happened."

"And so," Barbara chimed in, her eyes still not meeting mine, "After a lot of talk, doctor's advice, medical and marital absurdities, we have decided to adopt a baby and have been approved to be new parents."

I screamed in joy and jumped up, gathered Barbara's considerable bulk in my arms and hugged her with delight, babbling questions. Lincoln pumped Horace's hand, his smile splitting his face. "When? *When?*" I begged. "When is the baby *coming?*"

"In one to two weeks," Barbara's face was beet red. "You don't...you don't think we're too old?"

"Nonsense!" Lincoln boomed. "You're never too old to change diapers and stay awake all night rocking the creature and making goo-goo sounds to it."

"A boy or a girl or don't you know?" I danced with glee.

"A boy. He's being born in Boston. A young mother...she's fifteen...she can't cope with a baby and doesn't want to keep him anyway." Barbara told me the age-old tale. "The father is fifteen, too. And they don't really love one another. It was just a one-night teenage thing. They don't want to get married...at least not yet...and not to one another..." Barbara's words tumbled over one another. "Too young, but they refused to have the baby aborted. We've talked with both of them and they're relived that the baby will have a good home." Her words ran down.

"Oh, darling, I am so happy for you both. A *baby!*" I sighed in rapture, thinking of the joy that awaited these two nice people.

"They only want to let us allow them to choose his name," Horace grinned. "We told them sure."

"So, what will his name be?"

"Michael Joseph. That's what they both wanted." I nodded; a good, strong name.

"Michael Joseph Wyzinski." I tried it out.

"Sounds just right," echoed Lincoln. "Congratulations. He's going to be a lucky child." He began to laugh and then turned to me. "The name is fine for your name game."

"What name game?" Barbara wanted to know, and then I had to explain the whole thing, with the *"I love you, Michael"* and the *"Michael, you are now our Vice President"* situations. We all agreed that Michael, as a name, met every test in the grandest ways. A perfect name.

Horace opened his birthday scotch and we all drank to the health and happiness of a lucky little boy that hadn't yet been born.

"Oh, I'm going to give you a baby shower!" I exclaimed. "I'm going to be certain to embarrass the heck out of you! A big, gaudy baby shower with big blue bows and crepe paper and all!" Barbara blushed like a schoolgirl.

"You know, I'd like that."

"Goody. I'll get working on it right away. Maybe in two weeks?"

"Nice," she agreed. "I never thought that I'd ever get a baby shower."

"Well, you deserve one. Blue booties and all. Oh, it will be such fun!"

"We'd like the two of you to be godparents to Michael," Horace, too, looked as if he'd swallowed a candelabra. "Will you?"

I started to cry. "I'd be so...honored," I bawled. "Oh, I'm so happy!"

Lincoln hugged me and then mopped my tears with his white handkerchief. "You have a funny way of being happy," he kissed my eyelids. Right in front of Barbara and Horace.

That night, he held me tight and told me that his entire life had changed since we met. He said that had the clock been turned back about twenty or so years, he would have loved to have made me pregnant and had a baby with me. My heart soared and he put his hands on my stomach and said that it was too bad he couldn't have made it bulge with the fruits of our love. We giggled at this silliness, but when we finally came together, he called me his beloved, his darling, his own and I wept and we fell asleep, tangled in one another's arms. He slept beside me, cradling me in his arms and his lips brushed my shoulder and I think I heard him say that he loved me.

◆ ◆ ◆

It was a happy beginning to a week that...well...had a lot of things that happened.

◆ ◆ ◆

On Tuesday, I had a shock when I opened the door of The Loop Café and entered it, ready to work. Gerjeet greeted me civilly, but his face was like a black thundercloud. I almost commented something inane like, "What's the matter with you? Sleep on the wrong side of the bed?" But...something made me hold my tongue.

I walked back into the restaurant, tying my apron string around my waist and then…stopped dead and gaped, my mouth hung open with astonishment. Anoop stepped out from behind the counter. Her hair…her beautiful, long, glossy hair….was almost gone! She'd cut it! Short! I mean, really short, like an urchin boy! She looked stunning. Absolutely stunning. The new hairdo was a shining cap, glossy and close to her scalp, feathered to intensify her delicate features and her perfect, *café au lait* skin. Her eyes deadlocked into mine. She looked angry. And defiant. Her chin stuck up in the air and I saw – ohmygoodness – her forehead was bereft of the *bindi* that had always adorned her face. My eyes widened even more, if that was possible. "Anoop!" I exclaimed. "You look *won*derful!"

"Thank you, Reggie. You are the only human being who thinks that I have not lost my mind." Her voice was chilly with an undercurrent of tears. I noticed than that she was wearing different clothing. Not a sari, not a colorful Indian wrap. No, this new, modern woman was dressed in dark blue trousers, cropped at the ankle, a white, knitted tee shirt that clung to her curves, and white sneakers decorated her feet. Gone, too, were the leather, jeweled sandals. "No one else thinks that I look decent."

I heard a growl behind me and Gerjeet pounded his fist on the counter. "You look like an American whore!" he hissed, and then turned away.

Anoop's eyes filled with tears. She dabbed at them, trying to keep her fragile composure. I grabbed a napkin from the basket that held them and offered it to her. "He'll get over it," I soothed. "You look beautiful, my dear." I hugged her, feeling the slender bones shake under my hands.

"The mother is angry. Gerjeet is angry. They have both stepped on my heart today." Her lips trembled as she tried to regain her composure. The bell over the door rang as three customers came in.

"Good morning," I turned, picking up three menus, almost glad at the disruption in the tension. "Would you like to sit by the window?"

◆ ◆ ◆

The day seemed endless. Gerjeet and Anoop didn't speak directly to one another all morning. If Gerjeet wanted to convey something, he'd ask me if I would tell that stranger to make more tuna fish salad. If Anoop needed more supplies, she'd ask me to tell "my old-fashioned husband to please bring up some more carrots." It was a long morning.

Just before lunch, Mrs. Simha, Gerjeet's mother, came into the restaurant, holding Daria and walking stiffly. She avoided Anoop and brought the child to Gerjeet to hold. The two – son and mother – spoke bitterly in their native language, the generally liquid tones hissed in anger. Daria squirmed in Gerjeet's arms, calling, "Mamma! Mamma!"

"She is not your Mamma. She is a stranger woman." Misery made Gerjeet's voice hoarse. He marched out of the restaurant through the back and barricaded himself in the kitchen. His mother glared at Anoop.

"See what you have done, ungrateful one!" And she joined her son. Anoop began to cry in earnest.

"Ah, what have I done, *Ai, Ai.*" I patted her and tried to comfort her, but lunch was extremely uncomfortable for all of us, although every customer, with no exception, was fulsome in praising Anoop's new appearance. As each one complimented her, Gerjeet's face got angrier and angrier. After the meal was served, Gerjeet left the premises. I stayed late and helped Anoop clean up the dishes and put the food away.

"Will you be alright?" I was worried. After all, the poor child was so upset.

"I will be fine, thank you, Reggie." She seemed a little calmer. "I am not a child, you know." She tossed her head and looked slightly startled to not feel the weight of her hair. "I am not a possession. No woman should be her husband's possession, not to have a thought or an opinion." I agreed. "I am a grown up person now." She sighed, this beautiful, sad, upset, grown up woman, and straightened her narrow shoulders. "I *am* a grown up person now. I am myself."

◆ ◆ ◆

I joined the Fairweathers for dinner that night. We had meatloaf, mashed potatoes and green beans. Delicious. Maisie accepted my sincere gratitude and told us that sure, she could cook, but only plain and simple things. "My husband, Jacques, only liked meat and potato kind of food. Nothing fancy, no sauces, no wing-dings. Give him a dish of salmon and peas, steak, pork chops, that sort of thing…well, he was a happy man." I'd brought a batch of brownies for dessert, and we warmed them up a little and topped them with vanilla ice cream. "Jacques would have enjoyed these," Maisie enthused, as she spooned up the last drop of melted ice cream. I felt like a warm brownie myself, basking in her praise. Was I begging for scraps from the Fairweather table? You betcha.

Maisie brought a small jewel box to the table after Sasha had cleared the dishes. "Lincoln told me that you were curious about Lady

Pamela and the jewels that that rascal pirate had stolen." She opened the worn leather straps and opened the box. "I haven't looked at these for years. So." We all leaned forward and gasped. There, laying on a puff of stained purple velvet, were two earrings, a necklace and a ring.

"Oh, Grannie!" Sasha exclaimed. "Are these really Lady Pamela's jewels?" She put out a finger and reverently touched the center stone in the necklace. "From so long ago?" Maisie picked it up and handed it to her. The necklace was of heavy filigree gold, with an intricate clasp. The center stone was large, a deep blue jewel, about the size of a fifty cent piece. Leading away from it on either side were smaller blue stones. It was breathtaking. Sasha draped it around her neck, turned and let Maisie fix the clasp. She whirled to the mirror that presided over the dining room table. "Look at me!" she cried. We obviously saw a little girl dressed in a tee shirt and dungarees. But the jewels transformed her, turning her tumble of red curls into an aureole of light, echoing the highlights of her face, throwing her childish bone structure into a promise of astonishing future beauty. She looked like a queen. "I look pretty, don't I, Grumpy?" She preened innocently, while Maisie and Lincoln sat, stunned by the transformation. I know she must have looked exactly like her mother would have looked.

The earrings matched the necklace. I picked them up and fastened them to Sasha's ears, where they dangled like miniature stars. Lincoln managed to find his voice. "You are beautiful, my darling," he croaked, fighting tears.

I touched the ring. It was of heavy, old gold; almost an orange color, the gold woven in a ropy braid around the inset jewels. And what jewels! There were three red-colored stones; one huge one in the center, flanked by two smaller ones. The ring looked as if it should be on the finger of a queen or on a Medici princess in a portrait heavily guarded in some famous museum. "Is...is it a *ruby*?" My voice was hushed. Maisie reached into the box and handed me the ring.

"I think so. After all, I don't think they had fake jewels from The Shopping Network in those days." I held the ring, turning it around in my hands. I didn't put it on. It seemed a sacrilege for me to slide it onto my own finger. Only a King or a Duke should touch these things. Not a mortal like me.

"How did you get these?" I handed Maisie the ring back.

"How did you get them, Mom?" Lincoln took the ring in his large hands. Even in his hands, it was massive. "I knew you had some jewels from Lady Pamela, but I never thought much about it all. I've never seen these." Sasha turned from her reflection and wound her arms around her grandmother.

"Tell us the story, Grannie."

"Well," Maisie sat back, a small smile on her face. "It's a good story." Sasha bumped her until she moved out a little and then Sasha sat, gently, on her grandmother's lap, leaning against Maisie's comfortable bosom. "It was in, oh, maybe 1930 or so, during the Depression. I know that we old folks are always going on about how difficult things were back then…" Lincoln nodded, grinning…"Well, they were. People lost their jobs, their houses, sometimes even lost their children, if they couldn't afford a doctor or medicine. There wasn't much material-wise available, even if you were a well-off family." She settled Sasha more comfortably on her lap. "As my father was a doctor, we were fine. Oh, we didn't have fancy food, or too many toys, but, land sakes, no one had those things. We had one old car, which my father used to make visits to the people he treated who were too sick to come to the office." She snorted. "If you'd have told me that people would have three or four cars in the future, I would have laughed at you. What in tarnation would people need with three or four cars?"

Lincoln shook his head. "Enough about the old days, walking to school barefoot, in the snow, up hill both ways." We all laughed and Maisie continued.

"Well, anyway, it was winter, and there *was* snow." She shook her finger at her son. "And no snowplows like they have now. The roads were difficult and driving was perilous. We got a telephone call…did I say that we were one of the few houses that had a telephone? We needed it because my Poppa was a doctor. Well, the telephone rang and my father had a message that a little girl was sick down Brave Boat Harbor way. More than twenty miles from our house. My mother told him not to go out, that it was too dangerous. But my father was a good and kindly man. 'I couldn't sleep, Evangeline,' he said, 'if I don't try to get to that little girl and see if I can't help her.' There was no talking him out of it. My mother sighed, she knew he would go through the fires of hell itself to help someone who was sick. So she packed up some hot coffee in a flask, put newspapers on the floor of Poppa's car to keep the cold out as best she could, wrapped Poppa up with two sweaters, a jacket, a cap, and a long scarf wound twice around his head. And then he went out into the blizzard. Oh, didn't I tell you that it had started to snow hard? Oh my, it was so snowy that I could barely see out the window. I sat at the front window, up on top of the radiator where it was warm, and waved goodbye to my Poppa." She paused for a moment, perhaps reliving the scene in her mind. "At first, I could see the tire tracks where he had driven out of the driveway, but in a few moments, the tracks were all filled in by the falling snow."

"Go on!" urged Sasha. "What *hap*pened?"

"I fell asleep at the window, waiting for him. I heard Momma call me and I was all cramped and stiff. My face was pressed against the glass and it was colder than cold, and my bottom was hot from sitting on the radiator. Momma said that she was worried. It was late and Poppa wasn't home yet. I began to be afraid. We went into the kitchen and made three cups of cocoa. One for Momma, one for me and one for Poppa, for he would surely be home soon. We waited and waited. Momma and I drank our cocoa, but Poppa's cup grew cold and a skim formed on top of the milk."

"It was very late. The snow was still swirling and there were large drifts that had pushed up against the front door. Momma started to pace the floor. I was torn between falling asleep and terror." Sasha's mouth was open and her eyes were locked on Maisie's face. I think my mouth was open too, and I had trouble breathing.

"Go on," Lincoln whispered.

"All of a sudden, we heard a car. Momma's face lit up. She flew to the door and pushed and pushed, trying to open it against the drift. 'Come help me, Maisie. He'll be frozen and we have to let him in as quickly as possible.' I ran to help her and we shoved and shoved and finally opened the door. A huge shape fell into the house. It was covered with ice and snow. It was Poppa."

"He groaned with cold. 'Go and get blankets from the bed, Maisie. There's a good girl.' I ran as fast as I could and heaped the blankets around my father. His hands were waxy white and he was cold all over. 'Go and bring me the bottle of brandy in the front room, quickly now.' Again, I ran to help as best I could. Momma made him drink the brandy, and he coughed and sputtered and his face began to change from pale to pink."

" 'You're a big girl now, Maisie,' Momma said. "Go into the kitchen and heat up the cocoa. Be careful with the stove and don't burn yourself.' I nodded, very solemn, as I was only a little child and had never been allowed to use the stove by myself before. It was a big responsibility for me. I ran into the kitchen, leaving my mother with her arms clasped around my father. She was rubbing his arms and legs and murmuring soft words to him."

"I was ever so careful. I used a match to light the flame, poured the cold cocoa into a pan and stood guard watching to be sure that the cocoa didn't burn nor the house be set on fire. Then, when the little bubble appeared on the top of the cocoa, I shut the fire off. I took a cloth and wrapped it around the handle of the pan and carefully, oh, so carefully, poured the cocoa into the cup again. Holding the cup with both hands, I walked back to Poppa, not spilling even one drop." She smiled at her own recitation.

"Poppa was sitting up and Momma looked happy. Poppa took the cocoa from me and drank it, telling me that it was the very best cocoa that he'd ever had. Afterwards, he would always tell everyone that it was the cocoa that saved his life that night. Ha."

"But the jewels…what about the jewels?" Sasha wound her arms around Maisie and shook her. "Grannie Fair, tell me!"

Maisie smiled. "Oh, you want to know about the *jewels"*, she teased. "Well, in the springtime, a man came to our house. No one was home except me and the hired lady that did our washing. Traudie was her name. The man asked if I was the daughter of the house. I told him yes, I was. He handed me this box," she picked up the old box and turned it around in her hands. He told me that his little girl had gotten better because my Poppa came to help her in the middle of the night, even though it was snowing. I nodded and assured the man that my Poppa would always help other people."

"He was an odd old man, dressed like a sailor. He told me that he and his family were going away on a boat. 'I don't have a great deal of money and I wasn't able to pay your father for his visit or the medicine that he gave to my Millie.' He patted the box. 'You give this to your Poppa and tell him that this is the payment for him.' Well, I thanked him and told him that I would do just what he asked me to do. He took three steps out of the door and then turned around. 'Perhaps I should tell you about what's in the box', he said to me.

'Many years ago, my grandfather was a fisherman here on the Piscataqua River. One night, there was a huge battle out on the water and the news the next day was that Bold Charlie the pirate had been killed. But my grandfather knew better. His skiff was fishing out in the water when the battle started. He was frightened, my grandfather was, and he rowed with all his might to get away from the flames and the guns and the screaming of the horses and the men who were drowning. As he rowed, he saw a man in the water. My grandfather rowed to where the man was and pulled him into the boat. The man begged my grandfather to take him to the New Hampshire coast and leave him on the waterfront of Newcastle Island. My grandfather was afraid, but he thought the man might harm him and so he did as he was bid and rowed the man to the New Hampshire shore. The man was weary and slumped against the thwart of the skiff. My grandfather took off his coat and covered the man and gave him the bread and cheese and beer that he had for his own dinner. Meanwhile, behind them, the battle raged on and the waters were lit with gunpowder flares. As the boat bumped against the rocks at Newcastle Island, the man tried to stand up and get out of the boat, but he was wounded and couldn't get out himself. My grandfather helped him out of the boat. My grandfather felt sorry for the wounded man and told him to keep the coat and the sandwich of herring that was in the coat's pocket. He told the wounded man that perhaps, with the coat and something more to eat, he'd be able to get to safety. The wounded man laughed and gave my grandfather this box. 'One treasure for another,' the wounded man said as he gathered my grandfather's coat around himself. 'I'm Bold Charlie the Pirate and these were to decorate the neck and ears and fingers of my bride, Lady Pamela.' The poor man sighed and clutched the coat closer around himself. 'But I will never see her again. They are of no use to me now. You have been good to me, even though you were afraid. You have given me all that you have, even your herring sandwich.' My grandfather said that Bold Charlie laughed ruefully. 'And so, now these belong to you'. And then the wounded pirate blessed my grandfather and limped off into the night.

"I asked the sailor if that was a true story and he said that it was. 'Where I am going, I have no use for these baubles', the sailor said to me. 'Your father saved my daughter and now I will give them to you. One treasure for another. Use them to decorate your own neck and ears and fingers when you get to be a young lady.' And then he walked away." Maisie stopped her story.

"Is this true, Mom?" Lincoln asked.

"As true as my love for you," Maisie told us.

"Does anyone else know that story?" Maisie shrugged and said that she had never told it to anyone before. "I put the jewels away and never remembered them until tonight."

"Gee," Lincoln gloated. "Just think, everyone else thought that Bold Charlie died, but...if what the old sailor told you was true, he escaped."

"I wonder if he ever tried to find Lady Pamela again," I was intrigued. "After all, didn't you tell me she married the Governor?"

"Maybe he felt that his hide in one piece was worth more than Lady Pamela's perfidious love." Maisie giggled, a sweet sound from such a lovely lady. "She certainly didn't waste any tears over him. I think she married the Governor a few months after she thought Bold Charlie had died."

"She was beautiful, but her heart was fickle." Lincoln intoned in a solemn voice.

"Lady Pamela, the fickle woman. Her love wasn't really true." Sasha, sighing with a ten year old's world-weary wisdom, stood up and took off the necklace and earrings. She put them back in the box. "You ought to wear them, Grannie. They'd look so pretty on you." She grinned, gap-toothed. "I'm going to make some cocoa now," she told us and went into the kitchen.

◆ ◆ ◆

Later on that evening, I told Maisie and Lincoln about what had happened today at work between Gerjeet and Anoop. Maisie laughed gently. "They will work it all out," she prophesied. "I remember when I cut my own hair! I thought your father was going to kill me, he was that angry!" Lincoln gaped. "You were only about five years old. My hair was down to my waist. It was unruly and difficult to manage. I was tired of such a burden, it took hours to wash and dry. And if I ever got a tangle, well, my land, I was in agony trying to comb it out. I just upped one day and took a scissors and cut it off." She began to giggle. "I didn't have the luxury of going to a hairdresser. It looked like I stuck my head into a threshing machine. I looked awful."

"I never heard about this!" Lincoln was stunned. "I never even heard you and Dad argue, nevermind have a fight!"

"We...it was a different world then. You kept your problems and such to yourself. It would never have done to let your child see a disagreement between a man and his wife."

"So what happened?" I was agog at these glimpses into Maisie's life.

"Oh, we went to bed furious with one another...and then...well," she blushed, an endearing thing to see on an older woman. "We made up. Actually, your father got to like my hair that way, once I had it trimmed a bit."

"Well, I'll be dipped!" Lincoln shook his head. "I'll be dipped." His eyes looked at his mother in wonderment.

◆ ◆ ◆

My telephone rang late that night. It was Andrea, so excited that she could barely speak. "Mom! Oh, Mom! I'm coming to Boston in four days!"

"Boston! Oh, Andrea, what wonderful news! Will we...I mean, can I see you? Will you be able to stay here for a few days?"

"We're actually arriving on Thursday night, then, on Friday, they are going to shoot a scene in Boston. At some bar. I'll be able to rent a car and drive up to see you Friday afternoon, spend the night, but I'll have to be back early Saturday to catch a plane from the Boston airport – I think they call it Logan - at ten in the morning."

"Oh, Andie!" I rejoiced. "I can't wait to see you, darling!"

We were so excited that our words tumbled over one another. I planned to have a lobster cook out at my house. Jenn and Scott would drive up and I would obviously invite Lincoln, of course, and Barbara and Horace. I would be so proud to have the girls meet my new friends, and I was certainly looking forward to having Lincoln meet my daughters and son-in-law. We hung up after exchanging all our news. Andie was going to call Jenn and I was going to send everyone directions to the little martini-olive-green cottage. I gave Macduff an extra hug and explained to him that he was going to meet Andie and Jenn. Hooray!

◆ ◆ ◆

The frost was still in the air at work the next morning. It was obvious to me that there had been no lovey-dovey make up between the welterweights in the old-fashioned girl from Pakistan vs. modern woman battle. Again, I was the go-between.

Bob Micklewright appeared for breakfast, nice as pie. Left me his customary cheap tip and acted as if his temper tantrum had never occurred. Who can figure men?

I called Barbara and Horace and invited them to join us on Friday night. I then called Lincoln and told him that Andrea was going to be in town for one night. I waxed rhapsodic over the lobster fest. "I can't wait until you meet Andie and Jenna and Scott on Friday."

"Uh, yes. Um, Friday." I suppose I was on cloud nine and didn't quite realize that his reply was less than enthusiastic. I should have been...what? More perceptive?

But, innocently, I babbled on, "We'll have such a marvelous time. Please tell you mother and ask Sasha if she wants to include Eva. Oh, nevermind, I'll call them. I want to ask your mother to Barbara's shower anyway. Oh, Lincoln, it has been months since I've seen the girls and Scott all together. I'm so excited. I've told the two big girls all about the two little girls and they're dying to meet them."

"Uh, well, um, yes."

"I'll order the lobsters. Do you think everyone will want them, or should I also get hamburgers and hotdogs?"

"Hot dogs and hamburgers are fine. Uh, I, um, I have to go. We're busy here, Reggie."

"OK. I'll take care of it all. Are you excited to meet them?"

"I, um…ah, it's really busy here, Reggie. I have to go."

"OK, I'll see you at six tomorrow night." Tonight, he was on call. To-morrow, it was *his* turn to join me for supper. He harrumphed and hung up. I called Maisie and invited her to both the Friday evening party and the shower. "It will be in two weeks or so, and I'll call you with the exact date." She seemed as excited as I was, and I was gratified.

Should I have sensed that a huge problem was lurking? Was I really stupid when it came to men? Maybe, but all I was feeling was delight. My daughters were coming to see me (oh, and my son-in-law, too. I really did love Scott, but hey, it was the girls that I was dying to see). My darlings would meet my darling, my world would be rosy and eve-ryone would be happy. Was that too much for me to expect? Any rain cloud hovering above was completely missed by my Pollyanna-ish joy in showing Lincoln off to Andrea and Jenn. And vice-versa. I felt sure that they would all like one another and that Lincoln wouldn't wear tight silk pants or try to throw up his food in the bathroom.

The Café was extra busy that afternoon. Phil Moore came in, asked me if I would go out to dinner with him again. I declined, as nicely as I could. He seemed slightly annoyed, and took my refusal with bad grace, making sotto-voiced remarks having to do with women who teased men and then rejected them. I forbore to enter into any kind of meaningful dialog on anything so silly on his part. When he left the Café, I could hear the angry rumble of his truck's engine. I shrugged and got on with my chores, mentally planning the menu for Barbara's baby shower. Phil was forgotten in an instant.

Rod Kuntz came in, grabbed six brownies, winked at me and told me that he and Diane were having dinner and he had promised to bring dessert,. He waved the bag of brownies at me. "Dessert it is! Do I need ice cream with these?" I told him yes and he left to get it at The Golden Harvest.

Hank stomped in, ate her usual and left me a dime tip. I guess whatever warmth had been kindled from our last visit has disappeared. Again, I don't know why, but her very presence made me nervous somehow. I guess, no matter how I tried, I didn't like her. Oh well, one couldn't like everyone.

180

It was such a busy day…Zee came in with a green Mohawk haircut and two new eyebrow piercings, one of them a safety pin that could have held up a flag.. She sat with Pauli Rines, Christa Heibel and a group of people from the high school. Mrs. Cee and Elroy came in for coffee and a brownie and then Debby from Just Us Chickens. She told me that the store was doing quite well with almost thirty artists participating.

"Come and visit us, Reggie," she urged. I agreed that I had been remiss and vowed to pop over as soon as I could. Ed and John from We Care Dry Cleaners joined her at her table and then Ed's wife, Chong-Ye, came in carrying a small brown shopping bag tied with brilliant green and purple ribbons.

"See, Debby," she waved the bag aloft. "I just made you a rich woman!" She opened the bag and took out a small box marked with the Just Us Chickens logo. Always nosy, I loitered to see what she had bought.

"Oh, how lovely!" I couldn't help exclaiming as Chong modeled the intricate beaded necklace she had just purchased. The necklace was made of some glass beads, shot with gold flecks, and encased in fine golden wire that had been knitted into a glittering sleeve.

"Is this the kind of stuff you have?" I marveled to Debby. Trying to look modest, but only looking proud, she nodded with delight.

"Well, I will certainly trot over and inspect your wares!" I was impressed. This was first-class jewelry! And didn't I deserve to buy myself some nice bauble? I sure did.

I never got back to chat any further with Ed, John, Chong-Ye and Debby, it was ever-so busy. The customers never stopped. I ran my little feet off and was happy when the door closed at three. The atmosphere was still chilly, with Gerjeet still directing each remark in an icy tone through me and Anoop pretending that he simply didn't exist.

I went around the corner and into Just Us Chickens. The necklace that Chong had purchased was gorgeous on her, but perhaps I wanted something a little more utilitarian for myself. I met Julie-Anne, a weaver and a newcomer to town, who was manning the store that day. Her wares were gorgeous and I bought a fantastic woven throw to spread over my on a chilly night. The throw was woven of alpaca…a brilliant blue that reminded me of the ocean on a sunny day. I also bought a pair of earrings that were made of beach glass and a framed print of the beach at Seapoint painted by Debby herself. Julie-Anne and I chatted, liked one another immediately and promised to get together to go antiquing one day. Poorer, but very pleased with my purchases, I went on my way.

My way then took me to The Golden Harvest. I was in the mood for a salad and picked up three different kids of lettuce and a basket of local tomatoes. In addition, I bought dried cranberries and pistachio nuts for a batch of *biscotti* and a container of Eva's salsa and a bag of chips.

As Lincoln was working, I stopped in at the animal hospital to say hello and donate the salsa and chips to his night vigil of being on call. No one answered my "hoo-hoo" and I walked in to an empty waiting room. I headed towards his office, my sneakered feet making no sound. As I approached the half-opened door, I could hear his laughter and wondered who was there with him.

"We'll leave at about five....yes, yes......fine. A dinner jacket, too...." I poked my head into the room. He was in his office chair, slumped back with his feet on the desk, the phone cradled under his chin. He saw me and nearly leaped up, banging his shin as his feet came off the desk.

"Hi!" I mouthed silently. I waved and shook the bag of chips his way. He looked a little red-faced, but I thought at the time it probably was because he had almost fallen in his haste to get up.

He tucked the telephone under his chin. "Oh, hello. I, um, I'll be with you in a moment. Uh, can you, um, ah, get a bowl for those?" He pointed to the chips.

"Sure." I went into the little kitchenette and rooted around until I found a plastic bowl in one of the cabinets. I opened the chips and poured them into the bowl and then went back into his office, thus missing the end of his conversation. I thought nothing of it at all. Not then.

We shared the chips and the salsa, accompanied by two cups of coffee from the machine that stood on his sideboard. Our conversation was normal...we talked about his day, my day, his animal customers, my human customers, what I was doing that evening (baking for the Café), what he was doing (waiting to see if some dog or cat needed his attention), how Anoop and Gerjeet were still feuding, Sasha's grade of a B+ in spelling, Barbara's baby shower, and the loss that the Red Sox had sustained against the hated Yankees last night. We also talked about Friday night and the lobster party. That's how I remember it, but perhaps I was the one who talked about Friday night and he was the one who didn't.

The telephone rang...a Bernese Mountain Dog from York was

whelping for the first time. Could Lincoln come over and check that everything was going well? He gathered up his bag and implements and we kissed goodnight. I do remember clearly that it was a very satisfactory kiss and only the imminent confinement of the Bernese Mountain Dog kept it from developing into more.

My night was spent baking, enlivened by a visit from Mrs. Cee who had made braised short ribs and wondered if Macduff might be willing to assist her with trash removal. Macduff was quite amiable, and he and I exchanged a handful of freshly baked green and red flecked *biscotti* for a heap of luxurious bones. Lincoln, who generally called me while he was sitting around waiting for more night emergencies, must have been busy, as the telephone was silent for the rest of the night.

◆ ◆ ◆

In the morning, Jenn called and we chatted for a few moments about Friday night. "I can't wait to meet Lincoln." She told me. "Am I going to be crazy about him?" I assured her that he was a very nice man and wouldn't wear high heels, satin pants or too much jewelry. I told her about my new purchases and she was eager to come later in the fall to spend more than a few days with me so that I could take her shopping and show her how much I loved her by buying her some nice things. Laughing, we assured each other of our love and hung up.

At The Loop Café, the atmosphere was still frigid between Anoop and Gerjeet. I wanted to bang their little heads together, but, tactfully, ignored them both and got on with my work.

Lincoln stopped in for coffee. He looked tired and something else had put some worries in his eyes. I presumed that he had been working too hard. Goes to show you how perceptive I was...

He told me that the Bernese Mountain Dog, whose name was – incidentally - Bernice, for goodness' sake, was fine and had whelped four beautiful puppies with scarcely any help at all from him. "It was a long night, though, and it was too late to call you when I finally got home."

"No matter," I smiled. "Jenn called this morning. They're bringing champagne."

"Um," Lincoln said.

"I want to ask a favor of you," I dug into my apron pocket. "Can you order the lobsters?"

"Uh," Lincoln said.

"Let's see," I ticked off the names on my fingers. "You and me, Barbara and Horace...that's four. Jenn, Scott and Andrea. Seven. Your mother, Sasha and Eva. Ten. ...Who else?" I screwed up my eyes. "Oh, and Mrs. Cee and Elroy. And Gerjeet and Anoop, and hopefully, they'll be speaking to one another by then. That's fourteen. Do you think everyone wants a lobster?"

"I…uh," Lincoln said.

I handed him five fifty dollar bills. "Get fourteen lobsters…maybe a pound and a half each, please. And if they have steamers, get about twelve dozen." I giggled. "Too bad we don't have the chance to go and dig some."

"Um," Lincoln said. He looked at the money in his hand. Again, did I miss his dread? Did I even think that there was something amiss? No. Not at all. "I'll get some steaks and some hot dogs at Carl's. Mrs. Cee is going to make her everlastingly famous baked beans and Barbara is bringing bread and rolls." He stood up, the money in his hand, and I noticed then that not only did he look tired and a little off-color, but that he looked a bit sickly.

"Are you OK? You look…I don't know, a little pale. Are you coming down with the flu?" I put my hand on his arm.

"I'm…fine." He clenched the money. "Reg, um…"

I patted his arm. "Are you sure?"

Gerjeet called me from the counter. "Pick up, Reggie!" He waved a platter at me.

"Gotta go. I'll see you tonight."

"I'll…I…uh,"

"Reggie!" Gerjeet bawled.

"OK!" I laughed, a carefree, happy woman, secure in the love…well, in the extra-special *like*, of a marvelous man… and turned to get Judge Emery's order.

When I finished with the Judge and six other customers, I went to clear Lincoln's table. The five fifty dollar bills were lying there by the side of the plate. I picked them up, laughing at the absent-mindedness of Kittery's finest veterinarian, and pushed them back into my pocket.

The day sped by. We were so busy that I never even got to sit for a moment. Barbara stopped in at two-thirty for coffee and two sugar buns stuffed with a cream filling made from the new recipe my cousin MJ had sent me.

"These are *good*!" she exclaimed, eating one of them in three bites. "Where'd you get the recipe? Is it one from your old grandmother?'"

"Nope. Not this time. This one is from Cousin MJ. The one who runs the bakery in Greenwich." Barbara groaned with delight.

"I know. She's a wonderful baker. Puts me to shame." I modestly lowered my eyelids.

"You're no slouch, either, Reg." Barbara licked a few sugar bits from her fingers. "I ate three of those gypsy heads yesterday!" We laughed.

"I'll call you when I get home and we'll cement the date of your shower." I promised her. Waving goodbye to me, with the last sugar bun stuffed in her mouth, she left after telling me that she and Horace were going to look at cribs that evening. I was so happy…*so* happy for them!

Bathed in this aureole of sunshine, I left work, stopped at *Enoteca*, chatted with Chris and Cheryl, the owners, and admired their new baby girl, Brook. Chris wanted to know if I could do some baking for them. "We can sell as much as you can supply." He told me. "My customers are foaming at the mouth for me to have your stuff." As flattered as I was, I regretfully declined.

"Maybe I should give up waitressing and just bake," I laughingly told him.

"You'll make a fortune and never even have to leave your house," he encouraged me. "We'd sell everything you could bring in, honest."

I told him that several other places along the Kittery Food Mile had also asked if I could supply them with baked goods. I had declined all of them. "I really like being out at the Café everyday. I've met such marvelous people…friends, acquaintances…I'd miss the socialization if I just stayed in my kitchen and baked all day." Chris made a sad face and told me that if I ever changed my mind….

I shook my head and wandered off to peruse their enticing stock. After some discussion with Chris, I bought some imported *tagliatelli* pasta, a container of their home-made marinara sauce, a couple of pounds of gorgeous cold cuts*, soprasotta, proscuitto*, chunked *salami* and cheeses, a long loaf of crispy Italian bread and then rounded out my easy dinner with fresh tomatoes and lettuce and trudged next door to *Cacao* where Susan admitted me into the charmed circle and gave me the family discount on a pound of chocolates.

As I set the table, put water in my big pot for the pasta and fanned the cold cuts out on a platter, I called Barbara again and set the date for her baby shower. I then called and extended baby shower invitations to Rose and Joan and Susan and Hannah Clutterbuck, Zee and Rita, Christa Heibel, Rachel from the library, Pauli from Traip Academy, Lisa and Julie from Fair Tide, Diane and Holly Pearson. I smiled in a very satisfied way to think that I had found so many new and dear friends. Who could have imagined that little Reggie, everyone's dull homemaker in her old life, now knew all these people to invite to join her in celebrating Barbara's happiness. I would invite Anoop tomorrow and see if her mother-in-law might also like to join us. Maybe this invitation could mend the breach in their lives. I'd ask Maisie and Sasha and Eva to come too. Eva and Sasha would adore helping to open the wrapped gifts and I knew Maisie would glory in Barbara's happiness.

As I shut a kitchen drawer, the Victrola sprang into action and the cowgirl voices and I sang in cheerful harmony. I was *so* happy.

◆ ◆ ◆

How did it go so wrong? I lay in bed, tears streaming over my eyelids, running down my cheeks, my nose watery and red. Macduff whined and snuggled closer. He knew that I was unhappy and tried his doggie best to make me feel better, but it would take more than Macduff, as much as I loved him, to heal my shattered heart.

I'd greeted Lincoln and his kiss swept me off my feet and into that rose-colored dimension that only new lovers can find. We clung to one another, molded body to body and only a smidgen of common sense and a phone call in the middle of it all from Jenna kept us from tearing one another's clothing off. Giggling as I spoke to my daughter, I playfully slapped Lincoln's hands away from my body parts and finally, as I hung up, I grabbed him in a huge, delighted hug exclaiming, "I can't *wait* to have you meet my girls." I whirled around in glee. "I know you'll like them, Lincoln, and I know they will be very impressed by their mother's good sense in seeing a man like you!" I turned in his arms and....and then....I saw his face.

"What's the matter?"

"Reg," he started. "I...um, I don't know how..."

"What's wrong?"

"Oh, Reggie. I'm so sorry. I can't be here, um, on Friday. Um, not this Friday, Reg." His voice croaked and my eyes snapped into his. His eyes sought the kitchen sink, the phonograph, the window...anywhere, any place he could avoid looking at me.

A cold, clammy hand clutched my soul. I heard a clicking sound and the Victrola started.... "*A false hearted loooo-ver, is worse than a thief*"....

"What do you mean, not *this* Friday?" What *did* he mean? "What's wrong with Friday?" My body, so pliant and soft when in his arms, went rigid. His eyes, usually so bright and sparkly, were bleak and somehow ashamed; again, they looked everywhere but into mine. "What's *wrong*, Lincoln?"

"I...I ...just, um, can't be with you on Friday night?" His traitor eyes dropped to the floor and the cold, clammy hand squeezed my soul tighter.

"Why not?" I forced him to look at me.

"Because…oh, Reggie….please try to understand. I…I have a previous commitment."

"A com*mit*ment?" I'm afraid my voice went to fishwife proportions. I knew…just knew, that there was more. And that I would not like it, whatever it was.

"Uh, yes." He squirmed under my steely, suspicious gaze. "I, uh, won't be in town."

"I know I don't own you, Lincoln, so forgive me for asking, but just who will you be with on Friday night?" The light in my eyes was dangerous. I knew. I already knew.

"Uh…I, um, made a…a…an appointment to be at a convention." He tried to make it sound better, but my heart told me that the bad part was yet to come.

"And who will you be with at this convention?"

"Uh, well, um…" There was no way out for him. "Athena". Oh, Lord. I knew. I already knew.

"Athena." My voice was a whisper. "You'll be with Athena."

"But, Reggie. It isn't like that…" He tried.

"Isn't like *what*, Lincoln?" My whisper got a bit louder. "And how many days will you be with her, Lincoln?"

"We'll be back on Sunday evening," he mumbled.

"The whole weekend?" I know my voice squeaked. Visions of Lincoln and Athena…their heads together…them together…tormented my miserable mind…I saw her hands on him, her red nails pointed and glittering, twisting themselves into his ….oh, no!

"Reggie, please try to understand. She asked me to be the speaker at the convention. I…said I would. I…I have to be there." His misery was the only thing that made me feel better. Not much better, but a little better. He reached his hands to my sides. His touch made me burn and I wanted to scream and scream and never stop. *Athena!* "You know she means nothing to me." I could hear the guilt in his voice. It hung in the air, in big, capital letters, G. U. I. L. T.

"When did she ask you?" I had to know. If it was ages ago, before he met me, well….then perhaps I could deal with it.

"The night of the opera," he had the grace to flush red. He'd known since then and never said anything. Even when we made love, even when we talked and whispered and made plans….That was it…I couldn't deal with it. She asked him to join her to spite me, I knew it, I knew it. To show me that she was in charge. And that he marched to her song.

I stood straight and tall and pushed his hands away. I stepped back. "Fine, Lincoln. You go to your Goddamn convention with your Goddamn Athena. I'll be here with your mother and your granddaughter and my family and friends. And you'll be with Athena."

"Reggie," his voice rose. "Be reasonable…"

"I don't *want* to be reasonable. I hate her and I hate you for being her puppet. You could have said something this morning, Lincoln. Or yesterday. Before I asked everyone and their uncle to come and…and…I was so proud of you, Lincoln. So proud that I could show you my wonderful family and so proud that they could meet…" A sob hiccupped out. "You could have *told* me…You could have even told *her* that you couldn't go, Lincoln. You could have said no, Lincoln." I wouldn't cry. I *wouldn't*!

"I…I'm sorry, Reggie. I didn't know how to tell you. I can't back out on her now. I made a commitment."

"And your commitment to *me*?" Again, my voice went spiraling out of control. "When you made love to me, was that any kind of commitment?" Lincoln's head snapped back, as if I had slapped him.

"Reggie, please…" He started. "I…I lo…" I waited, hoping against hope. His mouth opened and closed, but he said nothing more.

So I finished for him. Maybe I should have shut up then but I couldn't stop myself. "You're going away for the weekend with another woman and you want me to feel just fine about it all?" Macduff's eyes went from one of us to the other. He whined softly.

I *tried* not to let the tears fall, but, hey, I was only human. One miserable human being, that was me. My heart hurt so badly that I couldn't breathe. My voice cried out despite my determination not to beg. "You…used me, Lincoln. I thought…I…." I dashed my hands across my face, smearing the teardrops. I took a huge, sobbing breath. "OK, I was a fool. I don't own you and you owe me nothing." I made my voice as steel. "I really, really want you to be with me on Friday night. It's important to me. I want my daughters to meet you…to see what kind of a man that their mother is…seeing. Please, Lincoln, can you make some excuse and be with me?" I hated myself for begging, but I wanted to give him every opportunity to choose me over her.

He lifted his hand and then let it drop.

A red haze of jealousy, anger and impotent fury swallowed me. "You'd better go now. You'll want to get ready for your commitment." And I turned, sweeping the dishes off the table into a heap of broken china and tangled food, and went upstairs.

I listened at the top of the stairs. Would he come after me? Would he explain? Would he sweep me into his arms and apologize? Had I been too horrid? Should I have let it all pass? Should I have begged? Was I really such a fool? My heart thudded so fast that I could barely hear. But I did hear. The closing of the door and his footsteps leaving.

CHAPTER SIXTEEN

I don't know how I got through the night. My face looked ravaged and bruised in the mirror. I gulped two aspirins. Should I call him? Should I apologize? Should I grovel? Should I never speak to him again? My heart ached and my soul was shattered. I fed the dog and let him out. The two cats appeared and twined themselves around my legs, mewing in sympathy. The Victrola sang its warning to me and to all girls who trust…"*but a false hearted looooo-ver, will lead you to the grave…..*" and I felt as if I were, indeed, dead.

The record spun… "*not one main in a millll-ion, a poor girl can trust…*"

I'd come full circle. Full, miserable circle. I'd recovered from being stomped on, being cheated on, by Steve. I'd mended my heart and then, when I'd met Lincoln, I'd let my heart believe again….I thought that he…I thought that we….ah, I was such a fool. And here I was, a woman with her heart splintered once more. A dumb woman, a dumb fool. "*They'll hug you and kiss you, and tell you more lies, than the cross ties on a railroad, or stars in the skies…*"

I splashed my face over and over with cold water, squared my shoulders and went to work. What else could I do? I had been so happy the day before, and now…oh, Lincoln, Lincoln.

At the Café, others were faring better than I. Anoop and Gerjeet had obviously made up their differences. Anoop was radiant, her shining face glowing with contentment and that special look that told me that all was truly well between them. Gerjeet, his chest puffed out in male-type happiness, was whistling. I was delighted, really, at their happiness. I gave them both my best watery smile and set to work scrubbing the tabletops within an inch of their wooden veneers.

"All is well, now, Regina," Anoop shyly confided. "He had told me that I am beautiful and that he has changed his mind about my hair and dress."

"I'm delighted that everything worked out, Anoop. You two are such wonderful people, that I never doubted that you would re-kindle your happiness." I felt like sobbing, but I simply hugged her and wiped a stray tear away with my bus towel.

The doors opened, the customers poured in, and the day began. I hid my unhappiness away as best as I could and got on with my job.

◆ ◆ ◆

I was astonished to see the old yellow Mercedes pull into a front parking space and Maisie get herself out and come into the Café at about ten o'clock. Her kind, sweet face searched mine as she sat down all by herself at a table away from most of the customers. I came right over to her, hooked out a chair and sat down. She reached across the table and took my hands. "So what has that fool of a son of mine done to you?"

I didn't want to cry. I sniffed it all back and dabbed at my eyes with a napkin. "Oh, Maisie, I'm so miserable. I didn't even give him a real chance to explain himself and I…well, I don't have any authority to tell him what to do with his life or his time." My lip trembled and I bit it hard, so that I wouldn't embarrass myself further than I had already. "He doesn't owe me anything…"

She snorted. "Hell he doesn't owe you anything, my dear. He does nothing but spend every waking moment with you, talks about you the rest of the time….Reggie this, Reggie that. Reggie is the sun, Reggie is the moon." She took one of my hands up to her mouth and kissed it. "He owes you his love, his loyalty and his alliance, that's what he owes you, fool man."

At that, I broke down completely and sobbed into my apron. A few of the customers looked curiously at me, but had the grace to pretend that a crying waitress was an ordinary thing. Anoop noticed my distress, made a step or two in my direction, but Gerjeet took her arm and whispered fiercely to her and she nodded and went to help two customers at the counter.

"I hate Athena!" I muttered.

"Oh, everyone hates Athena," Maisie's voice held a hint of laughter. "She's a first class bitch and she revels in it. She's attractive, in that hard, glittery way, and she'll stop at nothing to hurt you." She patted my hand and put it back on the table. "You know, Lincoln really doesn't like her at all, but he feels responsible for her lonely life somehow. I'm not excusing his behavior, don't get me wrong, but I don't think he really understood just how she manipulated him over this."

"I know he's your son, but...I ...I maybe shouldn't have made such a fuss about it all." She made a tich-tiching sound and shook her head from side to side. "You know that I...care dreadfully for Lincoln...." I looked into her wise eyes, my misery hanging all over my face. "I was married a long time to Steve...he was the only man...except for Lincoln...but, maybe, I took Lincoln's attentions too seriously. Perhaps he doesn't feel the same way about me. Maybe he...he...just...wanted..."

"Nonsense, Reggie. Lincoln's not a man to have careless affairs. I know that if he...if you...if the two of you..." She tipped her head suggestively and grinned like a young girl. "You know what I mean."

"Well, I thought...." I spread my hands out in frustration. "I had invited everyone to my house to meet him." I snuffled and wiped my eyes. "I was so proud of what we had and I wanted the world, and especially my family, to see him and love him like I do...." I was astonished at myself. Here I was, using the "L" word and to Lincoln's *mother*, of all people. My heart told me that I was so miserable that I was beyond shame. I agreed with my heart.

"And he's let you down badly here, hasn't he?" She was so wise, this lady that I also loved.

"Made me feel like a fool. All dressed up, lobsters on the grill, all my family there, a big party...and no Lincoln. Shit!"

"Well, sweetheart, I'll be there and Sasha too. We'll enjoy your daughters and your son-in-law and we'll make him feel like a right idiot." She nodded firmly.

"Do you think I did the right thing? Should I apologize and maybe back track on my anger?"

"No." Her voice was firm. "I think that if a man and a woman have this special thing between them, no rat like Athena should be able to squeeze her expensive fur-clad body in between. She meant to make trouble and she did. She meant to make you jealous and miserable and she did. She even meant to make Lincoln look like a donkey's hind end and she did. It's up to Lincoln to extricate himself out of this mess." She patted my hands again and stood up.

"Sasha and maybe young Eva and I will be there on Friday. I'll bring potato salad. We'll get through this, my dear, and Lincoln will have to live with his stupidity." She hung onto the back of her chair, her hands gripping it tightly. "Don't think that I don't notice how Athena treats Sasha; how she belittles and browbeats the child. I dislike her very much and hope that, when this is all over, we never see her or hear from her again." Her chin went up in the air.

I stood up too. "When this is all over? I think maybe it *is* all over. I think maybe that I have lost a very precious thing." My chin went up too. "But I am not going to beg or whine any more." I sniffed again and wiped my eyes. "He's a grown man with a grown man's mind. I'll miss him like crazy if he walks away from me, but...if he does, then I'll know that it just wasn't to be." I sniffed once more and stood tall. She bent and hugged me, kissed me on the cheek and told me that she'd be at my house, potato salad in hand, on Friday night.

◆ ◆ ◆

Anoop cautiously approached me. "Reggie, is it an unhappy time for you?"

"Yes, today is unhappy, Anoop, but perhaps tomorrow will be better."

"I understand. Look how unhappy I was a few days ago, and now, the sun has come back out in my life." She nodded her head. "Gerjeet and I will be at your party. Can we bring Daria?"

"Daria would be the most welcome guest. Bring her playpen and we can set it up in the backyard. Sasha and Eva will pretend that they are her baby-sitters and my daughters will adore her." I patted her arm and went to wait on our newest regulars, Sue and George. My smile clicked on and I held my head high. "Good morning, Sue. Hey, George. Where are those adorable cats and what yummy food tickles your fancy this morning?"

I put on a good show. The day dragged. My spirits dragged. My rear end dragged. To get myself out of the doldrums, I threw myself into an orgy of cleaning. I emptied and washed every salt and pepper shaker, scrubbed each tabletop, folded and re-folded the napkins and smiled at each customer until I thought my face would split. I was even overly cheerful to Hank Ormand when she dragged herself in for coffee and a piece of cake. She straddled a solitary chair, taking off her yellow slicker and putting her wicked-looking knife on the table next to her water glass. I wondered if I should mention the knife, but thought that she might be in a bad mood and slice my throat if I annoyed her. I approached her table, vowing to be pleasant. Maybe it was the change in her gastronomic routine, for she was pleasant to me, too. Her tip, however, was a solitary dime. I picked it up and put it into my pocket, smiling despite my misery, watching as Hank moseyed out of the Café and into her truck.

What an old tartar she was! And harmless, really. How silly I had been to have bad dreams about her and her Boston-Strangler sized hands.

As I waited on Lou and Cynthia Kochanek, the doors to the Café burst open and in tromped the Bethany Boys, yellow slickers flapping and a huge basket of lobsters in their arms. They saw Anoop, guffawed loudly and dropped the basket of lobsters in awed appreciation of her new Americanized glamour.

"Dang, but you look gorgeous!" Daniel dropped to his knees in stunned awe. "Good enough to eat!"

"You're stupendous!" Not to be outdone, Jonah grabbed her and whirled her around to the delight of the patrons and the annoyance of Gerjeet. Anoop laughed, thrilled to be so openly admired.

"Leave him," Daniel pointed at Gerjeet. "Leave him and run away with me!"

"Silly man," Anoop made a pushing motion at him. "I am a married lady with a baby and a mother-in-law."

"Yeah," Daniel shook his head in mock fear. "There *is* that!"

Jonah shoved his brother halfway across the room. "It's the mother-in-law part that really scares him!" Daniel nodded fervently. Despite my misery, I had to laugh at the antics of these two handsome, silly buffoons.

Daniel swung one boot-clad leg over the top of a chair and seated himself at the round table. "Where's the grub? We're starving!" I plunked two menus down and recited the specials for the day, adding that we probably also wcrc now featuring fresh lobsters. I walked away to bring them coffee and then, struck by a thought, turned and asked them if I could buy fourteen…no, thirteen lobsters from them.

"Sure, honey. I'll give you my special price" Daniel patted the chair next to him and leered at me. "Whatcha doing? Having a big party?"

"Something like that. My daughters are coming to Kittery."

"Daughters! How old are they?" Jonah's eyes glittered.

"Too young for the likes of you!" I laughed and put their coffees down.

"They're never too young for me," Jonah clasped his heart. "I love 'em all. Young, old, whatever…just as long as they're pretty."

Jonah asked for two hamburgers and a bowl of chili. Daniel wanted the roasted chicken with pilaf and some tomato soup. As I turned to put in their orders, I was smiling. They were something else, these Bethany Boys, goofy and harmless, but at least, for me, they banished a bit of my misery and even brought a special cheer to the whole restaurant.

I made arrangements with them to bring the lobsters to my house on Friday afternoon. "Can you get steamers, too?" They nodded in handsome unison and assured me that their price would be the one they used for their best-looking customers. Again, even though my heart was in pieces, I left their table with my face in a grin.

Gerjeet's face, however, was a thundercloud. "They make me mad, those boys," he confessed to me. "They make joking remarks to Anoop, but I know they say those things to make me jealous."

"I think they're harmless," I tried to lighten up the atmosphere. "They flatter everything in skirts."

"I do not like it at all. Not with my Anoop." He slopped the chili into a bowl. "I will be happy when they depart."

"But you like their lobsters," I smiled gently at him.

He glowered at me. "I like the lobsters, but I do not like the lobstermen."

"You can always trade their lobsters for Hank Orman's lobsters. She'll never make a pass at Anoop."

He glared at me, then smiled sheepishly. "Nevermind. We will keep the lobsters and the Bethany Boys both." He handed me the plates. "Here."

I set the food in front of Daniel and Jonah. Jonah grabbed my hand before I could turn away. "Hey, Reggie, honey. When are you coming out on our boat?"

Their boat? Why not? Why *not*? The hell with Lincoln. My chin shot up and my eyes glittered. Reckless, I thought that a day out on the water might be just the thing to take the cobwebs out of my life. After all, Lincoln would be…wherever he was going to be…away with Athena…and for the entire week-end. Why *shouldn't* I go with Jonah and Daniel? I turned back to the table. "Why not!" I echoed my thoughts aloud. "When are you going out again?"

Their blue eyes lit up, like double twin lighthouse beacons. "Dang! Well, well, well." Jonah twirled his moustache like a dime movie villain. "The little girl wants to go lobsterin' with us, Daniel! Hot diggity!"

"We're going out on Saturday morning." Daniel's grin split his face. "We'll pick you up at seven in the morning, is that OK?" I nodded, pleased to have plans of my own. *The hell with Lincoln*, I thought again. *Two can play this game.*

◆ ◆ ◆

Three customers took the four-top in the window. One of the women looked familiar. "Who is that?" I motioned with my head.

"The older lady is Roberta Winslow. She is the unfortunate one who found that other lady's body." Gerjeet whispered to me. "The other one is her daughter. I think her name is Phyllis. And that is the husband. They own that other place to eat...Fox's Restaurant."

I remembered when Lincoln and I had eaten at Fox's. I blinked back tears and went to wait on the trio, introducing myself. The husband's name was Steve. They were pleased that I had enjoyed my meal at their establishment and had heard that I baked for Anoop and Gerjeet. I smiled and waited. Sure enough, they wouldn't mind it if I were to do some baking for them, too. With a grin, I again declined, with a promise that if I changed my mind, they would be among the first to have the chance to hire me for my talents.

I turned in their orders for three roasted pork sandwiches on onion rolls, with onion *au jus* on the side and told Gerjeet just how lucky he was to have me as his own personal baker. "Everyone in town is panting for my baked goods." I gave him my best and most provocative look.

He grinned back at me. Fervently, with his hand at his brow, he flattered me, "Reggie, you are the best. I am a lucky fellow to have you here." We saluted one another.

"And I am very happy to be here." Thus, in a blissful state of mutual congratulations, we fed a few more customers.

As busy as I was, I was still feeling glum. I threw myself into talking to each and every customer, thinking that I'd work my way out of my doldrums. I stopped again at Roberta Winslow's table and asked her how she was coping. Mrs. Winslow was ever so sweet and thoughtful, telling me that she was praying every night for the soul of Candace Chabot. And then she confided, "One of these days, they'll find the men who killed her and then I'll pray that the murderers will roast in Hell," she affirmed. "The bastards!" And she shook her frail fist in the air. Nice, sweet old lady, I thought. I'm glad she wasn't mad at *me*!

As I brought her some more coffee, I wondered to myself why she thought there was more than one killer. Somehow, I had seen the killer as one demon, but Roberta definitely said "bastards".

◆ ◆ ◆

My mood improved when Chief Bridge and my Tall policeman entered and took seats at the counter. I really liked the Chief. He had been kind and considerate to me, yet business-like. I knew that everyone else in town respected him and that the Police Department of Kittery was a well-run, professional organization. In line with some of the reasons for my admiration, Chief Bridge acknowledged Roberta and her entourage and went over to speak somberly with them for a few moments while the rest of the customers looked on with interest.

Chief Bridge came back to his seat, winked at me and picked up his menu. Tall ordered the curry special with Nan bread and the Chief wanted a large salad and a diet soda. He patted his belly and told me that Claire had insisted that he try, once again, to lose a few pounds. "She said that I was *not* to eat any of your cookies or brownies." His basset hound face was glum. Tall, who was not only tall, but slender, grinned like a wolf and added a sugar bun to his order. The chief was in a talkative mood and spent ten minutes telling me about some of the terrible things he'd seen in his years as a policeman in Kittery.

◆ ◆ ◆

I went home an hour later, still shaking my head and bemused at Chief Bridge's stories. Was the Chief's reminiscing an omen to me to only worry about things that were really awful and let the rest, even including Lincoln's treachery and perfidy, settle itself? Had I, too, been over dramatic about my own personal misery and its ramifications? Maybe, but I didn't think so and even if I had, it didn't make me feel much better.

◆ ◆ ◆

My evening was long and lonely. Twice, I almost picked up the telephone to call and apologize, to mend the rift, to….well, make it all come out better. But I resisted, especially when I realized that the telephone went both ways. If Lincoln couldn't call me to apologize, to get us talking again, to explain, maybe, just why he did what he did…well, then. Stuffed with self-righteous misery, I tossed and turned and had a horrible night filled with Technicolor imagination of what Lincoln and Athena would be doing on their long weekend together. My vivid and evil thoughts gave me new impetus to perhaps try dating other men. After all, there were lots of them around and some of them seemed to want to wine me and dine me. Why shouldn't I try the field a bit and see if I could enjoy myself with some new men and try to forget about Lincoln forever and ever. My ever-busy little brain told me: *because you love the big lug.* I shushed my brain. Reggie was about to start a new phase in her life. Reggie was going to step out a bit more. Reggie was going to stop being Lincoln's patsy.

◆ ◆ ◆

On Friday, I rushed through my chores at work. Barbara came in for lunch and in one second flat, looking at my face, knew that something was dreadfully wrong. "I'll tell you about it tonight, Barb." I promised her. "If I start to talk about it now, I'll start to cry and then…" Her deep eyes bored into mine, and I know she wanted to sit down , take me in her arms and make me tell it all to her, even though she knew that I was terribly upset. But, wonderful and perceptive friend that she was, she had the grace to let me deal with my misery on my own time.

"It's Lincoln, isn't it?" She did say that.

I nodded, my face unable to hide my misery. She patted my shoulder. "We'll talk later, honeybun. Let me know if there is anything I can do."

"It's good just knowing that you're here for me." The glum expression on my face saddened her. "I'll get through it."

She blew out a deep breath. "OK, but call me if you need me." I nodded, wan and sad, and waved goodbye to her. I finished my work, with one ear cocked to hear a telephone call that never came. You know, the one that should have been from Lincoln.

◆ ◆ ◆

I took half a day off on Friday, leaving The Loop Café right after lunch was served. I needed a few hours to get everything ready, shop, clean and prepare the house for the fourteen minus one people who were coming over. I bought hot dogs and steaks at Carl's Meat Market, salad stuff, fruit and butter at the Golden Harvest, buns and bread, including four gigantic *fougasses* from The Beach Pea Bakery, pounds of *salami, soprasetta, provolone,* smoked *mozzarella* and three cases of assorted wines from *Enoteca,* beer and soda from Frisbee's, and five pounds of chocolates from *Cacao.* Jenn was toting her special brownies for dessert and I knew that most of the guests would bring along a dish that they wanted to share. No one would go hungry.

I was excited that Jenn and Scott and Andie were coming. I was excited that I was giving a party and that so many of my new friends would be there to meet them. I was. I was. But the sunshine was rimmed with the sadness that Lincoln wouldn't be with me. I just couldn't stop feeling sorry for myself.

Daniel Bethany came by as I was putting the finishing touches on my preparations. I knew he was arriving by the screech of brakes on his truck and an unusual growl from Macduff. Daniel yelled a greeting, then barged into the house, staggering under a green plastic tote filled with squirming lobsters. "We gotcha some nice two-pounders. Figure you gotta impress your guests," he picked up one gigantic crustacean and wiggled it at my face. Actually, as big as the lobster was, it was dwarfed by Daniel's hand. "Hey," he called to Macduff, who was sniffing at his boots.

Macduff watched him for a moment, then, overcome by the marvelously fishy smells, allowed himself to be scratched behind the ears. I took the lobster from Daniel.

"Oh, he's gorgeous!" My praise was honest and fulsome. Andie, who adored lobster, would be in seventh heaven.

"I gave you some ice and a damp tarp." Daniel opened the tote and re-deposited his hapless prisoner under the heavy cloth. "They should stay nice and fresh." His handsome face grinned at me. "You want me to stay and show you how to cook them?"

"Thanks, Dan. I can cope." I patted the top of the cloth. "How much do I owe you?" Macduff sniffed rapturously at the tote. "Get out of there, Macduff." I swatted at him. "Dogs don't eat lobster!"

Daniel laughed, a booming sound, "Oh, yes they do! Watch out for him." He lifted the tote easily and put it on top of the picnic table. "I'll just put it up here out of harm's way. You can pay us tomorrow. We'll be here at seven to pick you up."

I'd almost forgotten our lobstering date. Almost. "What can I bring?"

"Just your sweet self. That's all, baby. Just you." He patted me on my rear end, winked and was gone. Macduff stood, watching him leave, his tail up, but not waving.

"Don't get any bright ideas about these bugs," I warned him. He gave me one of those special doggie looks. I think he was telling me that he'd really rather have one of the steaks.

◆ ◆ ◆

Andrea arrived in a bright yellow rental convertible. With her was a tall, handsome young man. After our shrieks of welcome, our hugs and kisses, she introduced him. "Mom, this is Bryce Adams. He plays Blaine, you know, the guy who picked me up in the bar."

Fortunately, I remembered the intricate plot of the soap opera and hugged and greeted Bryce. "I know you didn't know he was coming, but I figured, hey, what's one more!" Bryce shrugged helplessly. I understood how my adorable daughter could run roughshod over a young man's plans and hugged Bryce again.

"He can sleep on the floor," Andie advised me. And he did. As far as I know, anyway. But that was later that night and now…they all began to arrive. Barbara and Horace, Maisie and the girls, Jenna and Scott…all of my friends and my children…everyone but Lincoln.

And we had a marvelous time. The food was plentiful and delicious. Scott and Horace did duty as lobster-cooker-men and steak and hot dog grillers, Sasha and Eva helped Jenna and Andrea to serve. Everyone ooohed and ahhhed over Daria and she was always in someone's lap and was fed dreadful amounts of food all night. Everyone ate and danced and laughed and enjoyed themselves, and everyone was treated to the Victrola's magical performance. The big girls and the little girls cleared and did the dishes while we older folks sat and drank wine and told stories and watched the lights on the Piscataqua. Macduff was in his element, getting in everyone's way, his tail smacking only two wineglasses over. Even the cats made their appearances known, sniffing delicately at morsels of lobster before munching. Everyone marveled over the Victrola and the cowgirl singing. Everyone had a great time. Almost everyone. I smiled and grinned and gamely tried to also have a wonderful time. I saw Barbara and Maisie's watchful eyes on me and I assured them that I was fine. Just fine. And have another brownie or a piece of Mrs. Cee's apple pie. And maybe another glass of wine. Isn't this party the *best?*

Jenna and Andie accepted the explanation that Lincoln's absence was unavoidable. I intercepted one sisterly look between them, but, as Lincoln's grand-daughter and mother were present, I don't think they had any idea whatsoever that a real problem had occurred. Whatever anyone thought, I put my best face on and smiled and smiled for seven hours during the entire celebration and even afterwards at the late-night rehash of the party with only Bryce and Andie and me.

◆ ◆ ◆

As I lay wide awake, I reviewed the evening. On the one hand, I was delighted to have had the girls with me. I smiled to myself at the thought of Andie in the little room next door. My sweet child, here at last, with me under my new roof. And Jenna and Scott and their happiness together. Oh, I was a lucky, lucky woman. With such good friends and neighbors, a good job, and yes, I patted Macduff's flank, and you, too, my faithful furry companion.

And then the other side of my evening's coin...the absence of Doctor Grumpy...Lincoln. My love.

My imagination was wild. I could see...actually see, them together...Agggh!

She'd be sure to be dressed perfectly, her make-up and hair immaculate. She'd be there, wining with him and dining with him – her red tipped fingernails running though his hair and....suppose she *wasn't* dressed perfectly! Suppose she was naked...Suppose...and.....I rolled over, a bundle of misery, and dry-eyed, watched the sun slowly rise.

◆ ◆ ◆

In the morning, The Bethany Brothers and Andie and Bryce collided at the front door. I could see the admiration in Daniel and Jonah's eyes and the mutual gleam in Andie's as she eyed these perfect specimens of Maine's manhood. Bryce and I stood back, watching the three of them watch each other. It made me like poor Bryce even more than I already did.

My eyebrows had asked Andie if there was anything more than friendship between her and Bryce. Her eyebrows had answered that they were friends…just good friends. He seemed a lovely young man and I was happy to have made his acquaintance. We made some tentative plans to meet in the fall in California.

Andie and I hugged and kissed one more time and then they were gone…off to Boston and then back to California and their own lives. I picked up a picnic basket filled with a few tasty leftovers and jumped into the big truck, nestled between the fellows. Macduff whined as I left, somewhat solaced by the huge porterhouse bone that I placed across his dish. The cats were nowhere to be seen.

CHAPTER SEVENTEEN

I had given a lot of thought as to how I should dress for a day out on a lobster boat. I was aiming for cute, but not too cute or suggestive. So I wore a black maillot bathing suit underneath it all, then a pair of tan shorts and a yellow tank top. Sneakers were on my feet and a fanny pack around my waist. Tied across my shoulders was a light-weight yellow sweatshirt that said "Maine – The Vacation State" across the front. Just in case it got chilly out on the water.

Jonah and Daniel seemed appreciative of how nice I looked and how nice Andrea had looked. They made a few salacious comments about pretty young girls and then settled down to a ride with some silly and amicable bickering.

They had brought the *Mary Anne Seven* to the Kittery Town Dock behind Frisbee's store. She was a lovely boat, freshly painted and as clean as could be. Jonah helped me on board and Daniel followed with my basket and another tote that the boys had brought along. The boat had a small, but cozy cabin at the front, a long, low open deck at the back, bisected with a waist high bench over the engine that was obviously used for work,. The boat was loaded with three large blue barrels of fish on one side. At the other side, dozens of empty green totes hopefully awaited the catch.

I handed Jonah a check. "The lobsters were wonderful," I told him. "Everyone truly enjoyed them."

"Didja have enough?"

"There wasn't a claw left untouched," I smiled. "Everyone was stuffed with crustacean." He nodded, pleased to have been of help and folded the check into his pocket without looking at it.

"We use the fish to bait the traps," Daniel told me as he started up the engine. "You sit here," he patted the seat next to the wheel. Jonah cast off the thick ropes that held the boat and we nosed out of Pepperell Cove and headed towards the ocean.

202

As we traveled, Daniel gave me an impromptu tour of the houses and forts that ringed the water. I saw, without commenting on it, Lincoln's house and Bold Charlie's island.

The day was a perfect one, sunshine and a light breeze which kept the smell of the fish bait under cover of the barrels. As we approached the ocean, Daniel turned the *Mary Anne Seven* to the left. "Our trap lines are over here," he waved his arm in a vast circle, "parallel to Driftwood Island". I sat up and looked to see if I could spot Steve and Brianna's house. Either we were on the wrong side of the island or I couldn't see it. Just as well.

Jonah began to set up the bait station. He explained to me that Daniel would drive the boat as slowly as possible toward their floating buoys. "Our buoys are blue and yellow…see?" He showed me. "Every lobsterman has his own pattern on his buoys, just so there's no nonsense of anyone else taking your lobsters." His normally cheerful face was stern. "It's a killing offense if anyone takes anyone else's lobsters."

Daniel pointed to the top of the inside of the cabin. There were two rifles tacked up against the white boards and three wicked-looking three-foot long knives. "Anybody tries to steal our lobsters, well…." The two brothers gazed at one another and nodded simultaneously. "We'll kill them."

Somehow, I didn't think they were kidding. Not at all. I shivered despite the sun.

"Really?" I had to ask.

"Really." Daniel's voice was flat.

As we approached their first line of traps, I saw the rhythm of two men who had worked in synchronization with one another their whole lives. There was beauty in their handling the crustaceans, hooks and lines and traps, sustaining a graceful dance with their boat and the sea. It was beautiful to see. The engine throbbed gently, almost at a standstill. As the lines were lifted, each lobster trap was pulled on board and rested on the engine cover. One brother took out the trapped lobsters, measuring them by eye and tossing one or two back into the water. "Shorts", Daniel muttered, showing me a measuring stick which they hardly had a need to use. He then flipped each lobster over and threw a few more back into the water, explaining that these were "she-males", female lobsters holding eggs, a no-no to take. The rest of the lobsters – the good ones – were banded – large yellow rubber bands were stretched over each of the claws – "Keeps them from eating one another and from ripping your thumbs off." Then the banded lobsters were piled into the omnipresent green totes to be taken to market. As each tote filled, Jonah covered the lobsters with the ice that had been stored below deck. As each lobster trap was emptied, it was re-baited with the fish from the barrel, then dropped back into the water and the next trap dealt with.

"How can I help?" I asked, ready to do my duty.

"You can help by sitting there and looking pretty." Always a good girl, I sat back, propped against one of the fish barrels, and enjoyed myself.

As they worked, I saw a large patrol boat come our way. "The fuzz," Daniel said, waving at the men on the boat. They waved back and I noticed that each of the men in the patrol boat held a rifle. "They never bother us much", Daniel commented.

"Nah. We are good little fellows and follow the rules." Jonah waved a large crustacean at the patrol boat and then men laughed and waved back again.

"Do lobstermen ever try to sneak lobsters that are too small into their catch?" I was curious.

"If ya do, and get caught, it's very, very steep fine." Daniel tsked and shook his head. "A couple a hundred bucks a lobster, not worth the trying."

"We never cheat on lobsters," Jonah's face was fierce. "It's a jungle out here and ya gotta play by the rules." I nodded, as if I really understood. He reached up and took one of the boathooks off the side of the boat. It was a sharp, lethal probe and could probably slide through a whale in an instant. "Nobody f..., um, screws with us." He jabbed the hook at some imaginary assailant and I flinched back at his strength. "Nobody."

Daniel finished baiting the last trap on a string, washed his hands in the exhaust wash hose and then wet down the large stack of filled totes. He then wet a pile of canvas cloths and re-stacked the green totes, covering the ice and lobsters in each tote with the wetted canvas. "Keeps 'em nice and chilly."

He pulled two large, shiny, greenish-black writhing lobsters out of one of the totes. "Ever see lobsters hypnotized?"

I bit. "Hypnotized?"

He laughed, his white teeth shining against his sunburned face. "Ayeh. Watch." He held one lobster under his arm. The lobster resented this intimacy and flapped his tail angrily. Daniel paid no attention and took the second lobster in his huge hand. He turned the

204

lobster upside down and bent its claws into a triangle behind its head. The lobster's tail flapped in agitation. Daniel smoothed down the lobster's tail and stroked the top of the tail in a firm and rhythmic motion. "Simmer down, Mr. Lobster. Simmer down." In a moment, the lobster stopped fighting and curled its tail downward. It stood straight up on the wooden engine top, upside down, as still as...well, a hypnotized lobster. I gaped. Daniel and Jonah both laughed as Daniel performed the same magic on the lobster that was under his arm. And there they stood, on their heads, upside down, two hypnotized lobsters on parade. I'd never seen anything like it!

"How long do they stay like that?"

"Oh, a few minutes....there he goes!" The spell had worn off and the second lobster began to squirm and flap. Daniel laughed again and tossed both hapless creatures back into the tote.

The brothers stopped the engine and hooked the boat up to one of their markers. "Time for lunch," Jonah said, and I was astonished at how fast the morning had flown.

The boys had brought veal and pepper sandwiches, sodas and beers and I added my donation of leftover sliced steak sandwiches on Beach Pea's best *ciabatta* bread, my special banana bread, Maisie's leftover potato salad, a jar of pickles, a container of *Cacao* chocolates and a tin of shortbread cookies. We sat in the sun, eating with gargantuan appetites, watching little sailboats and large oil tankers go by, feeding our leftovers to the ever-circling, every greedy, cawing seagulls.

It was a lovely time and I almost, almost, forgot Lincoln.

The afternoon was spent taking care of the remainder of the traps and heading the boat homeward. Jonah drove the boat and I spent some time sitting on the engine cover listening to Daniel talk about his life and the women to whom he'd been married. The sun was hot on my shoulders and his voice buzzed on and on, justifying the three divorces and how 'the bitches', for that is how he referred to them, had messed with him. I wondered what the bitches' side of the stories had been, but felt that this wasn't the time to question his reminiscing.

Once, during the ride home, Daniel went into the cabin to get a beer for himself and a Coke for me. When he came back out, he was carrying one of the long sword-like knives that hung inside the cabin.

He handed me my soda and popped his beer open. "I wish I'd stuck the bitches with this," he waved the lethal weapon in front of me. The knife was long, with a twisted hook-like edge at the end. I was sure that one thrust from it would disembowel any sea creature, or errant wife that might try to get away. It certainly would have killed a human being with ease. I shuddered and felt cold again as I thought of Daniel getting angry at one of his wives. I remember Barbara's warning that he could be dangerous, but then he laughed and feinted, jabbing the point towards me. "I'd never really use this," he laughed, throwing his handsome head back. His golden pony-tailed hair flew in the breeze and I thought that he might resemble a pirate of days of yore. Handsome and free and fierce and elemental.

His brother laughed from inside the cabin. "Don't let that pussy fool you," he tossed his own golden-haired head. "Daniel ran like a hound from each of his wives. He was scared shitless of all of them!"

"Yeah, you say!" Daniel laughed sheepishly. "One of them – Suzanne – she was scary!" He laughed again. "Thought she'd bash my brains in one night!"

"She caught him hound-dogging around," Jonah joined in. "Chased him for three miles!" We all laughed and the sun shone again on the waves.

The boys snubbed the *Mary Ann Seven* to the dock. They declined my offer to help them clean up. "Nah, that's not a job for a lady." We all got back into their truck and they drove me home. I hugged them goodbye, thanking them both for a wonderful and memorable day. Daniel tried his best to kiss me, but I wiggled my head so that his lips only brushed my cheek. He laughed, albeit hollowly, and said that he'd catch up to me one of these days. They left, in a roar of engine, to clean down the boat, get rid of the bait and bring the lobsters to the market.

Macduff sniffed me with great curiosity, wondering at the smells that engulfed my clothing. It had been a nice day. I was happy that I'd taken them up on their offer to spend the day on their boat. I'd give Barbara a call to let her know that I was safe and sound. She'd muttered dire predictions of the Bethany Boys gang-raping me on the boat while I was tied to the mizzen mast, or whatever, and I would be glad to inform her that my honor was intact. And, as a matter of fact, hadn't even been threatened.

◆ ◆ ◆

After my shower, I sat on the back steps, Macduff and Sunny and Blackie the Cat at my feet. I felt sunburned and salty and tired. I had checked my telephone messages to see if – maybe – Lincoln had called, but there was only a message from Jenn telling me how much fun she and Scott had and how much they liked my friends and lamenting that Lincoln hadn't been able to be with us. As I had fibbed, just a bit, when explaining to the girls just why he hadn't been there, I still wasn't sure that they accepted my explanation. I'd hated to sort of lie by omission to the girls, but as Maisie and Sasha were in attendance, I suppose they had no option but to think that his absence had been unavoidable. Oh, I *wished* that things had been different. I *wished* that Lincoln had been there. I *wished*…ah, what was the use? It was what it had been. I smacked myself metaphorically upside my own head. I *wasn't* going to let him ruin the rest of my life. I wasn't.

That night, I fell asleep right away, surprising myself. Unfortunately, I had horrid nightmares about cats and dogs drowning, being trapped underneath the ocean in green metal lobster cages.

◆ ◆ ◆

On Sunday, I awoke, gritty-eyed, shaking off the tail of some other terrible dream that I couldn't quite remember. I showered again, patting lotion on my slightly sunburned skin. The cats were nowhere to be seen, even when I let Macduff out for his morning ablutions.

I tried not to dwell on the fact that Lincoln would be home some time tonight. I tried not to dwell on the fact that he hadn't called me last night. I tried, but it really wasn't working. To keep my own personal cobwebs from blighting the rest of my life, I decided to ride my bike to work and let the sunshine drive my sadness away.

Did it work? Nah. And my misery seemed to have infected a few others. Although Gerjeet and Anoop were not back to their horrid non-speaking, they obviously had sustained some sort of problem. Gerjeet's face was stony as he greeted me and Anoop's generally sparking eyes were downcast. I hated to see them like this. Trying to set my own sorrows aside, I was as cheerful as possible, joking and cajoling them both into a better humor.

Bob Micklewright was first in line, settling himself at his customary deuce. His face seemed pinched and angry and my greeting to him went unanswered. Tired of all of the emotions in my own life, I simply ignored him and brought him a menu and his usual black coffee. With a peevish gesture, he shoved the coffee back at me, sloshing it all over my apron and sneakers.

"I didn't order this," he sniffed.

"No problem," I mopped up the mess, being sure to drip a bit of the coffee-soaked bus-rag onto his lap. I was damned if I was going to let him upset me even more than I was upset already. "What *would* you like?"

"Orange juice, a glass of water and a cheese omelet with wheat toast…and don't burn the toast."

I smiled with a serenity that should have had me canonized. "Certainly, sir." I almost saluted and turned away. Burned toast indeed!

207

Chief Bridge and his wife, Clare appeared. The chief looked grey, harassed and tired; Clare looked fantastic. She was a tall, rather exotic woman who sculpted magnificent jewelry. She was a living mannequin for her wares, being outfitted in a long, simple black dress festooned with a medieval necklace of gold and unusual chunks of glittering jewels. Long, dangly earrings complimented the necklace and her hair was skewered with – well, they looked like chopsticks to me – chopsticks decorated with pearls and emeralds.

I took their order. Clare was chatty and turned to talk to a table of women to her right. The chief sunk himself into a hot cup of coffee and ignored the chatter.

Micklewright's order came out of the kitchen. The omelet was beautiful, golden and puffy with cheese, the toast done just right. I placed it gently in front of him. He pushed it away. "I thought I told you not to burn the toast!" He hissed at me, loud enough to have several other patrons turn around to see what was going on.

I thought that I showed enormous restraint in not shoving the toast where the sun don't shine. "I'll have the cook re-do it to your liking," and removed the plate. I brought it back to Gerjeet who had been observing the entire transaction, his black eyes snapping.

"I will put the toast into his nose!" Gerjeet fumed. Anoop patted his hand, her own personal annoyance with Gerjeet superseded by her loyalty.

"I have two nice pieces of toast here," she reached under the counter. "They fell on the floor." She smiled at her husband and her best waitress. "I was going to save them for the next dog that comes in. Please to take them to our wonderful customer." And so, I did.

I felt much better after that.

The morning was a busy one, thank goodness. The rush of customers forced us all to pay attention to business. I was glad to note that Gerjeet forgot to be grouchy as he took platter after platter from Anoop's hands, and that I – even I – put my wretchedness temporarily behind me as I took platter after platter from Gerjeet to the crowded tables.

Everyone in town was there for brunch. Rodney Kuntz and Diane came in for banana crepes and mango sauce, Barbara and Horace joined them, scarfing down two orders of our new Dutch Baby Apple Puff with Rum Sauce and then settling in on the patio with the newspapers. Thane, Holly and their girls sat at the next table (well, Holly and Thane sat at the table, the girls lay quietly in a patch of shade below), Joan and Rose and Shotzy at the next. I waited on Roberta (with Gizer at her feet), Phyllis and Steve who told me they needed a break from their own busy restaurant

The day was lovely and everyone was talking and laughing. But, despite the laughter, I felt a sudden shaft of sadness. A piercing stab of memory came over me. I saw Jason Morant's body in my mind's eye as clearly as I had seen it that day on the island. Why did his image come to me this morning? Was it because I was so sad underneath? I felt bad for myself, and I felt bad for the families of Jason and Candace. I shivered. I looked up and thought I saw a similar cloud of sadness pass over Roberta's face. Like me, once in a while on a beautiful day, I wondered if she was remembering the body that she had found. I shook myself and the vision of Jason wafted away as Gerjeet yelled for me to pick up a plate of kedgeree.

Boy, were we swamped with customers. Practically the entire population of most of Portsmouth and Kittery was out there, in the morning sun, eating and eating and eating some more.

Bob Micklewright finished every mouthful, including the dusty and dubious toast, left without giving me a dime and my mood improved even more. I heard the exhaust from his truck roar off and even the exhaust sounded angry. The roar upset me more than I'd like to admit. What was it with me and trucks? A vision of two women chopped to bits flashed through my mind. I was certainly filled with the heebie-jeebies this morning, wasn't I? I cleaned off Bob's table, clashing the dishes together. Screw him, I thought and looked up as yet another truck pulled into the front parking space.

Phil Moore came in, hand in hand with a woman young enough to be his granddaughter. He glared at me, daring me to make a comment. I simply laughed to myself and, with a serene smile, greeted them both.

As the morning whizzed by, I felt better. Maybe what I needed was a series of small challenges to make me forget my own problems. I almost laughed, thinking that Bob Micklewright was a small challenge indeed. Very small. Gerjeet forgot whatever was bugging him and I found him patting his wife's rear end as I came into the kitchen. Giggling, they sprang apart. The morning got better and better.

As the hoards ate and left, new customers came and reclaimed the empty tables as fast as I could clean them. Diane and Rod left, and Barbara and Horace moved themselves and their newspapers over to Claire and Alexander Bridge's table. The chief still looked tired, but his grumpy mood had lightened and I caught a snatch of conversation about the Red Sox as I passed his chair.

At three, we figuratively closed shop. Barbara and Horace were still outside, and we chatted as I cleaned up and then stacked the chairs away. Their new baby was due in a day or two and they wanted me to come over and view the seven million toys that they had already bought for him. I promised to cycle over in a half hour and they left to walk home.

"Whoo!" I slumped at the counter as Gerjeet shut the doors and flipped the sign on the door from "WELCOME" to "CLOSED". "I'm pooped."

"We were so busy!" Anoop sat next to me. "So many customers and so much food." She opened the glass cake stand that held the detritus of my baked goods. "Only crumbs for the little mice left. You must bake a lot tonight, Reggie."

Gerjeet went behind the counter. "So busy today. I cannot believe how well we did." He ching-chang-ed the cash register and rummaged through the money. "We will be rich people soon."

I stretched and pulled a handful of money from my apron pocket. "Not that I didn't earn it, but I made a fortune today." I stacked coins into piles and smoothed out wads of crumpled bills. "Mmmmm," I wiggled my cramped shoulders. "I don't really feel like making cookies, but…a girl has to do what a girl has to do." I watched as Gerjeet came around the back of the counter and stood behind his wife's stool. He began to gently knead her neck and back. She leaned back into his chest. Whatever had been bothering them seemed totally forgotten.

"You go home now, Reggie. Get a good night's sleep."

I dumped my tips back into my pocket. The euphoria and odd moods of the Café's busy day ebbed slightly as I wheeled my bicycle towards Horace and Barbara's house. It would be a long night tonight. I knew I would brood over Lincoln and my highly imaginative thoughts of his weekend activities.

Barbara's joy and Horace's eagerness tamped my moodiness onto the back burner. For her sake, I allowed myself to share in their genuine happiness and anticipation. They had painted the baby's room a pale blue and put down a blue and white striped rug. Horace had found an old, comfortable-looking rocking chair and painted it a dark blue which matched the blue curtains at the windows. He'd put up shelving and piles of stuffed animals and boxes of newly-purchased tiny boy-type clothing were everywhere.

"What is there that you haven't already bought that anyone can give you at the shower?" I exclaimed, holding a stuffed hippopotamus in my hands. "This little boy is going to be the luckiest son-of-a-gun in the universe!"

"Not as lucky as we are." Barbara's face glowed.

I turned down their invitation for supper, begging that I had to bake. "You customers ate everything in sight."

I pedaled homeward, stopping to buy some sugar and eggs at the Golden Harvest. As I turned into Schooner Street, a wave of self-pity engulfed me. How could I bear my life now that Lincoln was no longer in it? I snuffled my way into the house.

Macduff greeted me with enthusiasm, but even his obvious adoration wasn't enough to lift my spirits past the soles of my coffee-spattered sneakers.

I threw myself into baking, complimenting my crummy mood with a CD by Lena Horne that sympathized about her man and how she loved him so. Lena understood men and their low-down womanizing ways. After four hours, I was exhausted, both physically and emotionally. I took off my apron and groaned at the aches in my back. My kitchen was piled with the fruits of my melancholy: cappuchino bars, *minni di sant'agata* cookies, brownies, *biscotti*, *pignoli* cookies, cakes and shortbread jostled for room and six ricotta pies were cooling, stacked on the cook top. I needed a glass of wine, a shower and a pillow for my head. Hopefully, I'd sleep well and not think about my former man and how I loved him so.

And then, a small - but horrid to me - disaster occurred. I was snapping off the light above the Victrola, when I jostled the table and lost my balance. Falling, I grabbed at the edge of the table, saving myself from a bad fall, but knocking the old Victrola to the floor. The crash broke the Victrola's horn and smashed my haunted cowgirl record to pieces. "Oh, Nooooo!" I mourned the loss as I picked up the Victrola and laid it back on the table. "Oh, Sunny, I am soooo sorry!" I tried to push the horn back on, but it was thoroughly broken off. Maybe Lincoln could mend...no. Maybe Horace could mend it for me. And as for the precious, mysterious record, it was in eight pieces. I should have thrown them away, but, in my sad mood, only placed them gently back inside the little wooden cabinet. "Sorry, girls," I lamented out loud. I'd miss their song. I shut the cover down, hiding Nipper, the horn, and the wreckage of my cowgirls' lament. I hoped the ghosts of Sunny Sunder-gaard and Catherine Black would understand.

I sighed, a deep, unhappy sigh. As I started up the narrow stairs, the telephone rang.

CHAPTER EIGHTEEN

"Reggie!" Sasha's scream froze me. "Help me!"

"What is it? What's wrong?"

"Grannie Fair! She's…I don't know…" Sasha groaned and I could sense that she was close to hysteria. "She fainted! I think she's…maybe she's…"

"*Sasha!*" I spoke sharply. "Tell me…*exactly*…what's the matter." A clammy hand squeezed my heart. What had happened?

"She's…I can't wake her up! Oh, God, Reggie. I don't know what to *dooooo!*" Sasha's voice rose spiraling out of control..

"Darling, is she breathing?"

"Yeeees, but not much."

"Is she awake?"

"No. I think she's not good. Her face is bluish, Reggie. I'm so frightened!"

"OK, pet. You call 911 and get the police there. Tell them where you live and make them stay on the line with you. I'm coming right now. I'll be there, darling. Hold on and don't be frightened. I'll be with you in a flash."

I flew out of the house, frightened, scared at what might be happening…my heart thumping in suspense, my gut ripped with fear. I tore out of my street, speeding and careening along the roads. "Come on, come on!" someone was urging and then I realized that I was praying aloud. My car screeched around corners and I sped through a red light, after slowing for a moment to be sure that no one else was impeding my stampede.

I skidded into Lincoln's driveway. The lights were on and Sasha was at the door as soon as my car stopped. She was dancing with frantic apprehension and I swept her into my arms for a swift hug. "Show me!"

I ran, following her into the kitchen. Maisie was on the floor, sprawled in a rag-doll position. Her face was pasty, grayish-blue. I bent

213

to her and listened. She *was* breathing, thank God. Shallow, strained breaths, but she was alive.

"I called 911. They're coming now." Sasha bent with me, patting her grandmother's face. "Grannie? Grannie? Can you *hear* me?"

"You wait at the door. Open it up and make sure that they see you. I'll…well…Go, now, darling." I turned back to Maisie's limp body, biting my lip. What the hell should I *do*?

"Maisie!" I patted her cheek, then patted it a little harder. "Wake up, Maisie!" Ohgodohgodohgod! What did I know about CPR? Nothing at all. I'd never taken any classes nor learned anything that was really useful! Castigating my lack of knowledge, I nevertheless, did what I thought might be helpful. I knelt be her side, pinched her nostrils together lightly, and breathed into her mouth. "Huf. Huf. Huf."

Then, I pushed on her chest, trying not to hurt her further. Ohmygod, suppose I broke her rib and killed her! "Huf. Huf. Huf." And then three short, light pushes. And again. "Huf, Huf, Huf." And again. And again. And again.

She coughed. A dry, husking sound. I screamed, "*Maisie!* Maisie, can you hear me?" She opened her eyes; they were dull and unfocussed. I breathed again for her. "Huf, Huf, Huf." And then she coughed again and sucked in a great lungful of air. I noticed with wonder that there was water on her face and then realized that it was my falling tears. She stirred, moaning and then tossed her head from side to side.

Gently, oh so gently, I lifted her head, slipping my arm under her neck. "Can you hear me, darling?" She nodded, a tiny, tiny motion, and her hand found mine. Behind me, I heard the sound of sirens and the crunch of tires on the driveway. Thank God, they had come.

They were gentle, swift and efficient. Worth every cent that they were paid and more. One lady and three men. They pushed me away, polite, but firm, asking me questions, and probing Maisie's mouth and chest. One attached a breathing apparatus to her face; one gently slid an IV into her blue-veined arm. Maisie's eyes flickered and she moaned and they reassured her that she would be fine and that she was a brave woman. They set a stretcher next to her and wrapped her securely before sliding her onto it.

Sasha and I clung to one another, drawing some warmth and hope from our frantic embrace. "How…is she…?"

The ambulance lady person, with a nametag that proclaimed her name as "JILL" gave me a quick nod. "You did well. I think she's going to be fine." Two of them men lifted the stretcher and Maisie was whisked outside and into the ambulance. "Follow us," Jill instructed us.

We drove in my little red VW, behind the ambulance, the siren undulating and out hearts beating in screaming rhythm.

At the hospital, Maisie's stretcher went into two doors that flapped closed, leaving us behind. A nurse guided us to a desk and took a sheaf of papers out. She smiled, so kind, and told us that we'd be helping best by getting the administrative part done...and by praying. Sasha was marvelous. She knew almost all that was needed, assisted by the hospital's medical records of Maisie's previous visits there.

"Let's get you two a nice cup of tea," the nurse guided us to a small sofa in a hallway. "The doctor will be with you as soon as he can." She smiled and patted Sasha's wild red hair. Try not to worry."

Sasha and I huddled around the transitory warmth of two mugs, our arms around each other, our faces creased with despair. After what seemed like hours, but was only 45 minutes, the nurse came back to us. She was smiling and our hearts leaped in our throats.

◆ ◆ ◆

"OK, I'll be back with Macduff and some clothes in twenty minutes." I settled Sasha back into the kitchen. "You stay here and keep trying to get Grumpy on his phone." I tried not to let my mind or my imagination interfere with anything but keeping Sasha soothed and at ease. "Grannie Fair is doing better and better. They'll take good care of her tonight and she'll have a good night's sleep. We can go and see her first thing in the morning." I smoothed the wiry red hair on the little girl that I loved. "You get lots of pillows on your bed and we can cuddle together with Macduff tonight." I kissed her and she clung to me.

"Will she really be all right?"

"Yup."

"*Really?*"

"Yup. I promise. She's going to be just fine." I patted Sasha's behind. "You did everything right, honeybun. You took good care of her and kept your head in an emergency. Your Grand...Grumpy...he'll be so proud of you." I grabbed her tight and we both cried a few tears of tension and relief.

"I'll wait right here by the front door." She was trying to be brave. "I'll be here, right here, until you get back," she sniffed and then tried once more to call Lincoln. The telephone buzzed and buzzed, but no one answered.

I cursed him mentally. Then, "Let's call Barbara and tell her very quickly what's happened." I took the phone and called. Barbara's shocked but relieved voice wanted to know if there was anything she could do.

"Not at the moment. Maisie's in Intensive Care, but she's stable and breathing well. I think it was a little stroke." I listened for a moment as Barbara mentioned her feelings about Lincoln and his parentage and discoursed on why he hadn't been at home for this particular evening.

"We'll keep trying to get in touch with him." I interrupted her rantings as calmly as I could. "Yes, Barbara, Sasha is right here."

"Oh," Barbara caught on. "OK for now, but when I find him…"

"I'm going back to the house to get some clothes and Macduff. I'll call you when I get back here. I'm going to stay here tonight with Sasha."

"Of course. I'm sorry that I blew up, but…"

Despite all of the evening's tension, I smiled. I sort of felt the same way, alleviated by a sharp, smug shaft of he'll-be-one-sorry-bozo-when-he-finds-out-what-happened-while-he-was-with-the-bitch satisfaction.

"Keep all the lights on," I kissed Sasha again. "I'll be right back."

◆ ◆ ◆

I drove as fast as I could back to Schooner Street. The house was just as I had left it several hours before with Macduff's face peering out of the front window. I know that there was no way that Macduff could have known why I flew out of the house, but, I swear, his grizzled face was creased in worry and his whines, as I came in, were frantic. I fell to my knees, grabbed his furry face and buried my head against him. "Oh, Duffers, thank goodness she's fine." He licked my face and reminded me that he needed to go outside.

I opened the back door, opened the screen and let him out. As he presumably did his business, I dashed upstairs to pack a few things for the night and tomorrow. As I packed, I tried Lincoln's cell phone again, forgetting about my own personal feelings and urging him to answer. "Come on! Come *on!* Answer the damn phone," was, I believe, how I put it. Whatever he was doing and wherever he was doing it, he didn't answer. I closed my little suitcase and started downstairs. I heard a screech of brakes and a pound of footsteps at my front door.

"*Thank goodness. Lincoln is here!*" I ran down the rest of the stairs as the door flew open.

CHAPTER NINETEEN

I stopped at the foot of the stairs in confusion. It wasn't Lincoln after all. It was Daniel Bethany. "Daniel? What…what are you doing here?" I was so dumb, I wasn't even afraid of him.

"I've come to see you, Reggie." He grinned, a handsome, wholesome grin and shut the door behind him.

"Oh, Daniel. I can't talk now." I stepped forward one step. "Maisie Fairweather's had a stroke and I…" I noticed that he was still grinning and that he had stepped one step closer to me. I felt a nervous jolt to my heart. What was going on?

"Who gives a shit about Maisie Fairweather," He loomed over me, so good-looking, so harmless. Like a big old dog with a wagging tail. "Me and you," he moved his arm and I could see the long, wicked knife he held. The one that usually was nailed into place on the wall of the cabin of *The Mary Ann Seven*. He waved it up in the air. "Me and you."

"Daniel," I tried to keep the rising panic from showing, "What's wrong?" I backed up and my heel hit the bottom step.

"Nuthin' wrong, honey. Just you and I going to have a little fun here." He lunged and grabbed me by the arm. I tried to draw back, but he was so much stronger than I was. He pulled me, like a puppet doll, forward and up against his broad chest. He smelled good, like fresh air seasoned with a little bit of salty tang. I was frightened out of my wits.

I pushed at his chest and he relaxed his grip. I shoved him and tried to turn – to run. I grabbed at the first thing that I saw, a square white vase that usually sat on the hall table. I threw it at Daniel's head. He ducked, laughing, as the vase sailed harmlessly by him and smashed into the wall.

"My, my, Reggie, honey," Daniel picked up one of the large pieces of glass. "What did you want to do that for?" He inspected the glass, rubbing his thumb against the sharp edge. "Nice vase like this. You want to take *care* of it." He made a tsk-tsk-ing sound and threw the glass back on the floor. "A girl like you might even cut herself on it." Horrid pictures of Sunny and Catherine flashed in front of me and I cringed. "Pity. I just don't think it can be repaired," he shook his head sadly, as if to himself. "You ought to be more careful."

Frantic, I tried to back away. If I made a dash for the door, could I open it and get away? I tried to judge the distance. He followed my thoughts and put out his hand. "You can't get away, Reggie, honey." I flattened myself up against the wall. Gently, he stroked my face as my heart hammered and my blood ran cold.

"Are you afraid of me?" I didn't know what to say. *Of course I'm afraid of you* didn't seem to be right. He shook his head and grinned his boyish grin. "No need to be afraid of me. Not yet, anyway."

Gently, he pulled me away from the wall and captured my boneless body into his embrace. I wanted to scream and rip his face with my nails, but I acquiesced, hoping that next door, the Clutterbucks could hear the hammering of my heart.

He kissed my hair, murmuring soft nothings while I tried not to writhe away; frightened that one false move on my part might send him careening further down this path of madness. But how silly, this was *Daniel*! He was my *friend*! And so I tried to reason with him.

"Please let me go, Daniel, you're hurting me."

His grin got wider. "Yeah." My flesh crawled. Ohmygod! He was enjoying it!

He half-pushed, half-carried me toward the sofa. "You've been askin' for it since I met you." He bent toward me and kissed me, hard and hurtful, his white teeth almost ripping at my lip. I tried, oh, lord, how I tried, not to scream. Maybe…maybe if I just let him…A thought flashed through my head. I remembered a PBS special about rape. You shouldn't try to fight it; just let them do whatever they were going to do. Being raped was not as bad as being killed. My body recoiled. Those PBS people, what the hell did they know.

"Stop, Daniel. Please." I twisted my head and tried to break his hold on me. Bad mistake. I should have paid more attention to the documentary. He hit me then, a heavy, hard blow across my face. My eyes watered and I gasped in pain. He was going to hurt me and then rape me and then who knew what. I screamed and tried to fight back. Another bad mistake, but what could I do?

He grabbed my fist in his hand and laughed again, a rich, rollicking sound. "Oh, you love it, don't you?" And he shook me then, like a spoiled child might shake a doll just before they threw it away. "Whassamatter? Don't you want me?" His expression was one of genuine hurt bewilderment.

What should I do, oh PBS? Capitulate? Pretend that I wanted him? What?

218

"Daniel, please don't hold me so hard. I want to talk with you before…" Oh well, I did try. He laughed again, but the laughter was evil, not so jolly, not so jovial.

"You little bitch. You're like all the rest." I sucked in my breath. *What rest?* "You women, you tease a guy…lead him on. All smiles and wiggles and then, you pretend that you never led me on." Had I led him on? No! Never! "You're like them women here last year." Oh God! Oh *God*! "Them lesbians." He held me up and shook me again. "Lesbos! Huh! All they needed was a good poke from a real man." He made a sound of disgust. "Show them what a man can do." He shoved me again, further into the living room. "But you're not a lesbian, Reg. No sir. You're a real, live woman!" He grinned at me and loosened his hands. I spun out of his grasp and backed away, frantically trying to think of where I could run, what I could do. My heart was hammering so hard, I thought I would die. Shit, I *was* going to die if I didn't figure out how to get out of this nightmare! He was going to butcher me just like he butchered Sunny and Catherine! *Oh, Lincoln, Lincoln, please! Save me, Lincoln!*

There was a sharp bark from the backyard. Macduff! Oh, *Macduff!* I heard his nails scratching at the screen. He began to whine and yip, high staccato barks. Perhaps someone might hear him and come to help! I opened my mouth to yell and he was there, grabbing at me again. He lifted the knife…the long, wicked sharp knife. The knife that had beheaded Catherine and chopped Sunny into pieces. Oh *God!*

A sound behind him…A needle dropped onto the record and a voice began to sing, *"On top of Old Smoooo-key…"* But the record was *broken*! *Broken!* Wha…? Wha…? The noise distracted him for a moment and his attention turned. At that second, Macduff burst through the screen door, his fangs bared and his hair on edge. He leaped through the air and sunk his teeth into Daniel's arm. Daniel tried to shake him off. I grabbed whatever I could get my hands on - a lamp from the table. I swung it at Daniel and it shattered against his head.

He howled in pain, swung the knife at me and …I screamed again as the blade bit into my left arm. Blood spurted, blinding my eyes for a moment and Daniel again tried to get away from Macduff's attack. Oh, Macduff! *Macduff!* Macduff was a big dog, strong and aroused, but Daniels's strength was even more prodigious and he smashed the dog against the counter and loosened Macduff's grip. Macduff fell to the ground, rolled over and sprang back up to his feet, making the most unearthly noise. Oh, *Macduff!* I hit Daniel again with the lamp as Macduff leaped again, aiming for Daniel's throat. Daniel raised the knife and stabbed Macduff, ripping through the rough coat into the flesh below. The knife slashed again and again, tearing into the dog. Macduff and I both screamed. Macduff's furry body fell in a heap and he lay still on the floor. I wailed and my cry of grief seemed to spur Daniel's madness. His arm was bleeding where Macduff had attacked him. He looked at himself with a curious look, then laughed and switched the knife to his other hand.

"Oh, babe. That was a bad thing to do to me. I'm gonna kill you good," he taunted, pushing his body up against mine and trapping me against the bookshelves, rubbing himself against me. I could feel his erection, pushing against me and I was afraid that I might vomit. Or maybe that was a good idea! Maybe he'd be so revulsed that he'd let me go. Whatever my face showed, it seemed to spur him on. His breath was hot and his own face evil. How did I ever think he was handsome? "You stupid bitch! You think your puppy dog could save you!" His knee rammed into me and my breath whooshed out. I tried to push against him, but my arm was now gushing blood badly and I was unable to move it nor feel any sensation in my hand or fingers. I was going to die. In the background, the record player galloped on… *"And a false hearted looo-ver…Is worse than a thief…."*

My right arm was twisted behind me. I groped madly; trying to find something…anything…I touched the smooth, cool side of the pewter jar…

"I was gonna make nice love to you, but now, well, you and your damned dog sort of knocked the lovin' outta me." He grinned evilly. "You wanna know how dangerous I am, babe?" His spittle hit my face. Not knowing what else to do, I tried to gain a hold on the jar, my fingers slipping on its satiny surface. "You wanna know about the other women I killed?" *Othe*r women…there were *more?*

I had to keep him talking. While he was talking, I would be breathing. I nodded. "What did you do?" My voice was a whisper. Let him tell me….let him tell me….give me a few more seconds of life, God. Please.

"Last year, those snotty bitches…" he spat. "I knew they wanted a good man. I knew it." He giggled and my heart contracted again. "They pretended, but they wanted me, I know. Bitches!" He spat again, his mouth just a few inches from mine. The spit hit me face, but I didn't flinch…didn't interrupt his stream of vitriol that was giving me a few moments more of living. Out of the corner of my eye, I could see the limp bundle that had once been my beloved dog. I wanted to scream, cry, rip Daniel's eyes out, but I could only crouch, trying to get my finger around the handle of the pewter jar.

"I hate bitches!" Daniel's face was suffused with venom. "My wives, all of them...Bitches. I could have killed them all." His eyes narrowed with craftiness. "But they would'a known it was me. I had to let them go." He laughed again, his head thrown back and I again marveled that he was so handsome. Even in his maniacal frenzy, he was beautiful. Lucifer must have been like this. His evil magnified because of his beauty. "So I killed some prosties instead."

"*What?*" I gasped, unable to stop myself. "Prosties?" The word was so...so..infantile. So childish...even in this moment of terror, I was taken aback. Prosties? What had he *done?*

I heard a faint sound outside. I stiffened, hoping that somehow, some way, a rescue was at hand. I couldn't be sure, but I thought I heard the sound of horses running. Galloping. I heard the rumble of their hooves. *Horses?* How could there be horses? Daniel raved on, his raspy voice unheeding the sounds behind us.

"I chopped them up. Little bloody pieces. I showed them. I showed them all." He laughed once more. "No one even guessed it was me." He made a sound of contempt and his hand curled around my throat. I gagged and tried to pull my head away. Tried to gulp at the air, tried to forestall my death. "Each time one of my wives left, instead of killing them, I killed a slut!" He laughed again, proud of his deeds.

"Who...?" *Keep him talking, Reggie*, I told myself. *Keep him bragging.*

"Shit, who cares? Who the hell knows who they were! Some cheap stupid whores. One in Portsmouth, one in Portland and I can't remember...shit. They were skags anyway." My horror was on my face. He let go of my throat, twisted my left arm and the blood gushed more and I screamed, despite myself. The blood was on me, on him. Intermingled. He dropped my arm and held me again by the throat, toying with my life. I gagged and coughed.

"You can't get away from me, you bitch," he snarled. "I'm a charmed man. No one suspected me at all!" His gloating was horrid. "And I killed that lady." My eyes asked him, *what lady?* "The old broad on the motorcycle. In the woods." *Candice? He killed Candice?* "She saw me driving drunk. She would have told on me. Maybe had me arrested, and then I couldn't go out on the boat. Stupid old bitch, I got her good." His grip on my throat tightened. "And I killed three more people, too." He was bragging. Bragging to *me*! My eyes widened, incredulous despite my inability to suck in a deep breath. I think it inflamed him more; that I couldn't believe that he could be so callus and evil.

"You don't believe me, bitch?" He shook me again and a red haze appeared before my eyes. I was dying now. This was what it was like. The air leaving me. Dying. My hand lost touch with the pewter jar and my body sagged. He loosened his grip on my throat. I choked and gasped, wheezing, madly filling my depleted lungs with air. He pulled my face closer to his. It was as if he couldn't stop telling me...he *needed* to tell me...everything.

I wet my lips. My throat was raw and painful. There was no feeling in my arm. I *was* dying. Maybe not this moment, but it would be soon. I could feel the life draining out, dimming. "Who...," my voice was cracked and tiny..."Who else did you kill?" I wanted to know it all. Somehow, at my own end, I was bonded to him. I wanted to know everything and he *wanted* me to know everything before he ended my life. There was a need for both of us to finish this insane conversation before he killed me. I wondered if he had confessed to Sunny and Catherine before he hacked them to pieces. Would he choke me first or would he just cut me up? I whimpered, defeated.

He loosened his grip. His voice softened and his eyes had a faraway gaze. "The kid...the kid that was stealing our lobsters. It was me and Jonah. We held his head underwater, the little bastard. He was trying to steal our lobsters." He shook his head from side to side, trying to be sure that I understood that they *had* to kill the boy. "We can't let *anyone* take the lobsters. That's our living, you know." I nodded. I tried to understand, I really did.

"And some other guy." Daniel's face was thoughtful. "I don't even know who he was. A couple of years ago. He tried to take lobsters, too. We drowned him."

"Who else?" I wanted to know so that it would all be tied up in a neat bundle before I closed my eyes. He nodded, glad that I understood.

"My mother." My eyes blinked wide.

"Your *mother?*" I gasped. His *mother?*

He had the grace to look slightly embarrassed. "Yeah," His eyes slid away from mine. "We didn't want to kill her, but she just *wouldn't* die! She hung on, week after week Sick and old, but she just wouldn't die." He sighed. "She never gave us any of the money, and we were

running out of time with out boat payments and all. We had to…well…
help her go."

"And no one ever suspected you of any of these killings?" Somehow, with all of the carnage, the part about his mother got to me. I
mean, his *mother,* for God's sake! "No one even talked to you about
the…the…um, killings?" I wanted to keep him talking. I listened hard,
but couldn't hear anything more from outside. Maybe I had just imagined the horses and the noises. Maybe I had hoped….

"Nope," he was almost cheerful again, practically bragging. "No
one knew." He stepped back and looked regretfully at me. "Nobody
but you knows now, Reggie." He bent and kissed me on my mouth, a
soft and gentle kiss. A kiss of goodbye. I knew then that he was going
to kill me in the next instant. I closed my eyes. *Goodbye, darling Andrea. Goodbye, Jenna, my love. Pray for me, girls. Goodbye, Lincoln.
Goodbye.*

There was an unearthly sound, a set of screeches that could only
have come from something beyond this world. Two small furry bodies
catapulted through the torn screen on the back door, tiny cat teeth
bared, claws extended. Two bodies, one black and one white, landed in
unison on Daniel's head, scratching and clawing. He let out a yell and
his hands left my neck to protect himself. He crouched, trying to grab at
the cats. The Victrola leaped back into action, the cowgirl voice shouting, "*…a false-hearted looo-ver, will lead you to the grave…*" With the
cats at his head, Daniel stumbled backwards.

My right hand touched the handle of the pewter jar. I grabbed at it
and brought it in front of me, swinging it as hard as I could in an arc
that smashed it against the top of Daniel's bent head. Dollar bills,
dimes and quarters flew all over the room, showering Daniel with
money. He staggered, flinging off the cats. His mouth was in a rictus,
grinning evilly. Easily, he lifted the knife and slashed at the cats, spearing Sunny on the tip. The cat yowled, a dying scream. "Ha!" Daniel
cried, exultant at the blood. There was another unearthly screech as he
drove the knife again into the body of the black cat. Blackie groaned, a
deep cry of death and her broken carcass slid to the floor. Daniel
watched, his eyes frenzied.

With my own scream, I raised the jar again and hit him once again.
He turned his attention to me, flailing at me, cutting me again on my
belly and thigh. A huge spurt of blood gushed out of me and he slipped
in it as he came forward to decapitate me. I grabbed at his arm with all
of my failing strength and deflected the knife away. As we both fell in

our grotesque dance, the knife turned in his hand. I screamed Lincoln's name again and we smashed onto the floor with Daniel's heaviness on top of me. The world turned dim…*Lincoln? Did I hear him?* I lost what senses I still had. *Lincoln? Lincoln!*

CHAPTER TWENTY

T he room swam into view. I wasn't breathing. My chest was crushed. I thought I was dead and this was my body's transition from one world into the next. Death was supposed to be peaceful, wasn't it? Then why was this noisy and bloody and hurtful? I heard a scream and a shout and prayed that the noise would cease and that I could sleep and be at peace.

"*Reggie!*" The voice was loud and intrusive. I groaned and closed my eyes, unwilling to look again on the animal corpses that littered the room; the innocent, precious animals who had given their lives to try save me. My dog and my two cats.

"*Reggie!*" Again. I opened my eyes.

"Lincoln." I watched him with dispassion. His face frantic and waxy white. "You left me and went with her." I was sad, so sad. I closed my eyes again and the darkness overtook me.

◆ ◆ ◆

Voices intruded again. New voices. It was hard for me to breathe, hard to focus. My eyes fluttered. Daniel's body was heavy on top of me. His blood and my blood gushed together. I wanted to push him off, but I couldn't move. Couldn't feel my arms or my fingers. I thought that Daniel had cut off my arm, hadn't he? Was that what happened? I was lost once again into the darkness of the horror and pain.

I saw Lincoln leaning over me. He pushed Daniel's body off me and to the side and knelt down next to me. Ah, now, he too was covered with blood. My blood, Daniel's blood, the animals' blood. We were all linked together. Everyone dead or dying except Lincoln. Lincoln, Lincoln, Bo-Binken...I watched him through half-opened eyes. His hand was lifted as if to touch me, but he didn't. His face was bleak, with his blue eyes pale, his cheeks sunken. I wanted to tell him that I still loved him even though I was mad at him, but my mouth wouldn't work. "*Reggie!*" his voice was a sharp whisper. "If you can hear me, know this. I love you and I have loved you from the moment I saw your rain-stained little face in my office. *Reggie?"* His voice shouted, and then another whisper, "Reggie, my love."

I watched him through hazy, blood-filled eyes. Did he love me, really? Really? Or was he just saying all of this because he thought I was dying and he wanted to be nice to me as I passed over.

He sighed, a deep groan, started to speak again and then was pushed aside by someone else who said something like, "We need to get her to a hospital." Lincoln heaved his large body to its feet, and shoulders slumping turned away. Perhaps always a veterinarian, even in a crisis with dead dogs and cats, he went to where Macduff's broken body was. I heard someone's harsh sobbing and saw Lincoln bend down. He groaned, then picked up the limp and bloody body of Macduff and went away, out of my sight. I tried to call to him, but the effort was more than I could sustain.

The heavy weight of Daniel's body was rolled completely off me and my lungs hurt as I breathed in and out once more. I opened my eyes wider. The room was filled with people. Chief Bridge, three more policemen, including my old friend Tall, a man in a white coat, Mrs. Cee and Elroy, the bloody body of Daniel Bethany, and some others in the uniforms of the Kittery Emergency Rescue Squad.

Someone pricked my arm with a needle. I felt a warmth and then my waning senses made the world swim. I saw Mrs. Cee bent over me. I tried to tell her about Candice, but my mouth wasn't working well. She kissed my cheek and whispered that it would all be fine. Mrs. Cee wouldn't lie to me or anyone else. I sighed, satisfied, and closed my eyes.

◆ ◆ ◆

I awoke suddenly with a strange voice in my ear calling, *"Reggie? Reggie, you cute thing, you. Open up your eyes."*

Cute? How inappropriate. I was dead, wasn't I? Maybe not, as my head pounded and my eyes were sticky. It was hard to open them. I tried to explain this, but couldn't get the words and my lips working at the same time. Some wise person wet my eyelids with a soft cotton ball saturated with warm water. The same wise person wet my lips with a cotton swab. "Better now?" this person asked me.

I nodded, carefully, oh so carefully, trying to keep my head from hurting any more. I blinked and slitted my eyes. I saw two worried blue eyes an inch or so away from mine.

"Reggie?" the owner of the eyes asked. "How're you doing, love?"

I licked my lips and croaked, "OK...just OK." The memories crowded into my brain and thundered against me. I lurched upward, grabbing at the blue-eyed person. My arm...one of my arms wasn't there..."Oh, Macduff!" I cried. "My dog...oh, noooooo!" I fell back against the bed, cognizant enough to know now that I was in a hospital. "The cats!" I closed my eyes, unable to cope with the images. "Oh, nooooo!"

Blue-eyes patted my cheek. "Reggie? Can you cope?" I sniffed and opened my eyes again as tears trickled down my cheeks and onto the sterile hospital pillow. Cope? I was tired of coping. I only wanted to howl and then go to sleep for ever.

Blue-eyes wasn't going to leave me alone, though, was he? "Reggie? Come on, now, wake yourself up."

With a touch of exasperation, I opened my eyes again. "Who are you?" I asked Blue-eyes. He grinned, a cute and slightly crooked grin and I thought that I couldn't quite be on death's door if I could admire the doctor's grin.

"I'm Jack Murphy, your new doctor."

"Did you take care of me?" I tried moving my head and the pain seemed to abate slightly. Dr. Murphy grinned again and nodded, as if I'd done something clever.

"Oh, I put some of you together, stitched you up a bit." He stepped back and another young man in a white coat stood behind him. This one had curly brown hair and soft brown eyes. There was no way that he could have been a doctor, however, as he seemed to be only about fifteen years old. I eyed him speculatively. Dr. Murphy introduced him to me. "But the tough work, putting your tendons and muscles and blood vessels together, the microsurgery, that was done by our own boy genius, Dr. Coleman." The youngster smiled shyly at me and ducked his head.

Doctor Blue-eyes introduced us. "Reggie, you brave and adorable woman, meet Allen Coleman."

"Hi, Reggie, nice to meet your face, at last." The shy, brown haired one said. "I got rather well acquainted with a few of your tendons over the last day or so."

"You can't be a doctor. You're a child," I grumbled.

"They all say that." Dr. Coleman grinned. "It's how I catch all the good-looking chicks." He patted my shoulder, one of the few spots that wasn't hurting. "You've got guts, Reggie. How is it going? You're doing OK?"

"I'm...fine." I let my memories flood back. "But...what happened? I remember...Macduff and the cats and the music." My face crumpled. "Is Daniel alive?"

"Nope." Dr. Murphy took my hand. His palm was warm and dry and I clutched at it. "He's dead, Reggie. He can't hurt you or anyone else anymore." He touched my face gently. "Are you up to talking about it all? Chief Bridge is waiting to take a statement from you, but I won't allow him to bother you until you're ready."

I smiled sadly. "It was awful." I tried to make my voice strong, but only a whisper emerged. "I want to tell him everything now."

"Doctor Coleman and I will be back to see you in the morning. You'll be well looked after and I promise that you'll feel a little better by then."

"Wait!" I called to him. "Is my arm....did he...Daniel? Did he cut off my arm? I can't feel it at all." I didn't want to feel sorry for myself and I steeled my heart for what he was going to tell me.

"Aw, honey, your arm is fine, thanks to Dr. Coleman. A little banged up, a lot cut, but fine." My eyes flew to those soft brown ones and Dr. Coleman blushed.

"Thanks, Dr. Coleman," I smiled at him, utterly captivated by his youth and sweetness. "I just didn't know if I still had it or not." I tried to lift myself up to look at where my arm might be, but I couldn't manage to see that far. "I just couldn't feel it at all."

"It's immobilized and anesthetized to the tenth power." Dr. Coleman assured me, blushing even more. "When the good stuff wears off, you'll feel it alright. It will hurt like hell."

"We'll see you tomorrow," Dr. Murphy winked and blew me a kiss. I turned my head away, embarrassed at the tears that tricked from my eyes. I was really happy that my arm was still with me. I mean, I could have stood it if I lost it, but heck, I was glad that I hadn't.

◆ ◆ ◆

I sighed and wiggled into a more comfortable position. I was in a biggish room. There was only one bed in it, but I could see that at some other time, there had been another bed. Afternoon sunlight came through the window at the other side of the room. My mind drifted. Maybe they removed the second bed so that I could be alone. I heard a sound in the hallway. The door opened again. A blonde, chesty nurse with huge blue eyes, dressed in colorful scrubs came in, followed by Chief Bridge and a Kittery policeman that I'd never seen. "Hey, Reggie," Chief Bridge greeted me, "We gotta stop meeting over all these crimes."

The nurse introduced herself as Kathie Hess and made sure that I was as comfortable as I could be. "You can talk as long as you want to, but if you're tired or sleepy, I'm here to toss these two out of your room." She gave the chief a glare and settled herself on a chair out of the way.

Chief Bridge brought a chair up to my bedside, sat down and leaned over so that I didn't have to strain to see him. The policeman, a huge man with a reddish moustache, was introduced to me as Detective Dennis Staer. He sat gingerly on a chair that groaned under his weight and took notes on everything we talked about.

The chief led me through the events of two days ago, as I learned that I had either been unconscious or in surgery for the better part of a day and a half. Slowly, with patience and close questioning, I told him everything. Well, almost everything. I left out the part about Lincoln and Athena. I wasn't *that* incapacitated.

As I told the story, I could see the different expressions that flitted across the chief's face. When I got to the part about the Macduff and the cats, I began to cry again. I just couldn't help it. Kathie, the nurse, leapt up, ready to tell the police to leave, but I assured her that I wanted to keep on talking. Little by little, the entire story emerged with all of its deaths and horror. It took the better part of two hours and by that time, I *was* exhausted.

"We've bothered you enough, Reg." Chief Bridge thanked me. He and Detective Staer got up.

"Wait!" I cried.

"*What?*" The chief almost jumped in the air. "What's wrong?"

"What *happened?* I mean, I know that Daniel died, but what about *Jonah?*" Good grief! Did they think I was going to let them slide out the door without telling me everything?

"Is she OK for us to stay a little while more?" Detective Staer asked. Kathie, almost as anxious as I was to hear the rest of the story, nodded fervently that it was fine.

"We went over to Jonah's house right away. The lights were on, the door was open and he was sitting on the sofa with a beer in his hand waiting for us."

"He knew you were coming?"

"Well he figured...let me tell it from my perspective." I nodded and behind me, I knew that Kathie nodded too. "Jonah just put his hands up in the air when we got to the door. 'Come on in, Chief,' he said. 'If you're here, then my lobstering days are over.' He waved a beer can around and we came in, nice and peaceful-like. I had Dennis here and Matt MacKinnon with me and we were armed. I guess he knew that he couldn't run anywhere, so he just gave up."

Detective Staer wiggled on his chair and the chair groaned in protest. "He was whipped, outgunned, outmaneuvered and out-classed." His luxurious moustache quivered with pride.

The chief continued, "We told him that Daniel was dead. He bowed his head for a moment. He said that Daniel sure had it coming to him. He asked about you and I told him that you were a tough little woman." I squirmed on the bed. "He said that he was glad that you were OK. 'Reggie is OK.' He said. 'I liked that girl, I did. I'm sorry that Daniel got so crazy and tried to kill her.'"

"Me, too." I intoned, touching the huge bandage that covered my abdomen.

"He told us that Daniel had been – I think he used the term 'wired wrong' – ever since he was a kid. Like a lot of psychopaths, Daniel loved hurting animals – torturing them. Hell, he told us a story that Daniel used to catch squirrels in traps, then, using big gloves so that the squirrels wouldn't bite him, he'd tie them up and bury them in the ground so that just their heads were sticking out and then he'd get a golf club and whack the squirrels' heads off – like he was practicing hitting golf balls." My eyes widened and I felt a sick jolt to my stomach. I could have been one of those squirrels.

"Anyway, Daniel was always hurting other kids, twisting their arms or smacking them around, but he was so personable and good-looking on the outside that no one really understood how rotten he was underneath. No one except Jonah. And the two of them, well, they were the most popular boys in high school. Great football players, leaders of the youngsters, always starting up a party or finding a way to get beer. Getting the kids together for a hot dog roast at Seapoint Beach…almost everyone looked up to them."

"Except the kids that they beat up," Detective Staer muttered.

"It really started to get out of control when his first wife left him. From what I understand, he beat her and cheated on her and was a terrible husband."

"Why didn't she go to the police?" I asked.

"I think she was scared shitless of him. She was a local girl…I think her parents still live up in Wells…One night she just packed up and got the hell out of town. She went to Nevada and started divorce proceedings, but I don't think he ever saw her again."

"And then he went to Portland and killed a prostitute? That's what he told me that night."

"I guess so. Jonah said that Daniel was pissed that she – the wife –

had left him and demanded alimony. Some judge in Nevada got her a good chunk of his money and he went stark, raving mad. He went out that night and never came back for three days. When he got back and sobered up, he told his brother that he'd picked up some whore, tied her up and raped her, then ripped her to pieces and left her body someplace over by the fishing docks off Commercial Street. We checked with the Portland Police and there were three unsolved murders of young women around that time. I'll presume that at least one of them was perpetrated by Daniel." Again, I felt the coldness around me. Daniel! I had thought him to be such a big puppy of a man. How wrong could I have been?

"Same sort of story for the second two wives. We can't find anyone unaccounted for who was murdered in Portsmouth, but the cops are checking, and we have bulletins out to all the police in New England to see about the third one."

"And their mother? Was Jonah involved?"

"So Jonah confirms. He says old Mrs. Bethany was hanging on and they had debts that couldn't wait. He says they looked at each other over her bed, picked up a pillow, and the two of them held it down over her face. She was sleeping when they did it, that's the only consolation." His face looked even more doleful than it usually did.

"Wasn't there any kind of post-mortem?" Kathie couldn't help herself. "No autopsy or anything?"

"Evidentially not. She was a very old lady, and had been at Death's door for weeks. I guess the doctor just put it down to respiratory failure – " He snorted. "Shit, it sure *was* respiratory failure!"

"So know one ever knew."

"Nope. They got clean away with it. They had been involved a few years back in a fracas with another lobsterman, but although there were threats and accusations on both sides, the matter was dropped. Then, Jonah said that they caught some man in a rowboat pulling lobsters from one of their traps. Instead of calling the cops or beating him up, they again looked at one another with some kinda brotherly telepathy, dragged the poor son-of-a-bitch out of the rowboat and held him underwater until he drowned. They scuttled the boat and went back to hauling traps, like nothing had happened."

"Man shouldn't'a been stealing their lobsters," Detective Staer mused.

"You're right. But they could'a just tied him up and no Maine police would'a had a problem with it."

"Who was the man?"

"Name was Edward Sansoucie. A man from Nova Scotia. Worked at the Naval Station."

"Didn't anyone report him missing?" I seemed to remember hearing about a man who had been missing....was it from Horace?

"Yeah, but he was a bachelor. A man who kept to himself. Word was that he had just upped and left the area. There was some sort of half-assed inquiry at the Yard, but nothing every came of it. It wasn't my jurisdiction, so I don't know how the investigation went."

"And then Sonny and Catherine Black. Poor souls."

"Jonah told us that Daniel had met them a few times and thought that they were two fine-looking ladies. He hated anything that smacked of lesbians and that sort of thing, found it an affront to his macho masculinity. Ha!" The chief made a leering face and a hand gesture that had Detective Staer guffawing. "He figured they needed one good rodger from him – a real man, as he considered himself. Then, they'd be begging him for it. The stupid prat just couldn't understand that a woman – a lot of women – might not give a rat's ass about him and his schlong!" We all chuckled, although the story really wasn't funny at all.

"What happened that night?"

"According to Jonah, Daniel had spent the night before drinking and nursing his fantasy of having two women, and avowed lesbians at that, at the same time. With every drink he took, his imagination of the scene became more and more inflammatory and by the time he decided to go over to their house, he was positive – in his own drunken, twisted mind – that he was going to have a high old time with Sunny and Catherine."

"They must have been horrified when he barged in." I shuddered, remembering my bewilderment and subsequent hysterical fright.

"I guess he lost control. When they spurned him – Jonah said that Daniel said that they laughed at him at first – he just went berserk..." Our faces reflected our thoughts of the consequences of Daniel's wrath, and then the could-have-been consequences of his encounter with me.

"If it hadn't been for Macduff and the cats, I don't think I would have survived," I whispered. They gave their lives for me." Kathie got up and put her arms carefully around me.

"Are you OK?"

The tears sprang. I couldn't stop them. "Those poor, brave animals." I almost sat up and was only impeded by the stab of pain that accompanied my move. "We have to bury them in some lovely place. Where...?"

A curious look passed between the chief and the detective. "Don't worry about that just now, Reggie. We've taken care of, well, the bodies" Chief Bridge held up his hand. ""We'll have a memorial service when you are a little better and maybe we can all donate a little bit to the animal shelters or something as appropriate."

I gradually stopped my sobs. "I want to…" I put up my one good hand to stave off any more conversation or condolences about Macduff and the cats. "I guess it's better for me right now not to talk about it."

"Just let time heal all of this a bit," Kathie offered her advice. I nodded, realizing that she was right. But, oh, Macduff! Macduff!

"Let's finish up Jonah's statement," The chief harrumphed. "The death of Candace Chabot." We all watched him as he stood and stretched. "She was just in the wrong place at the wrong time. " He watched me. "You better know about this now. The night before she was murdered, Daniel went over to your house. I don't know what was on his mind, but it wouldn't have been good for you. You weren't home and he drove away in frustration. He went to some gin-mill in Portsmouth and began to tie one on and went home very drunk. The next morning, he had a whale of a hangover. Jonah said that he goaded Daniel, making fun of him missing you and then getting pig drunk. In anger and to stave off the hangover, Daniel drank a few shots of whisky and got into his truck and drove away, screaming at his brother. I guess he was driving out of control and hit a deer and Candace saw him. In fear of losing his license, he turned around and rammed the truck into her, tipping her motorcycle over."

"Was there any paint from the scooter or dents in his truck?"

"No. He told his brother that he was careful to bump her enough to knock her over, but not to leave any traces. Then, wearing gloves, he got out of his truck and smashed her head with a big rock." My eyes were saucers of revulsion and I heard Kathie's indrawn breath behind me.

"Yeah, son-of-a-bitch. He dragged her and her scooter 'way into the woods and dumped them into a gully, figuring rightly that no one would find her for weeks. Then he went home and slept his hangover off."

"Gee," I said.

"Yeah," the detective agreed.

"What's going to happen to Jonah?"

"He's admitted to three murders that we know of. He'll spend the rest of his life in prison if they don't execute him first."

"I won't envy his life behind bars, either," Detective Staer opined. "They don't like kid killers or old lady killers – even in prison."

233

"I hope he rots!" I nearly fell out of bed in my agitation.

The chief grinned. "Sooner or later, he will." The detective stood up too and began to fold up his pad of notes.

"Reggie?" he turned toward me. "I've been reading all of the notes and confessions and statements. Even the newspapers." Newspapers? I hadn't thought of newspapers! I opened my mouth, but Detective Staer plowed on. "One thing I just can't understand about all of this." My face asked what.

"You said that you broke that record...that it broke into a dozen or more pieces..." I nodded, a half-smile on my face. "Right?"

"Mmmm-hmmm." I concurred.

"And you stated that the Victrola was smashed and the horn was half-broken off, right?" I nodded again.

"Then how the hell could the Victrola start up and how the hell could that broken record start to play?" His beefy face was twisted in disbelief. "Are you sure you heard it?" I nodded vigorously.

"I think maybe the record starting up might have helped to save my life," I grinned at him. "Those two dead women saved me."

His face was a study in disbelief. "Honest," I assured him. "Honest. It began to play. I heard it and Daniel heard it. I swear it. I'll even take a lie detector test to confirm it."

"How...? How *could* it?"

"You'll have to wait until you can ask Sunny and Catherine." And with that, I lay back and closed my eyes.

◆ ◆ ◆

Chief Bridge and Dennis finally departed. "I'm going to have these notes typed up and I'll come back to see you tomorrow. I've got a lot more to ask you, but, we can wait until tomorrow for the finer points. We'll go over everything and clarify anything else that needs clearing up. OK?"

I nodded OK. Chief Bridge's face looked exhausted. He winked at me, bent and kissed my hand, his bristles of whiskers scratching me and they left.

◆ ◆ ◆

Kathie took care of a few nursing type things, including an injection to stave off the pain some more, and then helped me to eat a light meal of broth and crackers. I didn't think I was hungry, but the broth felt terrific sliding down my raw and ravaged throat. Kathie chatted easily while she fed me. She told me that York Hospital was renowned for their marvelous kitchen and that as soon as I was able, I'd be ordering off a sumptuous patient menu. "You can even have lobster if you want!"

I gagged and told her that it would be a while before I wanted to face a lobster. Then, I suddenly sat up in a panic. "Maisie? How is Maisie?" I grabbed Kathie's sleeve with my good arm and twisted it.

Obviously, Kathie knew all the hospital gossip. She knew that Maisie had been brought in by me a few nights ago. "She's a tough old bird. She's out of Intensive Care and in a regular room. She'll be down to see you in a day or two." I nodded, too emotionally exhausted to ask more.

◆ ◆ ◆

I tried to rest...closed my eyes, but all I could think of was Lincoln, Macduff and the cats. I didn't want to cry anymore, but I felt very sad. I'd forgotten to ask if my daughters had been informed about what was going on, rang the bell for Nurse Kathie and asked her. She laughed and said that one daughter and son-in-law would be there in a few hours. "Your other daughter, the actress (and the nurse looked suitably impressed), will be here in three days."

Feeling a little bit better, I tried again to sleep. My mind was in a gallop. Lincoln, oh, Lincoln. No matter what had happened, I still loved him. And that was that. But what could I do about it? What should I do about it? The man had deserted me in my hour of need, left me to go away with the bitch, and yet, I wanted him back in my life. The big dope. The...the *man!* What should I do? Agitated now, I thought I might ring to ask Kathie for a sleeping pill so that I could forget about Lincoln for a few hours.

A noise. My door again opened to the grin of my blue-eyed Doctor Murphy.

"Why are you so gol-darned cheerful all the time?" I groaned to him, enjoying his crisp-doctor-like professional appearance despite myself.

"Can you stand a little more excitement?" he asked me. There was something about this man's charm that was irresistible.

"Sure. What is it?" I pretended to be annoyed, but neither of us were fooled.

His answer stunned me. "How's your heart? Can you find a little warm spot there? Can you see Doctor Fairweather?"

Lincoln! Poor Doctor Blue-eyes. I didn't think he had any idea at all of my thwarted love life. Again, dumb and helpless woman that I was, I began to cry in earnest. His face a study in dismay, he held my hand and told me that I didn't have to see anyone if I didn't want to.

He certainly had a kind and sympathetic manner, for I began to tell him – a perfect stranger, even though he had stitched my arm, my stomach and my thigh back together and probably seen parts of me that no one had ever seen – all about Lincoln and Athena and our romance and Lincoln's desertion of me in the last few days. I suppose I even got a little hysterical when I howled that Lincoln had gone away when I really needed him. "He deserted me! I *neeeeded* him and he left me!" I wailed into his white coat. I sneaked a look at his face and saw a tiny grin on it. Just a tiny one. I couldn't seem to stop, even though some of my story was a bit embarrassing to me. I sobbed and cried and hic-cupped until the story was all out of me. All the while, Dr. Murphy held my hand gently and patted it from time to time. His pleasant face held neither condemnation nor censure…he only listened until I was wound down.

"Reg, I have to confess to you that I have known Link Fairweather for more than thirty years," he started. *Link? Link?* "He's a good man, a kind man. I know he really wants to see you. If you think about it, he actually helped to save you in the end. Had he not gotten to you in time, you would have bled to death. I know it might not be the way you are able to think about it all right now, but I hope you can see it differently in time." He bent down and kissed my wet cheek. "You are both special people. Good people, and I think you both love one another. I think – I certainly hope - that you two will work out your problems in the near future. But for now, can you find it in your heart to see him for a mo-ment or two?" His blue eyes begged and I said well, OK and sniffed back my sobs. Dr, Murphy grinned an exultant grin and opened the door to my room.

I looked up at the intrusion of noise as a heavy metal hospital bed was trundled in. *Geez!* I thought to myself. *Here I am, ready to talk some serious talk to Lincoln, and another patient was being brought in.* I wish they'd waited a few days more to move a roommate in with me. The big, cumbersome metal bed, draped in white sheets, was maneu-vered through the door. I watched and was astounded to see that Lincoln was pushing the bed. Jack Murphy took the other end of the bed and helped to push it past the foot of my bed and into the space next to me. My eyes were wide with astonishment that Lincoln, of all people, should be pushing a hospital bed. And then…and then…I saw…under the white hump of sheets…a tail…a bushy, bushy tail like no other tail…Macduff…*Macduff!* Oh, my sweet Jesus, *Macduff!*

I couldn't speak…couldn't speak at all.

"It's the least I could give you, darling." Lincoln's face was a study. "Contrary to what he looks like now, he's going to be fine, although he'll probably have a little limp for the rest of his life." He patted the tail. "Look, Reg. He's OK".

He gave the bed a final push and pulled the sheets down so that Macduff's wooly head showed. My mouth was open in an astounded 'O'. Macduff was bandaged and shaved and had a cone of oxygen or some such thing over his muzzle. The oxygen was attached to a big cylinder that rested on the side of the bed. I could now see, through my tears of delight, that the chest on Macduff's body was rising and falling with the hiss of the machine.

"Oh, Lincoln!" I cried, half rising from my bed. "Oh, *Lincoln!*"

Lincoln came to my side and dropped to his knees. "Can you ever forgive me?" I gulped and gasped and then realized that Dr. Jack Murphy had tiptoed out of the room and closed the door behind him.

◆ ◆ ◆

I was in the hospital for three weeks. Macduff, being of stronger stuff than me, was out and about in a week and was presently basking at the Fairweather house in Sasha's care, with a few dozen assorted well-wishers to keep her company, and supply him with bones, squeaky toys, and doggie treats. Both of us had been very close to death. Both of us had been stitched up and sewn up and pinned together. Both of us had dozens of scars. But both of us were fine now…just fine.

"I had to use every favor in my book to get him rolled in here," Lincoln gloated. "I had to bring him to you. It was my only chance that you might forgive me." He patted Macduff's head gently. "I was afraid he was dead, but then I saw a little flutter, a tiny movement. I grabbed him and vowed that if I could fix him up, we'd all have some kind of future." His eyes probed mine. "The cats, however, I am so sorry to say, couldn't be saved. I wish I could have saved them all. They deserved to live, those brave cats." He sighed. "I'm sorry, Reggie."

◆ ◆ ◆

I had so many visitors that my sweet nurse Kathie threatened to nail my door shut. I had so many flowers that I was able to supply each and every room in the York Hospital with fresh blossoms for a week. "You are the most popular chick that I have ever treated," Dr. Murphy informed me.

Andie and Jenn and Scott were there, bringing me flowers and their love and their tears and astonishment. "Geez, Mom. You've had an ad*ven*ture!" was the way Andie put it.

Barbara and Horace were there every day. "The baby's been born. All is well. He's a little horse and weighs about 9 pounds. We'll get him in a week." Horace kissed my cheek.

"I called everyone and postponed my own shower," Barbara assured me. "We're going to hold it next Saturday night at The Loop Café." She beamed at me. "You'll be out by then. We just couldn't have it until you were better." She patted my good arm. "And don't worry, we've exempted you from baking or even having to buy a present."

They all came, all of my new friends and my own dear family, crowding into the room, bringing fruit and candy and gifts. But the best gift they brought was friendship.

Anoop and Gerjeet came. "To have no worry, Reggie." They assured me. "Your good friend, Rose. She is our new waitress until you are feeling better." My eyebrows climbed. Rose? Rose was *waitressing?* "She came right away to help." Gerjeet bent down and whispered, "She is a little clumsy yet. She has broken many dishes and makes many mistakes, but she is happy and the customers forgive her." I lay back, grinning. Amazing. Simply amazing.

And Rose came, smiling tightly, a little nervous that I might be upset with her usurpation of my job. "I thought...I thought that I could just help until you were better..." She sat down abruptly, her eyes wide behind their glasses. "Are you angry?"

"Angry? I'm delighted! Oh, Rose," I hugged her to me with my good arm. "Thank you for being such a good friend. I know you never wanted to work, and I'm so grateful; that you..."

"Who said I didn't want to work?" she harrumphed. "Nonsense. I never thought that I could manage to get it all straight. The orders and the timing." She threw her hands out. "I love it!"

"You *do?*"

She nodded, emphatic. "I feel useful again." She turned her hands palm up and then palm down. "I'm having so much fun!" She sat back and then, jumped back up, adding, "Naturally, when you're better, the job is, of course, yours again. I'm only filling in."

"I don't know if...or when...I'm not sure I'll be able to work..." I showed her the bandages that swathed my left arm. "It might be your job forever."

She tsked and patted me gently. "Let's see what happens." She got up to leave, opened the door of the room and then paused. "And, that nice man, Phil Moore. The one with the big gas station?" I nodded, wondering what the heck was coming next. "He's kind of, um, handsome. We went out last night to the movies and he asked me to have dinner with him next Friday."

"Rose!" I gasped. "Do you like him?"

She shrugged, trying not to show me how pleased she was, "He's nice. He's divorced, too. Has a very sweet sixteen year-old daughter." I sucked in a breath, thinking of how I had so wrongly condemned poor old Phil. "I'm having the time of my life at the Café," Rose continued. "Thanks, Reg." She laughed, winked and waved goodbye as she closed the door.

Rita and Zee came, together. I never thought I'd see the day! They brought me a mutually purchased basket of hand creams and stuff to rub into my skin, and a packet of some special dry shampoo that one brushed into one's hair and then brushed out. The two of them, together, held me up and gave my poor, dry, stiff hair a good cleaning. Afterwards, I felt marvelous and to top it off, Rita gave me a backrub with some of the cream that smelled like vanilla. Heaven.

Both of them assured me that I'd have a free haircut and shampoo awaiting me when I get a bit better.

Chris from *Enoteca* came with his pretty young wife Cheryl and their new baby, Brook. They toted in a huge basket filled to the brim with delicious Italian cheese, fruits and candies. Rod and Diane brought me some funny movies to watch. "Nothing scary, Reggie, only comedies."

Joan smuggled Shotzy into the hospital. The poor little dog was dressed as a nurse, complete with cap and all. Doctor Jack snorted with derision when he saw Shotzy's outfit. Joan drew herself up and told him that Shotzy *liked* being dressed up. "I'm going to train her as a hospital dog…one of those dogs who goes around cheering up patients." She told him hotly. Dr. Jack assured her that seeing a dog dressed up like that would make any patient laugh.

Christa came, bringing me a box of wild rice. "It's one of the only good things that they sell in International Falls!"

A contingent of relatives came from Greenwich. Uncle Pat and Cousins Joe, Joanne and MJ. They brought me Italian pastries, *cannoli, sfogliatelle,* and those little cream-filled *zeppoli.* Pastries or not, I was so happy to see family that I howled for ten minutes into Joanne's comfortable shoulder. After my tempest, I was fine and we spent three hours catching up on news. It was good for me to have them visit. We all promised to get together more often.

Tom came from the book store, carrying an armful of the latest British mysteries, the Kochaneks brought me a box of candied apricots, and Roberta and the Foxes gave me a lovely leather manicure set. Eva and her parents, Chris and Beth, brought me a beautiful nightgown, and Pauli, Debby and the artists from Just Us Chickens gave me some skeins of alpaca wool and a set of wooden needles, "So that you can keep yourself from being bored."

Bored! Who could be bored? There were so many visitors that poor Kathie Hess told me that she was looking forward to the peace that would come when I finally went home.

Barbara and Horace came every day. Sasha visited me and Maisie every day and Maisie, feeling perkier, wheeled herself down to my room every morning for tea and cookies. Holly and Thane trotted in several times, each time bringing me a stuffed animal, which I promptly turned over to either Sasha or Eva to stash on their beds. Other customers popped in, some sent cards, some telephoned. I was overwhelmed at the love and concern and friendship that came my way.

"Everyone misses you," Anoop told me. "Every single man and lady asks for you. You are beloved."

"I haven't heard from Bob Micklewright," I gently teased her. "He was supposed to be crazy about me and he never even sent me a fifty cent card." I pretended to be upset.

"He is unable to spend fifty cents," Anoop consoled me. "Only if he could find a ten cent card, maybe he would spend that." We both collapsed in laughter.

There were two visitors, however, that amazed me. The first was Hank Ormond. She shuffled in one afternoon, wearing her grungiest clothing, and carrying a small white box that contained two freshly filled *cannoli* from *Enoteca.*

"They said you liked these kind of things," she said gruffly. "I'm happy that you're better." Astonished, I thanked her and watched Kathie Hess out of the corner of my eye. Kathie had never quite seen anyone like Hank and it showed in her open-like-a-fish mouth. Hank shuffled her booted feet, made a sort of bow and then left. Gerjeet told me later that she had appeared at the Café carrying a basket of lobsters, explaining that we now needed her as our old lobster connection was no longer in service.

"And, of course, the lady…what a lady…is absolutely in the correctness!" He shrugged his shoulders. "Our former source is no longer reliable!"

And then, one morning as I was groaning myself out of bed, with Kathie's help, slowly, awkwardly and with many ouches, Steve came to see me. I was so surprised that I collapsed back on the bed, nearly ripping out some stitches.

He was uncomfortable, that much was easy to see. "I, um, ha..." he started, "I'm glad that you, um, survived, Reggie." He bit his lip. "I, uh, read about it all in the newspapers."

I nodded, not quite knowing what to say. He took a bouquet of flowers from behind his back and handed them to me. "Here, these are for you."

I thanked him as Kathie watched this drama enfold from behind my bed. She seemed tense, ready to leap out and defend me if he should upset me at all.

I didn't know what else to say to him. Should I have asked him how his new chick was? Or how was the house that we might have lived in together coming along? He didn't seem to know what to say to me either and stood at the side of my bed, biting his lip and growing more and more uncomfortable.

The silence stretched...Steve cleared his throat and sort of waved his fingertips, then turned to leave. As he passed through the door, a thought struck him and he turned back to me. "Aren't you grateful that I paid your insurance premiums?" he asked.

I thought hard for a moment. "Yes, yes, Steve. I am one grateful woman." I nodded graciously and let him slink away. Kathie and I laughed for fifteen minutes afterward.

◆ ◆ ◆

And Lincoln. Ah, Lincoln. He was there all the time. At my side, holding my hand, and he...

Well, we talked. And talked and talked, and cried, and swore and laughed and cried again and then talked some more.

"I hated leaving you here, Reggie. But I hated myself even more. I deserted you and let myself be used. I should have been strong. Should have been a man and told Athena 'no' from the very start." His face was red and flushed and I know he felt like a turd. As well as he should have.

"You hurt me, Lincoln. You hurt my heart."

"Oh, Reggie. I was such a fool," he groaned. And then...well, I don't have to tell you everything that happened....do I?

He confessed that he had been uneasy after we quarreled. He'd been tempted to pick up the telephone and capitulate to me, that he'd almost left Athena and come home. But he'd been embarrassed, been shamed by her, been out-maneuvered and out-witted by a woman who had no scruples and was determined to run roughshod over his feelings and senses. "I was a coward, Reggie. And I almost let you die."

He picked up my hand. "Finally, on Sunday, I told her that I was leaving. I felt so terrible, Reggie, there is no excuse for what I did. But it was even more than that. On Saturday night, she dragged me to a cocktail party. I wanted to leave then, but she pulled me here and pulled me there and I didn't want to cause a scene. Then, in the middle of the crowd and all the noise, I thought I heard the sound of horses galloping. I swear it. It was uncanny." His eyes focused inward. "I could only think of the ghost ponies and death." He made a face. "But I felt that was so silly, so…stupid…" His big hands waved helplessly. "I thought that I'd call you from the party, but I couldn't locate my cell phone." He looked sheepish. "I found out later that Athena had swiped it," I goggled at him. *She really was a bitch.*

"That night, the horses woke me up. I heard them galloping and the noise and sparks from their hoofs frightened me. I knew that something wasn't right and that I had to get home. I sat up in bed, afraid. I used the hotel phone and tried to call home, to be sure that my mother and Sasha were all right, but there was no answer. I then tried to call you, but again, there wasn't anyone answering. I began to really worry. I threw my stuff in my suitcase, got into the car and drove home." His face was doleful. "I was too late. Too late for my mother and too late for you." I patted his arm and he dropped off the chair and knelt on the floor, holding my hand as if he'd never let go. "I'll never forgive myself, Reggie. I nearly lost you."

"I heard the horses too. I thought I was losing my mind, but I hard them, honest, I did. What does that mean?"

"That there's more to this world, Horatio, than we mortals shall ever know, or whatever Shakespeare meant to say."

There were tears in his eyes and he dropped his head onto my chest. I stroked his hair and the other things that we said to one another were private and for ourselves.

◆ ◆ ◆

York Hospital was a superb place. Wonderful staff (witness my two adorable doctors and Kathie), wonderful food, lovely, soft sheets, changed every day, and gentle, caring attention to my every need. Generally, I read, even tried to knit, listened to music, tried without much success to watch daytime television, and was a good doobie when it came to doing the tortuous maneuvers that they called physical therapy. I slept, for the most part, rather well.

But…there were moments, even during the day, and most times in the deep of the night, when the memory of my attack and fear thundered upon me, waking me from my slumbers, sweating and afraid. A shadow suddenly blocking my light, a sudden sound of a truck's engine outside, the dropping of a dish or glass…for a moment, it would sweep my breath away and I would find myself writhing and shouting, pushing a phantom assailant and fearing again for my life.

Jack Murphy assured me that this was perfectly normal – good, even. "If you didn't get it all out of your system, Reg, it might warp your future. You had a real scare, a horrible experience," his blue eyes smiled kindly at me. "But, it is over. Really over. He's gone…dead, and I am sure that he is being punished as only God is able to punish."

Sometimes, it took Sasha climbing on my bed, her curly hair next to me on the pillow, reading the day's batch of get well cards, her voice grossly mispronouncing names and more difficult words, to jolly me back to my former sanity. I treasured her visits and she, more than anyone else, brought me back to some semblance of joy. I often told her what a wonderful child she was and how much I loved her. She'd smile and pat my hand. "And I love you, Reggie. You're the best. Just the best."

◆ ◆ ◆

The next morning, as I was bandying witticisms with Dr Murphy and that darling Dr. Coleman….don't think that I hadn't already thought of fixing him up with Andrea…Sasha trotted into my room pushing Maisie's wheelchair. Macduff, almost well, limped at their side, his hairy, mobile face expressing clearly that here was a dog who had suffered mightily and needed to be fed a biscuit. Sasha, as usual, threw herself on my bed. I held her sweet, childish body to mine and told her once again that I loved her.

"Oh, Reggie. I love you too!" she giggled.

Maisie and I hugged one another and we finally sent Sasha out to get us tea and cookies so that we could talk. Macduff, who had hero status throughout the hospital, was allowed to leap onto the foot of my bed where he pushed himself as close as possible to me. His tail whirled and he sighed, a happy dog, even as he begged me to pet him some more. His whimper of happiness conveyed again that he needed a lot of attention as he had been gravely wounded and was a true canine hero…everyone knew that, didn't they?. Honestly, I could see his doggie thoughts passing through his head. Maisie and I lavished him with praise and he looked smug and every inch the hairy hero.

◆ ◆ ◆

Both Maisie and I were to be released the following day. Lincoln told me, "And there is no discussion here," that I would be recuperating with him and staying at the Fairweather house until…"Well, we'll see about all of that," was how he put it. "We have a full-time nurse for my mother and she can peek in on you, too." There was no way, he insisted, that I was going to return to 236 Schooner Street. "And that's final."

"Of course, Lincoln," I meekly agreed. "Whatever you say."

CHAPTER TWENTY-ONE

So many things happened in the next few days. I went back to the Fairweather house and was treated like ...well, just like a queen. The steady stream of visitors that had begun in the hospital continued, except that this time it was even better. Maisie and Sasha and Lincoln and Macduff were all with me. Jenna and Scott and even Andie, who flew back and forth from California using my credit card, were underfoot as much as they could be. Jenn and Andie told me how dishy they thought Lincoln was and hoped fervently that something might just come of all of it. I smiled with what I thought was a mysterious and inscrutable smile, but I am sure that no one was fooled.

As my physical injuries would keep me from being a waitress extraordinaire for some time to come – maybe even for ever, Rose took over my duties at The Loop Café on a permanent basis. Gerjeet had a new cousin arrive in the US, complete with bindi, long, lustrous black hair and tinkly bracelets. She...her name was Danya...became waitress number 2, properly subservient under Rose's gimlet eye.

I was concerned, after all, I really needed to earn a living, even though there was some talk from Barbara of a settlement from the Bethany estate as a victim's compensation. Although I never thought that anything would come of this, I knew that Barbara would swing some cash my way if she could.

But before I could upset myself too much over how I was going to manage my future, Lincoln brushed aside my worries, telling me that everything would work out and for the time being, I had to be content with fretting in silence. I discussed my worries with Barbara and the two of us decided that I could always bake my cookies and cakes and sell them to local restaurants and shops, naturally, supplying The Loop Café first. I thought that *Enoteca*, Frisbees Store, Fox's Lobster House and The Golden Harvest would eagerly fight over the right to sell my goodies. Baking at home would give me some money to live on, as well as affording me the luxury of working only when I felt up to it.

"Maybe you won't have to worry about earning a living," Barbara leered at me in a suggestive way. I threw a pillow at her, but in the dark of night, propped up in Lincoln's spare bedroom, I wondered what my future would really hold, and prayed that it might hold exactly what I hoped it would.

◆ ◆ ◆

On Saturday, we had the baby shower for Barbara and Horace and that lucky, lucky child, little Michael Joseph. He was a gorgeous baby, huge and fat-cheeked and smiley like a little Buddha. He seemed to enjoy all the attention, being paraded from one person's arms to the next in some happy bliss. Barbara looked like the heavens were shining on her and Horace was so proud, I swear he was six inches taller.

Andie and Jenn were both able to attend the shower. Sasha spent the entire afternoon hanging onto them and they treated her just like a prized little sister.

And speaking of prized little sisters and becoming related...well, Lincoln presented me with Lady Pamela's ring, and a wonderful proposal of marriage that I will not share with anyone else. He also had a special license that would permit us to marry in a week's time. A clambake, we thought, but no lobsters....

◆ ◆ ◆

And so my future was changed. I no longer had to work. Lincoln confided to me, with a sweet smile that, sure, he wasn't rich, but he could manage to feed another face at the table without too much of a problem. I think that was just how he presented it all to me. And then, he fell on his knees in front of the couch where I was lying.

"But if you want to work, Reg, that's just fine with me." His blue eyes looked worriedly into my brown ones. "I mean. You are your own woman, and you can do whatever you want to do."

"I think that I might find full-time waitressing more work than I can manage," I said slowly, trying to think sensibly through the delirium of happiness that engulfed me. "I'd like to be here at home..." Oh, how I loved saying that... "for Sasha and for your mother." I leaned forward and patted his cheek. "I might do some baking, not because I'd *have* to, but because I'd *want* to." Lincoln kissed me and I almost forgot where my thoughts were leading me.

"Whatever Reggie wants, Reggie gets," he said, messing his fingers in my hair.

"Be serious," I swatted him. "I never want to be just Lincoln's wife...I need to be Reggie...my own person, too." He looked perplexed and I tried to explain.

"When Steve left me, I vowed that I would be myself...Reggie. I could be other things at the same time...Andie's mother, Jenna's mother...Sasha's grandmother..." I grinned and traced his mouth with my finger, "And, the best part...Doctor Grumpy Lincoln's wife." He captured my finger with his mouth and bit it softly.

"But you need your independence, right?"

"Right."

"Do you want to have a baking business? Everyone who tastes your stuff begs for more." He turned my hand over and kissed the palm. "We can re-do the mud room out in back of the kitchen, turn it into a little commercial kitchen where you can whip out your delicacies."

"Maybe, let's see how fast I mend."

"Do you think you might like to do something like that?"

"Yeah," I mulled it over for a moment. "I know that Gerjeet will buy anything I bake, the boys at Frisbees want my stuff, and *Enoteca* will also purchase whatever I can supply them with."

"Everyone wants your stuff. You can charge a fortune. You'll be a mogul." He made a face at me. "Isn't that what they call an extremely successful entrepreneur?"

"That will be me...Mogul Regina." I took his hand in mine and returned the favor of kissing his palm. "Maybe that's a good name for the business."

"A crappy name," he winced. "We'll put Sasha on to finding a better one. As long as you are able. Don't rush anything, darling."

"I like that darling bit." I leaned forward and kissed his lips. "I'll be careful and wait until I am sure that I am strong enough."

"Good," He grinned. "I look forward to having a rich wife who can support *me*!" We began to laugh and, well....I could see that married life with Lincoln was going to be great.

◆ ◆ ◆

Barbara came to see me the next day. "This is a business visit," she told me.

"Oh?"

"Yeah. What with your new status-to-be as Mrs. Fairweather, I presume you won't be wanting to live at 236 Schooner Street any more."

"Oh, what's happened with the house?"

"It's been cleaned up, repainted...poor little house," she commiserated. "It's a lovely place."

"Just happens to have a few bad things occured there." I chimed in.

"Still, the big bad wolf has been slain and I don't think anything like that will happen again." I shuddered, thinking of just how bad the big bad wolf had been and how close I had come to being snapped in two by his big bad knife.

"I don't think any of it was the house's fault," I tipped my head, considering it all. "There never was any bad karma about the house itself."

"That's how I feel. Anyway, Horace and I talked it all over and we are going to buy it from the estate."

"Really! What will you do with it?"

"Rent it to Rodney and Diane. They're going to get engaged and move in together."

"Super!" I exclaimed. And then, "Do they have any, um, feelings about what happened there?"

"They're level headed kids. They like the house and don't have any problems with cats and ghosts," She laughed, her rich, booming laugh. "And besides, they'll have Mrs Cee next door to hover over them. And," she shook her head in some perplexity, "the Goddamn Victrola is broken, so there won't be any more singing."

"Don't be too sure," I shook my head slowly. "That Goddamn Victrola, as you call it - damned if I know how - saved my life."

"Are you sure that it played?" Her face was creased with puzzlement. "I mean, how could it play, Reg? It was *broken*."

"I don't know, Barbara. But play it did." My own face was solemn. "*And* those women sang."

"OK, Reg., whatever you say." Barbara's voice was still skeptical.

"Hey, we both heard it play all the time," I considered. "Why would it be any different when I needed them to sing?" Barbara shrugged.

"Yeah, but it was broken then. Huh! Who the hell can know? The whole thing with the song…you have to admit, it is really peculiar."

"I'm a believer, whatever that means. All I know is that the cats, the record…all of it…whatever. I don't understand any of it." I gazed up at the blank, white ceiling above my bed. "Maybe the Man Upstairs is controlling it all. I'm not very religious, but there sure is *something* supernatural that went on there."

"Glad of it, what ever it was," Barbara agreed, getting up to leave.

"Whoa! They can rent the house, but, I want the phonograph." I figured that it really belonged to me now. "I *earned* it."

"You certainly did. It's yours. Who the heck else would want it?"

"I'm going to have Elroy fix it up and see if I can't get the record itself repaired. I'd...I'd really like to keep it."

Barbara grinned. "No problem, Reg. As I said, nobody in their right mid would touch it with a ten foot pole. It's all yours."

◆ ◆ ◆

Naturally, my wedding day was sunny and bright with blue skies and little white clouds that scudded across the sky. I wore a simple white dress and had Zee and Rita do my hair. They both fluttered around me and finally paid some attention to the fact that I only wanted a few small flowers twined into my curls.

Maisie was on the same track as me and did her own hair in the neat and dignified style that she always wore. The two hairdressers really had a ball, however, doing up Sasha's hair, bedecking her carroty curls with ribbons. She looked adorable. Rita even brought along some ribbons to twine in to Macduff's fur, but in three minutes, he had scratched them all off. He gave Rita a wide berth for the rest of the day, his expression saying just what he felt about ribbons on a dog.

Uncle Pat gave me away and Sasha and Andie and Jenn were my attendants. Horace was Lincoln's best man, with Chief Alexander Bridge performing the ceremony and Gerjeet and Lincoln's cousin Craig Newhouse, transported all the way from Texas as ushers.

Andie met the bashful Dr. Allen Coleman and I could tell...a mother always does...that they would be seeing something of one another in the near future. I wondered if Andie might give up the thrill of being a television actress to be the wife of a renowned surgeon who lived in the same town as her mother. Only time and my prayers could tell.

We had the party in the backyard at the Fairweather's house and half the states of Maine, Connecticut and New Hampshire attended. The Nosepickers played music and everyone but me danced. Well, I sort of danced, generally carried in Lincoln's arms.

Was I happy? Yes, I was. I was serenely, crazily, wildly, ecstatically, hysterically, delightedly happy. You betcha.

CHAPTER TWENTY-TWO

T he guests had left. Only family and a few special "almost family" people remained gazing sleepily over a lawn that was trampled from all the fun.

We sat in almost somnolent, over-stuffed splendor, reminiscing over what a wonderful wedding party it had been. The evening turned a little chilly. We all staggered inside and Lincoln lit the fireplace as we lolled on couches, chairs and the floor. Somewhere, music was playing, something light and pretty. Little Michael Joseph was sound asleep, cradled in Jenna's arms. She kept nudging Scott and they whispered together, perhaps planning a baby of their own.

I looked around the pleasant room. It felt like I had lived there forever. Comfy, overstuffed furniture, mellow old tables with highly waxed tops, wooden shutters at the curtainless windows that looked out on the white-capped waves of the Piscataqua inlet, squishy pillows, some embroidered with silly mottoes from places visited twenty years ago, slightly worn oriental rugs on the wide plank floors. Absolute heaven. I grinned as I gazed at my own addition – the refurbished Victrola atop its newly polished table. Unfortunately, the old black vinyl recording of Sunny and Catherine singing 'On Top of Old Smokey' was beyond repair. Elroy had tried his best, but there were just too many shattered pieces. He'd wanted to toss the whole thing out, but I insisted that he put the pieces into a small wooden box that I'd bought. The box resided on top of the Victrola. Who knew what might happen in the future with that magical recording? For certain, I'd never forget that little spinning disc. Never. Even if I couldn't explain to anyone, even myself, how than dratted thing had begun to play again when I most needed it.

Lincoln watched me eyeing the Victrola and pulled me even closer into his embrace. I put my head on his shoulder and sighed in happy satisfaction. We were postponing our honeymoon trip until sometime later in the year when I would be better able to travel and we knew that

Maisie's health was back where it belonged. I had no desire to go anywhere right that moment anyway. Nothing could be better for me than where I was right then.

Maisie yawned and declared that she was too pooped to even go to sleep.

I snuggled into the warmth of Lincoln's arm and Sasha's head lolled against my knee. And then Sasha's head came up suddenly. "Listen!" she said.

"What?" Her Grumpy Grandpa, and my new husband asked. I just loved saying 'my new husband' and planned to say it a lot from now on.

"Do you hear that?" Macduff's ears came up and he cocked his head in inquiry.

"I don't hear anything?" Horace leaned forward. "What is it?"

Macduff's body twitched and he got to his feet slowly, his nose pointed. His wooly hair seemed electrified. Sasha put her hand on his neck and pulled herself up. Her face was turned toward the front door. I heard it now...a scratching sound.

Together, Sasha and Macduff approached the door. The music had gone silent and the air seemed to hum with some peculiar tension. The scratching sound was a little louder. Sasha cried out, "Oh! The darling!" and opened the door, dropping to her knees. Macduff barked, one sharp welcoming bark.

Spellbound, we all watched as Sasha came back in, cradling a tiny, puffball of a kitten in her hands. The kitten was either black with white spots or white with black spots...and my heart beat a strange tattoo. Was this yet another manifestation of Sunny and Catherine? One black cat, one white cat...one black and white kitten? Nah, that made no sense at all...both the cats were females, weren't they? I turned to Lincoln to ask and found his mouth hanging open and his eyes glued with great incredulity and speculation to the tiny scrap.

The kitten yawned, its miniscule mouth wide-opened, its pink tongue curling like a tiny ribbon. I sucked in my breath and Sasha gently put the kitten into my cupped hands. I held it, and it was like holding a puff of dandelion.

"I think they left her for you. Her name is Hope," Sasha told me in a firm, no-nonsense voice. "I'll get some milk for her." She trotted into the kitchen as everyone gaped at the kitten and began to talk at once, trying to find some reason to explain our newest little miracle. Macduff stood in front of me, his eyes glued to the kitten, his breath huffing gently.

Sasha came back with a small bowl of milk. She put it on the floor and I gently deposited the kitten next to it. Hope, for obviously that was going to be her name, lapped the milk and then meowed, a tiny, thread-like cry. Sasha was enchanted and clasped her hands together in some maternal ecstasy. Never taking her eyes off the kitten, she plunked herself down on the couch next to her Grumpy. We all looked at one another, baffled and hushed.

Lincoln said what we all were thinking. "I'll be damned. I'll be double damned." He shook his head, bewildered, then hugged Sasha and kissed the top of her curly hair.

Macduff sniffed at the kitten, licked one last drop of milk from its tiny mouth and then lay down, circling the little body with his own. The kitten made a meowing cry and then snuggled into Macduff's chest fur. Sasha smiled a secret smile.

I know that no one – except those who were actually there and saw and heard - will believe me, but at that very instant, a scratchy song began to play...a guitar or a mandolin...on a record that was smashed to pieces... with the ghostly voices of two women who began to sing:

On top of old Smooo-key
All covered with snow
Our love that began there
Did blossom and grow

And all through the ages
We'll sing out our love
And we will be together
In the heavens above.

finis

These recipes are taken from the secret recipes of Zia Filomande

TORTA DI RICOTTA

The Crust (*Pasta Frolla*)
2 ½ cups flour
½ cup granulated sugar
½ tsp salt
½ cup softened butter

4 to 5 tbsp cold whiskey
Finely grated rind of 1 lemon
¾ cup sugar
1 tsp vanilla extract
3 tbsp all purpose flour

The Filling (*La Ricotta*)
½ cup raisins (optional)
¼ cup dark rum
2 pounds ricotta
½ cup slivered almonds (optional, nice to sprinkle on top)
2 large eggs, beaten
Zest of 1 lemon
Zest of 1 orange

1 extra beaten egg (for wash) plus some coarse sugar

La Pasta Frolla

On a marble slab or cold counter-top, place the flour, sugar, salt and lemon rind in a mound. Using your fingers and a circular motion, create a "well" in the center of the mound. Break the butter into little pieces and throw them into your well. Pull the flour mixture into the butter and combine them. Toss the whiskey and very quickly mix the dough so that it just holds together and is not crumbly. Wrap the dough in plastic and let it rest in a cool, but not cold, place, for about half an hour.

On the marble slab, roll out the dough with a heavy rolling pin...the dough will be fragile, so lightly dust with flour so that the dough doesn't stick. The dough is very tender, so if a tear appears, do not worry, you can patch it easily, as if you were playing with modeling clay. Wrap up the dough with the rolling pin and transfer it to a pie pan or a 3 inch high sided tart pan. Be gentle with the dough and lay it carefully down. Again, if it breaks, simply mend it as stated above. The leftover pastry should hang over the edges of the pie plate or tart pan. Cut off the excess dough and re-roll gently to make a long strip about 6 inches wide and about twelve inches long. With a crimped cutter, cut this dough into 12 long strips. This will be used to make a lattice crust for the top of the *torta*.

La Ricotta

Soak the raisins in the rum for 20 minutes. In a medium sized bowl, combine all the other ingredients. Add the raisins and the rum. Pre-heat the oven to350 degrees.

POUR the ricotta filling into the crust. Lay the dough strips in a neat criss-cross pattern.

BRUSH the top of the *torta* with the extra beaten egg wash and sprinkle the top with 1 tablespoon of coarse granulated sugar. Bake for 45 minutes to 1 hour until the top is golden brown. The crust should move a little – ever so slightly and be a little puffed up. Remove from oven and cool for an hour (the *torta* will shrink a little on cooling)..place on a serving plate and serve warm or cool, but not refrigerated.

FINOCCHIO ALLA SORRENTO

2 – 4 Fennel Bulbs
1 ½ sticks of butter
½ cup flour
1 cup chicken broth
1 cup grated *fontina* cheese
1 cup freshly made coarse bread crumbs, toasted

Butter the bottom of an oval baking dish. Cut the fronds off the fennel, leaving a few for decorating the top of the casserole after baking. Slice the bulbs into long, thin slices and put them into a frying pan and cover them with water. Boil for ten minutes or until the fennel strips are limp. Drain the water from the pan, BUT SAVE THE WATER…Put 1 stick of butter on top of the fennel slices and braise in the butter for 8-10 minutes more.

In a medium sized, heavy saucepan, melt the remaining butter, add the flour and cook the roux slowly until it loses its floury taste. Lighten the roux with chicken stock, adding a small amount at a time and stirring constantly. Then, add the cheese, bit by bit and stir until the sauce is thick and luscious. If the sauce is too thick, add some of the fennel water to thin it to the proper consistency.

Put the buttered fennel into the buttered baking dish and pour the sauce over it. Top the dish with the toasted bread crumbs. Bake at 350 degrees or until bubbly and fragrant. Enjoy.

TESTA DELLA ZINGARA VECCHIA
(THE HEAD OF AN OLD GYPSY)

The Domed Cakes
(La Testa)

3 cups flour
2 cups sugar
½ cup best baking cocoa
2 tsp. baking soda
1 tsp salt
2/3 cup vegetable oil
2 tsp white vinegar
1 tsp vanilla
2 cups strong cold coffee

The Ganache Topping
(i Cappelli)

8 ounces bittersweet chocolate
8 ounces heavy cream

Preheat oven to 350 degrees. Grease bottoms and sides of 12 dariole molds, or domed cupcake molds or oven-proof custard cups. Ideally, when the cakes come out of the oven and are turned upside down, they will resemble a domed mound.

In a large bowl, mix the flour, sugar, cocoa, baking soda and salt. In a small bowl, mix vegetable oil, vinegar and vanilla. Vigorously stir oil mixture and coffee into the flour mixture with a mixing spoon for about 1 minute, or until well blended. Immediately pour into pans.

Bake 20-30 minutes, until toothpick inserted in center comes out clean. Cool 10 minutes and then ease cakes out of pans or custard cups. If the cakes stick, ease them out carefully with a sharp knife point. Cool completely, upside down.

Make the Ganache as below. Place the testas on a wire rack and gently, using a large spoon, pour Ganache over each one. The Ganache should drip down the sides and look like the wild gypsy hair cascading over a gypsy's head.

To prepare Ganache:

Place chocolate in small, heatproof bowl. Bring the cream to a boil in a small saucepan over medium-high heat. Pour hot cream over the chocolate. Let stand for five minutes to melt chocolate and be sure that mixture is silky smooth. Set Ganache aside in a cool place to thicken to the consistency of cake batter (maybe 10 minutes or so). Proceed as above

Set the *testas* aside in a cool place to allow the Ganache to set. Enjoy as the men enjoyed watching the gypsy women.

ALSO WRITTEN BY J. TRACKSLER

THE TEARS OF SAN' ANTONIO

PART 1 – UNA FURTIVA LAGRIMA
PART 2 – UN DI FELICE

THE BOTTICELLI JOURNEY

MURDER AT MALAFORTUNA

THE ICE FLOE

DECEIT

CHERUBINI

AND COMING SOON......

THE ULTIMATE GAME

A FAT VIRGIN DEATH

PANIS ANGELICUS

Printed in the United States
56801LVS00006B/1-111